Harp of Winds

HARP OF WINDS

Book Two of the Artefacts of Power

Maggie Furey

LEGEND

Published by Legend Books in 1996

An imprint of Random House UK Limited
20 Vauxhall Bridge Road, London SW1V 2SA

Copyright © Maggie Furey 1994

Maggie Furey has asserted her right under the Copyright, Designs and Patents
Act, 1988 to be identified as the author of this work

An imprint of Random House UK Limited

Random House Australia (Pty) Limited
16 Dalmore Drive, Scoresby, Victoria, 3179

Random House New Zealand Limited
18 Poland Road, Glenfield
Auckland 10, New Zealand

Random House South Africa (Pty) Limited
PO Box 2263, Rosebank 2121, South Africa

Random House UK Limited Reg. No. 954009

ISBN 0 09 918922 4

Printed and bound in Great Britain by
Mackays of Chatham PLC, Chatham, Kent

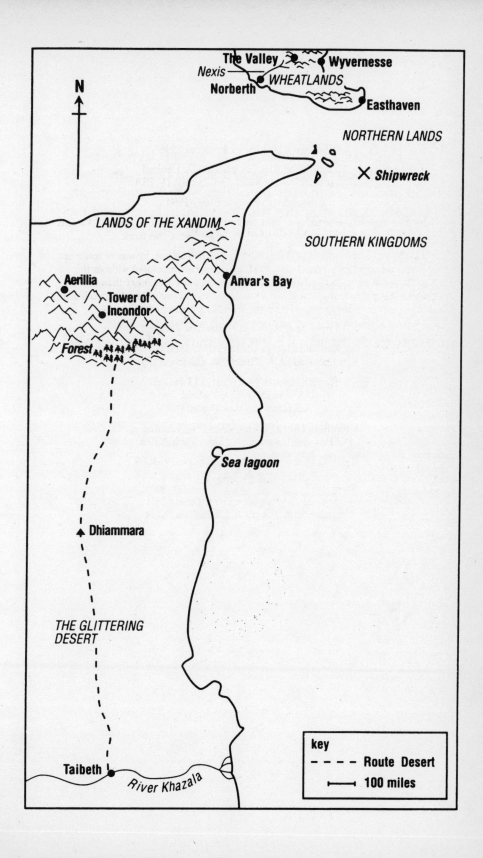

This book is dedicated to two very special people:
John Jarrold, best of editors, orchestrator of Legendary lunches,
and wonderful company at any time – for his enthusiasm,
his insight, his sympathy with the work in hand – and the
fact that he always lets
The Author Put It Right!
And:
John Parker, who was in this from the start, and to whom I owe
so much –
a clever and sagacious agent, a kindly mentor,
a sure guide through the trackless thickets of publishing –
and a true friend.

1

Between the Worlds . . .

'That temeritous swordsman!' growled Death. He was aware of all that went on in his domain, and could have stopped what was happening, had he wished – but instead he leaned upon his staff, and with a wry and rueful smile that was not untinged with respect, he settled down to watch the efforts of the brave and stubborn spirit that was trying to escape him – yet again.

The Door Between the Worlds was ancient; its weathered wood as grey and heavy as stone, the timeworn carvings on its panels obscured by the weight of years. With a grimace, Forral touched the splintered gashes that scarred the beauty of the complex, twining patterns – his own handiwork, from the first time he had tried to pass this way. Embittered by his murder, enraged by the unguarded folly that had led to his own untimely death, and frantic with fear for Aurian's safety, he'd been in no mood for obstacles. No matter that it was forbidden for the dead to return to the living – all he had cared about was his Mageborn love, and her unborn child – *their* unborn child.

Again and again, the swordsman's blade (Forral wondered why he had suddenly found a sword in his hand when he needed one) had hacked at this door in a frenzy of rage and grief until, shade though he was, he had become weak with exhaustion. Only then, as he leant against the cold grey wood and wept for Aurian, had he found the answer. Where no amount of violence would open Death's portal, love – if that love was strong enough – could take him through.

The door swung open to Forral's touch, at the sound of Aurian's name. He stepped through into a shining well of mist that obscured his vision and, by good fortune, concealed him within its silvery shroud. Although he'd learned how to pass this way, it did not mean that he was permitted to do so. The

1

swordsman shrugged. As if *that* could keep him from Aurian! He remembered the last time he'd seen her, in the City of the Dragons. She had been so sad and weary, with tear-tracks smudging the dirt on her haggard face and her belly rounding with child beneath her tattered desert robes. Tears came into Forral's eyes at the memory. It had torn his heart to be unable to hold her, to comfort her, to make everything right for her again. Instead, he'd done the only thing he could – he had shown her how to find the Staff of Earth. Death, the ruler of this eerie realm, had been livid at his interference.

As the swordsman reached the end of the overgrown track that led from the door, the fog dropped away to become a silken film, ankle deep, where the path opened out into the valley. Praying that he was unobserved, Forral strode the familiar way between rounded hills under a starry sky, with ground-mist roiling around his boots at every step. Sometimes, the way to the Well of Souls seemed short, but at other times, it seemed to take for ever . . .

'Forral – stop, I command you!'

The swordsman jumped guiltily, and swore. The hooded figure had appeared out of nowhere – a stooped old man it seemed; grey-cloaked, and leaning on a staff. He bore an intricate lantern that cast a single, silvery beam. As apparitions go, this one seemed fairly harmless – but Forral knew better 'Let me pass!' His hand went to his sword.

'You think to use that sword on *me*?' Death chuckled, the rusty, wheezing sound emerging from the sinister depths of his hood. His hollow, sibilant voice sent chills like corpse-fingers crawling down Forral's spine. 'Forral, will you never learn? No matter how you try, *you cannot go back!* What good does it do to haunt her? That one can manage quite well on her own – believe me.' The wry voice became soft, cajoling. 'Give it up, for everyone's sake. You are not permitted to linger here, Between the Worlds. Go back where you belong, and consent to be reborn. That is the only way in which you can return to Aurian.'

'Liar!' Forral spat, reckless now beyond all measure. 'You only want rid of me. How will rebirth get me back to Aurian? I wouldn't remember her, and she won't recognize me. What use would I be to her as a squalling brat?'

2

'Ah . . .' Death's voice was soft and cunning. 'An infant, yes, but *which* infant? Have you thought of the life that Aurian bears beneath her heart? What if . . .'

'What?' Forral bellowed. 'That's *obscene*!'

'Consider,' Death purred. 'In a brief span of Mortal time, you could be back in her arms, loving and loved . . . And perhaps, eventually, you might remember who once you were. Sometimes the memories slip through.'

For an instant, Forral was tempted. He was so desperate to return to Aurian . . . Then he thought about the torment that would be his if he *did* remember. 'Never,' he snarled. 'I've been a father to that lass, and I've been her lover – I'm damned if I'll be her son after that!'

To his acute irritation, Forral caught the flash of a smile, deep within the shadows of Death's hood. 'Enough, my belligerent friend – you pass the test.'

'Test?' The swordsman scowled. 'What test? Just what the thundering blazes are you playing at?' Then he gulped, backing away hastily as the Spectre suddenly grew, blotting out the stars as it loomed over him, dark with menace.

'Forral,' the chill voice hissed, 'It makes a refreshing change to deal with a Mortal who has no fear of me, and for that reason I indulge your courage – but never forget, for an instant, who I am.'

Forral breathed again as the Spectre dwindled back to human dimensions. 'But never believe that Death is not merciful,' it said softly. 'You and Aurian, and your friend Anvar, form part of a pattern that is yet to be resolved. Each of you has met me now, and been tested. Believe me, there is hope for you all.'

This was beyond Forral, and he was tired of being toyed with. 'If you've finished,' he growled, 'just get out of my way.' He took a deep breath. 'Please. I must see Aurian!'

Death sighed. 'Still you insist. Very well – but you have been warned. See her you may, but I will not permit you to interfere again.'

The ancient grove loomed dark on the shadowy hilltop, shrouding the secrets of its hidden heart. Forral strode forward confidently, knowing his love for Aurian would also cleave a path into this place, as it had opened the Door Between the Worlds. Death pushed him aside – a loathsome touch that was no touch, like the gruesome lack of feeling in a scar. It made the swordsman quake to the depths of his soul. 'Allow me,' the Spectre said with mock-politeness. 'The trees dislike you, Forral – your presence defiles their hallowed shade, and your unruly haste upsets them.'

Turning towards the grove, the Spectre bowed low, three times, and the trees moved silently aside to form a path. Forral, stepping in Death's footprints, could discern, almost beyond the range of his hearing, the rustling murmur of their anger as he passed beneath the arching boughs. Clutching the memory of Aurian to his heart like a shield, the swordsman told himself he was not afraid.

The pool at the heart of the grove was just as Forral remembered it. Cupped in its hollow of soft, mounded moss, it lay silent; still and solemn in its awesome power; all the worlds of the Mortal universe in its starry depths. The swordsman thrust forward impatiently. He had learned, long ago, that by touching the waters of the Well of Souls he could send his shade into Aurian's world.

'Wait!' The Spectre's voice was harsh. 'Before you approach the Well, I tell you once more – you may only observe. You may not go back, and you may not interefere. And if what you see in those waters brings you anguish – well, you were warned.'

'All right!' Forral growled. Kneeling on the mossy brink, he looked into the dark waters – and flinched, as always, as the starry universe spun out at him from the obsidian depths. But he had the way of it now. *Aurian*, he thought, yearning. *Aurian, my love* ... Though he remained firmly on the bank, the swordsman felt as though he were falling. Falling endlessly between the endless stars ... Then the waters cleared; became a mirror – no – a picture that moved and lived. Forral saw places, people, hours, days – all compressed into a timeless whirl, in a world that was heartbreaking in its sweet familiarity.

Bohan waited as he had waited for days; stubbornly keeping vigil on the ridge at the edge of the desert. He was not alone, though – his companions made sure of that. One of the others was always with him – one-eyed Eliizar, once the swordmaster of the Arena; or Yazour, the courageous young warrior who had fled his prince's service to join Aurian's odd little band. Always, always, they had guarded the eunuch as he watched the empty sands; never leaving him alone. Bohan was tormented by guilt at having let them gull him into leaving his Lady's side, and now he was unable to return for her – because they wouldn't let him.

Bohan's thoughts were bitter. They all assumed that, because he was mute, he was also stupid. Everyone, that is, except his beloved Aurian. Her kindness had won his devotion – but he had left her in the desert to die, together with his friends Anvar and black, flame-eyed Shia, the great cat with an intelligence that was more than human.

Though Eliizar had been forced to knock the eunuch unconscious to get him away from the Mages, Bohan still blamed himself. He had abandoned his Lady – and now, after the first lethal sandstorm had ravaged the desert, he was forced to face the truth. Aurian was dead; her breath choked off by the suffocating sands; her eyes and skin eaten away; her bones flayed bare by the knife-edged particles of gem-dust.

For a long time, Bohan had clung to hope – against all evidence, against all sense. Hope had prevented him, over the last few days, from simply setting out into the desert and defying the others to use their weapons on him. He had always believed that Aurian would win through in spite of everything – that any time now she would appear over the dazzling horizon of glittering dunes. That was why he had succumbed to the reasoning of the others. I must be stupid, after all, the eunuch thought. I let them persuade me: Yazour, Eliizar and Nereni, with their cunning words.

'If she comes, she comes, Bohan. Nothing we can do now will help or hinder that.'

'If anyone can come through this, she and Anvar will.'

'The last thing Aurian would want is for you to throw your life away.'

And now it was too late. Hiding his face in his hands, Bohan choked on a soundless sob, and tears drenched the gauzy veils that covered his eyes to protect them from the desert's blinding glare.

A hand, gentle in sympathy, touched his shoulder. He looked around to see Nereni, Eliizar's wife, and her voice, when she spoke, was muffled with tears of her own. 'Come away Bohan, it does no good to linger here. Eliizar says . . .' Suddenly she drew a sharp breath, and the eunuch felt her hand tighten on his shoulder. '*Bohan, wait! They come! They come!*'

The first one to reach the eunuch was the great cat Shia, with whom he had formed such a mysterious bond. She threw herself at him, purring ecstatically, and despite his great strength Bohan was hurled to the ground by her massive weight. But when he heard Aurian call his name, the eunuch could wait no longer, Untangling himself from his boisterous reunion with Shia, he hurled himself over the brow of the rise and plunged down through the steep cutting towards the flat expanse of the Jewelled Desert, kicking up clouds of glittering gem-dust as he ran.

Aurian staggered towards him, helped along by her fellow-Mage Anvar. She was clearly exhausted; her bloodstreaked skin was smeared with gleaming gem-dust, and her robe was a tattered rag. With tears streaming down his face the eunuch swept her into a crushing embrace, wishing desperately that he could explain that he had not wanted to abandon her in the desert; that Eliizar and Yazour had made him leave. He wanted to tell her how he had fretted and grieved for her; and, once the sandstorm had blown up, had despaired of ever seeing her again. Instead, all he could do was embrace her, putting all his heart into his eyes.

'Let me breathe!' Aurian gasped. She was laughing and crying all at once, and her face was radiant with joy. 'Oh, my dear, dear Bohan, I'm so glad to see you!'

'And he is glad to see you,' Yazour approached on noiseless feet, his voice, as always, soft-spoken and low. His handsome face was disfigured by a swollen eye that had darkened to lurid purple, but he was grinning happily. 'You have no notion of the time he's given us since we last saw you, Lady,' he went on. 'We had to knock him senseless to get him to leave you, and Eliizar and I have been forced to guard him ever since to stop him from

6

going back in search of you. When the storm came, we could barely restrain him – he went completely wild.' The young warrior touched his blackened eye and gave a rueful smile. 'What a blessing you arrived when you did. I think he knocked out all of Eliizar's teeth!'

'Not at all – just some of them,' Eliizar muttered through swollen lips. 'And I can spare them in a good cause!'

'It's a good thing Yazour got the bruised eye, and not you,' Anvar teased him. 'You couldn't spare another!'

Eliizar turned to pound the tall, blue-eyed Mage on the shoulder. 'By the Reaper, Anvar, I'd have given my eye to see you both alive and safe after that storm. What did I say?' he added in baffled tones, as his companions collapsed into gales of laughter.

'What could you see without your eye, old fool?' Nereni told her husband with a fond chuckle. 'Come, Eliizar – save this chattering until Aurian and Anvar are safe in our camp.' She turned to the Mages. 'Come, my dears – you need a bath, and a rest, and a good hot meal.'

The eunuch gathered Aurian into his arms and carried her up the sandy bank, with Nereni's good-natured cluckings following him every step of the way. Yazour and Eliizar, still grinning, helped the weary Anvar climb the steep incline. Bohan had to step carefully to keep from tripping with his precious burden, for Shia, who had befriended him when she and Aurian had escaped the Arena in the Khazalim city of Taibeth, was weaving her sinuous black body back and forth around his legs as he went, rubbing against him and purring with pleasure at seeing him again.

At the top of the rise was a narrow ridge, overgrown with low thornbushes and fat-leaved succulents, and dotted with scrubby, wind-twisted pines that had managed to survive the tearing blasts of the desert's lethal sandstorms. At the far side of the ridge the land dropped down again; and here, cradled in the arms of a long valley that swelled up on its further slopes to meet the foothills of the mountains, a dense forest arose like a vast green cloud.

Cradling Aurian gently in his great arms as though she might break, the eunuch crossed the plateau, bearing the weary Mage

7

along the rough path that had been hacked through the thornbushes. Then, stooping low to avoid the vault of overhanging branches, he plunged downhill and into the forest itself.

Because of its tenuous foothold at the edge of the desert, the forest had the tough, spare, weather-beaten look of a true survivor. The trees were cypress and pine; gaunt and darkly forbidding, but welcome after the harsh, arid Khazalim lands – and an unexpected blessing had brightened their grim and ancient gloom. Snow-melt from the dreadful winter that had locked the mountains had threaded the temperate foothills with lively new streams that sped down the boulder-strewn slopes to form shining pools in sheltered hollows. With this extra water, the forest had bloomed. Flowers splashed colour wherever the eye fell. Drifts of misty blue and lively pink; delicate, lacelike white and clusters of yellow gold like spilled coins – blossoms abounded in all shapes and sizes, attended by an ecstatic court of butterflies and bees, and mingling their perfumes with the tingling incense of the evergreens to make every breath a new delight.

Having spent his life in the arid Khazalim lands, Bohan was entranced by the forest's beauty. After the desert, this shaded green woodland seemed a miracle, and the eunuch smiled to himself at Aurian's exclamations of pleasure as they went on their way. He could hardly wait to show her all the wonders of this astonishing place.

The rough camp was not far from the edge of the forest, near the banks of a newborn stream whose rushing waters had washed out the roots of a gigantic pine. The tree had fallen to lean at an angle against its companions, its branches safely anchored in those of its fellows to provide a rough, slanting shelter for the wayfarers.

'This is but a temporary arrangement,' Eliizar was saying, as Bohan set Aurian down beneath the overarching tree. He knelt to kindle a fire as he spoke. 'We are too near the stream here – it is damp, and there is a risk of flooding. We thought to build a sturdier camp deeper in the forest – Yazour found a perfect clearing – but we could not move while there was a chance that you might come.' He looked up at the eunuch and smiled. 'Besides, Bohan would never have permitted it!'

8

Nereni, already advancing upon her cooking gear in a purposeful manner, shooed her husband away from the fire. 'Will you fetch some water, Eliizar? They must be parched, poor dears, and I must tend their hurts. Now where did I pack that salve? And Yazour, I need some cuts from the deer you shot this morning. Bohan can help you fetch it – and remember to bring a haunch back for Shia. On second thoughts, bring two. She looks starved.'

Forral rejoiced in Aurian's joyous reunion with her friends. Bohan was grinning from ear to ear. Lithe Yazour, his dark hair tied back in a long tail, positively glowed with quiet happiness. Eliizar and his plump, bustling wife were beaming with delight.

The swordsman listened with satisfaction as Eliizar showed his camp to Aurian and Anvar. Here they could recover from the hardships of the desert, and, thanks to the abundant gifts of the forest, prepare themselves for the next step of their journey. Everyone had been busy – even the horses, hobbled nearby, were grazing as though their lives depended on it. Making up for their near-starvation in the desert, they had spent the whole time in the forest eating, and the improvement in their condition was already visible.

Eliizar and his companions had worked together to build rough shelters of woven boughs. Nereni had harvested edible plants while Yazour and Eliizar hunted goat, wild pig, and deer. Bohan had discovered an unexpected talent for snaring rabbits. As he noted their achievements, Forral looked on with approval. He was sure that Aurian would be safe here – for the present, at least.

'And so we give the body of our brother Mage Bragar to the Fire, and his spirit to the gods . . .' The Archmage Miathan intoned the closing words of the death ceremony in a rapid monotone that was utterly devoid of any respect for the late Fire-Mage, whose shrivelled, scorched remains lay on the great stone altar of the rooftop temple on the Mages' Tower in Nexis. A waste of valuable time, Miathan thought irritably – Bragar, a stupid, shallow, over-ambitious bully, had done nothing to merit it.

'And let him go forth with our prayers and blessings.' He snapped out the final words with a contemptuous curl of his lip and, raising his staff, let loose a single bolt of crimson flame. It hit the corpse with an explosive flare that seared across the cloud-dark sky over Nexis, melting the glittering network of frost that silvered the temple's tall standing stones.

Before Bragar's body had even begun to sizzle and smoke, Miathan was striding towards the stairs that led down into the tower. As he passed Eliseth, who stood huddled in a furred cloak against the raw dawn chill, his glanced raked the Weather-Mage, and he had the satisfaction of seeing her cringe away from him, her icy hauteur vanished along with the beauty of her formerly lovely face.

Seeing the wreck of those once-perfect features, the Archmage smiled cruelly. Using the grail fashioned from part of the Cauldron of Rebirth, he had cast a spell that had reduced the Weather-Mage to a stooped and wizened crone. Eliseth had been vain about her looks. He could not have found a better way to punish her for attempting to lure Aurian to her death, by creating a vision of the Mage's murdered lover Forral. The ruse had failed spectacularly, resulting instead in Bragar's death.

As he passed her, Miathan saw cold hatred burning behind Eliseth's eyes, and warned himself that she would bear watching in future. For now, she would obey – he had made sure of that – but she would not stay cowed for ever.

With a shrug, the Archmage went on his way, ignorning the Magewoman's venomous look. He had much to do. The sight, in his crystal, of Aurian and Anvar emerging from the desert had spurred him to action. They must be taken before Aurian regained her powers – and while Eliseth was too subdued to interfere. Already, the net was tightening around the un-suspecting fugitives. His puppet, the foolish young prince, would be meeting the winged girl in the forest beyond the desert, and Miathan planned to leave his body and travel there to control Harihn's mind and make sure the youth obeyed his orders. But first, the Archmage needed to contact Blacktalon, High Priest of the Winged Folk.

Miathan regretted that Bragar's burning would prevent him

using the rooftop temple to carry out the dark, arcane ceremony that used the Death-magic of the Cauldron, and permitted him to cast his mind so far abroad. It would take more than one human sacrifice to give him the power he needed to travel as far as the Winged Folk's citadel of Aerillia. Still, he reflected with grim amusement, it was a bitterly cold day for working magic out of doors – and Mortals could be sacrificed anywhere, after all.

'Where in the Sky-god's name is that accursed Archmage?' Blacktalon screamed at the unresponsive crystal. 'Answer me, you worthless stone. I demand to speak to Miathan!' Seething, he kicked the carven plinth on which the crystal lay. As the darkly glittering gem spilled from its wooden rest, he made a frantic dive to save it, but it slipped from his straining fingertips. Hitting the floor in an explosion of sparks, it shattered into fragments.

'No!' the High Priest howled. Dropping to his knees, he scrabbled at the lifeless shards, scalding the air with curses. No matter what the provocation, how could he have been so stupid as to destroy his only means of communication with his ally? Blacktalon snarled with frustration. Why did Miathan not answer? He glared at his chamber walls, as though to wrest the information from their dark, reflective surface. It was vital he speak with the Archmage. The killing winter, through which he had gained and kept his supremacy over the Slyfolk, was faltering.

Blacktalon rose, shaking out his dusty black wings as he hurried to the wide, arched casement. Maybe this time he could deny the evidence of his own eyes? But the delicate spires of the city bore dripping fringes of ice-spears, and, as he watched, a slab of snow slid down the roof of the Queen's Tower to vanish with a rumble into the chasm below. Hearing voices, Blacktalon leaned out of the window to look across the city that he coveted. Winged Folk swept back and forth between the pinnacle-towers, crying out in excitement as they dodged the snow-slides. The sound of their joy was bile in the High Priest's throat.

Blacktalon was too preoccupied to heed the ominous

11

rumbling overhead. Leaning out as he was, the lump of snow from the roof caught him square between the shoulders, knocking the breath from his lungs and splattering his bald head with slimy slush. Ice slipped down the loose neck of his mantle, and slithered, melting and mocking, between his wings where he couldn't reach it. 'By the all-seeing eyes of Yinze, I won't stand for this,' the High Priest howled, as he danced about, trying to shake the snow out of his robe. 'Where *is* that damned Archmage?'

Slamming the window shut, Blacktalon cursed the loss of magic that had afflicted his race cince the Cataclysm. He'd spent hours poring over the wretched crystal in a frantic attempt to stretch his mind across the miles that separated him from Miathan. His efforts had resulted in nothing but a pounding headache and the loss of his precious gem. It would take too long to make another – and by then he might have lost his hold over the Winged Folk altogether.

Blacktalon was desperate to restore the dignity of his race. Before their decline, the Skyfolk had been one of the four great races of Magefolk – the guardians appointed by the gods to oversee the ordering of the world. Before they had been robbed of their powers in a disastrous magical war for supremacy, his people had charge of the element of Air. Together with the human Wizards, or Earth-Mages, they cared for the birds and all creatures that were borne on the wind. In conjunction with the mighty Leviathan, or Water-Mages, the world's weather had been under their control.

The loss of this power was a like choking briar that had twined itself about the High Priest's soul, growing greater with each passing year. The memory of his race's former greatness was a matter for pain, not pride. In Blacktalon's view, the Skyfolk, even in their ascendancy, had never fulfilled their true potential. 'Why?' he snarled. 'Why did we never have complete control of our element?' Every act of significance was shared, either with those groundling Wizards or the pathetic, soft-hearted Seafolk: the self-appointed conscience of the world. Blacktalon's driven mind had never paused to consider that all Elements and their controlling forces were interdependent; all interlinking and supporting one another in the complex web of life. He was only concerned with himself, his own race – and what they had lost.

In his youth, the High Priest had been more idealistic. The young Blacktalon had grown up in the sacred precincts of the peaktop temple of Yinze, dedicated to a priestly life by unknown parents – the usual fate among the Skyfolk for an unwanted child. But Blacktalon had been different. The others, accepting their fate, had become meek, obedient little priests, but he had always wanted more. Highborn females had rejected him – and the others, less proud and particular, he despised. Ugly, gaunt, and ambitious; underestimated by his teachers and mentors, he had clawed his way to power to spite them all, achieving his ends, within the temple, by becoming too good a student to be ignored.

In truth, in his loneliness and isolation, Blacktalon aspired to the family he had lost; the security and acceptance he had been denied. Lacking knowledge of his true parents, he had fostered the best possible dream – that he was truly a bastard scion of the Royal line. Fantasies filled his head each night, in which he took control of the Winged Race and restored them to their former glory – and brought himself to the position of supremacy in the world that had always been denied him.

Then had come the writings. Put to cleaning the temple by his superiors, who were still desperately trying to instil some seeds of priestly humility in his soul, Blacktalon, more zealous than most in his ambition, had discovered the secret, hidden journal of Incondor.

It was obviously meant to be. The young, arrogant, accursed Mage, co-instigator of the dreadful events of the Cataclysm, whose very name was taboo among the Winged Folk, had left his message to posterity to be discovered by Blacktalon in a dark, forbidden niche behind the altar. And nothing, in the view of the priest, happened by chance.

Incondor had been fearless; merciless in his ambition. Incondor had also been solitary and misunderstood by the lesser beings around him. Devouring the journal obsessively, night after night in his damp little cell, Blacktalon came to the obvious conclusion. That the journal had been left as a message, reaching out across the centuries, specifically for

13

himself to find. That he, in fact, was truly Incondor – newly reborn in order that he might bring his unfulfilled dreams of power to fruitation at last.

A timid rap at the door of his chamber interrupted the High Priest's musings. With a snarl, Blacktalon flung it open so hard that it rebounded on its hinges, almost knocking his visitor off the landing platform into the depths below. The messenger jumped back hastily in a blur of white wings to avoid the plaque of snow jarred from the porch above, and hovered, wary-eyed, out of danger. Blacktalon recognized him as Cygnus, a warrior-priest of the temple who had eschewed the way of the sword for the way of healing. The High Priest's lip curled in a sneer of contempt – yet Cygnus was a loyal, zealous follower, and his physician's knowledge of poisons had come in extremely useful of late.

'My Lord!' the young priest gasped. 'Queen Flamewing is dead!'

Blacktalon's heart leapt at the news. At last! By Yinze, it had taken her long enough – but she couldn't have chosen a better time. 'I'm coming!' he snapped, but as he spoke a muted tingle in his scalp pulled him back into the room. The High Priest turned – and gasped. On the wall opposite the window, a section of polished stone was glowing with a dim and ghostly flicker. Even as he watched, the luminescence took on depth and definition, resolving itself into the familiar, harshly carved features of the Archmage.

Blacktalon let out his breath is a sigh of relief. 'I will come as soon as I can,' he told the young warrior. 'In the meantime, I am not to be disturbed for any reason. Is that clear?' He slammed the door on the startled messenger, and bolted it quickly.

'Miathan, where have you been?' Blacktalon was too anxious to form the disciplined thought patterns used in mental communication. 'The snow is melting!' he gabbled. 'My winter is dissolving, and . . .'

'Shut up, Blacktalon, and listen.' The Archmage's mental voice seemed faint and far away. He sounded very tired. 'Eliseth, my Weather-Mage, has been attacked by those renegades . . .'

14

'She was attacked? Was she hurt? Can she restore my winter?' the High Priest insisted.

'Of course – if she knows what's good for her!' For a moment, there was naked steel in Miathan's voice. 'I shall deal with the matter on my return. More to the point, how fares that queen of yours?'

Blacktalon smiled. 'Dead,' he purred. 'The poison worked perfectly.'

'Excellent! Then you must seize power with all speed. My pawn, Prince Harihn, has duped your princess into betraying the fugitives. She will lure them to the Tower of Incondor – a superb idea of yours, that: it's perfect for an ambush – and if you provide the warriors you promised we cannot possibly fail. How soon can you be ready?' The image smiled: a self-satisfied, cruel smile that sent a shiver down Backthorn's spine.

'Ready?' he gasped. 'But the queen has only just died. I have had no chance . . .'

'Then I suggest you hurry, Blacktalon. You'll have sufficient time to prepare – our fugitives must make ready for a journey into the mountains, and it will take them some days to reach the tower. Take a firm grip on your city, and leave the rest to me. Have warriors ready to carry out the ambush on my word. Oh, and Blacktalon – I have no idea what has become of your crystal, but rectify the matter as soon as possible. Communicating like this is exhausting and inefficient, and I've better uses for my time and energy.' With that he was gone, leaving Blacktalon staring indignantly at a blank wall.

As the awareness of his surroundings returned, the High Priest heard a sound that did much to soothe his annoyance at Miathan's peremptory manner. Opening his window, he heard a wailing of many voices, mourning the death of Flamewing, Queen of the Skyfolk. Blacktalon allowed himself a brief smile of satisfaction. Then, composing his features into a suitable expression of sorrow, he straightened decisively and went to the door. He had a great deal to do, and little time in which to accomplish it all. Stepping out on to his landing platform, the High Priest spread his night-black wings and soared across the darkening void towards the tower of the queen.

Dark. Darkness and the smell of wet horse – both had become familiar companions to Parric since he and the others had been captured by the Xandim Horselords. The cavalry master cursed, but it was half-hearted. Even his endless store of profanity had run out. He was helpless, blindfolded and bound, and to be hauled like a sack of dung on one of the legendary Xandim beasts was a dire humiliation for a horseman. He was wet through; furious, frustrated and afraid. He could only speak with these people through Meiriel, but the Mage was stark-mad, and hated him besides. He had no way of knowing if she'd translate his words correctly – supposing these savages would give him a chance to speak.

Behind him, Parric heard the tearing sound of Elewin's cough. The elderly steward's illness had worsened during this gruelling journey. He might not survive it, for as far as the cavalry master knew, Elewin and the others were in a similar plight to himself – bound and gagged, and with their eyes tightly covered. Bereft of information, Parric fretted. Where are these bastards taking us, anyway, he thought – and how much longer will it take to get there?

The cavalry master bitterly regretted his rash decision to come in search of Aurian. How could he possibly find her in these vast, hostile lands? If only he had thought to find out more about the place from Yanis, the Nightrunner leader who had befriended the rebels, and had been running an illicit trading operation with the southerners. It had seemed a good idea, at the time, to beg a passage on one of his ships. Parric cursed again – had it not been for the gag, he would have spat. Idris, the superstitious captain who had brought them here, had been reluctant to carry a Mage, and the situation had not been improved by Meiriel's abrasive arrogance towards the man. It made no difference that she treated all Mortals in the same way – when his ship had been crippled by storms, Idris had dumped Parric and his friends on the nearest strip of land and abandoned them without even taking the time to repair his broken mast.

Gods, I'm a fool! Parric berated himself. Forral, his old commander, would have been disgusted. The cavalry master had abandoned his fellow-rebel Vannor to come on this fool's

16

errand, leaving the merchant, with no experience of warfare, in command. The gods know what a mess he's making of things, Parric thought ruefully. I wonder if he found the Lady Eilin? I wonder if she'll help us? Of course she will, he comforted himself. She's Aurian's mother. The Archmage murdered Forral and betrayed her daugher – she's sure to be on our side. If I could only find Aurian . . .

The horse paced tirelessly on. Parric, a horseman to his soul, found some solace in the appreciation of its smooth stride. Powerful muscles moved beneath his with fluid ease, and he rubbed his cheek against a thick but silken coat. He ached to see the beast; to run his hands along sleek flanks and powerful haunches. Oh, to ride this creature – to share such generous strength. Why, this horse could outspeed the very wind! Lulled by his mount's even paces and comforted by the warm, rough smell of horse, he dozed, and dreamed of riding the wind.

Parric jerked awake as the owl that had roused him gave another soul-freezing shriek. Only senses deprived of sight, as his had been, could have heard the soft rushing whisper of its wings as it ghosted away. It must still be night – it was black behind his blindfold, and he could feel a cool, damp breeze on his skin. The relentless rain had stopped at last, to his profound relief. He concentrated, using senses honed by years of scoutcraft to tell him what his eyes could not. Ah, the terrain had changed. The heady, crushed-hay fragrance of the grasslands had been replaced by the heavy musk of forest-loam, and he could hear the rustling murmur of wind among branches. The body of his mount was tilted, and he could feel its muscles straining as it hauled itself up a steep, uneven path.

The soft thud of the horse's steps was replaced by the hollow scrape of hooves on a paved surface. A murmur ran through the ranks of Parric's captors, and the beast came to a halt. Greetings were called out, and a babble of replies in the rolling Xandim tongue. Parric did not have to know the language to hear curiosity and consternation in their tone. Dim torchlight, interspersed with passing shadows, flicked across his blindfold. Then his horse stepped forward with an irritated snort, and they were moving again, climbing laboriously up the paved road. The cavalry master gathered his wits in anticipation of meeting the leaders of the Horselords. Wherever he and his companions had been brought, they had obviously arrived.

2

The Windeye

There were voices on the wind that whistled around the slopes of the Wyndveil Mountain, whispering secrets across the stiff, frost-cracked grasses of the plateau, long and wide and wildly beautiful, that was the heart's home of the Xandim. This meadow, once lush and green, and jewelled with poppies and starflowers in the summer that seemed to have fled for ever, was split by a turbulent stream running out of a dark, narrow valley that vanished into the shadow of the mountain's limbs. Within this haunted vale lay the barrows of the Xandim dead. Only for a burial would the Horselords pass the avenue of standing stones that guarded the valley's entrance, and only the Windeye knew its secret heart: the twisted spire of rock cleft from the mountain, that stood like a tower at the valley's end.

The apex of the spire had been hollowed out in some long-ago age to form an eyrie, open to the elements, with walls of air and a roof of stone supported by four slender pillars. This Chamber of Winds was reached by a scanty stair of crumbling footholds cut into the mountain's face and connected to the spire by a cobweb bridge of twisted rope. Only a Windeye would attempt the risky climb, and dare the perilous crossing. Only a Windeye would have the need.

The keening wind shredded the misty weave of Chiamh's shadow-cloak, hurling handfuls of sleet into his face as he sat hunched and freezing on the chill stone floor of the chamber. He tried to ignore the storm's distractions, reminding himself that he was the Windeye of the Xandim – blessed (or cursed) with the power to see beyond the vision of normal men; to perceive and understand the tidings of the winds. This storm, he knew, bore more tidings than most. The tortured, scream-ing air was swollen with portents.

The storm tore at his soaked and shivering body, flattening

19

his tangled brown hair across his face, and the young seer flinched from the evil Power that rode the wind like the shadow of dark wings. Coming from the north, it had haunted his nightmares since the onset of winter. Slim, strong fingers on the wind clawed him with icicle-nails. Eyes that held the merciless chill of eternal winter glinted in the darkness. Silver hair flowed like a deadly glacier as the snow-laden winds formed the image of a face: flawlessly beautiful, its cold lips curved in a cruel, mocking smile. Her gaze passed over him, unseeing and dispassionate but painful as a blade drawn across his shrinking skin. Despite the windspun cloak of shadows that concealed him, he shuddered. If she could find him . . .

Chiamh shrank down on the exposed platform, withdrawing deep into the elusive depths of his shadow-cloak until the dark-bright shadow of her passing had sped away across the mountain. Tonight there would be more, he knew. Something had forced him from his bed to dare this lonely, freezing perch, and the terror of the Snow Queen's passing. Turning his back on the evil north wind, the Windeye swung his blurred, nearsighted gaze towards the mountains; drawn like the nether point of a lodestone towards the south.

A sense of chill dissolution, like a wave of icy water, washed over him. Chiamh felt his weak-sighted brown eyes melting – glazing – turning to reflective quicksilver as his Othersight took control. The night turned bright and clear around him; the mountains changed from the dense solidity of stone to glittering translucent prisms; the writhing winds became turbulent rivers of silver light. The Windeye caught his breath in panic and screwed his treacherous eyes tight shut. Though it had been with him since childhood, he would never get used to this unnerving change.

The lure of Vision tugged at him; demanding that he follow. Chiamh bit his lip, bribing his undisciplined fear with the promise of a jug of wine as soon as he got down from this dreadful place. From the past, he seemed to hear the voice of his beloved grandam: '*Eat your meat, Chiamh – then you may have the honeycomb!*' As always, her memory eased his fear, and Chiamh smiled. What a fierce old lady she had been. How wise! How strong! A warrior born, and the greatest Windeye in

20

the history of the Xandim. She had borne this burden unflinching, and it was up to him, her heir, to bear it now. Scraping his dripping hair out of his face with cold-stiffened fingers, Chiamh opened his eyes, and directed the piercing silver beam of his Othersight across the mountains.

Spurning his earthbound body, the Windeye's mind ripped loose to soar aloft and ride the unruly winds in pursuit of his vision. Like a rainbow of jewels, the translucent mountains spun beneath him. A scattering of bonfire sparks seared his eyes; each vivid light a single, living soul. O goddess – it must be Aerillia, the Skyfolk citadel. He had spun too far . . . Out of control . . . Right over the mountains to the crystal lacework of the forest beyond, with its scintillant backdrop of desert sands . . .

Far away, in the Chamber of Winds, the breath fled Chiamh's body in one shocked gasp. More Powers! Another Evil One like a dark, writhing cloud – and two others, far to the south, in the forest beyond the mountain. Their lights shone clear and bright, united in love and honesty and clarity of purpose – then suddenly they were gone, eclipsed by a wave of black and overwhelming force that reeked of hatred and menace and merciless lust. Chiamh shrieked and fled. The forefront of the wave smote him – engulfed him. Somehow his awareness clawed its way back into his body. Chiamh sobbed with terror, hiding like a child beneath his shadow-cloak until the evil had passed.

It was a long time before the shaken Windeye dared raise his head, but when he finally looked out again with his silver gaze, the streaming air ran clean. To his utter relief, there were no tidings of death on the wind. He understood then that he had been vouchsafed a vision of warning. The Powers – those bright and lovely lights – they still lived. But what would happen when the Dark One reached out to take them as he had foreseen? He had to help them – that was why he had been drawn here tonight.

Chiamh's excitement faltered as dismay overtook him. 'How can you help them?' he said aloud, in the way of those who live alone. 'You have no idea who they are, what their purpose is. But you can find out – if you dare.'

21

The storm wailed and tugged at the Windeye still, like a fretful child. Its violence would make a seeing hard to control, the danger being that he was likely to find out far more than he would wish. Such visions were perilous – yet he had to take the risk. He alone of the Xandim knew the cause of this grim winter that paralysed the land, though not one of his people believed him. He knew that if the Snow Queen was not opposed, it would spell the end of freedom for his race – and others. By himself, he was helpless but if he could somehow help those bright Powers . . .

Turning into the storm, Chiamh gathered a skein of wind around his fingers. As he poured his Othersight into the knot of air it took fire, flaring into a shining tangle of moonspun silver. With the greatest care he grasped it, then, pulling his hands gently apart, he began to stretch and mould the gleaming stuff until at last, between his hands, he held a glimmering disc of silvery air. Narrowing his quicksilver eyes, the Windeye looked into the mirror.

And the visions came; a flood of images that flickered and changed and ran into one another in their urgent haste to reveal themselves.

The Snow Queen's cold and deadly beauty; the haggard face of the Dark One, with eyes of burning stone – and all the world in chains beneath their feet . . .

The forest beyond the mountains. A solitary tower, crumbling to ruin, and the lean, fleet shape of a running wolf. The Bright Ones – a tall woman with hair of burnished red, her body rounded with child; the blue-eyed man who never left her side – and behind them, half glimpsed, the spectre of a warrior, who hovered over them protectively . . .

Another forest, far away in the north, that woke in Chiamh a conflicting tangle of fear and longing, and the wrenching pain of separation and loss. A fiery Sword, sealed in crystal, that marked the end of evil – and the annihilation of the Xandim . . .

A face, lone and narrow, bony of nose and high of cheekbone; too young for the silver that streaked the dark hair and echoed the sly, sidelong glint of hooded grey eyes. It was the face of a rascal, a malcontent, a maker of mischief – the face of Schiannath, the misfit, who had actually dared to challenge the Herdlord Phalihas for leadership several moons ago. Chiamh had no idea of his whereabouts now. His failure had meant his exile from the tribe, and he had vanished into the mountains, together with his sister Iscalda – a particular cause of anger to Phalihas, since the girl had been the Herdlord's betrothed.

'*Schiannath?*' The mirror rippled and clouded, as Chiamh almost lost control of the seeing in surprise. Schiannath a part of this business? 'O sweet goddess,' the Windeye muttered, 'how in the name of your mercy can he be concerned with this?' With an effort he steadied the image – and saw the woman again, her hair a flaming banner, her body wreathed in a rainbow aura of magic. The Dark One stretched forth his hand to take her, but the vision of Schiannath lay between them like a barrier. She reached out to take the Sword, and destroy the Xandim . . .

'No! Chiamh shrieked. The mirror dissolved into mist between his fingers as he collapsed on the very brink of his eyrie, heedless of the lethal drop. To his Othersight, the meaning of the vision was horribly clear. Only the Bright Ones could forestall the encroaching evil – but at the cost of the entire Xandim race.

The seer wrestled with the conflicting possibilities, but whichever way his thoughts turned, he came up against one inescapable truth – whether or not the Evil Ones succeeded, the Xandim were doomed. The Windeye bowed his head and, with tears streaming down his face, he turned north, to look out across the heartlands of his people.

He had forgotten that the Othersight still held him in thrall. Chiamh's body stiffened, left behind on the brink of the platform as his consciousness fled on the wings of his Othersight; arrowing down the valley along a path of silver towards the source of the vision. Across the snow-scoured meadow of the plateau he sped, following the crystal course of the ice-locked stream. Down the broad, shallow steps of the cliff path, beside the diamond-lace curtain of the frozen waterfall, and along the well-travelled track that skirted the foot of the cliff until . . . until . . .

'Iriana of the Beasts!' Chaimh reeled in astonishment.

23

There, approaching the blocky fortifications of the Xandim fastness, he saw the prisoners. Strangers from across the sea! A man and a woman, warriors by their garb; a silver-haired grandsire, clinging stubbornly to life ... And the other. Goddess, the other! She was one of the Powers – but bright or dark, Chiamh could not tell. Her mind was hidden from his Othersight by a cloudy labyrinth of madness.

The Windeye was aware that these outlanders were somehow connected with the Bright Powers. And he also knew, with a chill of certainty, that as foreigners in the Xandim lands they would be executed out of hand. But they must not die, or the Bright Ones would be lost. The vision was telling him to save them!

But saving the strangers was easier said than done. How would he persuade the Herdlord? Chiamh knew he had failed to win the respect accorded to his grandam. She's had the advantage of venerable old age. The Windeye grimaced. His grandam had not always been old, but she had proved herself as a warrior against the marauding Khazalim. He had never done so and never would – the weakness of his normal sight prevented it. Why, before he saw his enemy, he'd be dead meat. Face it, Chiamh, he thought, you're a laughing-stock – and so you hide in your valley, living in a cave like a hermit. They will never believe you – they'll mock, as they have mocked so often.

None the less, he had to try – and there was no time to lose. By the light in the sky, half-glimpsed between the scudding clouds, Chiamh knew that dawn was on its way. Stifling his doubts, the young Windeye scramble down from the tower; slipping and slithering and scraping himself painfully in his haste as his Othersight faded back to his own defective vision. He fell the last few feet and landed, winded and bruised, on a pile of gravel. Without waiting to catch his breath, he picked himself up and pelted down the valley, stumbling and rolling and getting up only to be tripped again by rocks and roots and hampering drifts of snow that massed in this narrow, sheltered place. But he kept on going, driven by sheer determination. The Bright Ones must be helped. He *must* get there in time to save the strangers. With the forgotten tatters of his shadow-cloak streaming out behind him, Chiamh ran as he had never dared run before.

The Windeye burst out of the woods at the lower end of the valley, and passed the standing stones that were its gate. The smooth, inviting grass of the plateau beckoned, and he heaved a sigh of relief. No longer did he have to worry about breaking a leg on uneven ground – on the plateau, he could really move. Chiamh stopped in the shadow of the great stones and collected himself, turning his attention inward. Then – he changed.

To an observer, he knew, the transformation would have taken place in seconds. To Chiamh, time seemed to stretch, as did his body; his bones and muscles gaining a tingling elasticity as they lengthened and grew thick and strong. There was a moment of blurred confusion, as impossible to register as the instant between consciousness and sleep – and in the lee of the stones that had previously shadowed a young man stood a shaggy-maned bay horse.

Chiamh pawed the ground, enjoying the power of his equine body, and the tapestry of rich scents that swirled around him. His ears flicked back and forth, hearing the slurring of the wind across the plateau's snowswept grass, and the creak of branches back in the woods. His eyesight, unfortunately, remained unchanged in his Othershape – flatter in depth and more peripheral and encompassing than that of a human – but still as blurred as ever. Still, at least in this form he had other senses that could, in some measure, compensate.

Woolgathering! Chiamh snorted disgustedly. That was the trouble with this shape – one's thoughts tended to become those of a horse, and the longer one stayed this way the greater was the risk of losing all vestiges of human intelligence. But enough. Time was passing. At the far side of the meadow, he would have to change back again, to descend the steep cliff path, but in the meantime it was worth it – both for the saving in time and the sheer, exuberant joy of the run. With a flick of his heels, the Windeye was off, racing the wind across the plateau.

In the lands of the north, yet in a place unreachable within the boundaries of the mundane world, the palace of the Forest Lord, with its treelike towers and innumerable gardens and glades, lay deceptively tranquil in a waiting silence, within and upon its massive hill. Upon the craggy slopes of the mound, a ferny hollow cupped a crystal pool, fed by a silvery filigree of water that twisted and tumbled down a stony precipice from the heights above.

The Lady of the Lake sat by the water, combing the silver-shot strands of her long brown hair. Warily, the great stag watched her from its thicket on the other side of the pool; safe, he thought, and unobserved – until the Earth-Mage lifted her eyes to him and smiled. 'Do you prefer that form, my Lord?' Her voice was low and musical. Hellorin, chargrined, stepped forth, shifting to his magnificent human shape. Only the branching shadows of the great stag's crown above his brow remained as a reminder that this was no ordinary Mage or Mortal – for indeed, the Lord of the Phaerie was more than both. His feet, clad in high boots of supple leather, caused nary a ripple as he walked towards Eilin across the surface of the pool. 'The eyes of the Magefolk were ever keen,' he complimented her. 'Many's the Mortal huntsman I have lured and deceived with that shape.'

The Lady Eilin laughed. 'Aye, and many's the Mortal maid, I'll wager, that you have lured and deceived with the shape you are wearing now!'

Hellorin chuckled, and made her a flourishing bow. 'I have done my best,' he told her loftily. 'After all, my Lady – the Phaerie have a certain reputation to uphold!'

Sitting down beside her on the fragrant turf, he turned to more serious matters. 'I did not expect to find you here. Are you tired, then, Lady, of your vigil?'

Eilin's brow creased in a frown. 'Not tired, Lord – not weary, at any rate. It helps to see what passes in the world outside. But oh, it galls me to be reduced to an onlooker, when I long to be free – to go where I am so badly needed, and do my part.'

Hellorin, hearing the tremor of tears in her voice, turned the starry depths of his grey eyes upon her. 'But that is not the sole cause of your unhappiness. There is more, Eilin, is there not?'

The Earth-Mage nodded. 'The window in your hall shows my Valley,' she said sadly, 'it shows Nexis, and all the northern lands – but it doesn't show my Aurian! Day after day I bend my will upon the thought of my daughter, but she is nowhere to be found. Where is she?' Her voice caught on a sob. 'Trapped in this Elsewhere, I might not know if she died. Surely, if I cannot find her, then she must be dead.'

The Lady's hopeless weeping scalded the Forest Lord's heart. Since losing D'arvan's mother, the Mage Adrina, grief had been a constant companion to Hellorin, and he sorrowed for Eilin's heartache. Putting an arm around her shoulders, he drew her close to his side. 'Take courage,' he told her. 'Your fears may yet be groundless. If you cannot see Aurian's image in my window, it may only mean she has voyaged across the ocean to the south.'

Eilin stiffened. 'What!' Her head came up sharply; a spark of irritation lit her eyes. 'Do you mean your wretched window doesn't work across the sea?'

Hellorin, amused by her transformation from sorrow to anger, and her sudden abandonment of the courtly manners of the Phaerie, struggled to hide a smile. Ah, it took little provocation for the Magefolk to revert to type. And how much she reminded him, in that moment, of his dear Adrina. 'Did you think to try to look?' he asked her gently.

The Earth-Mage reddened. 'Why, yes!' she blustered. 'I mean – no! How the blazes should I know what the southlands are like? I thought your window worked in the same way as scrying – I concentrated on Aurian, and even had she been in the south I was relying on it to take me to her.' To Hellorin's astonishment, she flung her arms around him and hugged him. 'Gods,' she cried, half in laughter, half in tears, 'what a relief it is, to hope again. For days I've been convinced . . .'

It had been years since Hellorin had held a woman – of any race – in his arms. After the loss of Adrina, he had never had the heart to do so again. As the Earth-Mage looked up at him, their eyes caught and held, until Eilin looked away. 'Tell me,' she said, in a voice that sounded strained and unnatural to the Forest Lord's ears, 'why does the range of your window not extend beyond the ocean?'

'The salt seas are a barrier to the Old Magic the Phaerie use.' Hellorin found his voice with difficulty. 'A fact that your ancestors, Lady, employed to their advantage, and our detriment.'

27

'How so?' The Mage was frowning now, and Hellorin felt a fleeting pang of regret that the bitter troubles of an age long gone should mar their accord. He sighed.

'Lady, forget that I spoke. What good can it do us, to dwell upon the quarrels and injustices of the past?'

'I want to know!' Eilin snapped; then her expression softened. 'If the forebears of the Magefolk wronged you, then only their descendants may make amends. And since I am the only Mage to whom you can speak at present . . .' She tilted an eyebrow at him, and Hellorin realized that her anger had been directed, not at him, but at those ancestors, long gone to dust, who had imprisoned his folk out of the world. And so he began to speak; telling her things that no Phaerie had ever told a Mage. He told her how the world had been long ago, before the Artefacts of the High Magic had been crafted, and the Magefolk had gained ascendancy over the elder races who possessed the powers of the Old Magic.

The Lady Eilin listened, wide-eyed, as Hellorin spoke of the gigantic Moldai, elemental creatures of living rock who existed in an odd but mutually beneficial association with the Dwelven, the Smallfolk, who make their homes within the mountainous bodies and went out into the world to be their eyes and ears and limbs.

'When the Magefolk wished to weaken the Moldai, what better way than to separate them from the Dwelven; exiling the latter in the northern lands where they could no longer reach the Moldai, who lived in the south?' Hellorin's voice was bitter. 'And what apt justice, to use the sea to do so; for it was Moldan – a mad, wild giant – who seized the powers of the Staff of Earth and used them to fracture the landmass that was once both north and south together. He caused the sea to enter, drowning the lands between, with the loss of many lives, both Mage and Mortal alike.'

Eilin frowned. 'I didn't know,' she said. 'These tales of the Ancients have vanished from our history.'

Hellorin laughed sourly. 'Then the more fools you, to misplace such vital knowledge. Lady, are you not aware that the Mad One – the Moldan who caused the destruction – is now the only one of his race to survive in the north? And had you no

28

idea that he still lives, chained and imprisoned by spells, within the very rock on which you Magefolk built your citadel?'

'What?' Eilin gasped. 'In *Nexis?* Dear gods, if the Archmage should discover this . . .'

'We must pray that he does not,' Hellorin agreed grimly. 'Miathan has already placed the world in gravest peril by his profligate summoning of the Nihilim. A Moldan, mad already, and bearing a grudge that has lasted centuries, might not care about limiting his revenge to the Magefolk who imprisoned him.'

The thought of the Moldan existing all those years beneath the Academy was too frightening for Eilin to dwell on. Wishing to distract her mind with other matters, she turned her back to the Forest Lord. 'You said that my ancestors used the sea against the Moldai,' she told him, 'but what has that to do with the Phaerie?'

Hellorin shrugged. 'Little, in truth,' he admitted, 'but when the Moldan created the sea that had not existed before, the Magefolk found that the power of the Old Magic could not pass across the salt water. Also, the catastrophe convinced the Mages that elemental beings such as the Phaerie were too dangerous to be left at large in the world. They used the Artefacts of Power to exile us – and not content with that, they also took our steeds.'

A wistful smile softened the Forest Lord's sculpted mouth. 'What beasts they were! What fire they had; what power; what beauty and spirit! They were fleet and strong, and terrible in battle – and they could outspeed the wind.' Hellorin sighed, his eyes shadowed with ancient memory. 'In winter, when the moon was full, we rode across the land like comets, with our great hounds, like my Barodh, at our sides, and the coats of our horses glistening like moonlight. The Mortals would lock up their beasts and hide quaking in their beds when the Wild Hunt was abroad.'

Hellorin's voice shook with emotion. 'The loss of our horses represented the loss of our freedom. Perhaps that was why the Magefolk took them – or perhaps, as I believe, they wished to tame them for their own use – as if they had a chance! At any rate, when they exiled us, they forbade us our mounts, that we loved, and sent them to the southlands, across the sea where our magic could not reach. We only had time for one last desperate spell to confound our foes, before we lost our steeds for ever.'

'What did you do?' Eilin asked breathlessly.

'To protect our precious beasts from conquest by Magefolk and Mortals alike, and help them survive in an alien land, we gave them human form,' Hellorin told her. 'They became – and as far as I know, they still are – capable of changing shape from human to equine at will.' He looked at her sadly. 'We will not regain them until we have been freed from our exile – and even so, there may be difficulties, for we Phaerie cannot cross the sea. And who knows, in these long ages, how their race may have altered?' His voice grew harsh. 'Truly, Eilin; if this Magefolk interference has cost us our horses for ever, all the endless ages will not suffice for them to make recompense!'

His words, recalling the bitter enmity that had existed for so long between his folk and hers, were enough to strain the fragile bond that had been building between Forest Lord and Mage. Eilin was frowning, and suddenly the evening seemed darker. Hellorin shivered wondering what damage he had unwittingly wrought. The Earth-Mage twisted her hands in her lap. 'Speaking of recompense, Lord, there is something I have long been meaning to ask you.'

Hellorin, his curiosity piqued, nodded. 'Say on, Lady.'

'I . . . Do you remember, so many years ago, when I summoned you to find my child, and the swordsman Forral, who were lost in a blizzard?'

'Aye, Lady, I recall it well – the first time we met.'

'You told me then what I already knew – that in dealing with the Phaerie there is always a price. You said . . .'

'*Remember that this matter is not resolved between us. We will meet again – and when we do, I will claim my debt,*' Hellorin supplied.

Eilin flinched. 'What made you say that?' she demanded. 'How did you know we would meet again? Had I wished to renege on our bargain, I only needed never to summon you.'

'As indeed, you did not,' the Forest Lord rebuked her. 'This time, it was my son D'arvan who did the summoning.'

30

'Thanks to which, I now owe you another debt for saving my life.' Eilin turned anxious eyes to the Phaerie Lord. 'How long will you keep me in suspense? I am a prisoner here, no matter how kindly a captivity it may seem. How can I rest, not knowing what you may see fit to ask of me?'

Hellorin sighed. 'Eilin, I understand your concern. Sooner or later, a price must be paid, for our law cannot be set aside. Why, I was unable even to spare my son and his beloved, who paid a heartrending price for my aid with their endless vigil in the wildwood to guard the Sword of Flame.' He shook his head. 'But alas, I cannot name what I would demand of you. This is not cruelty on my part – I simply have no idea what to ask, which in itself is strange, as if it formed part of the workings of some destiny that I cannot foresee. When first we met, I hated the Magefolk – I scarcely knew you, and I had no idea of the existence of my son. When you asked for my aid, so many notions leapt into my mind . . . to exact revenge on your race, through you . . . But –' he spread his hands. 'I could not. I must hold your indebtedness against some future need.'

'I see,' snapped Eilin. 'Your actions say little for your trust in me – and a great deal for my lack of trust in you!' She rose to her feet and strode out of the clearing without a backward look.

Eliseth sat in her chambers, bundled in cloaks and huddled over a roaring fire. Since Miathan had set his ageing spell on her, her bones had ached with the cold. The Weather-Mage stared into the blaze, her silver eyes reflecting the glare of the leaping flames. Her body was racked with shivers, but her hatred smouldered on, unquenched. She would not endure this loathesome condition much longer. 'Don't think you'll get away with this, Miathan!' she grated. Her rheumy eyes tracked blurrily around the room, registering drifts of shattered crystal that twinkled frostily on the lush white carpet. After Miathan had wrought his hideous change in her, the Weather-Mage had smashed every mirror in her chambers.

Avoiding slivers of glass, Eliseth shuffled across the floor, leaning on her staff for support. With stiff, twisted hands she

31

poured spirits into a goblet, cursing herself for succumbing to the dubious comfort of drink – the very thing for which she had once derided Bragar.

Bragar! Eliseth emptied the glass in one swallow, and refilled it quickly. The Fire-Mage had been a fool – he had deserved to die. So why was she haunted by the sight of his blackened, smoking face? Why did she still feel the ghost of his clawlike grasp on her hand's aged skin?

Bragar loved you! Who will love you now, old crone?

That insidious, persistent thought. A snarl of rage bubbled up in Eliseth's throat. The goblet flew across the room, impelled by the force of her magical will, to smash against the wall, its contents streaking like dark blood down the pure white surface. 'Oh gods!' Eliseth buried her face in shaking hands. 'Pull yourself together!' she growled. 'If you panic, you'll ruin your only chance.' Taking another goblet from the shelf, she filled it and returned to the fireside to wait. *He* would be coming soon. By now, he must have discovered what she had done – and if she wanted to regain her youth everything depended on the approaching confrontation.

The door flew open, rebounding against the wall with a reverberant crash. *'You treacherous bitch! What in the name of the gods are you playing at?'*

Eliseth jerked upright, scrambling her wits together to meet the ire of the Archmage. Miathan slammed his fist on the table, the gems that had replaced his eyes burning crimson with rage. 'You have one minute to begin restoring the winter in Aerillia before I blast you to cinders!'

This was her moment. Eliseth willed her shaking body to stillness, and forced the illusion of nonchalance. 'I don't care if you do.' She shrugged. 'Do you think I want to stay in this wrinkled, sagging shell? Do your worst, Miathan – ah, but I forget – you already have.'

'You call that my worst?' Miathan howled.

The Weather-Mage cringed as a roaring inferno leapt up around her. The flames closed in, reaching for her greedily. Eliseth felt their searing heat; felt her hair frizzle and flame. Her skin was beginning to blister and crack. She clenched her fists so hard that blood ran through her fingers as her nails cut into her palms; clamped her teeth so hard to stop herself from screaming that she thought her jaw must surely break. 'It's just an illusion,' she told herself. 'An illusion.' But oh – the unspeakable pain!

'Restore the winter!' the Archmage roared, his voice cutting into the depths of her agony. Eliseth shuddered, ignoring the insistent voice. Everything was at stake – *everything*! I *must* endure, she told herself. I must. But it was too much – how could anyone bear such suffering? The mind of the Weather-Mage twisted and writhed in panic within its cage of tortured flesh, desperately seeking to escape the agony. And then – something changed.

Eliseth's senses reeled as her vision blurred and doubled. Though she could see the inferno surrounding her, and beyond that the gloating face of the Archmage, she also viewed the scene from above, as though she looked down from overhead. The Magewoman, needing all her strength to fight the pain, closed her eyes against the dizzying distraction, and suddenly she understood. As though her eyes were open, she could still see the second scene – the view from above. In order to flee the agony, her mind was trying to escape her body. Her faltering crone's brain had almost missed the solution, but her instincts had not led her astray. Eliseth laughed out loud as she gathered her remaining energies and slipped easily free from her outward form.

Oh, blessed relief! The Weather-Mage paused, conscious only of the absence of pain, steadying and balancing the energies that formed her inner self. Then a howl of thwarted rage drew her attention. The flames had vanished. Hovering close to the ceiling of her chamber, she looked down to see Miathan, white with fury, standing over the discarded shell of her body, heaping curses on her head.

Eliseth's confidence returned in a glorious surge. Her inner being was not old and ugly. Here she was young and strong again, and beautiful as ever. If I could only stay like this, she thought. But without the arcane power generated by such as Miathan through the shedding of Mortal blood, a Mage could not sustain life outside her earthbound body for long. Due to the aged fragility of her mundane form, and the dreadful

33

depletion of the energy she had spent to withstand the Archmage's onslaught, Eliseth could already feel herself weakening. She must go back, she knew, or remain lost and bodiless for ever – but still she lingered, hoping to drive Miathan into a frenzy as he saw the last chance to restore his winter slipping away. Ah, now she had him where she wanted him! Eliseth smiled in satisfaction, then shuddered at the thought of abandoning this glory to cage herself once more in the weak and aching body of the crone. 'But it won't be for long,' she assured herself, as she swooped, closed her eyes, and sank back into the shackles of her earthbound form.

The Weather-Mage looked up, and Miathan's tirade choked off as though he had been throttled. Fleetingly, Eliseth wished he still possessed his eyes; not through any kindly feeling, but because the expressionless gems that had taken their place rendered his face unreadable. But whether it was due to relief or anger, the Weather-Mage gave thanks for his hesitation, and was quick to seize the initiative.

'You've had your vengeance, Archmage; will you not be content? I defied you, and I have paid. Won't you put the past behind us? For still you need my help. A bargain, Miathan – my youth for your winter. We must trust each other now, for with your ageing spell you'll always have a hold on me, as I have the winter that is so essential to your plans. How can such cooperation not benefit us both?'

'I'd sooner bed a viper than trust you again!' Miathan spat. The Weather-Mage hid a smile. He's beaten, she thought triumphantly. She said no more; only waited for his rage to cool. His surrender had come sooner than she'd expected, and Eliseth wondered just what had passed during his communion with the High Priest of the Skyfolk.

'Very well,' Miathan snapped at last. 'But be warned – one more attempt to thwart my plans, and I will use the Cauldron to blast you so far from the living universe that not even the gods will be able to find you!' The Archmage raised his hands, his face taut with concentration. A wave of weakness flowed over Eliseth; her body seemed to blur and shimmer; there was a flash of excruciating pain as the old bones straightened; a tingling sensation suffused her skin as the sagging flesh filled out again with the healthy bloom of youth. Powerful blood coursed like wine through her veins, restoring suppleness and strength to stiff old muscles.

'Thanks be to the gods!' Eliseth leapt to her feet, flinging aside her swathing cloaks.

'You'd do better to thank me,' the Archmage told her flatly. 'Count yourself fortunate, Eliseth, that I still need your aid to accomplish my plans.'

'Whatever I can do to help you, Archmage, I will.' The Weather-Mage did her best to sound chastened.

Miathan gave her a long, hard look. 'Very well,' he snapped. 'To begin with, you must undertake a task that I had planned to entrust to Bragar. Since your meddling killed him, you must take up his work in his stead.' He scowled at her. 'At least it should keep you from mischief for a while.'

Eliseth went to her cabinet and poured wine for them both. Miathan took the goblet without thanks, and sipped before continuing: 'I wanted Bragar to investigate the disappearance of Angos and his men. We must assume they are dead, and since their last message said they were tracking the rebels towards the Valley, I suspect that Eilin had a hand in the matter – possibly aided by D'arvan.'

Eliseth's fists clenched with rage at the thought of the ones who had slain her lover Davorshan, but despite her anger she felt a shrinking knot of fear within her. She discounted Davorshan's weak-willed twin as a threat, but the Lady of the Lake had destroyed a Mage far younger and physically stronger than herself, and, seemingly, had slain about two dozen hardened mercenaries. Obviously, they had underestimated Eilin's power. The Magewoman shivered. Is this some new plot of Miathan's invention, to get rid of me? she thought.

'You want me to go to the Valley?' she asked quietly.

'No!' the Archmage barked. 'Use subterfuge – use spies. You're good at such underhanded work. But whatever you do, find out what is happening in that Valley.'

'The only reason I do not ask you to go yourself,' he went on, 'is that I need your skills to restore winter over Aerillia. Is it possible, though, to keep the worst of the storms away from the southern part of the mountains?'

Eliseth looked at him through narrowed eyes. Now what is he up to? she thought. She frowned, trying to reconstruct the area in her memory, for her ancient charts had been lost in the destruction of her weather-dome. 'I think so,' she said at last. 'The range broadens south of the country of the Winged folk –if I monitor the airmass carefully, those mountains form a natural barrier . . .' She frowned. 'Why?'

'Eliseth, if you think I'll trust you with my plans, so soon after your treachery . . .' the Archmage began heatedly, but smoothly she forestalled him.

'Miathan, please. That was all a regrettable mistake. I only want to make amends, but how can I help you when I don't know what is going on?'

'I'll tell you my plans in my own good time,' Miathan snapped 'At the moment, all you need to know is that, in order for my trap for Aurian to succeed, she must have access into those southern mountains. You will facilitate this, will you not?' His voice sank to a sinister purr. 'For remember, Eliseth – the ruin of your youth that I accomplished once, I can easily wreak again.'

The Weather-Mage met his gaze, her face expressionless. 'I promise, Miathan, that you will never again have the need,' she lied. 'You can trust me, I swear – for it's as much to my advantage as yours that Aurian should be captured.' Eliseth turned away to hide a smile. And once you have captured her for me, Miathan, she thought, you and Aurian must look to yourselves!

3
Raven's Fall

Within the pine-scented shelter of the fallen trees, Aurian rested against a pillow of packs and folded blankets. Shia dozed beside her, her lacerated feet covered in salve and swathed in rags. She purred in her sleep as she lay with her head in Aurian's lap. Anvar was curled on the Mage's other side, his dazzling blue eyes closed in the profound sleep of pure exhaustion. His fine, dark-blond hair, lightened and sun-streaked now from their trip through the desert, had fallen across his face, moving lightly in time with his breathing. He deserved his rest, Aurian thought. He had saved their lives when Eliseth attacked, and for a half-trained Mage he had acquitted himself admirably.

Aurian shrank from the fact that Anvar's devotion was based on feelings far deeper than friendship. The memory of Forral was still too strong. Yet she had chosen to stay with Anvar rather than follow the shade of her murdered lover into death . . . Aurian shook her head as if to jolt away the pang of guilt that accompanied the thought, but there was affection in her gaze as she gently brushed the errant strands of hair from Anvar's face, and pulled up the blanket that had slipped from his shoulders.

Aurian's unborn child moved restlessly, disturbed by his mother's unease, and the Mage reached out with her mind to reassure Forral's son.

'Do you never rest?' Shia's mental voice was tart, but Aurian heard an underlying note of concern. The cat regarded her gravely with an unblinking yellow gaze. 'Aurian, why must you burden yourself so? The cub has a claim on you, true; but that other who concerns you is dead, and beyond your help.' As Aurian flinched from her blunt words, Shia's tone softened, carrying an echo of what the Mage had come to recognize as a smile. 'As for Anvar, you need not worry about him. The strength in him is growing all the time. He will wait.'

'I never asked him to wait for me,' Aurian objected.

Shia's projected thoughts held the equivalent of a shrug. 'He will wait – whether you ask him or not.'

Aurian dozed again, and was awakened by the delectable aroma of roasting meat. Anvar was already up and about, helping Nereni finish the preparations for her feast. The little woman had been working all afternoon, having sent Bohan and Eliizar out into the forest to find tubers to bake in the ashes of her fire, and berries and greens to go with the venison she had prepared. Yazour, seeing what was coming, had promptly volunteered to go fishing. He returned near suppertime, whistling and empty-handed, to a scolding from Nereni. 'What could I do?' he protested innocently. 'They were simply not biting.'

Aurian exchanged a grin with Anvar at the success of the warrior's ploy. How good it was, to have their group all safely back together again. Then suddenly it hit her. Something had been nagging at her, and now she realized what exhaustion and the joy of the reunion had put out of her mind. 'Where on earth is Raven?' she asked.

'Raven keeps wandering off to hunt in the forest,' Nereni replied. 'She brings back birds and such, but I worry so. What if she should meet a wild beast?'

'You worry too much,' Eliizar told his wife. 'If a wolf or a bear should come, she has only to fly away.'

'That's true,' Aurian agreed, but none the less, she wondered at Raven's solitary behaviour.

Raven perched awkwardly among the spiny branches of a fir, watching twilight steal through the dark and tangled trees. In the north, the high peaks were still gilded with the fiery light of sunset, and the winged girl scowled at the sight. Accustomed to the long days of her mountain home, she could never get used to the fact that the light faded so early from these wretched lowlands.

She blinked back tears of frustration. It was not her kind of hunting – skulking in a smother of trees. She missed the vast arena of the open skies; her joy was in the speed and skill of the chase. Back in Aerillia, her lost home, she had hunted for sport, releasing her feathered prey to sing and soar in peace. She had never known, then, what it was to be hunted herself – to live as an exile without shelter; to be ruled by the demands of an empty belly. Now she knew only too well.

Raven cursed Blacktalon, who had forced her to flee in terror from her rightful place as princess of the Winged Folk. He had to be stopped – and, by the Sky-god Yinze, she meant to do it! If her companions of the desert had failed her, at least she'd found one who would not. At that thought of Harihn, she suppressed a shiver of guilt. Skyfolk mated for life, and her people would revile what she had done with a human. But he'd been so good to her . . . At the thought of him, her grim mood softened. She would show the others. Aurian, who would not listen to her plea for help – and Anvar, of whom she'd had better hopes . . .

It was a sore point, but Raven forced the thought away as her growling belly reminded her to concentrate on the hunt. Waiting with wary patience, she weighed a stone in her hand as she watched the layer of ground-mist that accompanied the forest dusk. There was a rustle in the bushes, followed by a harsh cry. Raven hurled her stone. In a blur of wings the pheasant broke cover and she launched after it with the clean swift grace of a hawk. Swooping on the bird, she grabbed it in an explosion of feathers, and with a practised jerk broke its neck in midair.

'Well caught, my jewel!' The voice came low but clear from a gap in the trees below. Raven's blood sang in her veins. Harihn had come at last! Glowing with excitement, she turned in a breathtaking sideslip to angle down through the narrow slot between the tangled boughs. It had been days since she'd seen Harihn, and it had been so lonely without him! Her wings stirring the mist in gossamer swirls, Raven, panting from the exhilaration of the chase, swept down to meet her lover.

Harihn emerged cursing from the bushes and ran his hands through his tangled hair, dislodging leaves and bits of twig.

This clearing was so well hidden that only the winged girl could reach it with ease. Dusk had fallen sooner than he had expected, and he'd been forced to blunder his way from his camp in near-darkness. By the Reaper, this had better be worth it, he thought.

'Harihn?' There was a rusle above his head, and a creak of branches; then Raven landed beside him. The prince of the Khazalim hesitated, torn as always between awareness of her oddly alien beauty and revulsion at the thought of coupling with a creature that was not human. Then the Voice was in his mind, spurring him on impatiently. *'Get on with it, fool – before she suspects!'*

Harihn moaned, fighting the quick surge of his blood as his treacherous body succumbed to his rising desire. It was always the same; ever since he had begun her seduction at the prompting of the Voice that had probed his mind on the day he had entered the forest. Sometimes, he wondered if he'd been right to trust the Voice – but it had offered him what he wanted: power to gain his father's throne – and revenge on Anvar for corrupting the loyalty of Aurian, who could have brought him that power, and so much more.

'Come, what's wrong with you? Take her, if it's what she wants!' the Voice snapped. *'We need her cooperation!'*

To Harihn's horror, he felt himself taking an unintentional step forward, his limbs moving of their own volition as the intruder took control.

Raven looked at her lover, hesitating. Harihn seemed strange tonight. His curling black hair was bedewed with silver droplets, turning him grey before his time. He looked as though he had aged, she thought. His gentle features were hard-etched; as though an older, harsher face had been laid over his own. His eyes blazed into hers, and for the first time she felt a pang of fear.

'It's time,' Harihn grated. Just that – no smile, or kiss, or word of welcome. Before Raven could move he grabbed her, one foot hooking her ankle, tripping her to the ground, trapping her with his weight. Feathers flew like black snow as her wings caught in the bushes. He tore at her tunic, stopping her protests with bruising kisses, his hands mauling her breasts. His knee was between her legs, thrusting them roughly apart. 'Harihn, no!' Raven gasped. Cursing her, he drew back his hand, and her cheeks flamed as he slapped her into silence. Tears leaked down her temples, ran cold into the tangled cloud of her hair.

Hard and urgent, he thrust himself inside her, and Raven hissed with pain. 'No!' she shrieked, hurling curses in the Skyfolk tongue. Her nails, like talons, raked him, snatching at his eyes.

Harihn flinched aside, deep gashes scarring his cheeks. 'Savage!' he spat. His blood dripped hot on her face as he kissed her again, more gently.

'Forgive me,' he whispered. 'We were so long apart, and you are so beautiful . . .'

His hand squeezed between their bodies, slipped between her legs, and Raven whimpered with pleasure and arched against him. 'I hate you,' she gasped. 'I hate you,' she chanted over and over, to the quickening rhythm of their thrusting. 'I'll kill you! Oh!' Her talons gouged him as she climaxed, ripping his robe and scoring the skin of his back.

They rolled apart stickily; filthy, bleeding and brusied; gasping for breath. Harihn blinked, as though emerging from a dream. Raven watched through her eyelashes as he reached out to brush away the sweaty tangles of hair that clung to her cheeks. He kissed her bruised face, his breath tickling her damp skin. 'Poor child – can you forgive me?' he murmured. Raven, in the aftermath of the passion that had seized her at the last, simply nodded. He had changed, just in time – as if, for a while, he'd been someone else, then the real Harihn had returned to save her from humiliation. She was thankful for that. Little did he know, the princess thought, that she was forced to forgive him. Skyfolk mated for life, and now she was committed.

A shiver ran through her, but Raven was not a princess for nothing. She touched the scratches on Harihn's face, with a little curling smile of smugness as he flinched. 'I paid you back,' she told him, and the shadow cleared from his eyes.

'Vixen!' he muttered.

41

'It serves you right!' It was one of Nereni's phrases, and at the reminder Raven shot bolt upright. 'Yinze on a treetop! Nereni expected me long ago.'

Harihn's smile switched off. Like the sun passing through a cloud it reappeared, but more sinister, now. As it had been at the start, when he had taken her so violently . . . Raven flexed her talons, but Harihn made no move towards her. 'I have a surprise for you, Princess,' he told her. 'The Mages have come safe from the desert, and Nereni plans to celebrate with a feast.'

'A feast?' Raven cried. 'While my kingdom goes to wreck and ruin, and not one of them will lift a finger to help me . . .'

'Hush.' Harihn kissed her into silence. By the Reaper, what a credulous fool she was! 'You have no need of them, my jewel, for our time is ripe. You know I have a powerful ally. If we help him capture Aurian and Anvar, he will give you whatever assistance you need to recover your kingdom.'

'I hope so. I've had precious little help from the others.' The winged girl's voice betrayed her bitterness, and in the darkness Harihn smiled. It was so easy to manipulate her. 'Persuade your companions to head into the mountains and make for the Tower of Incondor, the ancient watch-post of your people,' he told her. 'If they reach it before Aurian regains her powers, they can easily be ambushed by my folk.'

Raven thought of Nereni, and hesitated. 'Harihn – you promise they won't be harmed?'

'Dear one, I promise.' The darkness hid the lie in Harihn's face. Nereni's husband had betrayed him, as had that renegade Yazour, and the eunuch Bohan. They deserved to perish, and Nereni with them. Harihn smiled at the thought. Unable to resist the idea of taking her again, he stroked her hair and bent to capture her lips once more.

Later, as he groped his way back to his camp, Harihn was still smiling; while Raven struck for home, flying high over the trees as the mountains faded into night.

Within a short time, the prince had stirred his people into a frenzy of activity. 'My remaining warriors leave tonight for the north, where I will join them shortly,' he told his household folk. 'In my absence, you must stay here and amass supplies

for us. Winged folk will come to take what you have gathered.'
His followers, startled by this sudden change of plans, eyed
their prince warily, whispering behind his back. He had never
been the same since he had entered the forest, and sometimes
they had even caught him talking to himself, when he thought
he was unobserved. And as for his association with the winged
creatures – that went far beyond the pale of decency.

Harihn's behaviour had been growing ever more bizarre.
Soon after their arrival at this place, he had sent most of his
soldiers, their horses laden with supplies, away north with a
winged warrior as a guide, leaving his folk with only a token
guard – and now he planned to abandon them completely.
But they were Khazalim, schooled in subservience to
authority; and Harihn was their prince. He had promised to
return for them, and with that they must be content. Harihn's
people sighed – but they obeyed.

The Xandim had never been a race that attached importance
to roofs and walls. It had been fortunate, Chiamh thought,
that folk so lacking in the skills of construction had found a
ready-made stronghold. No one knew who had built it; the
Windeye's grandam had attributed it to the ancient race of
Powerful Ones from across the sea. Chiamh doubted that,
though its creatures must have wielded incredible power, for
it had survived the depredations of time – and not surprisingly. It would take more than passing centuries to
humble such a solid construct.

Set in a deep embayment in the cliff, the fastness was a
massive keep extending out of the towering curtains of stone
that were part of the Wyndveil. The building formed a hollow
square around a courtyard, with the main living areas backing
on to the cliff. Though the fortress seemed impressively large,
its size was deceptive, for the building had been extended
back into the cliff itself, with mile on mile of corridors and
chambers hollowed out of the mountain. In times of need, the
stronghold was large enough to accommodate the entire
Xandim race – but that was not its most staggering feature.
*The entire edifice – both inside and out – had been formed from a
single stone!*

The green slope below the fortress was scattered with other, lesser buildings. With their outlines softened by growths of green, cushiony moss and gold and silver lichens, they looked from the outside like rough-sculpted rocks that had fallen from the cliff above. Their appearance, however, belied their true nature. Chiamh's investigations had proved that the structures were not boulders at all. They extended underground and seemed, like the fastness, to be outgrowths of the mountain bedrock. Each had a small, square door, and a hole in its top to admit light and allow smoke from the hearth to escape. Still more astonishing were the interiors, for the walls and floor were raised and ridged to form beds, shelves and benches. Like the fortress, their origin was a mystery, but the Xandim accepted these structures as part of the landscape. Unless the weather was extreme, they rarely bothered with these ready-made homes.

The Xandim were a hardy, active, outdoor folk who preferred the freedom of temporary shelters in the sweeping foothills or the open plains to fixed settlements and walls of stone. As humans they hunted, fished, gathered and traded – when in equine shape, their food grew in abundance around them. They had a basic written language of signs, but rarely bothered with such niceties. Instead they told stories, the taller the better, and sang many songs. Their history was simply passed down by word of mouth, much to Chiamh's frustration. He was certain that much of it was missing, and most of what remained was muddled.

The Windeye arrived, soaked, bruised and gasping for breath, at the massive, arching gate of the fortress. The building gave him a feeling of unease, as though unseen eyes watched him from under its eaves. He looked nervously up at its looming structure. The unusual silver veining in the rough brown stone gleamed softly in the afterglow of dusk, and in the deceptive ghostlight the towers and windows, balconies and buttresses of the building's fascia seemed to suggest, to Chiamh's imperfect vision, the dignified lineaments of a craggy old face. For the first time, he wondered why he had never thought of viewing the fastness with his Othersight. The goddess only knew what such a seeing might reveal – but there was no time now for such frivolous experiments.

First, he needed news of the outland prisoners. Had they arrived yet? His visions were accurate as to context, but they could be confusing and uncertain where time was concerned. And although he was the Windeye, Chiamh lacked sufficient standing with the Herdlord to enter the dungeons. The rescue of the strangers must be contrived after their trial, when they could be reached. Besides, the Windeye wanted to know more about them before he committed himself further. Luckily, there was a way to find out what he needed – so long as the strangers were already there.

It was time for the change of sentries – an informal business at best, for the independent Xandim took badly to formality and regimentation. Chiamh sighed. What a time to arrive, when he would have twice as many guards to deal with. As he approached the sentries, Chiamh recognized the ranking officer as Galdrus, a muscle-bound idiot whose head was thicker than the stone of the stronghold, and his heart sank. Lacking intelligence and imagination, Galdrus found great sport in mocking the nearsighted Windeye. But the guards had already seen him, and he had no option but to go on. Doing his best to assume the dignity of his station, the Windeye straightened his shoulders and walked up to the group of warriors who stood gossiping at the gate.

As Chiamh had expected, the mockery started before he had even reached the top of the steps.

'Come out of your hole, have you, little mole?' Galdrus jeered, earning a laugh from his companions.

Chiamh clenched his teeth. 'Let me pass,' he said softly. 'I have urgent business within.'

'Oh! The Windeye has urgent business within! What is it, Chiamh – have you come for your laundry, by any chance?'

Chiamh ignored the sniggers of the guards as they mocked his filthy, tattered appearance. The goddess only knew what he must look like after his headlong, tumbling rush down the mountain. Cursing the blush that heated his cheeks, the Windeye lifted his chin and marched determinedly inside – and fell flat on his face on the threshold, his legs entangled in the butt of a spear. 'Oops – sorry, Great One,' Galdrus snickered. His eyes grew wide with feigned terror. 'Please don't turn me into a horrible beastie!'

The Windeye picked himself up, rubbing the knee he'd cracked on the edge of the stone steps as the guards howled with laughter. Chiamh's face burned. His only thought was of escape, before his tormentors baited him further.

'Do you intend to let them get away with that?'

Chiamh whirled, seeking the voice that had whispered in his ear. The guards were convulsed with laughter – surely it had not been one of them? The voice had sounded much deeper – older, somehow, than their sneering tones.

Galdrus had noticed his hesitation. 'Yes?' The word was an open challenge. 'Did you want something, Chiamh? Directions to the bathing rooms, perhaps?' Putting his nose in the air, he held it between his fingers, and his appreciative audience laughed all the harder.

'Face them, you fool! If you walk away from this, they will torment you for the rest of your days.'

Goddess, thought Chiamh, only the mad hear voices! He tried to flee into the fastness, but as his foot touched the threshold . . .

'GET BACK THERE AND DEAL WITH THEM!'

It was no whisper this time – the roar nearly knocked him off his feet. Surely the guards had heard – but no. They were still holding their noses and making stupid jokes. Suddenly Chiamh had had enough. Wherever the voice had come from, it was right. Though the storm had faltered, the wind was still gusting round the corner of the building; there was more than enough for his needs. Chiamh's vision glazed and then cleared as he summoned his Othersight. Seizing a great double handful of the shimmering wind, he twisted it into the form of a hideous, slavering demon, and flung it into the faces of the jeering guards.

Galdrus fell to his knees screaming. Some men drew their weapons, their faces slack with fear, while others tried to flee, but were trapped in the corner of the great stone bastion at the side of the door. Chiamh laughed. Before the howls of the guards could draw the attention of those within the fortress, he gathered the vision back to himself and, flinging his hands wide, freed and scattered the winds, dispersing the demon.

The guards picked themselves up slowly, their faces an ugly mix of anger, resentment and humiliation. By the stench, more than one had soiled himself. The Windeye chuckled. 'Perhaps you should direct yourselves to the bathing rooms,' he said brightly, and went inside.

The Othersight left Chiamh as he entered the fastness, and with it his heady sense of triumph. His revenge had been sweet and well merited, but its aftermath left him with a sinking sense of shame. I was not given my powers to abuse them, he thought, remembering the fear and hate on the faces of the guards. I may have taught them not to mock me, but I made no friends today.

'Nonsense, little seer! They were not your friends, and never would have been. They feared your powers and so they mocked you – but today you taught them to respect you, which is all to the good.'

'Who are you?' Chiamh cried, drawing curious glances from passers-by in the corridors. There was no reply – already he had learned not to expect one. 'I'll get to the bottom of this,' he muttered, 'come what may.' But this was not the time to indulge his curiosity. First, and more important, the Windeye had to find the prisoners.

Chiamh looked around the entrance chamber of the fortress, and shuddered. Goddness, how he hated this place! His body was damp with the clammy sweat of fear. As always, he was aware of the tremendous mass of stone surrounding him, leaving him feeling stifled and crushed. As he stumbled along half-blind he felt lost and insecure, for, bereft of the winds in this enclosed stone tomb, Chiamh was forced to depend on his wretched, imperfect eyesight.

In happier times, the torchlit corridors of the fastness would be almost deserted. Even the Herdlord spent little time within, and most of the Xandim progressed from birth to death without ever setting foot in the place. The edifice was guarded by warriors who took it in turns, for no one wanted to be stuck here permanently. Now, however, the sinister winter that locked the land had altered the place beyond recognition, for the Xandim had brought their most vulnerable kin – the young, the sick and the aged – to shelter within the stout protective walls.

Children were everywhere, their noise almost deafening in the constricted space as they played underfoot in the corridors, hurtling past Chiamh like screeching projectiles. Grandsires and grandams, dragging bags and bundles of belongings that turned the passages into a maze of obstacles, raised their voices in querulous protest against the youngsters, and did nothing but augment the din.

The news that foreigners had been caught in Xandim lands had spread like wildfire, arousing great curiosity. In addition to those who sheltered within the stronghold, many others had come in the hope of seeing the strangers, and to witness the trial which would take place on the morrow. Through overheard snatches of talk, Chiamh discovered that the outlanders had already been brought here and imprisoned in the dungeons to await the Herdlord's justice.

It was with a tremendous sense of relief that Chiamh finally reached his chambers, after several false and confusing turns. He stepped inside, wrinkling his nose at the musty odour. His rooms had not been cleaned since his last visit, several months ago. His feet smeared trails in the dust that coated the floor, and the Windeye sneezed. He sighed. This would never have happened to his grandam. Her chambers had been in the outer part of the keep, where there were windows to let in sweet breezes and the cheerful light of day. He, Chiamh, was forced to content himself with this obscure rat-hole deep within the bowels of the cliff, but at least it was conveniently close to the dungeons – and right now that was exactly what he needed. Once he contacted the prisoners, he might find out their connection with the Bright Powers – and also, he hoped, some clue as to the part of Schiannath the Outcast in what was to come.

The Windeye remembered with shame his part in the ceremony that had exiled the warrior and his sister. When Schiannath's challenge had failed, he had been exiled, according to tradition, and Iscalda, utterly devoted to her brother, had insisted on joining him. Chiamh had been forced to use his powers to erase both their names from the wind, and supposedly from the memory of the tribe.

The Herdlord had added a cruel twist to the punishment of

Iscalda, his betrothed who had abandoned him out of loyalty to her brother. Though the Xandim possessed the ability to change at will from human to equine form, they could only breed as humans. There was, however, an ancient spell, passed from Windeye to Windeye, that could prevent the change, trapping the victim in its equine body. The Herdlord had insisted this binding be placed on Iscalda, so that she and her brother could never create a child.

Chiamh tore his thoughts from the memory. Though the deed had been forced upon him by the Herdlord, what he had done still filled him with shame. But dwelling on it would not bring him any nearer his goal of finding the prisoners.

Chiamh walked over to the wall and ran his hands over the stone, seeking a crack in the smooth surface. Though the building was made from a single, seamless rock, these chinks were everywhere. The Windeye suspected that the fastness was ventilated through these tiny gaps that honeycombed the stonework. His nearsighted vision was little use to him, but over the years his hands had developed an uncanny sensitivity to the air currents that were the tools of his power – he only had to find the slightest draught . . .

Once again, the Windeye felt the familiar melting coolness as his Othersight took over. This time, so intent was he on his work that he never thought to be afraid. Ah, now he had it! He could see the draught – a tiny, curling slip of silver . . . Chiamh poured the mystic awareness of his Othersight into the moving thread of air, and began to follow it; his consciousness leaving his body to slip like an eel through the tiny chink in the stone, following the stream of air through a labyrinth of minuscule passages.

Chiamh crept slowly forward, feeling his way blindly through tiny fissures in the rock. He followed the minute changes in the flow, moving always towards the noisome and damp. At last, after several false trails that led him to deserted chambers and cells, his patience was rewarded. He felt a tingling sensation as the air around him vibrated with the odd burr of voices speaking in a foreign tongue. Triumphant, the Windeye slipped his consciousness through a chink in the rock – and found himself in the deepest part of the dungeons, confronting the outlanders of his vision.

Back and forth, back and forth, Meiriel paced the narrow limits of her cell. There was no light. *They* had put her here, condemned her to the torture of endless darkness in this subterranean tomb with its door that was locked and barred with magic. *Them.* Eliseth and Bragar. The Healer clenched her fists until the nails cut into her palm, and a bubbling snarl came from deep within her throat. They held the power now – they and the blind, twisted creatures that had murdered Finbarr.

Meiriel's lips stretched back in a feral snarl. 'I know you, Miathan,' she hissed. 'You cannot deceive me! I see everything, down here in the dark. I see you writhe in the agony of those black charred pits in your head – the blacker pits in your soul! I see the child in Aurian's womb – the monster you created – the demon that I must destroy . . .'

During a wild and eventful lifetime, the cavalry master had discovered that all prisons look very much alike. Parric, no stranger to the cells of the garrison in his younger days, might have been transported back in time by the damp stone walls, the smouldering, smoking torch, the verminous, foetid straw in the corner. But thanks be to the gods, they were all together. Had he been imprisoned alone, and left to contemplate the fate of his companions, he might have given way to his fear. As it was, he could look at the others for the first time in days, though the sight was not reassuring. Sangra's face was blotched with dirt and bruises; she looked resolute but grim in the dim light. Elewin, his eyes dark-circled, was coughing blood; and Meiriel – gods, if only she would stop that endless pacing! She was muttering about death and darkness, her expression fell and fey with madness. Parric was angry. More than that, he was furious and frustrated. He forgot his own peril, he only saw his companions, and how they suffered.

'Let me out of here!' The cavalry master hammered on the unyielding door. 'Curse you, let me talk to someone!' He spun, and rounded on Meiriel. 'You speak their language! Tell them, you bitch! Tell them we aren't their enemies!'

'*Are you not?*' The voice was soft and elusive, and it seemed to come from everywhere.

'Great Chathak!' Sangra breathed. 'Is that real?'

Parric gaped. The dungeon, already chill, had turned suddenly colder. Wind blew through the cell, clearing away the noisome damp. There, in the corner, stood a young man, perfectly ordinary – except that the cavalry master could see, quite clearly, the guttering torch and rough stone walls of the prison – right through his body.

Parric stepped back, his scalp crawling, his mouth gone dry. A *ghost*? Normally the cavalry master would have scoffed at such nonsense, but after living through the Night of the Wraiths in Nexis his belief in the unseen had altered. His bowels tightened, and chills chased across his flesh. He found himself reaching reflexively for the sword that had been taken from him by his captors.

'Who are the Bright Powers?' The apparition demanded. Parric was puzzled, for the words seemed to be in his own northern tongue, yet, watching the lips of the spectral figure, it was quite clear that it was speaking another language. Parric frowned. It seemed as though the words, on leaving the lips of the ghost, were somehow twisting themselves in the air, to come to his own ears in a form he could understand. The apparition was still speaking, however, and Parric forced his attention away from the mystery in order to concentrate on what was being said.

'I must know,' the spectre insisted. 'Who are the Evil Ones who ride the north winds with winter in their train?'

'The Archmage Miathan is evil.'

Parric was relieved that Meiriel had snapped sufficiently back to reality to speak up at last. The supernatural was the province of the Magefolk, and an answer was more than he could have managed in that moment. The apparition frowned. 'What is the Archmage Miathan?'

The cavalry master was glad to leave it to Meiriel to explain the Archmage. Unfortunately, the ghost seemed scarcely satisfied by her rambling account of Miathan's perfidy. 'Explain!' it demanded. 'You have spoken of the Dark Ones, but what of the Bright Powers? Who are the Bright Ones that you have come to assist?'

'I don't know about any Bright Ones, but I've come looking for the Lady Aurian.' Finally, Parric found his voice. He looked to Elewin for assistance, but the old man was too far gone in fever to reply. The cavalry master was forced to take on the burden of the tale himself, but it wasn't easy. He found himself prey to a growing sense of unreality as he sat in a dungeon in a foreign land, telling a ghost of his friendship with Forral, and Aurian, who was carrying Forral's child when the commander was murdered by Miathan. Stumbling over his words, he told how Aurian and her servant Anvar had fled Nexis, and were thought to be here in the south. Finally, he told the ghost how he and Vannor had formed their band of rebels – and how he had left them to undertake this rash, impulsive quest to find Aurian.

When he had finished, Sangra spoke. 'Now we've answered your questions, what about answering ours? Who are you? How can you walk through walls? Why . . .' But the ghost had vanished.

As Chiamh made his way back to his chambers, following the fresher currents of air through the crevices in the stone, his mind was awhirl with excitement. Though he still had gained no clue as to Schiannath's part in this business, he had heard most of what he wanted. The Dark Powers, the Bright Ones – at last all had been made clear, and he knew now, more than ever, that he had to rescue these strangers from his own people. But how?

Lost in thought, the Windeye was not concentrating on what he was doing. Engrossed in a series of plans of increasing complexity and impracticality, it took him some time to realize that he should have reached his chambers long ago. Chiamh came out of his reverie with a jolt, to discover that he was utterly lost in the trackless labyrinth of crevices within the body of the fastness. He had no idea where he was – and no means of returning to his body.

4
News from Wyvernesse

When the Archmage had left once more to supervise his southern pawns, his departure came as a tremendous relief to Eliseth. Though Miathan was gone only in spirit, the atmosphere in the Academy was considerably lightened by the absence of his brooding thoughts, and the Weather-Mage could relax at last. Within the sanctuary of her chambers, she felt her face with anxious fingers. Her skin was smooth now; taut and silken where it had been rough and sagging before. Suddenly, she wished she had not smashed all the mirrors. What a joy it would be to see herself, and not that hideous old hag. Thank all the gods – but then again, why thank them? Eliseth had saved herself through her own cleverness.

None the less, the Mage was quick to keep her word and restore winter – a simple matter, though her weather-dome had been destroyed in the backlash of the battle with Aurian. Her spells had not had much time to unravel, and it took only a little effort to rebuild them, working from the open rooftop temple on the Mages' Tower, from which the ashes of Bragar had now been cleaned. Her work completed, Eliseth wandered downstairs, enjoying the supple response of her young-again body; savouring the peace of the silent tower. When she came to Miathan's door, she stopped. His body would be lying beyond, untenanted and helpless while his mind was away in the south, overseeing his plans for Aurian's capture.

Eliseth stood at the door, studying the honey-rippled pattern of the grain. The temptation was overwhelming. It would be so easy . . . As she lifted her hand to the latch, a blast of tingling cold smote her palm. From the corner of her eye, Eliseth glimpsed the illusory shimmer-haze of a wardspell. She snatched her hand back with an oath, rubbing the palm against her skirts. I should have known, she thought. The old wolf

53

would never put enough trust in me, or anyone else, to leave his body unguarded in his absence. She wondered what spell Miathan had placed on the door; what fate would have been hers, had she been foolish or unwary enough to lift the latch. It would be something unspeakable, Eliseth was sure. Now that Miathan wielded the power of the Cauldron . . .

Shuddering, the Weather-Mage moved hastily away, and continued her descent. The next rooms she passed belonged to Aurian. After a moment, Eliseth pushed open the heavy door. The rooms were tidy – as tidy as Anvar had left them on the night he had fled Nexis with his mistress. Eliseth wrinkled her nose at the smell of mildew. The dank air of the room was stale with neglect; the void of the ash-furred hearth was cold and grey. Cobwebs and dust shrouded the furnishings like a ghostly veil, and the mouldering cushions had been nibbled by mice.

The Weather-Mage smiled. If the Archmage had his way, Aurian would soon experience similar desolation within her soul. *It's as well I didn't kill you, Aurian,* Eliseth thought. *Miathan can make you suffer more intensely than I!* Turning on her heel, she left the dreary chamber without a backward look, seeking her own rooms on the floor below.

While the Mage had been busy above, one of the few remaining menials, a ragged, pinch-faced brat, had been cleaning her rooms. As Eliseth entered, the child shot her a scared look from beneath a curtain of snarled brown curls and bobbed a sketchy curtsey, her cleaning-rag clutched tight in grubby fingers. 'I – I filled your bath, Lady,' she whispered nervously. 'I hope I done right.'

The scullion had done a fine job of restoring the chamber. The broken mirrors had gone, and not a particle of glass remained on the gleaming floor. The furnishings had been dusted, and the liquors and goblets put away. The stains from her thrown cup had vanished from the wall and a fire flamed bright in the clean-swept grate. Eliseth nodded approval. At last! she thought. One of these slatterns knows how to work. She dismissed the girl, sending her back to the kitchen with orders for a meal to be prepared.

When Eliseth entered her bathing-room she was further

54

gratified. A fire had been lit in the squat iron stove, the tub was filled with steaming water, and soap and scented oils had been laid out for her. Fresh-laundered towels had been hung to warm near the glowing stove. The Mage was delighted. What a difference these attentions make, she thought. Her maid had been slain by a Wraith when Miathan's abominations had run amok, and since then they had been so short of help at the Academy that she'd never found another. But this girl had potential . . . Eliseth smiled. Perhaps my luck is changing, she thought. She pulled off the robe that she had worn as an ancient crone, and her face darkened into a scowl at the reminder. Spitting out a curse, she crumpled it into a ball and thrust it into the stove, slamming the door on it as it burst into flames.

As she slipped into the scented water, regret for the loss of Davorshan twisted like a knife within Eliseth's soul. She missed the Water-Mage keenly. Under her tutelage, he had grown ever more talented, in magic and in her bed, proving a willing, useful tool in her schemes until Miathan had sent him to kill Eilin, and he himself had been slain. Eliseth was glad of Miathan's sanction to discover the identity of his murderer, for eventually she meant to avenge him. But in the meantime Eilin's Vale remained a mystery fraught with direst peril. How to find out what was going on there? As the Mage lay musing in the soothing water, the seeds of a plan began to form in her mind.

Emerging some time later, cleansed at last in body and spirit, Eliseth returned to her bedchamber and put on a loose robe of thick white wool. Having conjured a warm breeze to take the last of the damp from her hair, she curled up on the white velvet cushions of her window-seat and began to brush the silvery strands.

It would take a while for the grim clouds of her winter to return to their place over Nexis. In the meantime, the heavens seemed to be making the most of their chance. A spectacular sunset flooded the Academy courtyard with honeyed light and cool blue shadow, turning the shattered shell of her weather-dome to fire and crimson blood. *Bragar's blood.* At the reminder of her failure and disgrace, Eliseth drew in a hissing breath. 'Just wait, Aurian,' she snarled. 'One day I will have my revenge!'

The topaz glory of sunset faded to the sapphire and amethyst of twilight. To Eliseth's relief, night threw its shadowy cloak over Nexis, hiding the ruin in the courtyard. High in the deepening vault above, the diamond-points of stars were beginning to appear.

'Lady Eliseth? Are you there?' There came a timid tap at the door of her bedchamber.

'How *dare* you interrupt me!' The Mage flung open the door to find the ragged girl-child on the other side.

'But Lady, your supper . . .' Her words ended in a wail as Eliseth slapped her.

'Never answer me back, you guttersnipe!' she hissed. The girl's fists clenched, and behind the greasy tendrils of hair her eyes flashed defiance. Eliseth raised an eyebrow. It seemed she had underestimated the little baggage! What a diversion it will be, to break her to my will, she mused. 'What's your name, child?' she asked.

'Inella, Lady,' mumbled the brat.

'Speak up, girl! Tell me, why haven't I seen you before?'

'Wasn't here before.'

Eliseth's hand itched to slap her again, but she kept her temper reined. She required fear and respect from the girl, but she also needed her loyalty. With an effort, she managed to produce a smile. 'Are you hungry, child?' The girl nodded, her large eyes fixed on the serving dishes that crowded for space on Eliseth's supper tray.

Her mouth quirking in an odd little smile, Eliseth divided the contents of the tray, serving herself with generous portions of beef stew and steamed vegetables, but leaving enough in the covered dishes to feed the starveling child. She took one of the sweet apple pastries, spicy with cloves and cinnamon, and left the other for Inella. 'Here, child.' She handed back the tray. 'Take that off to a quiet corner and feed yourself – by the look of you, Janok keeps you on slender rations. Report to me first thing tomorrow and we'll replace those disreputable rags you're wearing.'

The dull, resentful look had vanished from Inella's face.

Already, it seemed that Eliseth's ill-tempered slap had been forgotten. 'Oh, Lady – thank you!' The child's eyes were bright with gratitude as she took the proffered tray, which tipped perilously as she curtsied, and Eliseth steadied it quickly before the dishes could slide to to the floor. 'Off you go,' she said. 'Enjoy your supper, child – and when you report back to Janok, tell him that from now on I shall want you as my personal maid.'

When the girl, still babbling her gratitude, had departed, Eliseth sat down to enjoy her first hearty meal since Miathan had cast her into the shape of a hag. It was good solid fare – a far cry from the broth and gruel that were all she'd been able to manage with the toothless gums of an old crone. The Mage ate with great appetite, but, more than the food, she was savouring the thought that once again she would have a willing tool, enslaved by her false and easy charm, to do her bidding. Eliseth smiled. She was sure the little maid would prove useful eventually. Mortals usually did.

Eilin's Valley cupped the rich sunset colours like a handful of jewels. In the glittering waters of the lake, a unicorn disported in the shallows, striking starbursts of spray from her bounding hooves and scattering a rain of diamond droplets with her silvery horn. D'arvan, watching, smiled. Gods, she was breathtaking! The most beautiful creature that had ever lived, and he was the only one privileged to see her – yet he would have traded the marvel in an instant to have his Maya back. Her hearty laugh and sense of fun; her blunt common sense so richly mingled with compassion; her slight, wiry form with its strong, sun-browned limbs; her glossy dark hair, neatly braided warrior-fashion, or lying loose in crinkled waves across a pillow . . .

As though he too were emerging from the waters of the lake, D'arvan shook himself free from the dreams of longing as the unicorn approached, the deepening twilight blue-silver on her moonspun hide. D'arvan put his arms around her neck and the two of them – Mage and Miracle – embraced; sharing, for a moment, their loneliness. How long would this wretched isolation last? D'arvan wondered. He and Maya were doing all that his father, the Forest Lord, had asked. His magic, augmented, he suspected, by the ancient powers of the Phaerie, had kept Eliseth's deadly winter out of the Vale, which glowed with burgeoning life like a solitary emerald set into the iron-locked lands around. Trees, aware and wakeful, filled the great bowl from brim to brim, providing shelter, protection and sustenance for the enemies of the Archmage. D'arvan and the Lady Eilin's wolves patrolled the Valley, protecting those who dwalt within from invasion and danger. Maya guarded the lakeside, and the wooden bridge that led to the island and its hidden secret – the legendary Sword of Flame, forged in ancient times by the Dragonfolk to be the greatest of the Artefacts of Power.

D'arvan sighed. Were it not for the accursed Sword ... But wishes were useless. The Weapon of the High Magic did exist, and until the One for whom it had been forged came to claim it, as had been foretold long ago, he and Maya must fulfil their lonely guardianship. The Mage wondered, as he often did, who the wielder would be. It's all very well, he thought, for us to assume that this person will be on our side. It could be anyone! What if it turns out to be the Archmage? His guts twisted in terror at the thought.

Maya – or, rather, the unicorn – nudged him sharply in the stomach with her nose, making him totter backwards to keep his balance. 'All right,' D'arvan told her. 'I know. I'm wasting time with my foolish notions, while you want to take a last look at your friend Hargorn before he leaves.'

Darkness was falling, and all was still, save for the rhythmic chirp of frogs in the rushes. Ghostly tendrils of silver mist were swirling over the dark, smooth surface of the water. D'arvan held up the Lady's staff, and the trees parted before him, bowing their leafy heads in homage over the path they had created. Together they left the lakeside, Mage and unicorn, vanishing into the shadowed forest like the last, fading memories of a dream.

It was not far from the lakeside to the camp of Vannor's rebels. Though D'arvan and the unicorn were invisible to the Mortals, they remained in the thicket that edged the clearing.

58

D'arvan had tried, once or twice, to enter the camp, but had been unnerved by the blank expressions of Vannor's fugitives, as their eyes looked right through him. It was lonely enough being invisible, the Mage had decided, without being reminded of the fact.

Invisible or not, D'arvan had done the rebels proud by way of a camp. His father had told him to shelter Miathan's foes, and he had done his best by way of preparation, even before Vannor's folk had arrived. With the protection of the trees uppermost in his mind, D'arvan had taken every precaution to eliminate the need for the fugitives to cut living wood. The rounded shelters that ringed the clearing were made from saplings and shrubs that the Earth-Mage had persuaded to embrace and intertwine, leaving hollows within their hearts where men might live. D'arvan made sure that a pile of deadwood appeared each day, transported by an apport-spell – taught him in his brief apprenticeship by the Lady Eilin – from the furthest reaches of the forest. Paths appeared, wherever Vannor's people wished to go. The filbert and fruit trees that throve by the lakeside had been cajoled into producing early harvests, and though the island, with Eilin's garden, was forbidden to the outlaws, D'arvan had rounded up most of her scattered goats and poultry, and had left them where they had soon been found.

The young Mage smiled, remembering how unnerved the rebels had been at first – and how quickly they had settled in. Vannor's redoubtable housekeeper Dulsina had, of course, been the first to point out that they were clearly being helped and protected, so they ought to make the most of it – as, indeed, they had. D'arvan's haven, apparently, was a vast improvement over their hideaway in the sewers of Nexis!

It was with great reluctance that Vannor had eventually pointed out that this idyll in the forest was accomplishing nothing. Accepting the need for tidings of their enemies, and also wishing to increase his forces and bring more people from the city to this place of safety, he had decided that someone must return to Nexis. Hargorn, to Maya's palpable dismay, had been selected for the mission.

*

'Are you sure you have everything?' Dulsina asked Hargorn. Vannor, who sat watching on a nearby log, grinned to himself at the disgusted expression on the veteran's face.

'For goodness sake, woman,' Hargorn protested, 'I've been packing for campaigns since you were a little lass at your mother's skirt. Of course I have everything!'

Vannor, alerted by a familiar, wicked twinkle in Dulsina's eyes, leaned forward expectantly.

The veteran sighed, and raised his eyes heavenwards. 'Food, water flask, change of clothing, blanket, flint and striker . . .' he counted various parts of his clothing and boots where daggers were concealed. 'Cloak . . . Anything else? Or are you willing to concede defeat?'

Smiling sweetly, Dulsina thrust her hand into the pocket of her dress and pulled out a small but bulging leather pouch. 'Money?' she suggested. 'Or were you planning to sing for your supper when you get to Nexis? I've heard your singing, Hargorn – I wouldn't like to think of you having to depend on it!'

Vannor, who had given the silver – the last of his slender supply – to Dulsina to pass on to the grizzled warrior, burst out laughing.

'Seven bloody demons!' Hargorn said feelingly. He turned on the chortling merchant. 'This is your fault – she's *your* housekeeper!'

'How is it my fault?' the merchant protested. 'You brought her along – you've only yourself to blame. Besides, I dismissed her long ago – but she refuses to leave.'

'Indeed you did dismiss me – and came back about ten days later, begging me to return because the house was falling apart around your ears,' Dulsina snorted. Now it was Hargorn's turn to chuckle at Vannor's discomfiture. 'It always ends the same way,' Dulsina told the warrior. 'The truth is, he can't survive without me.'

'Be quiet,' Vannor growled, putting an affectionate arm around her waist, 'or I'll beat some respect into you, as I should have done long ago.'

Far from being impressed by his threat, Dulsina howled with mirth.

'Stop laughing, woman!'

'Stop playing the fool, then,' Dulsina chuckled, and slipped away before he could think of a retort.

'Do you ever manage to get the last word with that woman?' Hargorn asked.

'I've known her more than twenty years, and I haven't managed it yet.' Vannor looked across the clearing at his housekeeper, who was checking the contents of Fional's pack. 'On the other hand,' he said, 'I would place my fortune, my children, and my life in her hands without hesitating.' He shrugged. 'To be honest, Hargorn, I don't know what I'd do without her. I'm glad she talked you into smuggling her along with us – but don't you tell her so!'

Hargorn chuckled. 'I knew you'd see sense eventually. At least, Dulsina assured me you would.' The veteran smiled to himself at the rueful expression on the merchant's blunt and bearded face. What a pity, he thought, that Vannor is still obsessed with the memory of that sly little bitch he married. It's such a waste! It's plain that he's fond of Dulsina – and by the looks of it I suspect she's been in love with him for years. A lovely, clever, sensible woman like that is what a man like Vannor needs – not some damned miller's daughter half his age who was only ever after his riches. Hargorn sighed. Poor Dulsina – wasted on a fool without the wit to appreciate her. Why, were I ten years younger, I'd court her myself – not that I think for a moment that she'd have me.

Just then Fional approached, and the sight of the young man's anguished expression gave Hargorn second thoughts.

'Vannor, Dulsina is emptying my pack out all over the ground,' the young archer complained. He ran a distracted hand through his shaggy brown curls. 'Tell her to stop it.'

Vannor was sending the bowman to the Nightrunners with messages. He wanted to let his daughter Zanna know that they were safe in the Valley – and he wished to arrange for Yanis, the Nightrunner leader, to be able to contact Hargorn in Nexis, where the smugglers had an agent in concealment. Since the escape of the rebels, Miathan kept the city well guarded. Movements were monitored, so if Hargorn found folk who wished to leave – and Vannor was certain he would –

he wanted to be sure that the smugglers could get them out by river. At the moment, however, it looked as though Fional would be lucky to get away at all.

'You were supposed to *pack* this, Fional,' Dulsina scolded, 'not stuff everything in.' She was holding the young archer's spare tunic, which had been wadded into a ball in the bottom.

'What difference will a few creases make?' the bowman protested. 'I was busy making new arrows – I didn't have time for fancy folding.'

Dulsina sighed. 'It's not the creases. If you fold things properly, like *this*, you'll have more room for food. You haven't put in nearly enough.'

Fional sighed, with the air of one who already knew that it was hopeless. 'I thought I could shoot rabbits and birds on the way.' The young archer was justifiably proud of his skills, but Dulsina was unimpressed with his practicality.

'Have you forgotten it's winter out there?' she told him. 'There'll be few creatures out and about on those moors – and besides, you won't have time to spare for hunting.'

Beneath his beard, the young man reddened, and Dulsina patted him on the arm. 'Never mind,' she said. 'It was just an oversight. I'll fetch you some extra provisions.'

Vannor and Hargorn exchanged sympathetic looks with the younger man. 'I know,' the merchant told him. 'Believe me, I know – but the thing is, she's always right.'

D'arvan, watching from his hiding-place, was dismayed. He had known that Hargorn was going – but Fional too! In addition to Maya, the archer had become his friend when Aurian had first taken him with her on her visits to the garrison. The two of them, Mage and Mortal, had discovered a common passion for archery – one that, in D'arvan's case, was only exceeded by his love for Maya – and in Fional's case was exceeded by no one and nothing at all. Not so far, at any rate, the young Mage thought, remembering how his own passion for Forral's dark-haired second in command had taken him so completely by surprise

When the Archmage had seized control of Nexis, D'arvan had fretted for Fional's safety, and had been relieved to find him, safe and sound, among the rebels seeking sanctuary in the Vale. Here, at last, the Mage had been able to protect his friend – but to think of him roaming those freezing moors alone; exposed to all manner of dangers . . . Yet Fional was a level-headed young man who could more than hold his own with a blade, and who was, of course, lethal with his bow. Furthermore, he was an experienced tracker who was unlikely to lose his way on the moors – which, of course, was the reason Vannor had chosen him. D'arvan, in his heart of hearts, was aware of all these facts, but nevertheless he worried. Oh, if he could only leave the Valley and accompany his friend, to see him safe! But that would mean abandoning Maya – and besides, he and the unicorn were unable to leave. They were guardians here, and had their allotted tasks to perform.

Suddenly D'arvan stiffened, alerted by a disturbance among the nearby trees. Sending out his consciousness into the forrest he perceived the warning message of the arboreal guardians. Intruders! There were people at the boundary of the Valley, trying to gain entrance. He turned to Maya. 'To the bridge, my love – and hurry!' With a flash of her heels, the unicorn was gone. D'arvan, taking the opposite direction, hurried off to the edge of the woods to see who the intruders might be.

'Gone? What do you mean, she's gone?'

Tarnal took a hurried step backwards in the face of Vannor's rage. It had been bad enough, the young smuggler thought, entering this unnerving place. He and Remana had been trapped for some time, pinned against a tree by a pack of the meanest looking wolves he had ever seen, when suddenly the sheltering trunk behind him had simply picked up its roots and *moved*! When he looked round again, the wolf pack had vanished, and a broad, leaf-arched avenue had opened before him, heading down into the crater. Tarnal sighed, and cursed Yanis roundly under his breath. Terrifying though the encounter with the wolves had been, it was nothing in comparison to having to tell Vannor that his daughter had vanished.

63

'What the bloody blazes does Yanis think he's playing at?' Vannor's tirade continued unabated. 'How could Zanna have slipped out like that, unobserved. What a fool I was, to trust my daughter to that halfwit imbecile! And as for you . . .' His rage turned on Remana. 'I thought you were supposed to be looking after her. I trusted you . . .'

Remana looked stricken. Tarnal sighed. Might as well get it over with, he thought. 'I was on guard that night,' he interrupted the furious merchant. 'I never thought she'd . . . And then she knocked me out . . .' The words dried in his mouth beneath Vannor's withering, contemptuous glare.

'She had tried this trick already with Tarnal, before you came to join us.' Remana came to the young man's rescue. 'Honestly, Vannor, we never thought she would do it again. But she had quarrelled with Yanis, because she thought he should be doing more to help you, and, I think, because he wouldn't take her when he went south to trade. He went off to sea that very same day and didn't tell us what had happened between them, and Zanna never said a word, though I thought she was rather quiet. She left that same night.' Remana bit her lip. 'If you blame Tarnal, you might as well blame me, too. It was I who taught Zanna to sail, and to navigate the passage outside the cavern. Yanis is still in the southern oceans – he doesn't even know. Tarnal and I thought we should come at once to tell you. Gods, Vannor, I'm sorry. Dulsina, you were wrong to trust me.' There were tears in Remana's eyes. 'She left a note, explaining what had happened, and what she planned to do. She's gone to Nexis.'

Vannor maintained a stony silence. Tarnal wished he would do anything, even hit him with those tight-clenched fists, rather than just stand there with that look of loathing on his face. Dulsina stepped forward and took hold of the merchant's arm. 'Vannor, don't blame them too harshly. You know what Zanna is like – she takes after you. There's no stopping her once she gets an idea into her head.'

'And that makes it all right, does it?' Vannor growled, turning on Dulsina. 'They should have taken better care of her. She . . .'

'They didn't, as it happens.' Dulsina's flat tones brought the merchant up short. 'Now,' she went on, 'the question is, what are we going to do about it? Raging at Tarnal and Remana won't get Zanna back.'

'You're right.' Vannor seemed relieved to be doing something positive. 'Hargorn, there's a change of plan. You're still going to Nexis – but I'm coming with you.'

'Vannor, you can't!' Dulsina gasped. 'There's a reward out on you. You'll be recognized. And what about the rebels? You're their leader . . .'

'Then they had better choose another bloody leader!' The expression on Vannor's face brooked no argument. 'Dulsina, fill a pack for me. Fional, you're still going to Wyvernesse. Get a couple of ponies from these idiots – it's the least they can do in atonement.' He turned a scornful look on Tarnal and Remana. 'And bring my son back with you. I want him safe here with Dulsina.'

'But . . .' Fional stammered.

'*Don't argue with me!*' Vannor roared. 'Dulsina, is that pack ready yet? What's keeping you, woman?'

As Dulsina, for once knowing better than to contradict the merchant, came running up, Tarnal swallowed hard, and went to Vannor. 'I want to come with you,' he said firmly.

Vannor scowled at him. 'Come with me? After what you've done? You've got a nerve, boy! Get out of my sight. I never want to set eyes on you and your Nightrunner friends again.'

When the travellers said farewell to their companions and walked out of the clearing along the path that opened out before them, D'arvan closed his eyes, unable to watch as they left the haven he had created and went out again into danger. He could have stopped them, he knew. For the son of the Forest Lord, it would have been simple to change the paths between the trees, and deny the wanderers egress; to bring them back in a circle to the safety they had left. But he would have been wrong to do so. They must play their parts in the fight against Miathan, even as he must, and all he could do was pray for their safe return.

Hargorn wiped his numb and dripping nose across his sleeve.

65

'By Chathak, I'd forgotten how cold it can be out here,' he muttered to Fional, who would be leaving them for Wyvernesse once they had cleared the trees. Remana and Tarnal would be following him as soon as they had rested from their arduous journey, but Vannor had not permitted the archer to wait for them. Once more, Hargorn wished that the rebels had been able to bring horses to this desolate place. But in these days of famine, horses were a scarce commodity, for most had been eaten long ago. Unless they could find any on their journey to Nexis, he and the merchant would be forced to go without.

Before the three men stretched the endless bleakness of the moors; the black rock of their wind-scoured bones poking out in places from a ragged cloak of shrivelled bracken and heather, patched with night-grey turf that was harsh and brittle with a skin of crackling frost. Behind the wanderers, the trees that ringed the precipitous edge of the Vale thronged tight and close, as though huddled together for warmth. Goaded by the bitter, whining wind, their bare, twisted branches clawed at the clouding sky.

The archer nodded, his usually smiling mouth twisted down into a grimace. 'It was easy to forget, in there.' Frowning he turned to the older man. There was no point in talking to Vannor, who had remained grimly silent ever since they had set out. The others did not dare mention their concern for Zanna in his presence, and Fional racked his brains for another topic. 'Hargorn, what do you think was protecting us in the Valley? Do you think it was Aurian's mother? If it was, why didn't she show herself?'

The veteran shook his head. 'I've no idea, lad – though I remember Aurian saying that her ma was a pretty solitary sort. Still, after all that happened, you'd think she would show herself – if it was the Lady who was taking care of us in there.'

'But who else could it have been?'

'The gods only know ... but your Mageborn friend D'arvan was supposed to be coming out here with poor Maya. I've been wondering lately what could have become of them?'

'D'arvan and Maya would never have stayed in hiding if they knew we were there,' Fional protested indignantly.

Hargorn sighed. 'Maybe not. But there are strange things going on in that Vale, lad. It's easy, when you're in there, not to think about it too much. But coming out, and thinking back . . .' He turned to the younger man with a wink. 'Don't you feel your curiosity stirring? Don't you want to find out what's going on in there, and what happened to D'arvan and Maya? Do you think Parric, had he been here, would have been content to sit around and not find out what was going on? Do you think that Forral would?'

Fional grinned. 'Why no, now you come to mention it. After all, it's our *duty* to find out what happened to our missing friends.'

'Good lad!' Hargorn clouted the archer on the shoulder. 'Tell you what – once we've done what we set out to do, and returned to the Valley, let's you and I get to the bottom of the mystery once and for all.'

'Done!' The archer thrust out his hand, and Hargorn clasped it to seal the bargain.

'Well,' he said briskly, 'the sooner we go, the quicker we'll get back and get on with it. Take care, young Fional – and don't go bedding *all* those pretty young Nightrunner wenches!'

Even in the gloom, the young man's face was darkened by a blush, and Hargorn grinned. Fional was notoriously awkward where women were concerned. 'Would that I had the chance,' the bowman retorted. 'Go well, you old villain – and don't go drinking *all* the ale in Nexis!'

With a parting salute, the two warriors, the old and the young, made off in opposite directions across the dark and freezing moors; each towards his separate goal. Vannor strode along at Hargorn's side, wrapped in an impenetrable cloak of silence.

Hargorn twitched his heavy pack to a more comfortable position on his shoulders, and stepped out with the steady, ground-devouring stride developed from years of arduous marches. He was anxious to cover as much ground as he could before dawn; for although no enemies had come into the Valley after the massacre of Angos and his men, he had no idea whether or not the moors were still being patrolled.

Fifty-two was a rare age for a soldier to reach, and the veteran had not managed to get this far without a bit of common sense and caution – and, he thought in all modesty, pure skill. In this business, knowing how to avoid trouble was as important as knowing how to deal with it.

Vannor, unfortunately, was trouble that could not be avoided. Hargorn shot a worried, sidelong glance at the merchant. This uncanny silence was due to shock, and not surprisingly. Poor Vannor, losing both his precious wife and his beloved daughter in a matter of months. Hargorn only worried about what the merchant would do when the shock subsided.

None the less, despite his concern for the man at his side, and that poor daft girl, all alone and in danger, the veteran found his spirits lifting with the promise of action ahead. A warrior to his bones, he'd mistrusted the easy life in the Vale –it was all very well to say that some mysterious power had been helping the rebels, but while they were lolling around at their ease they weren't doing much to oppose the Archmage. In fact, the soldier thought, whatever is keeping us cocooned in there has taken us out of the fight as surely as if we'd been imprisoned.

It was a relief to have found, in Fional, an ally at last. Hargorn had been forced to go very carefully within the Vale, and keep his doubts to himself. Something was plainly lending its aid to the outlaws – a something that didn't want its idenity to be known. You never knew, in that place, just what might be overheard. But Parric, or a real commander such as Forral, would never have been content to sit still in the midst of a mystery, without investigating further.

Nor, come to think of it, would Maya – and that brought Hargorn to his third, and most important, concern. He was desperate for news of the girl. He had known her ever since she'd first joined the garrison as a shy and raw recruit, straight from her parents' farm in the south, and he had followed her increasingly successful career with fondness and respect ever since. If she had come to the Valley with D'arvan – and Maya had always accomplished what she set out to do – then where was she? Where was the young Mage? What had happened to them? 'Vannor or no Vannor,' the veteran muttered, 'one of these days I intend to find out!'

5

Soul of the Stone

There was no denying that Nereni's feast was a good one. As usual, she had worked wonders with the materials to hand. The succulent vension was flavoured with herbs. There was a stew with a tantalizing aroma that, to everyone's astonishment, turned out to be wild goat cooked with mosses and the bulbs of certain flowers. Bohan had come back from foraging, his round face blotched and swollen with stings, clutching a parcel of honey-comb wrapped in leaves. He had also brought several impressively large trout, earning Yazour a hard look from Eliizar's wife. 'So they weren't biting, eh?' she accused the sheepish young warrior.

Luckily for Yazour, Raven returned at that precise moment, her wings stirring up clouds of smoke and ash from the fire and raising twin whirls of dust and pine needles as she landed. Nereni's wail of anguish for the ruination of the food was cut short when she saw the state in which the winged girl, her special pet, had returned. 'Raven! Reaper save us, what happened?' She rushed to assist the princess, who thrust her gently aside, and turned to the Mages with a smile.

'By Yinze, I am glad to see you,' she said simply.

'Raven, what happened? Did you fly into a tree?'

Raven faced the penetrating gaze of the Mage, and warned herself to be on her guard. On the way back, she had cleaned herself as best she could in a forest stream, but she had known that there would be consternation at her bruised and tattered appearance. Fortunately, Aurian's words had given her the very cue she needed.

'How perceptive you are,' she replied, with a rueful grin. 'When Nereni warned me about flying after dark, I should have listened. Game was scarce –' she held up her solitary, mangled pheasant. 'I misjudged the swiftness of nightfall, and flew, as you guessed, right into a tree!'

70

As Raven had hoped, any further explanations were cut short by Nereni's fussing with hot water, salves and fresh clothing. The winged girl smiled inwardly at her own subterfuge. *You have no idea how glad I am at your return, Aurian,* she thought over the cheerful babble of greetings, *for now I can put my own plans into motion.*

As the companions ate, the talk turned inevitably to the future, and Eliizar began to enlarge on his plans to build a more elaborate camp in a better site that Yazour had discovered. Aurian listened carefully. Anvar knew that, now she had rested and eaten, the Mage's restless mind would already be planning the next step in her journey.

'You have some good ideas,' Aurian told Eliizar. 'Though I hate the delay, we must make preparations before heading up into the mountains. The horses must be rested, for one thing – we're short of mounts, since Anvar and I lost ours in the sandstorm – and apart from finding some way to make warmer clothing, we must lay in a stock of food . . .'

'Surely there is no rush, Aurian,' Nereni interrupted. 'How can we travel further until your child is born?'

'What?' Aurian stared at her in dismay. Anvar, watching, held his breath.

'Did you not think of that?' Nereni looked shocked. 'Aurian, how can you set out now? Do you want the little mite to be delivered in the midst of a snowdrift?' She lowered her voice persuasively. 'It's less than three moons now – surely you can wait, for the sake of the child?'

Aurian turned very pale, and Anvar, watching her as he always did, felt his heart go out to her. Nereni's words about the risk to her child had struck her deeply. *Gods, they had only just survived the desert, and now this. Must we always be so driven?* he thought. He understood her urgent need to take the fight to the Archmage, but the child was her last link with Forral. Anvar looked around the firelit circle. Yazour and Eliizar were nodding in agreement with Nereni. Only Bohan, always faithful to his beloved Aurian, looked unhappy and torn. Only Bohan – and himself. Aurian, as though reading his mind, turned troubled eyes to him. 'Miathan knows where we are,' she said. He heard the uncertainty in her voice. 'He may attack us here.'

'He may, it's true.' Remembering their last confrontation with the Archmage, Anvar found it difficult to keep a level voice. 'But so far we've managed, and it's a question of weighing the risks. If you attempt those mountains now, you'll certainly endanger the child.' He bit his lip and looked away, struggling with his own conscience. 'I want to advise you to wait, but with every day that passes Miathan's advantage grows. I'll help you in any way I can, Aurian, but in the end this must be your decision. You know I'll support you, whatever you decide.'

From his vantage point beyond the Well of Souls, Forral was grinding his teeth with frustration. That stupid lad was going about this the wrong way. 'Why don't you help her?' he muttered. 'If only I had been there, I would have . . .' Forral hesitated. Just what would he have said to Aurian? Poor lass – how torn she must be, between the need to protect her child, and the urge to hurry north to deal with Miathan's depredations.

Forral, as a soldier, knew all about duty. But the one thing he hadn't bargained on was the fierce, protective love of a parent for a child – even one as yet unborn. Suddenly, the swordsman was shamefully glad that the decision was out of his hands. But what would Aurian decide? He peered into the Well once more, anxiously scanning the forest for a sight of his love.

Aurian hesitated, looking unhappy and grievously undecided. Raven, sensing that the moment was slipping away knew she must act quickly. 'Aurian.' She leaned over and touched the Mage to gain her attention. 'It would be safer to leave as soon as we can.'

'What do you mean?' Aurian swung around, scowling. Raven took a deep breath. She had agreed with Harihn only to use this information if all else failed, but seemingly she had no choice.

'I discovered something today, while I was out hunting,' she said. 'Harihn and his folk are camped here too, on the northern edge of the forest.'

'What?' Aurian cried in dismay. 'Harihn is here? How do you know that for sure? You've never seen him.'

'It must be the prince,' the winged girl replied hastily. 'They were wearing similar clothing to you – and who else could it be?'

Anvar cursed. 'Raven, you idiot! Why the bloody blazes didn't you tell us before? If Harihn should find us . . .'

'But he may not,' Nereni put in hopefully.

Anvar grimaced. 'I wouldn't care to count on it. Dear gods, what a mess! Aurian and her child will be at risk in the mountains, yet we're all in danger if we stay here.'

This was Raven's moment. 'Anvar,' she said persuasively, 'it may not be so bad as you think. There is a place in the mountains, a watchtower built by my folk long ago, to mark the far boundaries of their kingdom. From here it should be . . .' she shrugged. 'Some fifteen to twenty days' travel on the ground, I would guess. The building is secure and sturdy. We would be safe from attack and from the elements, and there is a coppice nearby for firewood. If we could get as far as that, then surely it would be a safer place than the forest for Aurian to have her child?'

As she saw the hope that brightened Aurian's eyes, Raven's guilt almost choked her. Think of Harihn, she told herself. Think of your people! But to look the Mages in the eye and answer their questions calmly, knowing all the while that she was betraying them, was the hardest thing the princess had ever done.

'What would we do about food?' Aurian asked her. The winged girl shrugged, glad that she and Harihn had thought out these problems in advance.

'There must still be some hunting in the mountains – ptarmigan, goats, winter hares and such. But for the journey, and for settling in, we must take all we can carry from this place. We can leave a cache of food here in the forest, and if we run short, or there is no game to hunt after all, I can easily fly back for more.'

'And think,' Nereni added, 'how good it would be for Aurian to have sheltering walls around her when she comes to bear her child.'

Aurian nodded. 'Oh, I don't disagree. The problem is, what shall we do for mounts? Anvar and I lost ours in the desert, and if we want to take enough food to last us, we'll need a packhorse or two besides.'

Everyone looked at one another. Just as Raven was beginning to wonder if she'd have to suggest *everything* herself, Yazour came to her rescue. 'We could always,' he said, with a wicked twinkle in his eye, 'steal some from Harihn. Not now,' he added, forestalling their protests. 'The last thing we want is the prince's men combing the forest for missing horses. But could we not do it when we are about to leave, with Raven and Shia to scout for us?'

Aurian grinned. 'Well done, Yazour!' She turned to the winged girl. 'Raven, you have my heartfelt thanks.'

It was late when everyone went to bed. Because of Harihn, there were watches to be organized, though Eliizar insisted that Yazour, Bohan and he himself would undertake them, to allow Aurian and Anvar a good night's sleep after their trials in the desert. From the next day onwards, Shia and Raven would keep watch on the Khazalim, to make sure that they stayed away from the companions' camp.

Aurian was utterly relieved when at last she was able to curl up with Anvar in one of Eiliizar's rough shelters. Even so, her mind was seething with plans, and she found it difficult to settle down to sleep. 'How soon do you think we'll be able to get away?' she asked Anvar.

He shrugged. 'Who knows? Our friends have been working very hard since they got here, but there's still a lot to be done.'

'And in the meantime, we must leave someone free to keep an eye on Harihn and his folk, to make sure they don't come wandering in our direction,' Aurian agreed.

Anvar nodded. 'It's a big forest, apparently, and Raven says they're camped near the northern edge. Presumably they plan to head north, so they probably won't come back this way.' He paused, frowning. 'Something is bothering me about this. Why are they still here at all? They were well ahead of us, and they took all the gear that was stored in Dhiammara, so they must already be equipped for crossing the mountains. Why are they delaying?'

Aurian felt an unpleasant prickling between her shoulder-blades. 'Anvar, could they be waiting for us? I mean, Yazour escaped with horses, so they must have known that we could get out of Dhiammara after all . . .'

Anvar shook his head. 'Surely, if it was an ambush, they would have scouts posted throughout the forest? And what better time to attack than when we first came out of the desert? The others were distracted by our arrival, and *we* were certainly in no condition to defend ourselves.'

'To be honest, I'm not in much better condition now.' Aurian yawned. 'I'm so tired I just can't think straight.'

'You poor old thing,' Anvar teased her.

'Poor old thing, indeed,' Aurian growled, but she was chuckling as she lay down beside him.

Forral, watching, sighed. Though he knew he was being foolish, and tried to be generous in spirit towards his lost love, there were times when her growing closeness with Anvar seemed a bitter betrayal. The longing in the swordsman's heart was an all-encompassing ache. 'It should have been me . . .' His hand crept towards the surface of the pool . . .

'*Enough.*' Forral shuddered as the chill non-touch of Death clamped down upon his shoulders, hauling him away from the Well. 'You have seen enough,' said the Spectre. 'Did I not warn you it would cause you pain? Come, now. You know that Aurian will be safe for a time in the forest. Be content, and leave the living to their own concerns.'

Hot words of protest formed on Forral's lips, until he remembered his last sight of Aurian, curled up at Anvar's side. He had told himself that he was only concerned for her safety – but Death was right. He knew she was safe now, and this further watching amounted to spying on her, which wasn't doing either of them any good. Forral, grieving for the years together that he and Aurian had lost, suffered himself to be led away.

Aurian, who had been finding it increasingly difficult to keep her eyes open, fell asleep at last. Perhaps it was the aftermath of the battle in the desert, or the natural consequence of such an emotional day. Perhaps it was the relative coolness of the forest, or Nereni's highly spiced stew, that made the Mage dream of Eliseth that night. Perhaps it was more than that.

Aurian dreamed that the Weather-Mage stood on the top of the Mages' Tower in Nexis, arms outstretched to the midnight skies, calling down the storm from boiling clouds that gathered above the city. In one hand she bore a long, glittering spear of ice. Snow swirled around her, mingling with the streaming skeins of her silver hair as she climbed up to stand on the low parapet that circled the top of the tower, the cold perfection of her face alight with exaltation. With a shrill, wild cry she leapt – out, out and up, as the ice-wings of the storm bore her aloft. And south she came. South across the ocean, south across the lands of the Xandim, riding towards the mountains on winter's wings . . .

Aurian awoke suddenly, shivering, her heart racing. 'Stupid!' she told herself briskly. 'It was only a dream. Nothing but a dream. Eliseth is dead . . . Isn't she?'

Lost beyond his body in the depths of the fastness, Chiamh panicked, fleeing blindly through the labyrinth of fissures that ventilated the building. What would happen to his body if he couldn't find his way back? Would it die? What if they found it, and thought he had died, and . . .

'Come now! Such a premise is utterly ridiculous.'

The first time he had heard the mysterious voice, it had almost scared him out of his wits, but this time it was very different. Chiamh had never been so glad in all his life, to hear another living creature. 'Who are you? Where are you? Can you help me to get out of here?' he pleaded.

'Had you been concentrating, you would not need my aid,' the voice scolded. *'However, since you seem to be the only one of your puny race who can hear me, I must assist you – but let this teach you to be more careful in future. Watch the air, little Windeye – and follow my light!'*

Chastened, Chiamh collected his wits, concentrating on the silvery strands of moving air. He followed them until he came to a dividing of the ways – and gasped as one of the strands split away from the others. Glowing with warm, golden light, the errant strand plunged sharply into a crack on the right. The

Windeye followed, as it twisted this way and that through the network of fissures, until at last, with a squirm and a bound, Chiamh's roving spirit tumbled out into the familar dusty clutter of his own chambers.

Weak with relief, the Windeye returned to the welcome security of his body. As he rubbed his cold, cramped limbs with shaking hands, he realized that he had not thanked his mysterious benefactor. 'Are you still there?' he asked tentatively, somewhat embarrassed to be speaking aloud to empty air.

'I am everywhere within these walls – and you need not speak aloud. Use your mind, as you have been doing.'

'I – I want to thank you for rescuing me,' Chiamh stammered. 'I don't know how you knew the way, but . . .'

'How could I not know the way?' the voice retorted. *'Though when Mortals start crawling around inside my body . . .'*

'Inside *what*?' Chiamh gasped. The voice burst into great peals of laughter.

'Do your people lack all lore and legend, that they know not what they inhabit? Has the world forgotten the Modai so soon? I am Basileus, little Windeye – the living soul of this fastness!'

Time ran slow for the Moldai; time ran fast. Time, in the sense that Mortals understood it, did not exist at all for these ancient creatures of living stone. The passing of a day was as the blink of an eye to them, but the days ran into one another in a changeless eternity. The roots of the Moldai ran deep into the heart of the earth; their heads, decked all in caps of dazzling snow and veiled in skeins of cloud, were crowned with the very stars. Oldest of the Old were the Moldai; the Firstborn; as old as the very bones of the world. In the birth-pangs of the world they had come into being and they did not die – save the parts of their bodies that were hacked away by lesser, heedless creatures.

'I can scarcely believe it!' Wishing that he had some specific point to look at when speaking to this peculiar entity, Chiamh addressed the room at large. 'Never in my wildest dreams did I imagine talking to a *building*.'

'I am not a building. Buildings, as you call them, are hacked and murdered chunks of our flesh piled upon each other by Mankind. I and my brethern are living entities – and we take on these shapes of our own accord.'

The ire of Basileus was awesome. The walls of Chiamh's chambered shuddered, and the torches flickered in a sudden swirling draught. Fine dust pattered down from the ceiling. The Windeye hastened to apologize – he had already discovered that his new companion was inclined to be touchy.

It was truly a day of surprises. First, the vision that had led to his discovery of the Bright Ones, then the arrival of the foreigners – and now this! Chiamh's mind was reeling. On his return from the dungeons, he had groped his way to the kitchens for some food, for he had not eaten since the previous night, and had travelled fast and far, both physically and with his Othersight, in the intervening hours. Back in his chambers, the exhausted Windeye had slept for a while, but on awakening he had been swift to resume this bizarre conversation with Basileus.

One thing about mental communication – you could eat at the same time! Chiamh stuffed bread and cheese into his mouth. 'You mentioned brethren – are there more of you?'

'Of course. All the mountains around us are Moldai. Your lack of awareness astounds me – especially since you have actually dwelt within another part of my body.'

Into Chiamh's head came a vision of his own spire, with the Chamber of Winds on top. The Windeye frowned. 'But how can that be you, if this is you?' he gestured around the room. 'How can you be in two places at once?'

Basileus sighed. *'Raise your hand,'* he instructed. *'Is that hand a part of you?'*

'Well, of course it is!'

'Good. Now raise the other. See, you have two hands, each of which is distinct and apart from the other – but both of them are equally part of you. My consciousness resides within the entire Wyndveil peak, and the roots of a mountain – and a Moldan – go out a long way! It is the same principle as you and your hands. Both this place and the tower are part of me – as, indeed, are all the smaller dwellings on the hillside.'

'Really?' The Windeye's interest was truly pricked. He had wondered about those mysterious structures for so long. 'Why did you build them?' he asked eagerly. 'Are they dwellings, as they seem? Who were they for?'

The Moldan's response made him regret his curiosity. Chiamh cried out, holding his hands to his head, as a wave of grief washed over him; a sorrow so profound that it was more than a Mortal soul could bear. 'Stop,' he cried, tears streaming down his face. 'I beg you – no more!'

'It must be told,' the Moldan grated. *'Only by the telling do we obtain surcease.'* In a voice that was heavy with sorrow, he spoke of the Dwelven, the Smallfolk, the companions without whom the Moldai were wrenchingly incomplete. *'They were our brethren,'* he sighed, *'and for them we made dwellings from our bones. We nurtured them; we who were strong and wise but rooted and fixed. They cared for us, husbanding our lands and guarding us from human hewers of stone. On reaching maturity, each one would travel out into the world; returning, if they returned, with gifts, and tales of mighty deeds, and news of far-off places.'* The Moldan paused. *'The arrangement worked perfectly down the ages, until the Wizards – those you call the Powers – intervened!'*

Chiamh pricked up his ears. The Powers again? Surely this could be no coincidence?

'In their arrogance,' Basileus continued, *'the Wizards created the Staff of Earth. The temerity of those puny creatures – to tamper with the High Magic in* our element!' The building shuddered with the Moldan's wrath, and Chiamh trembled.

'What did you do?' he asked.

'What could we do? In vain we sent Dwelven emissaries to protest – the Wizards told us to mind our own concerns. Then –' A shiver passed through the stone of the fastness. *'Then came the blackest day of our history. The Wizards were experimenting with the Staff, and Ghabal, the mightiest among us, discovered a way to tap its power. He used it to escape from the constraints of his stony flesh. As a giant he appeared; a human form, but the size of a mountain!'*

Basileus sighed. *'The power of the Staff proved too much for him. He became crazed and violent. He wanted, he said, to put a barrier between the Moldai and the Wizards. In those days the north and south was a single landmass, with no sea between – until Ghabal*

79

broke the bones of the earth, creating a rift between the two lands where once a fair and fertile kingdom lay.' The voice of the Moldan was hushed with regret. 'Thousands of lives were lost as the seas rushed in, and I believe that Ghabal felt every death-pang. They punished him, of course. Combining their powers, the Wizards wrenched the Staff of Earth back to their control, and used it to master him. And they possessed the perfect prison. They had made a great artificial hill of stone in their city, and built their citadel atop, and there they imprisoned Ghabal's tortured spirit, sealing it into lifeless stone. Then they came here, and destroyed his body beyond hope of returning.'

'Steelclaw!' Chiamh gasped, thinking of the Haunted Mountain that lay beyond the Windveil. No Xandim would set foot there – legend said that anyone who spent a night on Steelclaw would return insane, if they returned at all. The mountain itself was enough to discourage the bravest or most foolhardy soul – Chiamh had always known that some unthinkable disaster had befallen it. The rock had been riven and twisted, tortured and melted, almost down to its roots, leaving three jagged stumps to claw the sky. The very sight of it made the Windeye think of pain.

'Steelclaw indeed,' Basileus answered. 'The remains of Ghabal, once the tallest and fairest of us all. Had the Wizards let the matter rest there . . . But in their wrath, they punished us all. They took the Dwelven – our eyes and ears in the land and the only ones, save themselves, who could hear us – beyond the sea whence they could not return. The Wizards sent them underground and laid a spell on them, that if they emerged into the light, they would perish. Without them we have languished in isolation, trapped in a waking dream. But now, we may dare to hope again, for the world is changing. Not long ago, my mind began to awaken and reach out again – to find you, though you were not the reason. The Staff of Earth is abroad once more. I feel it coming closer.' The Moldan's tone betrayed his excitement. 'Those wizards are up to something, or I'm a pebble! Little Windeye, know you aught of this?'

Chiamh frowned. 'Perhaps,' he said. 'Last night I had a vision, and now outlanders have appeared in our lands . . .' Quickly, he told Basileus what had been happening.

'Indeed,' the Moldan agreed, when he had finished. 'These

80

matters cannot be unconnected. And you believe your leaders will execute these strangers?'

'For certain. That is our law.'

'In that case, we must act swiftly to save them.'

'Could you help me get them out?' Chiamh asked eagerly. 'Could you open a passage out of the dungeon, maybe?'

'Alas,' Basileus sighed, 'it would take far too long to create such a passage – and it would be of no avail. The prisoners have been taken elsewhere.'

'What?' Chiamh shrieked. 'But their execution is not until tomorrow!'

'You have lost track of the hours, little Windeye. You were long within my body finding the dungeons, and longer coming back. And when you returned you slept before we spoke. By your lights, it is already tomorrow. To save the captives, you must act swiftly – if it is not already too late.'

6
Steelclaw

In contrast to the close and narrow gloom that shrouded Chiamh's Valley of the Dead, the plateau of the Wyndveil was a place of air and light. Towards its southern end, the land broke up into a series of crags and canyons, rising to the sheer white walls of the Wyndveil and its brethren. At its northern brink the land dropped, sweeping down across dark, pine-clad slopes to the verdant plains, and finally to the bright expanse of the sea. It was a windswept perch between peak and plain, belonging neither to earth nor sky – an open temple, designed by the goddess for the contemplation of her world. The Xandim used it as their Place of Challenge and a court of justice. Only here, in the airy Hall of the Goddess, against the stunning panorama of her creation, could matters of life and death be decided by the tribe.

Now, in the chill dark close of a winter's night, the snow-scoured plateau was redolent of awe and mystery. In the narrows of the meadow, beside the sinister stones that guarded the gate of the Deathvale, a figure stood braced against the storm. He was a stern-faced man of middle years; bald, save for a silvering of cropped hair at the back of his head. His gaze was proud and uncompromising, like a keen-eyed hawk. He held his years well; his belly was flat, his body as muscular as it had been in his youth, when he first won the leadership by Rite of Challenge. Phalihas was his name, and he was chief and Herdlord of the Xandim.

The Herdlord stood by the hallowed stones, awaiting the prisoners; showing no movement save where the snarling wind worried at his heavy cloak. At a respectful distance stood the curious folk who had come to watch the trial of the outlanders. Awed into stillness by the numinous ambience of this sacred site, they huddled together, whispering softly, in reassuring groups around bonfires whose streaming flames were pressed flat to the ground by the gale. Phalihas saw the restless dark shadows of their flapping cloaks, like the wings of carrion birds, and the occasional vivid spark of brightness where fitful firelight caught a rough-hammered torc or an armband, or the polished beads of stone or bone that they threaded into their braids.

To one side, in an uneasy, muttering knot, stood the Elders; men and women old in wisdom, though not necessarily in years. Though any of them might advise Phalihas, the final verdict would be his alone. They were present by law and tradition, but this time their contribution would not be needed. The matter before him was straightforward: strangers were not permitted in the Xandim lands, and the penalty for trespass was death. It was as simple as that.

Phalihas sighed, and pulled his cloak more tightly round his shoulders in a futile effort to block out the icy wind. It was his own fault, he told himself, that he was out here freezing, instead of being warm and asleep in his bed back at the fastness. The Elders had objected to this trial as a waste of time, and only his insistence on adhering to the law had dragged everyone out here. Though he held to his conviction that traditions must be upheld for the good of the tribe, Phalihas had not realized that this trial would stir acute and painful memories of the last time he had stood here in judgement.

The face of Iscalda, his former betrothed, was seared into the Herdlord's memory. Pale and wild-eyed with terror she had been; her flaxen hair, unusual among the Xandim, of which she had once been so proud, had hung down around her face in ravelled snarls when she had stood before him in this place, her face set in a stony mask of defiance as she repudiated the one who had condemned her beloved brother to exile. Phalihas made a small sound of anger, a low growl deep within his throat, at the memory of the one who had dragged his beloved Iscalda down into ruin. Schiannath! he thought. If only I had slain him when I had the chance!

Alas, under Xandim law, execution was saved for strangers. The only time one of the Xandim could kill another was in the

Rite of Challenge for Herdlord – and Schiannath had already undergone that trial. Though he had lost, he had survived, and the Challenge, by law, could not be repeated. Schiannath, on losing, had not accepted his lot with good grace. A malcontent and a troublemaker, he had undermined the Herdlord's authority in every possible way, and the tribe had suffered as a consequence. Exile had been the Herdlord's only option, but it burned his heart that the transgressor could still be alive somewhere, among the trackless mountains. And Iscalda – did she still live? Did she remember anything, now, of her human existence? Had she died of the cold, or been eaten by wolves, or the Black Ghosts that haunted the peaks? Was nothing left of her but a jumble of stripped bones at the foot of a precipice?

With a muttered curse, the Herdlord tried to shrug the dreadful visions away. What did it matter whether his former betrothed had survived or perished? She had rejected him. But ever since that day, when his hurt and rage had betrayed him into condemning her to live as a beast, he had been haunted by guilt and bitter regret. 'The truth is,' Phalihas sighed to himself, 'that if it were permitted, I would undo what I did that day. But it can never be.'

Above the seething wrack of the storm, the sun was lifting her crown above the jagged mountains, and day crept forth on dragging feet to infuse the plateau with a feeble, ghostly half-light. Across the meadow the prisoners were approaching, bound and desolate, between their guards.

Phalihas, glad to be distracted from his dawn-bleak thoughts, observed the outlanders as they were cast down before him and forced to kneel on the iron-hard ground. They made a strange group – the wiry little man whose very posture spoke defiance; the tall, fair warrior-maid, whose ripe body promised joys uncounted, but whose eyes were cold and hard as an unsheathed blade; the old man, sick and fevered unto death, unless the Herdlord missed his guess – and the other. The bony woman with the mad, fey eyes. Merely to look at her sent chills down the Herdlord's spine. He tore his eyes from her and forced himself to speak, rushing through the sentencing in his hurry to get as far away as possible from her relentless, burning stare.

'You are here to answer the charge of trespass and invasion,' he told them; wondering, as he spoke, whether he should have had that wretch the Windeye present, in order to translate for the prisoners. Truth to tell, since Chiamh had pronounced the words that cast Iscalda for ever into equine shape, he had not been able to bear the sight of the half-blind seer. The knowledge that he was being grossly unfair to the Windeye – after all, Chiamh had only been acting under his own orders – did nothing to improve the Herdlord's mood. What does it matter, he thought. Within hours, these strangers will be dead – and whether they understand the reasons for their execution or not, it will scarcely matter then.

Straightening his shoulders, Phalihas continued, in the age-old formula: 'You need not speak, for you have no defence: you were caught by my warriors the midst of an illegal act. The penalty for your crime is death . . .'

'How dare you!' The strident voice, cutting abruptly across his own, robbed Phalihas of his carefully prepared phrases. The madwoman! How did she come to know the Xandim tongue? Her eyes grew larger – they were burning into his soul, as her voice shrilled on and on . . .

When Chiamh arrived, late and panting, on the plateau, he found utter confusion. The Herdlord, looking shaken, his grey face twisted with rage, stood in a knot of Elders who were gesticulating wildly and shouting at the tops of their voices. What in the world had happened? The Windeye strained his weak-sighted gaze, but could see no trace of the prisoners. Had they been executed already? Had they escaped somehow? 'Gracious goddess,' Chiamh muttered. 'Iriana of the Beasts – don't let me be too late!' He took one look at the stricken Herdlord, and gave up any hope of speaking to Phalihas. Instead he found a wizened old grandsire, who was standing to one side, sucking his gums and watching the commotion with avid interest. 'What happened?' Chiamh demanded, clutching at his sleeve.

'Hola, young Windeye! Missed the trial? You missed a sight,' the dotard confided with relish. 'Herdlord was passing sentence when up speaks that skinny witch, and demands safe passage through our lands, if you can credit it!' The oldster was

85

frowning with the effort of recalling the madwoman's words. 'She has business in the south, she says, that can't wait on the whims of a bunch of savages!'

'What?' Chiamh yelped, horrified.

'It's true as I'm standing here.' The grandsire nodded sagely, delighted with his role as the imparter of such momentous news. 'That big bonny wench is nudging her, trying to shut her up, and the little fellow is shaking his head like he can't believe it. Then the witch says if our Herdlord tries to stop her, she'll curse him to the end of his days! Well, stirred like a hornets' nest, the Elders was. But the Herdlord put his foot down, and they've taken the foreigners up to Steelclaw, to stake them out on the Field of Stones to be breakfast for the slinking Black Ghosts, and . . . Hey, come back . . .'

Chiamh heard the whining voice trail off into the distance as he ran, as fast as he could, past the standing stones towards his valley. Luckily the guards wouldn't dare take the straighter route through the Vale of the Dead. As Windeye, he had access to a shortcut . . .

The Field of Stones was not, in fact, a field at all, but an unusually level area of the mountainside that was littered with more of the low, flat-topped hollow boulders that appeared to be dwellings, though they were never used as such by the Xandim, for the altitude was too great, and the climate too harsh. Instead, the Horselords had found a more sinister use for the structures. Manacles and chains had been bolted to the flattened tops, and outland prisoners (usually marauding Khazalim, captured on raids) were staked out here as sacrifices to appease the fearful Black Ghosts of the mountains.

The Field, with its grim associations of death and bloodshed, was located on a long spur, high up the mountain, where the Windveil was joined to its neighbour, Steelclaw, by a saddle of high, broken rock known to the Xandim as the Dragon's Tail. Like the tortured stone of ruined Steelclaw, this sheer, knife-edge ridge was twisted and fractured partway along its length, preventing human access to the other peak, but that was fine by the Xandim, who never set foot there in any case. Steelclaw was the haunt of the fearsome Black Ghosts who ate human flesh – and the Ghosts could cross the ridge with no trouble at all.

Chiamh's shortcut took him through his own valley, and so he was able to stop briefly at his cave and put on an extra tunic and a warmer cloak against the freezing air of the higher altitudes. He bundled up some of his blankets, with a flask of strong spirits packed carefully in the centre of the roll, and fastened the resulting bulky package to his back with rope. Then, picking up a staff shod with an iron spike, to assist him up the icy reaches of the mountain, the Windeye set off to rescue the strangers.

The secret way up the flanks of the Wyndveil led past the place where the flimsy rope bridge to Chiamh's Chamber of Winds was attached to the mountain. First came the icy flywalk ledge that led as far as his bridge, then the cliff seemed to fold over upon itself to form a narrow gully with towering walls that was invisible from the plateau below. It slanted up the mountain's flank to eventually merge with the main trail that zigzagged up from the plateau round an outthrust spur of the Wyndveil. For Chiamh, with his blurred, chancy eyesight, it was a dreadful journey. Though he was accustomed to climbing the cliff, its slender ledges were glassy with ice. Even so, he preferred the perilous scramble up slippery, precipitous rocks to the heavy going in the gully, where the way was darkened by the steep walls of stone, and he was forced to plough his way through waist-deep pockets of drifted snow, and scramble around thickets of stunted firs that had rooted themselves in this sheltered place whenever there was a crack in the rock.

Weary and panting, his limbs numbed and aching with cold, the Windeye finally arrived at the junction with the main trail – and found, as he had expected, that this would be the worst part of the climb.

The gale slammed into Chiamh like a giant fist as he left the sheltered gully for the faint, icy tract that snaked across the exposed mountainside. On his left, the bleak snowfields sloped steeply upwards, with nothing, not even a tree, to break the force of the wind. On his right – the Windeye shuddered. Better not to think of it! Stray too far in that direction, and he would be falling down a slope that, though not a cliff exactly, was far too steep to let him stop. There would be an ever-quickening slithering plunge – until he reached the edge of the cliff and hurtled to oblivion on the rocks at the bottom. For the first time since he had experienced his vision, Chiamh began to have serious doubts about whether the strangers were worth this trouble. None the less . . : Cursing under his breath, the Windeye drove the spike of his staff down hard into the ice, and took his first, tentative step along the perilous trail.

After what seemed to be a lifetime, the track, climbing steeply, curved sharply to the left and rounded an outcrop of broken black rock. Chiamh noted thankfully that boulders had begun to appear on his other side too, cutting off the drop to his right. As the way began to narrow, he heard voices, borne to him on the wind from the Field of Stones.

Thank the goddess! Though he'd been forced to go slowly and carefully, testing his footing with each step as he blundered up the slippery track, Chiamh had reached the Field of Stones before the guards escorting the prisoners were ready to depart. The last thing he'd needed was to meet them coming back, and have to explain what he was doing up here! Blessing the shortcut that had bought him the extra time, the Windeye slipped into the midst of a cluster of boulders at the side of the trail. Praying that the wretched guards would hurry, he settled down to wait.

Luckily, the escort had no wish to linger until the Ghosts appeared. The snow had begun to fall again, whipped into swirling flurries by the howling wind. Within a short time, Chiamh heard the squeaking crunch of footsteps in the snow as the guards passed his hiding place, cursing as they slithered down the treacherous trail and grumbling in the typical manner of soldiers. Their complaints came to the Windeye on the voice of the gale: 'Because of the Herdlord and his accursed law, *we* risk our necks in this storm . . .'

'Aye, and for what? The stinking outlanders will likely freeze to death before the Ghosts come . . .'

'Why we couldn't simply have run a sword through them down on the plateau, I'll never know . . .'

'It would be a waste to run that wench through – not with a

sword, at any rate! We could have had some fun with her, had it not been so cold . . .'

Hearing the hectoring tones of Galdrus, the Windeye fought to suppress the hope that the fools would fall over a cliff on the way down. Once they had safely gone, he left his hiding place and made his way along the rocky track to the Field of Stones – until a spate of curses and shrieks, coming from ahead, made him stop in his tracks. Oh goddess – surely the Ghosts could not have come already? Quaking with more than the deathly cold, Chiamh waited until the sounds had ceased. Then he crept forward, more slowly now; afraid of what he might find upon the Field of Stones.

Parric lay spreadeagled and helpless on the flat-topped Death-stone. The icy chill of the shackles burned into his wrists and ankles. By all the gods, he thought, I didn't know it could be so cold! Already the snow on the rock beneath him, which had melted in its initial contact with his body, had frozen again, sealing him to the stone. Already, as the lethal temperature claimed his body, his anger against the Xandim was giving way to despair. Anger had been better. At least with anger, you could fight – but how could he fight in any case, shackled and frozen as he was?

Nearby, the others were chained down on great boulders of their own. Sangra was somewhere behind him, out of sight. Meiriel he could see from the corner of his eye; now here, now gone behind the drifting grey curtains of snow. The cavalry master bit down on a flash of rage. Due to some strange effect from the spell of tongues that the Mage was using on the Xandim, he had been able to understand her words at their trail, and it was likely that she had brought them to this end. If she had only let him speak to the ruler and explain that they were only passing through his lands, and wanted nothing, and would soon be gone! Parric had worked it all out, but instead of translating his words Meiriel had flown into a typical Magefolk tirade – just like the one that had got them thrown off the Nightrunner ship and into this mess in the first place! Her arrogance had killed them all.

Elewin, to his left, lay grey-faced and unmoving, not even

coughing now. Parric was afraid that the gruelling journey up the mountain might have finished the old man.

'As this cold will soon finish us all.' The cavalry master was unaware that he had spoken aloud, until he heard Meiriel's shrill cackle from her nearby rock.

'Oh no, you stupid Mortal – it won't be the cold that will finish you. That was not the reason you were brought here. The guards were talking, I heard them. There are demons up here, Parric – Black Ghosts that haunt this place. A sacrifice, that's what you are – you and your pathetic Mortal friends – but they won't get *me*!'

As the Magewoman spoke, the chains that shackled her wrists and ankles flared into painful brilliance and crumbled to dust. She scrambled, crowing, to her feet – and Parric's glad cry died in his throat as she turned her back on her erstwhile companions and scuttled, with her tattered skirts flapping scarecrow-fashion in the wind, away down the broken ridge towards the other mountain. In no time, she was lost to sight among the drifting snow. 'May you rot, you accursed Mortals . . . They won't get me!' Her mocking cry floated back to Parric on the wind, and he struggled furiously against his bonds, cursing bitterly.

'Come back, you bloody bitch!' Sangra was shrieking.

Then, once again, there was silence, except for the whistling moan of the wind across the stones.

May Chathak curse her! the cavalry master thought. I should have suspected something like that from Meiriel – she's a Mage after all, and mad besides. Elewin warned me from the start. But her betrayal pierced him like a sword to the heart, somehow setting the final seal on his fear and misery. What a fool he'd been to come south! Now he would never find Aurian – and still worse, he'd dragged Sangra and Elewin along with him to their deaths. Alone and wretched, Parric closed his eyes and wept – until, with horror, he discovered that the tears had frozen, sealing his eyelids shut and blinding him. At least I won't see the Ghosts when they come; he thought wryly, remembering Meiriel's words – and that was a mistake. Now that his eyes were sealed, his imagination took over.

Parric began to hear noises coming nearer and nearer – the

90

hoarse huff of breath through fanged jaws; the blundering, scraping sound of a massive body moving among the rocks, as it came to rend his helpless body . . . It was coming – it *was* coming! Parric gave a whimper of terror. 'Dear gods,' he gasped, 'no!' Then something touched him. 'No!' he howled, thrashing against his chains.

'It's all right,' a voice said hastily, in a tongue that was, and was not, his own. 'I am Chiamh. I came to rescue you.'

'You festering idiot!' Parric screamed, on the knife-edge of hysteria. 'I thought you were the bloody Ghosts!'

'Sorry,' the voice said cheefully. Warm air, moist and smelling faintly of herbs, tickled Parric's face as Chiamh breathed on his eyelids to melt the ice. By the time he could open his eyes, his heart had stopped trying to claw its way into his throat and he had recovered sufficiently to feel embarrassed by his outburst. Then all such thoughts were driven out of his mind by the sight of the round-faced, brown-haired young man who stood before him. It was the apparition – quite real and solid now – that had visited him in the Xandim dungeons.

After all that had happened, the cavalry master was feeling dangerously overwrought. The 'ghost' was groping short-sightedly on the ground, and somehow the sight of that amiable, foolish face only fuelled Parric's anger. 'What do you want with us anyway?' he snarled unwisely. Chiamh stood up abruptly, his grin vanishing like the sun behind a cloud, and Parric saw the rock in his hand. For a moment, the cavalry master ceased to breathe.

With a quick jerk of his wrist Chiamh brought the rock smashing down on Parric's manacle. Parric yelled, as the edge of the manacle bit into his flesh. Though he was too numbed by cold to feel the pain, he felt the flow of hot blood across his hand, and knew it would hurt like perdition later on. 'They aren't locked, you jackass!'

'Oh.' Chiamh didn't bother to apologize. He simply started to pry with the hilt of his dagger at the stubborn metal catch, which his blow had bent sadly out of shape. 'Just as well, really,' he added, as the clasp finally gave way, 'because it seems the Ghosts have found us.'

'*What?* As the other wrist came free, Parric shot bolt upright,

91

groping frantically at his manacled ankles with fingers that were too numb to work.

'Out of the way.' Chiamh pushed his hands aside and quickly freed the remaining chains. 'Stay you quiet, my friend – they're right behind you.'

His skin prickling with dread, the cavalry master turned to follow the Windeye's gaze. Not a man's length away from the stones were two of the Ghosts – not spectral beings at all, Parric discovered, but great cats of an awesome size. He swallowed hard, seeing the size of their claws, like scimitars of steel, and their great white fangs as they snarled in a low and menacing duet. The gleaming pelt of one was stark black against the snow, the other was black with patterned dapples of gold. The blazing lamps of their watchful yellow eyes were filled with a weird and arcane intelligence. Parric's breath froze in his throat.

'You know,' Chiamh said in a soft, conversational tone, 'I believe these cats to be more than simple animals – and for all our sakes, let us hope I'm right.' Then, to the cavalry's master's horror, he appeared to go utterly mad. Advancing on the Ghosts, he seemed to Parric's fear-glazed vision, to be twisting his hands, as though tying an invisible knot in the air. Both cats started, their golden eyes widening as they stared, hackles rising – then, with bloodcurdling yowls, they shot away as though Death himself were hot on their heels.

'I was right!' Chiamh laughed. 'It takes imagination to be scared by an illusion.'

Parric stared at him, amazed. 'Why did you save me?' he whispered. 'What do you want from me?'

'You had best ask the goddess,' Chiamh replied shortly. 'For I'm sure I don't know. But our Lady of the Beasts has a task for you, and it was her vision that sent me to you.' His sternness vanished as he put a shoulder under Parric's arm to help him rise. 'Come, let us free your companions.'

'About bloody time!' Sangra's voice came faintly from the direction of her stone, and Parric and Chiamh shared a grin.

'Here.' The young man shrugged the bundle from his shoulders and unwrapped it, handing the cavalry master a flask that, to his delight, contained something very close to raw spirits that went searing down his throat like a bolt of lightning.

'Aah! Good!' he gasped. Seeing that Chiamh was already loosening Sangra's chains, Parric threw one of the young man's blankets around his shoulders, and went quickly across to help Elewin.

The old man did not move as he approached. Elewin's face was sunken; his skin was a sickly bluish-grey. As he loosed the shackles, Parric found no signs of breathing. 'Ah gods, no,' he muttered. 'Poor old bugger. All this way he came, and only to die.'

'Let me see.' Chiamh pushed him aside. Lowering his shaggy brown head to the old man's chest he listened for what seemed an endless time, then put his face close to Elewin's own. 'Not quite gone, but close,' he muttered. 'Too close for my liking, but . . .'

Chiamh laid his hands on the old man's chest, then on his face – then he lifted and moved them in a series of fluent gestures; seeming, as he had done when he banished the great cats, to be writing invisible figures in the air. Sangra, wrapped in a blanket, approached with tears in her eyes, and the cavalry master put an arm around her. They looked on, entranced, as Chiamh's hands moved fluidly across the old man's body, seeming – so distinct were his actions – to cocoon it in some invisible weave from head to toe.

After a time, Chiamh looked up, and Parric saw that, despite the dreadful cold on the mountain, the young man's face was glistening with the sweat of exertion. Chiamh mopped his brow, and reached out wordlessly for the flask that Sangra still held. 'It may hold long enough,' he said, and took a long, gasping pull at the liquor. 'Your friend is old and tired and very ill, and this cold was almost enough to finish him. But I have done – something – that will keep the air moving in and out of his lungs for the present. If I can keep him breathing until we can carry him down the mountain and back to my home – well, my grandam taught me much about herblore and healing. It may be that we can save him after all. It is a hard thing to ask of you, but if you could spare him your blankets . . .'

Parric looked doubtfully at Sangra. She was shivering,

white-faced, and bedraggled, and leaned wearily against the stone as if her strength was scarcely sufficient to keep her upright. Frankly, he felt little better himself.

'Pox rot it!' Sangra muttered. She sighed, shrugged off her blanket and handed it to Chiamh. 'Come on, then,' she said briskly. 'Let's get off this blasted mountain before we all freeze to death.'

While they were wrapping the unconscious Elewin for his journey, Chiamh suddenly looked up, frowning. 'What became of your other companion, the madwoman?'

Parric scowled, and shrugged. 'Forget her,' he said.

Chiamh soon realized that getting the sick old man down the mountain was going to be appallingly difficult. His companions were incapacitated by their own weariness, and they were almost stupefied with the cold besides. Time and again, as they crossed the slanting track across the snowfield, the Windeye's heart was in his mouth as one of the outlanders slipped, almost sending themselves and their unconscious companion hurtling down the precipitous slope to their deaths.

Time stretched into eternity as they crawled like flies across the endless white expanse; two of them struggling along with the motionless body of the old man slung between them, while the other took a turn to rest. It was as well that their route was chiefly downhill. As it was, Chiamh found before too long that he was forced to take constant charge of Elewin, while the others rested for longer and longer periods, trudging behind. They had no idea how to move safely on a mountain, and their carelessness gave the Windeye some moments of alarm, but at least they had the sense to know that they must keep going, though Parric's face was creased with fatigue, and Sangra looked ready to drop. None the less, she still had the strength to fetch Chiamh a telling clout that almost sent all four of them over the edge, when he saw that the tip of her nose had turned pink with impending frostbite, and without thinking to warn her he clapped a handful of snow to her face.

By the time they had reached the branching trail that continued down the gorge, a thick cap of dark stormclouds was rolling down the face of the mountain, portending another bout of evil weather. When Chiamh paused, it was as though the others had been puppets, and some playful god had finally cut their strings. Setting the old man down in the snow, they leaned against one another, sagging.

Chiamh could see that both of the outlanders were completely foredone. How could they carry the old man through the rougher going of the defile? And what about the approaching storm? If they could not get down before the blizzard hit, they stood little chance of getting down at all. Sangra, shivering, her hair straggling around her face, gave the Windeye an accusing look, and cursed bitterly. 'Is it very much further?' she whispered.

Chiamh nodded, and the three of them looked at one another in silence. It was Parric who finally voiced what everyone was thinking. He looked at Elewin, and bit his lip. 'Are you sure you can keep him alive until we get back?'

'I think so.' The Windeye hesitated. 'But if I do, I will not be able to use my powers to hold off the storm until we reach safety, which I otherwise might have done.'

The cavalry master looked down again at the old man, refusing to meet Sangra's eyes. 'Are you sure you can save him if we do get him down?'

For a moment, the Windeye's confidence wavered. Parric was asking him to make a decision that might either kill the old man, or kill all four of them. Is it worth it? he found himself thinking. Is it worth the chance of preserving one spent and fragile life, if the alternative is for us all to die here on the mountain? Then suddenly, into his head came a vision of his grandam – and the old woman was scowling at him fiercely. Chiamh flinched as though she had clouted him and stiffened his spine. 'Of course I can save the old man, and we *will* get him down,' he said, with confidence he was far from feeling. As he spoke, he was uncoiling the rope that had originally bound his bundle of blankets.

'Help me tie this around him,' he instructed. 'The gradient is steep in the gorge – if we cannot carry him, we may be able to pull him, like a sled.'

'Don't be daft, man! All that jolting around will finish the poor old beggar,' the cavalry master protested.

Chiamh sighed. Parric was right, but the alternative was the one thing he had been hoping to avoid. To change in front of these outlanders – to betray the secret of the Xandim . . . Not to mention, he thought wryly, the risk of breaking a leg down there among these rocks! But if the old man was to be saved, there was nothing else for it.

'Listen carefully,' he told Parric. 'Don't be alarmed by what you will see in a moment – I'm going to alter . . .' He knew he should be explaining this better, but the words were sticking in his throat. He hurried on, before they could ask questions: 'Tie the old man to my back and I will take him down the gully. When we reach the bottom take him off again – I'll need my human shape to get down that last part of the cliff.' As he had been speaking he was backing away from them, trying to avoid their puzzled eyes lest they should start asking difficult and untimely questions. 'Now, you folk – stand back!'

And with that, the Windeye changed. The shocked cries of his companions shrilled loudly in Chiamh's equine ears, and their outlander stink burned his nostrils. He began to tremble all over. What have I done? he thought wildly. Gritting his teeth and blowing hard, he edged nervously towards the others. He had already betrayed the secret of the Xandim – there was no going back now.

Sangra was the first to recover from her shock. 'Seven bloody demons,' she breathed, and swallowed hard. 'Right,' she said crisply. 'Come on, Parric, stop dithering! Help me get Elewin up and get these ropes tied – a horse is the one thing you *do* understand.'

For Chiamh, the descent of the gorge was a nightmare. He was unaccustomed to carrying burdens in his equine shape, and though the old man's weight was slight in comparison to the Windeye's strength, the unfamiliar bulk of the body unbalanced him, making it hard for him to pick his way down the slippery track, especially with the added distraction of keeping Elewin breathing. Also, in this form, he could feel the storm; the pressure of its forefront prickling against his skin and filling him with the instinctive, animal urge to shed his burden and flee. Before they were halfway down the gully, a wild-eyed, shivering Chiamh was dripping with sweat, despite the freezing weather.

'There, hush – it'll be all right soon. Soon we'll be down.' Sangra's lilting voice was low and soothing. A hand smoothed his neck; stroked his nose. Chiamh flung up his head and snorted in surprise, but her voice helped calm him, and her touch was astonishing pleasant.

'Sangra, what the blazes do you think you're doing?' The Windeye heard Parric's frantic whisper from his other side. 'He's not a bloody *horse*, you know!'

Sangra's hand never paused in its gentle soothing. 'For now, he is,' she said. Chiamh blessed her understanding.

When they reached the bottom of the gorge and removed his burden, Chiamh barely had the strength to change back. Once he had done so, he slumped in the snow, trembling all over. Spots were dancing before his eyes. Sangra draped one of Elewin's blankets around his shoulders. 'Are you all right?' she asked, her eyes wide with wonder.

He nodded. 'Thank you for your help. As a horse it's hard to think straight.' His words lost themselves in a half-shamed smile.

Parric shook his head. 'That was the most incredible . . .' he began, but the Windeye cut him off.

'Ask me later.' Snowflakes were beginning to swirl around them in the rising wind. Chiamh got swiftly to his feet. 'Come, we must get down the cliff before the storm hits.' In fact, he had no idea how to accomplish the final part of the descent. That crumbling, icy ledge would be difficult enough for him, and he was used to it, but for inexperienced, exhausted outlanders . . . Chiamh was crushed by a weight of despair. After he had brought them so far . . .

'Have courage, Windeye, for I am also the mountain. Take up your burden and trust me. I will not let you fail.'

'Basileus!' Chaimh cried joyfully. Clearly, the others thought he had lost his mind, and only the proximity of the storm persuaded them to trust him when he assured them that the ledge was not so difficult as it seemed. Even then, they would only follow him when at last he hoisted Elewin across his shoulders, staggering under the weight, and set off alone down the narrow path. Behind him, he could hear them swearing horribly as they began their descent.

But as Basileus had promised, it was easy. It was as though their feet clung tight to the stone of the ledge; as though a vast invisible hand held them safe against the rough cliff face. Chiamh's burden seemed to weigh nothing, as the Moldan's strength poured into him to take him over that last, desperate lap. None the less, when they finally reached the pinnacle-spire at the head of the valley, the Windeye had never been so glad in his life to see his home.

7

The Roof of the World

As the peaks beyond the forest turned from rose to blazing gold
in the sunrise, Raven came banking low over the campsite,
skilfully avoiding the trees. From her vantage point aloft, she
could see a great deal of early-morning activity. Yazour and
Eliizar were skinning two deer by the stream, watched by Shia,
who, no doubt, had played an enthusiastic part in the hunting
of the animals. Bohan was coming through the trees from
another direction with the rabbits he had snared dangling
limply from one huge hand, while Nereni, cooking breakfast by
the fire, looked up and waved to her. The winged girl noticed,
with a twinge of annoyance, that Aurian and Anvar were
missing – again.

Raven landed, the whirls of wind from her wings making the
fire spark and glow. She exchanged warm greetings with
Nereni, and handed over her catch – two pheasants and a wild
duck that she had caught napping further up the course of the
stream. 'Where are the Magefolk?' she asked.

'Fishing, perhaps, or rounding up the horses.' Nereni gave
her a cup of steaming broth in exchange for the birds. 'By the
Reaper, I'm glad we leave tomorrow. The sooner I have walls
around me again, the better it will please me.'

'And I,' Raven muttered, thinking of Harihn. How she had
missed him, since he had left for the tower! For the better part
of a month she had laboured like a drudge, helping the others
prepare for the gruelling journey into the mountains. As well as
ostensibly keeping an eye on Harihn's encampment, she had
helped to build the rough shelters of woven boughs that were
dotted around the clearing, caught birds for Nereni to cook,
and scouted for the hunters to locate deer, wild pigs and other
game among the trees. Her scathed and roughened hands bore
testimony to the fact that she had hauled wood and water as

99

though she had never been a princess, and she had still found time on top of these tasks to help Nereni with her endless sewing.

After the baking heat of the desert, the cold of the mountains had presented a problem, for the robes they had been wearing were too thin for these colder lands, and the clothing stored in Dhiammara to equip the Khisu's raids to the north had been taken by Harihn. The companions had been lucky, however. At the forest's edge, Bohan had found the desert tents that the prince's party had abandoned. Nereni, who had guarded her case of needles like a royal treasure all the way across the desert, was making new clothes for everyone from the silken cloth; sewing it in double layers quilted with wool from wild goats, the fur of rabbits snared by Bohan, and soft warm down from Raven's birds.

It was tedious and painstaking work, which took up most of Nereni's time, and as much as the winged girl could spare. The others helped as they could; with Bohan, to everyone's astonishment, producing miracles of deft and delicate stitchery with fingers so thick that they obscured the needle. Aurian had proved to be useless at sewing, and though she was now in no condition to help with the heavier work around the encampment, she had, to Raven's disgust, still managed to find ways to get out of the detested chore.

The hunters, including Shia, had been bringing in all the game they could find. Some they ate, glad of it after the privations of the desert; but most they smoked and dried for the journey. Even the horses had been busy, foraging for tender new grass. The improvement in their condition was visible to all, while the days had flowed past as swiftly as the forest's running streams – until at long last, just as Raven's frustration had reached breaking point, the Mages had decided that it was time to leave.

'Surely we must have enough now.' Aurian looked at the pile of speckled trout that glittered on the streambank, and straightened her aching back with a grimace.

'It's better than sewing, though, isn't it?' Anvar teased.

Aurian grimaced. 'Anything is better than sewing!'

'Anything is better than your sewing,' Anvar chuckled. 'Apart from its appalling effect on your temper, I had visions of your clothes falling to pieces on us halfway up a mountain.'

'And you could do better?' Aurian retorted.

'Not I! We Magefolk may have many talents, but needlework seems not to be one of them, somehow.'

Aurian had managed to escape the dreaded sewing by taking up fishing, and so it was that Anvar had mastered the art of trout-tickling at last; not in the sea, but in the icy forest streams, with Aurian as his tutor. Forral had taught her the skill long ago, in Eilin's lake, and Aurian's heart was wrenched again and again by the memory of her younger self, a skinny, tangle-haired urchin, elbow-deep in the still lake waters as she copied the swordsman's every move, her eyes filled with adoration, her face alight with excitement. Ah, those had been happy days! Now she was grown, and had drunk the bitter cup of grief and hardship to its very dregs. Another head, blond instead of brown, nestled close to hers as she peered into the amber forest streams, with Anvar's brilliant blue eyes straying from the waters again and again, to peer longingly into her face.

Anvar, seated on the streambank, was cleaning the fish with quick, deft skill. 'Are you coming with us tonight?' he asked her conversationally, as she bundled their catch into one of Nereni's woven baskets. Aurian knew that the question, casual though it sounded, was anything but; and could easily provoke another of the squabbles that were all too frequent between them nowadays. Since they had escaped the desert, Anvar's protectiveness was beginning to grate on her, but Aurian knew there were limits, now, to what she could do.

'What?' she asked him in scandalized tones. 'You want me to go out stealing horses? In the forest, in the middle of the night, in *my* condition?' She grinned at the quick flash of relief in his face. 'Got you!'

'Wretch!' He flung a fish at her, and Aurian clawed the slippery creature out of the air just before it hit her.

'Do you mind?' she protested. 'We have to eat that.'

'In fact,' she returned to their original conversation, 'I intend to be in bed and asleep by the time you leave tonight, so don't make a noise when you go.'

'I'll believe that when I see it,' scoffed Anvar. 'Really, though, do you mean it, Aurian? You don't mind?'

The Mage looked at him gravely. 'Anvar, I mind it more than I can say. But what use would I be? I can't move quickly, and I'd find it hard to fight if I had to. But what if it's a trap? Have you thought of that? For the life of me, I can't see why Harihn's folk have stayed here so long. And I'm amazed they haven't found us.'

Anvar shook his head. 'How can it be a trap?' he argued. 'They don't know we're going to steal their horses, and with Shia and Raven guarding our camp, none of them could have come near enough to spy on us. If you ask me, I don't think the prince is there at all.'

'What?' This was news to Aurian.

'Well, think about it. Raven had no idea of their numbers, but when Shia scouted, she said that half of them were missing – mostly men-at-arms. You know how callous Harihn was about leaving *us* behind – I think he's gone ahead with soldiers, abandoning his housefolk who were likely to hold him up on his way through the mountains. If those people are trying to settle here, that would explain the hunting and gathering, and their lack of exploration.'

'Dear gods, I never thought of that.' Aurian frowned. 'It would be just like Harihn. If you're right, it should make tonight's expedition much easier, but all the same . . .' She leaned across and laid a hand on his arm. 'Anvar, for goodness sake be careful, won't you?'

'Of course.' He reached out to hug her – and Aurian, with a wicked grin, dropped the fish, that she had been saving for just such a moment, down the back of his tunic.

'Shia, are you ready?' Anvar peered through the bushes at the dim and shadowy shapes that grazed, content and oblivious, in the clearing.

'How fast do you think I can move in this tangle?' Shia's terse mental voice came back at him. 'Do you want me to scare the stupid creature all the way back to the desert?' There was a moment's pause, then: 'I'm in position now. Can you see them?'

102

'They're right in front of me. Any sign of a guard on your side?' Because Anvar possessed the night-vision of a Mage, he had been the one selected to go in close with Shia to steal the Khazalim mounts.

'Only one – where Raven said he'd be,' the cat informed him. 'The fool is fast asleep!'

'Perfect!' Anvar grinned. 'Move in slowly, so that the horses don't get panicked. We don't want to wake him.'

'I know, I know!'

In the bushes, Anvar waited. Somewhere on the other side of the clearing, he knew, Shia would be creeping up carefully on the Khazalim beasts. She was upwind of them, and at any time now ... One of the horses flung its head up and snorted, scenting the predator. Hobbled as they were, they could not stampede. Instead, as the sense of unease spread from one beast to the others, they began to move in a tightly-gathered knot away from the danger. Out of the clearing they came, away from the sleeping guard – and, Anvar thought with a grin, right into his arms!

'Come, my beauties,' the Mage crooned softly, slipping a rope around the neck of the leading horse. In normal circumstances, they might have tended to shy away from a stranger; but now, with the cat at large in the forest, they knew that a human meant protection. Anvar whistled softly, and Yazour, Eliizar and Bohan came melting out of the forest to help him. Cutting the hobbles on four of the horses, they led them away, back through the forest to their camp, where everything was packed and ready for them to leave at dawn, before the Khazalim discovered their missing mounts.

Anvar, who could see better than the others, was in the lead. As he walked, only part of his attention was given to picking out the best trail through the dense, crowding woodland. He was conscious of a sense of relief, that the stealing of the horses had been so easy, but at the same time there was a nagging suspicion at the back of his mind. It had been easy, all right – too bloody easy! Just what, Anvar wondered, is going on? All things considered, he would be glad to get out of this forest at last.

As the horses picked their way up a tortuous goat-track in the dappled light beneath the trees, Aurian looked around, saying a last farewell to the place that had been her haven for the last month or so. Ironically, now that it was time for the Mage to leave, she was reluctant to quit the forest's shelter. But it was not the beauty of the place that made her hesitate. It was pure fear.

Since her powers had left her, Aurian's vulnerability terrified her almost to the point of paralysis. After months of flight and fighting, her body had betrayed her, forcing her to pause in her struggle. Her fears, however, emerged while she slept, filling her dreams with nightmare Wraiths, horrific visions of Miathan's depredations back in Nexis, and the suffering of Raven's Winged Folk, until she woke each night, sweat-soaked and trembling. The Mage had been impossibly torn between continuing her journey, or remaining in safety in the forest until her son was born, for now that she could feel his thoughts, the reality of the child had truly come home to her, and she had found herself loving him with a fierce protectiveness that had stunned her. She had found herself unable, even, to confide in Anvar, and unbeknown to her companions she had fought a tremendous inner battle in the forest to find the courage to go on with her quest. The last thing she wanted to admit, even to herself, was that her fear and indecision stemmed from the loss of her magic.

Now, however, Aurian could delay no longer. It was vital that she make some kind of stand against the Archmage, and Raven's tower would be a step in that direction. What other choice was there? She and Anvar perforce must travel north. The Mage was glad that the proximity of the Khazalim camp in the forest had made the decision for her, but by Chathak, she was not looking forward to this journey!

All day the companions rode a twisting course through the forest, scrambling upwards via the rough game trails that threaded the increasingly rocky slopes. By early evening, they had reached the end of the trees. Looking out across the bleak waste of boulder and scree that sloped up to the knees of the hostile mountains, the travellers decided to spend one last night within the forest's shelter. Already the air was ominously cooler, and they gathered gratefully around a cheerful fire, roasting rabbit and pheasant from the previous day's hunt while Shia made short work of a haunch of venison.

After supper, Aurian offered to take first watch, afraid that if she slept, her evil dreams would return. Sword in hand, she sat close to the fire, watching its dancing light make ruddy shadow-faces on the rough bark of firs, and wondering what was happening to the friends and enemies she had left behind in Nexis. Ever since her dream of Eliseth, she had felt uneasy – and the sight of the continuing snow that cloaked the distant peaks had added to her disquiet. Surely, if Eliseth is dead, her winter should be diminishing by now? the Mage thought. Beyond the comforting ring of firelight, she could feel the looming presence of the mountains, as though they watched her with unfriendly eyes. As though they were waiting for her.

As the Magefolk and their companions climbed through the convoluted chain of valleys that led up to the high mountain passes, the going became more difficult as the biting cold increased. The barren, stony landscape, hemmed in by ragged cliffs and unclimbable slopes of scree, was profoundly grim, though sometimes they found a rare green valley, protected from the incessant, whining wind by a trick of the cliff formations. They gladly stopped to rest in these havens, giving the horses a chance to graze, and themselves a respite from the overwhelming bleakness of the landscape; but as they went on, frost whitened the trails with a slick film that made the horses stumble, and slowed their progress to a snail's pace. The fear that someone would sustain a serious fall was always with them. Bohan wrenched a shoulder when his mount went down, and it was sheer good fortune that the beast had not been lamed. Often they were forced to climb on foot, leading the animals – a gruelling business which left everyone exhausted, dispirited and out of temper by the end of each day's freezing march.

The journey took its toll on everyone. Food for humans and horses was rationed, and there was never enough to sustain them against the enforced activity of the climb and the deadly cold. Tempers grew short among the little band, and even gentle Bohan was often seen to be scowling. He had taken a marked dislike to Raven, but without speech was unable to tell them why. Anvar was deeply concerned about Aurian. Day by day, she grew more gaunt and hollow-cheeked as the babe took her food for its own growth, leaving its mother all belly and bone. Lacking the energy to talk, she no longer refused his aid as she hauled herself upward step by step, leaning on the Staff of Earth that she clutched in frozen, rag-wrapped fingers. At night, though Bohan and Shia curled up beside her and Anvar held her close to warm her body with his own, she never stopped shivering. Anvar, to his increasing frustration, could think of no way to ease her suffering, and he wished with all his heart that he could end the torment that Miathan was causing for his beloved, and countless others besides.

As the days went on, and the companions continued their cold and miserable climb, the thought occurred to Anvar again and again. Why should Aurian risk herself and her child? He had his own powers now, and the Mage had been training him intensively before she lost her magic. Perhaps he could find some way of fighting Miathan by himself. Had he confided in Aurian, she would have disabused him of such brave but foolish notions, for without the missing Weapons the two of them together stood little chance against the Cauldron, and might bring about a war between two equal powers that could destroy the very world. But Anvar kept his thoughts to himself, and the idea remained with him, growing in his mind like a canker. This, he was convinced, would be the way to repay Aurian for his part in Forral's death.

The companions had been travelling for about a score of days when the blizzard struck. All morning as they had climbed, leading horses that were strangely uneasy, Aurian had felt spits of snow in the wind – hard, tiny pellets that stung her chapped hands and face and blew in skeins across the rocks to collect, unmelting, in every crevice. The sky grew black and heavy, as though the clouds were sinking to meet them as they climbed. The force of the wind was increasing, and Raven, who had been flying ahead of them, landed suddenly by the side of the tired Mages. 'I think we should turn back,' she said. 'There's no shelter ahead – we're nearing the top of the ridge, and it looks bad up there.'

Aurian swore. The slopes around them were naked scree, and it had been the same lower down. 'There's no shelter for miles, the way we've come,' she said. Everyone looked at one another, reluctant to lose any of their hard-won progress. Before a decision could be reached, the air was full of fat white flakes that bore down on them with a shocking suddenness; so thick as to make breathing difficult, and cutting them off from each other's sight.

'Stay where you are!' cried Yazour. Aurian reached out to grab Anvar's sleeve, and felt his hand clutch tightly at her own. At her other side, she felt Bohan's big hand grip her shoulder, and hoped that her other companions had also located each other by touch.

Eliizar's voice penetrated the rising howl of the wind. 'Stay together,' he shouted. 'Tie the horses in a circle and get inside.' It was difficult to follow his advice, blind as they were and with frightened horses to contend with, and hands that were numbed and clumsy with cold. After a struggle, they found themselves huddled within the minimal shelter of the circle of beasts as the snow heaped itself around them, counting one another by touch and afraid to sit, lest they never rise again.

The companions clung together, sharing each other's warmth, which was quickly leached away by the merciless wind. Aurian had long ago lost all feeling in her frozen feet, and the cold was pervading her body with a drowsy numbness. It took her back to her childhood, when she had searched for Forral in the endless snow . . . She awakened in the warm, glowing kitchen of her mother's tower on the lake, to see the swordsman's anxious face looking down at her . . .

'Aurian, wake up!' It was Anvar's voice. Aurian's dream melted like snow – oh, dear gods, the snow! She opened her eyes with difficulty and pulled herself upright. Anvar was shaking her. 'Thank the gods you're all right! You fell asleep, you idiot! Had I not felt you go down . . .'

Aurian groaned. 'I was having a wonderful dream.'

'I should hope it was,' Anvar told her grimly, 'because it was almost the last one you ever had.'

For the first time, the befuddled Mage noticed that she was hearing Anvar's voice quite clearly. The wind had dropped.

The snow was still falling, but more gently now, and Aurian could see her surroundings for a few yards around. Not that there was much to see . . . Only snow, and more snow – and her companions, who were so encrusted with the dreadful stuff that they were difficult to distinguish against the stark white background.

Raven, with her race's inborn resistance to the cold, seemed the most alert of them all. 'We should be fairly close to the tower now,' she said. 'If you will wait, I'll fly up and see where we are.'

Nereni sighed. 'I wish we could have a fire. We all need something hot inside us.'

Nereni, however, would have to go on wishing. They had exhausted the slender stock of firewood that they had brought with them from the last valley, some days previously. The companions had not long to wait, however, before Raven returned. 'I thought so,' she told them. 'The tower is at the far end of the next valley. We should reach it before dark, except –' her face fell. 'For you flightless ones, there may be a problem.'

Grim and silent, the travellers urged their weary, frozen horses through breast-deep drifts to the top of the ridge. Near the top the going became easier, for the wind had scoured the snow away until it was only a thin speckling over the dark rocks. They paused on the windswept ridge, looking out over the next stage of their journey. Below them, the way opened into a broad sweep of valley; its stark, snow-choked whiteness alleviated here and there by dark clumps of twisted evergreens, bent like worn old men by their wintry burden. Above, oppressive with their looming weight, peaks like jagged fangs shouldered one another as though jostling to attack their puny human victims.

The Mage, looking out across the way they had to travel, felt her heart sink. Now that the companions had reached the summit, she could see only too clearly what Raven, with masterly understatement, had described as a problem. The pass below them, the only way down into the valley, was choked with snow.

'That's all we need,' Aurian sighed. 'How will we ever manage to dig our way through that lot?'

Shia, born and bred in the mountains, surveyed the snow-clogged pass. 'The way looks very steep,' she said. 'An avalanche might sweep it clear, at least sufficiently for us to get down. If only we could start one . . .'

'A what?' Anvar squatted beside her, his cold hands tucked beneath his cloak, while the great cat told him of the massive snow-slides that sometimes occurred in the mountains, crushing everything that stood in their path. He frowned, looking down at the pass. 'Do you think it would be possible to start one?'

'Surely.' Shia paused. 'So long as you are willing to sacrifice the one who starts it, for the risk of being swept away is exceedingly great.'

'Oh.' Anvar's face fell, but the great cat's words had set Aurian thinking. 'Anvar – Do you think you could set the snow in motion with the Staff of Earth?'

He turned to her, his face alight with excitement. 'Aurian, you're brilliant! That is . . . if you wouldn't mind lending it to me again?'

Aurian shrugged. 'If it's a choice between that and freezing my backside off on this accursed mountain, there's no question. But Anvar, for the sake of the gods, be careful. The Staff has a way of taking over, it's so powerful; and Shia just told us how dangerous this is. Think it through first, before you do anything, and – '

'I know, I know!' He grinned at her. 'Don't worry, Aurian. I'll be all right.'

The Mage fumbled the Staff from her belt and handed it to him, seized with misgivings as she did so. These were different circumstances from the first time he had handled the Staff, during the desert battle. Then he'd been fighting for his life – and he had also had her steadying hand on the Staff to take up some of its awesome energy. Me and my bright ideas, Aurian thought. For an alarming instant, she saw in Anvar what he must have seen in her, when she had first won the Staff. He seemed taller, his body wrapped in an aureole of power. His eyes glowed with sapphire fire as he strode to the head of the pass, where the snow deepened and the way began to drop towards the valley floor.

'Stay back,' Anvar called cheerfully. Aurian swore under her breath. She knew how he felt – she had experienced this euphoria when she'd first held the Staff. Over his shoulder, she could already see his spell beginning to take effect as a web of glowing green lines snaked their way through the snow, right down to the bottom of the pass. But he only needed to dislodge a little of the snow at the top, Shia had said. 'Anvar, don't!' Aurian yelled.

The force-lines flared with a blinding emerald light. With a rumble growing to a deafening roar, the snow began to thunder down the narrow defile, rumbling and rolling and crashing down in an inexorable wave as the ground shook and shuddered and great clouds of powdered white crystals erupted into the air and the plaque of snow on which Anvar was standing began to move, sliding forward, down and over the edge. Anvar, flailing wildly to keep his balance, cried out once in shrill desperation – and was gone.

8
The Tower of Incondor

The ground shook and the ears of the companions were battered by the receding roar of the avalanche. Snow, hurled high into the air, came spattering down on top of them. Raven took wing like a startled bird. The terrified horses reared, trying to pull their lead-reins free of the eunuch's hands. One broke free and shot forward, vanishing over the edge of the slide with a shriek that was abruptly and sickeningly cut off. Bohan and Nereni had fallen to the ground beneath the hooves of the plunging animals, and Aurian fought to keep her balance by hanging on grimly to the bridle of her wheeling mount. Then, mercifully, the world began to settle.

'Anvar!' Heartsick, Aurian tried to scramble towards the edge of the slide, but hands were holding her back. After a frantic struggle she realized that Yazour and Eliizar were hanging on to her arms. 'Wait, Aurian,' the young warrior told her urgently, 'lest we lose you too!'

As the echoes of the avalanche died away, Aurian, her knuckles clenched tight against her mouth, stepped forward with Yazour and Eliizar, and looked down into the pass. Crystalline clouds of powdered ice hung in the air as a silvery haze above the snow-slide, obscuring what lay below. Raven landed beside them. 'We must wait until it settles.' She sounded very subdued. 'I can see nothing down there.'

Aurian cursed. 'You wait. I'm going now.'

'Let me – I can move faster on that slippery surface.' It was Shia. 'Follow – but take care, my friend. We want no more falls today.' With a bound, the great cat was gone.

Behind the Mage, Bohan and Nereni were picking themselves up. Barring a bruise or two, the eunuch seemed unhurt, and went limping off to gather up the reins of the horses. A shaken Nereni had to be helped to her feet by Eliizar. Her face was streaked with tears, and blood poured from a cut in her forehead, where she had been caught by a flying hoof. Aurian, numb with shock over Anvar's disappearance – she would not let herself call it anything else – found herself thinking that the woman was lucky to be alive. With that, the Mage's thoughts returned to Anvar.

At the top of the pass, the rocky trail had been swept almost bare of snow. What was left had been smoothed and impacted in patches by the avalanche until it looked like glass. Aurian felt a shiver of dread. Automatically, she groped in her belt for the Staff of Earth to help her balance – and stopped dead, her eyes wide with horror. Dear gods, if the Staff had been lost . . . Flinging caution to the winds, she started down.

Luckily, Yazour caught up with her before she had gone more than a step or two – and even that had been almost enough to send her hurtling to the bottom of the defile. He caught her arm as she floundered for balance. 'Take care!' he scolded, handing her one of the stout walking staffs that Bohan had cut for her companions before they left the forest. 'You should have waited.'

'But . . .' Aurian protested.

The warrior hushed her. 'I know,' he told her sadly. 'We have no choice, however – we must go slowly, if we hope to reach the bottom intact.'

Though Aurian was frantic with fear for Anvar, not to mention the fate of the Staff, it was impossible to descend the pass with any speed. Visibility, between the heavy grey sky and the steepening walls on either side, was poor, and the trail was like glass underfoot. She had to test her footing with each step before she could put her weight on it, and, to make matters worse, she was continually unbalanced by the bulk of the child she carried.

Partway down, they came across the unfortunate horse. It lay broken and bloody beside the trail, its neck and limbs wrenched askew at impossible angles. Aurian turned away, with tight throat and clenched teeth, unable to stop herself thinking of Anvar. Yazour's hand tightened on her arm. One look at his grim and pallid face, and Aurian knew that his thoughts were similar to her own. 'Perhaps we should wait for the others?' he suggested tentatively.

112

The Mage shook her head. 'It's no use putting it off.'

It was then, in that darkest of moments, that Shia's voice burst into Aurian's mind. 'Anvar is alive!'

It was as well that the avalanche had already spent itself. Aurian let out a whoop that unbalanced her again, and sent her slithering down the trail. Yazour caught at her, and they slid for several feet before coming to an unsteady halt against the rocky wall of the defile, while Yazour blistered the air with curses. Aurian hugged him. 'He's all right, Yazour! Shia says he's all right!'

Abruptly, the warrior stopped swearing. 'You sorcerers! How in the Reaper's name did he manage that?'

Anvar, lying half-stunned in a pile of snow at the bottom of the trail, was wondering much the same thing. Shia looked him over anxiously, poking him from time to time with her great black muzzle. 'Nothing broken?' she asked sharply.

'I don't think so . . . I can move my arms and legs . . .'

'I suggest you move them, then, before you freeze!'

Anvar groaned, and used the Staff, which he'd clung to with all his strength down every inch of the wild and terrifying slide, to help pull his aching body to unsteady feet. Shia pushed her massive bulk against him, propping him as he stumbled. 'Idiot!' she snarled. 'Aurian warned you to stay back!' She looked at him over her shoulder, her golden eyes ablaze, and the Mage, his hands buried in the thick, warm fur of her back, gave her a sheepish grin. Her mental tones, though sharp with the aftershock of fear for him, lacked the stinging edge of true anger, and he knew she was thankful to see him alive and in one piece, more or less. Anvar's head was still swimming from the fall, and he sat down abruptly in the snow, hugging the cat for more than warmth.

'I'm glad to see you too,' he told her sincerely.

He was even more glad to see Aurian come slithering down the track with Yazour, whose face split into a grin of relief to see him. The warrior clapped Anvar hard on the shoulder, making him wince, before fading tactfully back up the slippery defile to help Eliizar with the horses, leaving the two Magefolk alone with Shia. Aurian looked wretched, a grim expression on her ashen face. Anvar braced himself for the storm of her wrath, certain that this time, at least, he deserved it. 'I'm sorry,' he told her. 'You warned me, and I should have listened.'

The Mage dropped to her knees in the snow beside Anvar, wanting to curse him, to pound him with her fists for putting her through this ordeal. But she couldn't. When she saw him there, blue-lipped and shivering, his clothing torn and wet, his skin scraped and already beginning to bruise in places – well, how could she be angry when she was so glad to see him alive? She wanted to embrace him – she was almost ready to weep with relief to see him safe. But the sick feeling of horror when she thought she had lost him remained within her, like a ball of lead in the pit of her stomach. Instead of his face, she saw the cold, lifeless features of Forral, after the Wraith had struck him down.

Aurian felt her hands beginning to shake. Rather than face the bleak and horrifying possibility of another loss, she took refuge in briskness. 'I understand, Anvar. I should have known – the Staff has so much power. I remember how it was in Dhiammara, the first time I held it, and the city fell apart around me.'

Anvar looked startled. 'But that wasn't your fault. That was a spell of the Dragonfolk, surely.'

'Well, maybe,' Aurian conceded; 'but even if the destruction *had* been my fault, I couldn't have prevented it. What happened today was my mistake, Anvar. Since you'd already used the Staff in the desert, I thought you would be all right, but that time, the power was channelled into the battle – it had somewhere to go. When you disappeared in that avalanche – gods, I thought . . .'

Aurian knew she had betrayed herself when Anvar put an arm around her shoulders. 'And Shia called *me* an idiot!' he scolded. 'Why blame yourself? You trusted me with the Staff, you warned me to be careful – how could it be your fault? In fact,' he went on, 'it was the Staff that saved my life, I think. Its power seemed to surround me and cushion me from the worst of the fall. I remember rolling and sliding, very fast . . . Thank the gods, the worst of the avalanche had already gone before I started to fall, or I'd have been dead for sure.' Anvar, shuddering, fell silent.

Aurian didn't want to think about it. 'Come on,' she said brusquely, 'you mustn't sit and freeze. Let's find you some dry clothing in the packs. We ought to go on now. We stand a better chance of surviving this night if we can find the tower before dark.' She helped the shaken Mage clamber to his feet, and retrieved the Staff of Earth from his grasp. Without looking back at Anvar, she scrambled up towards the place where Eliizar and the others were bringing the horses down the trail.

Taken aback, and not a little hurt by the swift change in Aurian's demeanour, Anvar cursed. 'Gods help me, I'll never understand her.' Though he had been talking to himself, Shia caught his eyes.

'Her behaviour seems perfectly clear to me.'

'You can read her bloody mind!' Muttering under his breath, Anvar limped towards the others.

Eliizar was looking utterly disconsolate. 'We lost another horse, coming down,' the swordsman was telling Aurian, as Anvar approached. 'When he slipped, I could not hold him.'

'The animal broke its leg,' Yazour put in quietly. 'We had to end its suffering.' He sighed.

'It wasn't your fault,' Aurian consoled them. 'I thought we'd have trouble bringing the horses down that trail. You did well to get the others down in one piece.'

'Very true,' Yazour told her grimly. He gestured at the weary, drooping beasts, and Anvar saw that one was holding a foot carefully off the ground, and another was cut about the knees. 'We would have lost those also, had it not been for Bohan's strength to hold them back when they slipped.'

Eliizar cheered up at Anvar's approach, and Nereni, her face bloodied and bruised, gave a squeal of delight and hugged him. Aurian, examining the injured horses, left it to Nereni to plaster salve on his hurts and find him some dry clothing, and took no further notice of him at all.

The descent through the deep-piled snow at the foot of the defile was as gruelling as the climb to the pass had been, and it took the companions a long time to plough their way through the congested drifts as they came down into the valley. The sky began to darken as they struggled on; whether with dusk or another storm, Anvar had no idea, for he had lost track of time in the blizzard. In fact, it proved to be both.

The tower was situated at the far end of the valley, perched atop a craggy, tree-clad hill. By the time they reached the clump of twisted pines and saw the sturdy shape of the building looming above them, snowflakes were thickening the air once more. Thinking of the freezing peril of the night, everyone worked to gather broken boughs, which they loaded on weary horses for the last ascent of the steep, slippery path.

The squat crumbling silhoutte of the ancient tower loomed black against the sky. The door was frozen shut, and Bohan had to exert all the strength of his mighty muscles before the heavy slab of wood finally shuddered open with a grating complaint. The interior was pitch dark, and the companions, not knowing what to expect within, hung back, reluctant to enter. Yazour tugged at Anvar's sleeve. 'Anvar, can you make a light?'

Chilled and exhausted as he was, with his mind still numbed by the shock of his headlong fall, Anvar had to force himself to focus on the warrior's words. Eventually he nodded, and tried to summon the strength to create a fireball. Nothing happened. He cursed and tried again, closing his eyes and concentrating so hard that sweat sprung out to freeze on his brow, but still nothing happened. His tired mind simply refused to obey his will.

'Here.'

Anvar opened his eyes to see Aurian holding out the Staff of Earth. After his recent mishap, and her coolness towards him afterwards, he was astonished that she would trust him again with the precious Artefact. 'Are you sure?' Behind his question were a thousand others. The Mage simply nodded, and thrust the Staff into his hand. Once again, Anvar felt its power running through him like molten fire, as unquenchable hope rekindled in his heart. He lifted the Staff, and heard muffled gasps from the others as its tip burst into sizzling flame, lighting the way into the darkened maw of the building.

The companions surged into the tower behind Anvar, and into the single, circular chamber that they found within. Bohan snatched a bundle of wood from the back of one of the horses and hurled it into the gaping fireplace. Anvar thrust the blazing Staff into the heart of the kindling, and everyone cheered as the wet wood smouldered, sparked and burst into flame. Only then did he allow the fire of the Staff to die. It was hard to surrender such glory. When he went, reluctantly, to return the Artefact to Aurian, she grimaced and shook her head. 'Keep it,' she muttered, 'for now at least. It's no good to me while I'm in this state.'

Oh, he was tempted to accept her offer, but . . . 'No,' Anvar told her. 'You found it. You recreated it – by rights it belongs to you. You'll be able to use it again in no time.' But she had already turned away. Sighing, Anvar carefully propped the Staff against the wall in a shadowy corner, where it would be out of harm's way.

The bare tower room soon warmed with the roaring blaze and the steaming heat from the bodies of the horses and companions that were packed inside. While Nereni, who seemed to have drawn a new reserve of energy from the presence of secure walls and a fireside, raided their provisions to produce one of her heartening stews, and Yazour doctored the injured horses, Eliizar and Bohan made torches and went to explore. They returned after a short time with the news that the tower consisted of three stories. Above the rough stone chamber was another circular room with a flimsy ladder leading up through a trapdoor to the flat roof above. Below the ground-floor chamber, down a narrow flight of steps, a damp but solid dungeon had been hewn out of the foundations.

Supper was a silent affair among the weary, famished group, with everyone paying too much attention to the food to talk. As time passed, however, and some degree of comfort was restored, everyone began to relax – with the exception of the Mages. Nereni had to press Aurian to eat, and she sat silent and abstracted, not joining in their conversation. Anvar was almost as bad, and could do little justice to the excellent meal. Later, when the others had drifted into an exhausted slumber, he found himself unable to sleep. His frustration with Aurian was reaching the point of anger now. What was wrong with her? Surely she couldn't be holding that fall against him? True, he might have lost the Staff through his rashness, but all had turned out well in the end. After tossing and turning for a while, Anvar gave up trying to sleep. He kindled a torch and crept upstairs to the roof, seeking the chill solace of the snowy night to ease his thoughts.

Aurian awakened from a sleep that had been long in coming, disturbed by the restless kicking of the child within her. Grumbling drowsily, she turned over to find a more comfortable position and Shia, disturbed by the movement, opened one eye. 'Still brooding?' the cat asked pointedly.

Aurian sighed and sat up, heartily wishing for a bottle of the peach brandy that she and Forral used to enjoy. Oh to get gloriously, obliviously drunk, and escape, for a time, the tangle of conflicting emotions that consumed her whenever she thought of the only two men she had ever cared for. Shia was still watching her, waiting for an answer.

'All right,' Aurian told the cat resignedly. 'When Anvar fell in the avalanche today I thought he was dead. It hurt, Shia, as it hurt when I lost Forral. I don't want to feel that way – not ever again, not for anyone. Once was more than enough.' She swallowed hard against a tightness in her throat. 'Besides,' she went on doggedly, 'I'm letting the whole ridiculous business distract me from the fight against Miathan, and that's our chief concern. I don't have time for this, Shia. It could cost us our lives.'

'So you withdraw from Anvar, and try to bury your feelings,' Shia mused. 'Well, in a small company such as this, you cannot avoid him. You must send him away, it seems, or go yourself.'

Aurian stared at Shia, aghast. What, face her quest alone, without Anvar? 'But I can't do that!'

The great cat sighed. 'Why must you humans complicate matters? I suspect that once you stop fighting your own feelings, your distraction will vanish.' She looked deep into Aurian's eyes. 'Listen, my friend. Why torment yourself? You have loved him since the desert at least, though I suspect the seeds were sown long before. No one lives for ever, Aurian. I will not. I flatter myself that you would feel some measure of anguish at my loss – do you wish to discard *our* friendship?'

'Of course not!'

118

'Then why make poor Anvar suffer?' Aurian felt Shia's mental equivalent of a shrug. 'After all,' the cat went on slyly, 'there is every chance that *he* may outlive *you*!'

Aurian, with a guilty glance at her sleeping friends, muffled her snort of laughter. 'My dear Shia, what would I do without you? You have the most amazing talent for making me feel better, while pointing out that I'm a fool!'

'You give me a lot of practice, you and Anvar,' Shia replied. 'Go and talk to him – he is on the roof,' she added helpfully, as Aurian, feeling lighter of heart than she had done in a long time, sped up the tower stairs. She was so preoccupied with thoughts of Anvar that she never noticed Raven was missing.

Blacktalon was uneasy in the pinewood below the tower. It hemmed him in on all sides, cutting off the open sky and enclosing him so that he could scarcely breathe. For all his race's resistance to the cold, he shivered as he tried to peer through the whirling snow and tangled mess of trees that concealed his quarry. 'Is it not time we made our move?' he whispered to the prince. 'My warriors weary of this endless wait.'

'Be patient, you idiot!' Harihn snapped. 'By the Reaper, High Priest, recall the plan! The princess will come to tell us when they sleep. We must wait for her word – then, when my men attack the tower, your warriors will go in from above. And Blacktalon – remember that I want them alive!'

The High Priest of the Winged Folk nodded impatiently, biting back his irritation. By Yinze – did his ally think him a complete fool? But fear held him back from a scathing reply. For behind the foolish, vacuous expression on Harihn's handsome face, there burned the harsh and terrifying gaze of the Archmage Miathan!

'Harihn?' Raven stumbled through the bushes, wishing that the night were lighter, so that she could safely take flight. It would be easier, and less painful, she thought, as she sucked blood from yet another scratch, to locate him from the air. By the eyes of Yinze, where was he?

To the winged girl's relief, the springy branches gave way

before her at last, and she found herself in a clearing. Raven frowned, puzzled; and stamped in irritation. Harihn had promised to meet her in a clearing close to the tower, but this was obviously not the right one. Yet . . . Raven squinted into the gloom. Was that not a movement, over in the bushes on the opposite side? Surely that shadow was not a tree, but the tall, straight figure of a man?

'Harihn?' Raven stepped forward. Too late, she heard the rustling behind her, and on either side. Before she had time to take wing, a heavy weight hurtled into her, bearing her to the ground and grinding her face into the snow and fallen pine-needles. Then many hands were upon her, grabbing at her wings and limbs. Though she struggled and fought, lashing out with flailing pinions and clawed fingernails, she was hopelessly overpowered. Before she could cry out for help, a hand seized her jaw, thrusting a heavy wad of cloth into her mouth and tying it in place with another scrap of material. Her wings, wrists and ankles were bound tightly with strips of leather, but tighter still was the hand of fear clenched round her heart. Harihn, she thought desperately, where are you?

Raven soon found out. A booted foot rolled her on to her back, and she looked up through tear-filled eyes to see the face of her former lover. 'No!' The word was only a muffled whisper through Raven's gag – it was her mind that shrieked in rage and anguish. The prince had betrayed her!

'Ah . . .' The heart of the winged girl twisted within her at the sound of the dry, familiar voice that had haunted her nightmares for so long. Cloaked in the dusty black of his wings, the High Priest Blacktalon stepped out from behind the prince. 'Mine at last!' He knelt down beside her, and Raven closed her eyes, shuddering at his touch.

'Get moving, Blacktalon – you can enjoy your plaything later.' Harihn's voice was harsh and cold. 'My side of our bargain has been fulfilled, but we need to take the others before your prey is secure.'

'Mind your tone, when you address the new king of the Skyfolk!' Blacktalon snapped stiffly. Nevertheless, he obeyed, and got to his feet at once. Raven stiffened at his words. *King*? But that could only mean her mother was dead! As the sound of receding footsteps faded from the clearing, Raven closed her eyes in utter despair, and sobbed.

The Mage had a tremendous struggle to haul herself up the rickety ladder to the roof. When she saw Anvar, huddled out of the wind in the corner of a crumbling embrasure, her courage almost failed her. But he looked up, aware, as always, of her presence, and the sight of his sad, tired face strengthened her resolve. She crouched down beside him, but her words were drowned by the howling of the wind. 'Come inside, Anvar,' she yelled. 'You're frozen!'

The upper chamber of the tower boasted a fireplace, and a few cobweb-draped bits of old furniture of peculiar design that must have used when the Winged Folk maintained a guard. Anvar smashed a tall, backless stool against the wall and flung the pieces into the hearth, lighting them with a sizzling fireball. As the flames flared up he began on the remains of a spindly table, and Aurian, seeing his grim expression, took an involunatary step back. His first words took her completely by surprise.

'Aurian, you are an utter idiot to risk that rotten ladder. If you'd fallen, you could have lost the child!' Then he seemed to become aware of what he was saying, and turned away from her. 'Not that it's any of my business,' he muttered, his voice thick with bitterness.

Aurian took a deep breath, and laid a hand on his arm. 'It is your business, Anvar,' she said softly. 'That is – if you still want it to be.'

For a moment he simply stood, unmoving. Then he turned to face her. 'What do you mean?' he asked.

Aurian swallowed hard, her throat gone suddenly dry. 'I should have spoken sooner – after the desert, maybe, or certainly after the avalanche today. But I was afraid.' Her voice began to tremble. 'Oh, curse it!' She sniffed, wiping her nose on her sleeve. She tried to pull away from him, but he held her fast.

'You know, I don't think I'll ever break you of that revolting habit!' The anger had fled from Anvar's face. He led her to the fire and sat her down on the floor beside the hearth. Taking pieces of the broken table, he fed them to the dying flames, while Aurian plunged on before she lost her courage.

121

'I let you think I didn't love you, but I lied. I was lying to myself, too. I was afraid, because after Forral was killed I never wanted to go through that pain again! And we're in such danger . . .'

'And that was the problem? You were afraid I'd be killed too? Oh, my dearest love . . .' Anvar put his arms around her, holding her close, and at long last Aurian gladly returned Anvar's embrace, rejoicing in his touch, his closeness; feeling the racing of his heart that matched the joyous beating of her own. But there was one vital thing that she had left unsaid.

She took her face from Anvar's shoulder to look at him. 'I can't forget Forral, you know,' she said softly. 'Even if I could, I don't want to.'

Anvar shook his head. 'I don't expect you to forget him, my love, and neither will I. Forral was a true friend to me, and I honour his memory. Things have happened so quickly since he died, and I'd rather you came to me heart-whole than plagued by doubts.'

Aurian reached out to touch his face. 'I've had enough of doubts.' She ran her palms across the breadth of his shoulders, leaning into his embrace – and stiffened, as a scraping noise above her head shattered the web of love and longing within which she and Anvar had sheltered.

'Anvar – did you hear that?'

Anvar's eyes were wide with alarm. 'It's on the roof . . .'

The trapdoor in the ceiling burst open, its burden of snow dropping to the floor with a slither and thump as a blast of wintry air ripped through the faint warmth of the room. With a curse, Aurian scrambled to her feet as a pair of legs appeared on the frail ladder. Reaching for the sword that was always by her side, she swung with all her strenth in a wide sideways swipe, her wrists taking the impact as the blade bit through flesh and wood alike, and into bone. The ladder splintered as the man fell screaming; one leg severed at the knee, the other spraying blood. Aurian jumped back clumsily, cursing the hampering bulk of her child, and Anvar steadied her as she fought for balance.

'Winged Folk!' Anvar cried, as he pulled her away from the flailing pinions of her writhing victim. Another figure dropped through the opening, wings folded to fit the cramped space. Aurian tried to engage the new foe before he could recover himself, but his sword was already in his hand, and he drove her back easily, knowing she was disadvantaged by the need to protect her unborn child. Inexorably he pressed forward, clearing space for more of the enemy to enter.

From the corner of her eye, Aurian saw Anvar dive under their flashing swords to snatch the weapon of the first, fallen warrior, but she was forced to concentrate on her own opponent, until a shriek of agony turned her cold. She tore her eyes from her assailant to glimpse Anvar pulling his bloody blade out of the chest of the next man through the trapdoor, but another followed, kicking the corpse aside. Another, behind him, dropped lightly through the opening.

Sensing her distraction, her opponent lunged, almost breaking through her guard. Oddly, Aurian felt no fear, just a surge of anger that he was blocking her from going to Anvar's aid. She twisted her blade in Forral's deft, circling flick and, as her enemy's sword went flying, she snicked his throat on the follow-through, regretting it as his blood sprayed into her face. Freeing a hand to wipe her eyes and gagging on the metallic reek, she leapt across his body – and jerked to a halt as his hand closed in a dying spasm around her ankle, trapping her foot in an iron grip.

Anvar had two opponents now, they were attacking him mercilessly, backing him into the lethal trap of the corner between the chimney-breast and the wall. Unable to free herself and with no time to waste, Aurian flipped a knife left-handed from her sleeve with the deadly accuracy she had learned from Parric, and heard a grunt of pain as it sank hilt-deep into the back of its target, between the great wings. The other warrior glanced around as his comrade toppled – a fatal mistake. He doubled over screaming, clutching at the slithering loops of his gut, ripped out by Anvar's blade.

Aurian severed the limb that held her with one stroke. As the hand fell away she shot across the room, pulling Anvar towards the door as more foes dropped through the trapdoor above. Someone was hacking at the hole with a sword, enlarging the opening. The chamber was becoming impossibly cramped, and the Mages were forced to scramble backwards over the bodies of the fallen, fighting a desperate rearguard action. But when they reached the door, Aurian's relief turned to horror as she heard the sound of fighting in the room below. They were surrounded!

Then the Mage remembered Shia, and a wild hope rose in her heart, only to be dashed as she touched her friend's mind. The reply came brief and stilted, as the cat fought for her life downstairs, even as Aurian was fighting for her own. 'Bohan fights – Eliizar hurt – can't reach you . . .'

'Run, Shia!' Aurian told her. 'Take the Staff and run!'

'Have you lost your mind? I'm not leaving you!'

'You must. If we lose the Staff, we're finished.'

For a moment there was silence, then: 'I have it. I go!'

Aurian caught a blurred impression of claws and blood as the great cat fought her way to freedom; then she was gone, into the storm. Someone grabbed the Mage from behind, jerking her backwards, as unseen assailants came pouring up the stairs. A handful of her hair was seized and yanked, and she felt the chill bite of steel at her throat.

'Drop your weapons!' Aurian recognized the voice that came from behind her. Harihn! In league with Winged Folk? She stiffened with rage, and the blade bit into the taut-stretched skin of her neck, drawing a trickle of warm blood. Fuming helplessly, she let her weapon drop, and saw rage mingling with dismay on Anvar's face. His sword fell clattering to the floor as he was surrounded by winged warriors and dragged away, struggling, to be held against the opposite wall. Aurian saw his eyes flare bright with icy rage as he gathered his powers and . . .

'Don't try it, Anvar,' Harihn snapped. 'At the first hint of magic from you, my warriors will slit her throat.' Aurian saw the fire in Anvar's eyes die away; his anger fading into a look of bitter defeat. Then her hands were seized from behind, jerked back, and bound, while Anvar's winged captors dealt with him in a similar fashion.

'How good of you to join me.' Smiling sardonically, Harihn stepped out to confront the Mage. 'Thanks to the treachery of little Raven, you are now my prisoners.' Ordering the knife to

124

be removed from Aurian's throat, he hit her across the face. Unbalanced by the blow, she fell, but her guards caught her, forcing her to her knees. Through the ringing in her ears, she heard a scuffle.

'Leave her alone!' Anvar's yell was cut short by the sick thud of a blow, then the prince's hand lashed across the other side of Aurian's face. Her head jolted sideways, and she tasted blood where her teeth had cut into her lip.

'I warn you, Anvar,' Harihn said menacingly. 'One more move from you, and she will be the one to suffer.'

His voice was not the voice of the prince. Aurian looked up through tears of pain, and her heart turned to ashes within her. The handsome, familiar features were those of Harihn – but the grim malevolence that burned behind his eyes could only belong to the Archmage!

9
Schiannath

The snow-laden wind hurtled through the narrow mountain pass like a river in spate; powerful, inexorable, and deadly. The pass, a strait corridor between cliffs of incredible height, was the gateway to the kingdom of the Skyfolk. At the end of the pass, a tower had been built high on a spur of rock, where in the past the Winged Folk kept a guard. A dark and tangled wood of pines below the spur provided fuel for fire.

The wind keened shrilly around the Tower of Incondor, prying with chill claws at the solid stack of man-piled stones like a living beast, seeking to reach the puny humans who had taken sanctuary within. Beyond the tower, the way opened out into a broad sweep of valley; its stark, snow-choked whiteness alleviated here and there by dark, skeletal clumps of trees bent over like worn old men by their wintry burden. Above the vale, oppressive with their looming weight, great peaks like jagged fangs shouldered one another as if jostling for the privilege of attacking the squat and sturdy building that stood bravely at their feet.

The man who hid behind a pile of tumbled boulders at the mouth of the pass spared the threatening mountains not a single glance. He was more concerned with the strangers who were sheltering within the tower. In his cloak of silvery wolfskins he was camouflaged against the snow-and-shadow backdrop; as was his horse, Iscalda, the white mare who stood patiently at his shoulder, showing less movement than the whirling snow that piled in drifts around her feet.

Schiannath stared at the tower, silhouetted on its wooded mound, and cursed bitterly. Of all the vile, unbelievable, impossibly bad luck! The abandoned building was the best of his refuges, the only one in which he and Iscalda could shelter with any degree of comfort from this deadly, preternatural winter. His other lairs, discovered in months of wandering these inhospitable mountains, were either dense woodland thickets or caves: the former were pathetically inadequate in this bitter weather, and the latter were damp and draughty, tending to fill with choking and conspicuous smoke if he lit a fire. He and Iscalda had made a long, perilous journey to this place in the teeth of the storm and had arrived here wet, frozen, and unutterably weary – only to find the tower already occupied.

Once more, Schiannath cursed the interlopers, whoever they were. And who could they be? The Xandim never came so far south. These lands were quite outside their province, which was why he was here. The outlaw flinched from the memory of his trial and exile, when the bumbling, half-blind young Windeye had uttered the spells that erased his name from the wind, and from the memory of the tribe. He bit his lip to keep from crying his shame and agony aloud. Oh, goddess, why did I do it? he thought wretchedly. Why was it so important to me, to be Herdlord?

How had it come about? Why had he always been the outcast: solitary among a people where the tribe was all; secretive among folk who shared everything? Time and again, the sharpness of his wits had got him into trouble. He was cleverer than the lot of them, and they hated him for it. Well, a plague on them all! Curse his mother, for leaving him in the coastal settlement with his father when they parted, while she kept the children of her other mates with her in the hills! If not for that, Schiannath would have grown up with his brethren in the tribe. As it was, when he'd come to the fastness after his father's death, he had never been able to settle; clashing with the Herdlord again and again over his wild, undisciplined behaviour, until it seemed that the only way to be free of Phalihas, and his tiresome rules and restrictions, lay in becoming Herdlord himself. Only his sister Iscalda had cared about him, had tried her best to dissuade him from his folly – and, when that had failed, had insisted on sharing his exile.

Grief pierced Schiannath's heart like a knife. The Xandim had no death-sentence for their own; that fate was reserved for foreigners and spies. Instead, they had done worse – they had

127

taken his name, and driven him out with curses and stones. For defying Phalihas, Iscalda had been transformed into her Othershape and locked for ever in that state by the Windeye. Now she was no different from a normal horse, with the needs, the instincts – and the mind – of a beast.

His throat tight with unshed tears, the outlaw glanced over his shoulder at the white mare, wishing that he could find surcease from his painful memories. There had been times, in his despair, when he had thought of ending it for both of them – with his blade, perhaps, or simply by riding Iscalda over a precipice. But he had never found the courage. There had always remained that tiny, unquenchable hope in the depths of his soul, that one day he would somehow find the means to change her back.

The mare made a low chuckling sound deep in her throat and dropped her nose into his palm, lipping gently at his fingers. Schiannath sighed. 'I know, Iscalda – I'm hungry too. Come, it's time to go.' He had another lair nearby; a small cave set high in the towering walls of the pass. It would be cramped and uncomfortable, but he had left a small store of food there for emergencies, and dried grasses for Iscalda that he had harvested from the valley during the long-gone days of milder weather.

Schiannath glanced up at the tower for one last time, scowling at the thread of smoke that trickled from the crumbling flue. Curse them! Who were these folk? Why were they here? He hesitated. If they were not Xandim, then they could not know he was an outlaw. If he claimed to be a strayed traveller, they would surely take him in!

Hope, painful in its intensity, swelled in Schiannath's heart. After months spent with only Iscalda for company, the sudden hunger for people, for kind faces and the sound of human voices and laughter, overwhelmed him in a flood of desperate longing. His lean, weather-beaten face creased into its first smile in months as he took hold of the mare's bridle, and began to step out of his hiding-place.

A new sound drove him swiftly back, like a hunted animal into its lair. With the sharp-honed senses of a wild creature, he heard on the wind the sound of wings, drumming through the valley towards the pass. Schiannath huddled behind the boulders, the mare tucked in behind him. He was shivering, and not from the cold. Had he become a Windeye, that the storm's tidings brought such dread foreboding? Then, as he peered up beyond the stark limbs of the tower's encircling trees, the outlaw saw winged figures dropping from the sky. He caught his breath in horror. By the Fields of Paradise, what were those abominations doing here?

Then, to Schiannath's astonishment, a group of human warriors – who must have been well concealed to have escaped his careful observation – left the pinewood at the sound, and came briefly within his sight as they fanned out towards the tower. Schiannath heard a mutter of voices in a harsh, uncouth tongue, and stiffened with rage. Accursed Khazalim! What did they want here? With a muttered oath, he shrank back behind the rocks as the Skyfolk hovered over the copse, then dropped out of sight amid its branches.

Common sense warned the outlaw it was time to leave. If the invaders sent out scouts ... Yet, he lingered, drawn by curiosity and the irresistible urge to be near humans – any humans – again. Iscalda would warn him of approaching danger, and with his knowledge of the surrounding terrain it should be easy to elude pursuit in the flurrying snow. So he stayed, and watched as the winged warriors soared up to land on the roof of the tower, and the Khazalim scum who seemed to be in league with them assailed the door. It was an ambush! Whoever might be within the tower, Schiannath found himself moved to pity for the poor wretches.

Yazour awakened abruptly, disturbed from his sleep by some faint, unplaceable sound. He opened his eyes, and glanced around a strangely depleted chamber. Shia was stretched out, catlike, in the warmest place beside the fire. Bohan lay nearby, his head pillowed on the hearth, and Nereni and Eliizar were curled in a tangled nest of blankets. But where were the others? He tensed in alarm, until a murmur of voices from the floor above him told him the whereabouts of Aurian and Anvar. Yazour smiled. They were making the most of the opportunity to be alone, and who could blame them? That only left Raven

– but why should *she* be missing? He was rousing himself to go and investigate as the door of the tower flew open, and Harihn's men burst into the room.

Yazour sprang to his feet and drew his sword. 'Foes,' he roared. 'Awake!' His heart clenched with the anguish of betrayal as he recognized each familiar face. Before he left the prince's service, these had been the loyal troops that were his to command. Now he was their enemy. Yazour felt sick at heart. If Harihn was his captor, he could expect no mercy from the prince. Then his foes were upon him, and there was no time for further thought.

Shia leapt up with a snarl as the door burst open. The first two men had fallen to her claws before Yazour had drawn his sword, and then her companions were beside her, defending each other against the overwhelming numbers. From the corner of her eye, she saw Eliizar go down, and moved back to defend him – but Bohan was already there, fighting with the strength of three. Nereni, shrieking, darted in to help her husband, and in a moment Eliizar was up again, fighting one-handed with the other clasped to his bleeding side, while Nereni, yelling angry curses, was flinging burning brands from the fire into the knot of Harihn's men who were still forcing their way in at the door.

The great cat clawed out right and left, with a deadly economy of motion, inflicting dreadful injury on her foes – but there were so many of them! Despairing, she glanced back towards the stairs. Where were Aurian and Anvar? Why had the Mages not come to help? Linking with Aurian, she saw the scene upstairs through her friend's eyes. Winged Folk. Aurian and Anvar captured. A bolt of fear streaked through Shia for the safety of her companions. She was already fighting her way towards the stairs when she heard Aurian's voice in her mind, telling her to run.

'Have you lost your mind? I'm not leaving you!'

'You must. If we lose the Staff, we're finished.'

Shia snarled with frustration. Abandoning the fight with reluctance, she leapt towards the shadowy corner by the chimney-breast, where stood the Staff of Earth. The great cat

130

tensed herself, to close her jaws on the hated magical object, then: 'I have it. I go!' Although she was hampered by the long, unwieldy object that was clutched between her teeth, she was determined to wreak as much destruction as she could manage, on her way to the door.

When Shia, with the Staff clenched in her jaws, erupted into action, Yazour moved with the speed of pure instinct to take advantage of the confusion. They were badly outnumbered here – it made sense to have as many of the companions as possible free, and on the outside. Swinging wildly, he hacked his way out behind the great cat, caring nothing, in his desperation to escape, that these men had once been under his command. The crowded room had erupted into chaos. Swords were flailing, and men were falling over one another to get away from the fearsome teeth and claws of the great cat. The floor was slippery with blood, but Yazour, fighting for his life, gained the door at last, and charged out into the freezing night.

Cold seared his lungs with every gasping breath, and the snow was thick and treacherous underfoot. Yazour knew he'd be finished if he fell, yet dared not risk slowing his pace. Behind him, he heard a call for bowmen. Reaper, no! Wasting a breath on a curse he faltered briefly, until the jolt of terror gave new impetus to his flying feet. He began to zigzag like a hunted hare to confuse the archers' aim, his feet slipping on the treacherous ground with every turn. Deadly shafts peppered the snow around him, and the skin between his shoulders cringed in dread anticipation, expecting at any moment to feel the impact of an arrow.

When it came, it knocked him from his feet. Fire in his left shoulder forced a shriek from his throat, and Yazour went tumbling, over and over in the snow.

Schiannath had listened, dismayed, to the sounds of fighting within the tower, and had wished with all his heart that he could go to the aid of the strangers against the accursed Khazalim raiders and filthy Skyfolk. Luckily, common sense had prevailed. He had no idea who the victims were – why risk himself? Yet if they were fugitives, did he not have something in common with them? Some fellow-feeling?

Then the night erupted in a terrifying cacophony of snarls and roars, punctuated by screams of pain and fright. Iscalda reared in terror, pulling at her reins and trying to break away from him. Engaged in quieting the mare before they were discovered, he had failed to see Shia bolt out of the tower and vanish into the wood. What he did see, when he turned his attention back to the fight, was a man fleeing in a staggering, zigzag half-run, downhill towards the pass. A Khazalim bowman appeared in the doorway of the tower. Afraid to call out a warning and draw attention to himself, the outlaw could only watch as the bolt flew, hitting the man in the left shoulder.

The victim stumbled, driven off balance by the force of the arrow, and fell on his face in the snow. Schiannath held his breath, willing the man to get back on his feet. The bowman took aim once more, his fallen prey an easy target. The man staggered upright – the bolt flew – and swerved wide of its target as the long shaft loosed by Schiannath entered the bowman's eyes with swift precision and pierced his brain.

Schiannath fell back with a curse, his hand slippery on the shaft of his bow. What had possessed him? This was not his fight. But only when the victim staggered almost within touching distance did the outlaw realize the gravity of his error. The fugitive was Khazalim too. Schiannath let fall the hand he was extending to help the man and melted into the shadows, letting him pass. Let the storm and the wolves take care of the wretch. Let the accursed southerners track their fugitive, and let the renegade lead the bastards far away from himself.

Aurian heard the scuff of feet on stone steps, and one of Harihn's men entered the upper chamber, bowing to the prince who had Miathan's burning eyes. 'The tower is secured, sire, and the princess is in the hands of the winged priest. The others are in the dungeon, but the cat escaped, alas, as did the traitor Yazour. I could swear that one of our bowmen winged him as he fled, but we lost him in the storm.'

'No matter. He will not survive out there for long.' The prince shrugged, dismissing the man with a curt nod. Picking his careful way across the bodies of the fallen, he crossed the room to face Anvar, his face contorted once again with Miathan's feral, pitiless expression. 'Now, half-breed,' he snarled, 'at last I have the chance to rid you of your miserable life. But we need not hurry – I want Aurian to appreciate every lingering moment of your agony!'

He wrenched Harihn's knife from its sheath and stooped to thrust it into embers of the fire until the tip glowed red. Removing the blade, he held it close to Anvar's face. Anvar shrank back, white with horror, unable to take his eyes from the searing metal. Sweat streaked his face, catching the crimson glow as though his skin was already smeared with blood. With a swift, swooping movement, Miathan pressed the knife against his cheek, and Anvar screamed horribly, thrashing in the grip of his guards.

'Miathan, stop!' Aurian shrieked.

'Ah, so you recognize me.' With a triumphant smile, the Archmage removed the knife, and Anvar, limp in his captors' grasp, raised his head to look at Aurian. A livid burn scarred his cheek, and his face was contorted with pain as he spoke to her through gritted teeth. 'Don't watch,' he grated. 'Don't . . . give them the satisfaction.'

'Oh gods,' Aurian whispered, her grief a physical agony as though she shared the pain of Anvar's burning. The Archmage put the knife back into the fire; watching her with a calculating expression; mocking her tears. He seized Anvar's hair, pulling his head back, holding the knife a hair's breadth from his flinching face.

'Now comes the first of many reckonings, Aurian. Do you remember burning out my eyes, so long ago? Did you enjoy your petty triumph? Now I intend to pay you back for that – an eye for an eye. But not your pretty eyes, my dear. Let Anvar suffer in your stead.' His hand tightened on the knife hilt, poised to strike at Anvar's unprotected face.

'Leave him alone!' Aurian raged, struggling to escape, but her guards hurled her down with insolent strength. She fought wildly, and with a curse one of them twisted her bound arms behind her back until she screamed with pain.

'Stop!' Miathan dropped the knife, sweeping across

133

the room to thrust the man angrily aside. 'She is not to be harmed.'

To Aurian's relief, the pain in her arms subsided, allowing her to breathe again, and, more important, to think. She knew she had very little choice about the means she could employ, no matter how repugnant the terms of the bargain would seem to her. She struggled to her knees, looking up at the possessed form of Harihn and trying to quell the hatred that flared within her at the sight of Miathan's expression on the prince's face. 'Miathan,' she begged. 'Don't hurt Anvar – it's me you want. If you leave him alone, I'll do anything you want – I swear it.'

The Archmage twisted Harihn's face into a sneer of contempt, his eyes full of wry amusement. A chill went through Aurian, as she realized just how great was his hold over her. 'Indeed?' he mocked. 'Whatever I desire, I can take, including Anvar's life – and you. But I intend to possess more than your body.' He dropped his voice to silken, caressing tones, and the Mage felt her guts twist with loathing. 'I require your support and power to further my plans. Put that power at my disposal, and I will spare Anvar's life. Indeed, the wretch will be most useful as a hostage to ensure your loyalty, my dear.'

The horrific implications of Miathan's words cut through Anvar's haze of pain. 'No,' he shouted desperately. 'Aurian – don't do this. Don't put yourself in his power.'

'Silence him!' Miathan snapped, and one of the guards delivered a sharp blow beneath Anvar's ribs that drove the breath from his body. While he fought, in agony, for air, the Archmage turned back to Aurian. 'Well? Do you agree?'

Bleak-faced, Aurian nodded. 'I have no choice,' she whispered. 'Just don't hurt him any more.'

Miathan smiled. 'Very sensible,' he purred. 'The half-breed will ensure your loyalty until the child is born, for it is too late to rid you of it now without endangering your life.' Miathan chuckled – a chilling sound that reminded Anvar of the Death-Wraith that had killed Forral. 'More to the point, however,' he went on, 'Anvar will act as a hostage for your continued obedience once I've put an end to the brat – for when you see it, you will beg me to put it out of its misery. Your child is cursed, Aurian – I cursed it myself, long ago, using the power of the Cauldron. You carry a monster within you.'

Anvar saw the blood drain from Aurian's face. Her mouth opened, but no sound emerged. 'You bastard, Miathan!' he screamed. 'I'll kill you for this, I swear it.'

The Archmage laughed again. 'Swear away, Anvar – you're in no position to threaten me. You are in my power, and you will help me to manipulate this renegade slut. My problem lay in making her use her powers for my benefit, once I had killed her child. Now it will be easy, since she has obviously transferred her allegiance from that oaf of a swordsman to you.' Miathan snickered crudely. 'It must be the Mortal stain on your ancestry – she could never resist defiling herself with your sort.'

Anvar's mind went blank with horror at the simple cruelty of Miathan's plan. His eyes went to Aurian, and he saw the sick dismay on her face. Not her child – her last, precious link with Forral. He couldn't let this happen – and at least he could spare her the agony of choosing. He had provided Miathan with a hold over her, but if he should die, that hold would cease. Aurian, once her powers were restored, might be able to protect the child after it had been born. Through his mounting terror, he felt relief, and a dawning hope. His own life might be forfeit, but it would be well spent, if Aurian and her child might have a chance.

Anvar made his decision. It was no good attacking Miathan – he would only destroy Harihn's body, and the Archmage was too close to Aurian. The backlash of the spell could kill her. But he had one other, desperate option . . .

Miathan's attention was locked on Aurian. Anvar's expression turned grim as slowly, surreptitiously, he began to gather his powers for the last time. He felt his eyes beginning to flare with a dark and muted glow from the mounting energies within him, as he turned his magic inward, upon himself, to his own destruction. Searing heat swept through him, his heart began to race and labour as his bubbling lungs clamoured for breath. He felt his organs, his senses, falter and start to fail . . . His vision was clouding with a red haze from the destructive might of the pent-up forces he had summoned. Unable to resist, he sought Aurian's eyes before it was too late, trying to tell her, in a

135

final, appealing glance, that he was sorry – and that he loved her.

It proved his undoing. Through misted vision, he saw her eyes widen with sudden understanding – and horror. 'Anvar no!' she shrieked. Miathan, alerted by her frantic cry, spun round with a curse. In a swift, brutal blow, his fist crashed into Anvar's face. Shock and pain ripped through the Mage, dissipating the powers he had gathered so carefully. As he slumped against his captors, half-stunned and spitting blood, he was dimly aware that his body was stabilizing, returning to normal. With a sinking heart, he realized that he had lost his chance. Oh, Aurian, he thought despairingly, why did you stop me?

Miathan was berating the guards, spitting with rage. 'You fools! I told you to watch him!'

Anvar felt the grip of his warders tighten, their fingers bruising his bound arms. Using the pain as a focus, he wrenched his slipping consciousness back to the room, through the sheer force of his Mage's will.

The Archmage had turned his anger on Aurian. 'So much for that!' he snapped. 'What use will he be as a hostage, if the fool kills himself at the first opportunity?' Then he brought himself swiftly under control, the cruelty of his expression distorting Harihn's handsome face. 'It seems, my dear, that I must impose a further condition on our agreement. You know that my powers will not transfer to this Mortal body. You have no magic until your brat is born, and that makes us even – but Anvar will always be a risk to me that must be dealt with. Therefore, when your own magic returns, Aurian, you will remove his powers, as I removed them once before.'

Aurian's face twisted with anguish as she fought against overwhelming tears. Never had Anvar seen her look so cowed. 'Very well,' she whispered. 'If that's the only way to save him.'

'No!' In a flash of panic, Anvar recalled the time, long ago in his youth, when Miathan had torn away the power that he had not even known he possessed – remembered the agony, the despair, the dread sense of utter helplessness. It couldn't happen again – he would rather die.

Then he caught the obdurate glint in Aurian's eye, and

cursed himself for a fool. Of course she would never do such a thing. Distracted by pain and fear, he had been slow to realize that she was engaged in a desperate gamble, playing for time to save them both. For a moment, Anvar's pain vanished in a glow of love and pride. Despite the appalling shock of the news about her child, she had kept her head. He prayed that Miathan would be deceived.

'What are your plans for us, Miathan?' Aurian asked in a dull, hopeless voice, and Anvar knew she was trying to draw the Archmage's attention away from him.

Harihn's dark eyes glittered. 'Anvar will be imprisoned elsewhere, as a surety for your cooperation. I hope he knows better than to try any further tricks to end his own life, for if he should succeed, I intend to make you pay for his folly in ways that neither of you could even begin to imagine.'

Anvar shuddered. Miathan could have thought of no better way to ensure his compliance.

'As for you,' the Archmage continued, 'you will be shipped back to Nexis once your child is born, and disposed of. Once there, you will surrender to me, or see Anvar dismembered before your eyes.' Swiftly he bore down on Aurian, grasping the front of her robe and ripping it apart. Naked lust leered from Harihn's borrowed features, and one of the guards snickered. 'I can't think why you want her, Anvar,' Miathan taunted, 'ugly and swollen as she is with another's brat! Personally, I prefer to wait until she is in better condition before I use her. Though perhaps I may give her back to you afterwards – if you still want her.' He paused in calculated reflection. 'Still, why should you not? You can have no objection to used goods. You were not too proud to pick up Forral's leavings.'

Anvar's heart burned at the sight of Aurian kneeling there, stricken and shamed. Fighting back the tears of rage, he glared coldly at Miathan. 'There speaks jealousy,' he sneered. 'She was too proud to take you, was she not? Do your worst – you'll never defile this Lady, who is far beyond the reach of such as you. Used goods? You deceive yourself. If you take from Aurian what she would never give you freely, then the shame is on you, not her. You may take her body, but you can never sully

137

her brave spirit or touch her heart. No matter what you do, you've already lost.'

The Archmage stood as if turned to stone by Anvar's words, but they restored Aurian's tattered courage. Turning away from Miathan, she lifted her chin proudly and spoke directly to Anvar, as though they were alone in the room. 'My love,' she said softly. 'As long as I have you, I have hope.'

Anvar looked at her, his heart in his eyes. 'You'll always have me, I promise.'

Miathan spat out a vile curse, and gestured to the guards. One of them drew his sword, and clubbed Anvar hard with the hilt. Without a sound, he crumpled to the floor as his captors loosed their grip.

'You said he wouldn't be harmed!' Aurian cried.

'Did I?' Harihn's face was disfigured by Miathan's ugly scowl, and Aurian saw jealousy burning livid behind his eyes. 'I remember no such thing. Anvar's continuing good health depends entirely on your future conduct towards me.' He leered into her face, caressing her body. Though his attentions sickened her, Aurian bore them without flinching, concentrating instead on Anvar's words.

Cheated of his sport, Miathan ceased his torment and, with a snarl of rage, struck her until she sobbed in pain. 'When I return, I expect to find you in a more accommodating mood – for Anvar's sake,' he snapped, and stalked out, followed by his men, who dragged Anvar's unconscious body with them. Aurian's guards threw her down, bound as she was, and left her lying on the cold hearth with its dying fire, alone in her despair.

Yazour staggered through the pass, weak and faint from his wounds, buffeted mercilessly by wind and driving snow, and no longer even certain that he was still heading away from the tower. Blood streamed from the bolt that pierced his left shoulder, but amazingly, the pain had been numbed away from the wound, and from the tender bruise on his skull, and the sword-cut in his thigh that he had received, almost without noticing, in the heat of his fight to escape. Blessed snow! Kindly snow, to take away his pain.

What am I doing out here in the snow? Why can I not

remember? he wondered. It seemed to Yazour that there was something he should be remembering ... Some danger ... Was he not running away from something or someone? But why worry? The wonderful snow would take care of him. It lay all around him, like a thick, soft blanket. It would hide him, as his blankets had hidden him in his childhood, when nightmare-dreams had threatened from the darkened corners of his room. Of course! That was the answer. He would hide here, and rest in the soft warm snow ... Dropping to his knees, the wounded warrior pitched forward, giving himself gratefully to darkness, and winter's deadly embrace.

Miathan swept downstairs, enjoying the disciplined vigour of the prince's youthful body. He smiled to himself, putting Anvar's disquieting words out of his mind. It would not be long now before Aurian was rid of the monster she carried – then he would have her, with this wonderful new body that promised such pleasure ...

When the Archmage reached the lower chamber, even the scenes of carnage that awaited him did nothing to damp his spirits, though far down at the back of his controlling mind he felt a faint stir of protest from Harihn. The great cat, it seemed, had proved a formidable opponent. The room resembled a battlefield, its floor awash with blood and entrails. Men were dragging bodies out of the door, or tending groaning wounded. Miathan shrugged. So long as enough remained to guard his prisoners, the ills of these Mortals were none of his concern.

Blacktalon approached with a rustle of wings; his bald head gleaming in the torchlight, his hooded eyes bright with satisfaction. 'It went well,' he said. 'The princess has already been taken to Aerillia.' He smiled. 'When I felt the touch of your mind that first night, it turned out to be a most auspicious meeting – for both of us.'

'Indeed,' Miathan replied brusquely, thinking that when he turned to the conquest of the south, he would have to find a way to eliminate his new ally. In a struggle for power, Blacktalon could turn into a dangerous opponent. However, in the meantime ... 'I need a favour, Blacktalon,' he said.

'Will you take this wretch to Aerillia, and guard him?' He gestured towards Anvar. 'He is to be a hostage.'

Blacktalon shrugged. 'Of course. The Winged Folk will keep him safe for you.'

'Listen, High Priest.' Miathan held the other's eyes in an icy stare. 'I must emphasize the risk – and responsibility – involved in guarding this renegade. Anvar is a sorcerer. He may be able to escape as easily as . . .'

'Be easy, my friend,' Blacktalon interrupted. 'I have studied ancient records of this sorcery of yours, and precautions will be taken. There is a cave in our mountainside set in sheer rock with a thousand-foot drop beneath. Believe me, it can only be reached by Winged Folk.' He laughed harshly. 'Unless his powers of sorcery extend to flight, he'll be safe enough. Food can be lowered from above, and none of my people need go near him.'

Miathan smiled, betraying his keen sense of relief. 'I chose well, in selecting you as an ally,' he said. 'You will take the best possible care of my prisoner, will you not? Remember, I need him alive – for now.'

10
Aerillia

Raven had been put back into the old turret room in the Queen's Tower, with its walls of rose-pink marble, that had been hers for all the years she could remember. It was unchanged; exactly the same as she had left it when she'd fled into that stormy night – how long ago it seemed, now. There were her familiar furnishings: the round scoop of her fur-lined bed, where she had curled up to sleep so many nights beneath the shelter of her drooping wings; the same warm rugs on the floor; and the night-table, made of scarce and precious wood, with its mirror of polished silver. There, wrought in a sturdy filigree of gleaming iron, was the tall backless stool with its cushioned seat, on which she'd sat for hours by the window, watching the changing sweep of cloud and sunlight across the mountains.

There were her frayed old wall-hangings, which she had loved too much to have replaced, with flights of Winged Folk soaring like eagles across a backdrop of snow-bright peaks and valleys that had once been green. In the niches concealed behind them, Raven found the favourite playthings of her childhood still in place; old and battered now, but too beloved ever to throw away. The only change in the room was the grille of sturdy iron that now barred the window.

Her mind still numb with the shock of betrayal, Raven surveyed the room with an increasing sense of unreality. Her escape, and all the adventures that had followed it, seemed like a fading dream amid the old, familiar surroundings of her childhood. Or had that brief time of freedom been the only reality, and was this the dream?

The chamber might be the same, but Raven had changed beyond all recognition from the young innocent who had climbed out of that window some three short moons ago. In

141

that time she had grown up – and, it seemed, grown old in bitterness and regret. Oh, Yinze, how she hated herself. How could she have been so blind, so gullible, so false to her new friends? She had betrayed the companions who had helped her in the desert and taken her in as one of their own. She had betrayed poor motherly Nereni, who had taken such good care of her. Who had trusted her. She had defiled herself, beyond all redemption, with an alien, an outsider, a ground-grubbing human who had used and discarded her like the worthless offal she had become. And now she had come full circle. She was back in the vile clutches of Blacktalon – and no doubt it was all that she deserved.

Her mother, the queen, was dead. Due to the terrible and terrifying things that had happened to her, that brutal fact had barely begun to penetrate the winged girl's mind. Flamewing had never been gentle and kind like Nereni – she was a queen, after all, with many responsibilities to occupy her mind and time. She had been forced to rear her daughter in a hard school, to fit her for her future burdens. Among the Skyfolk, the monarch must rule and stand alone. None the less, Raven knew her mother had loved her, and had shown it whenever she could. Flamewing had been proud of her, and the princess's stomach turned sick at the thought of how she had abused that pride. Did her mother know? Did the dead know everything, once they had passed Beyond, as the priests of Yinze claimed? Raven flung herself, weeping, on to her bed. 'Mother, I'm sorry!'

The winged girl wept for a long time, but at last the storm passed; she was too drained and exhausted to weep any more. Wiping her eyes on the bed's fur covelet, Raven looked again around the room that was her prison. Food had been left for her, but she was too sick at heart to eat. She felt soiled and defiled, and her tears had done nothing to wash the stain of guilt from her conscience. There was wine on the table in a silver flagon. Raven poured a brimming goblet and drained it in one gulp, choking slightly at the unfamiliar burn in her throat, and remembering, with a guilty pang, that Flamewing had never allowed her to drink the stuff. But her mind was turning, now, from the guilt of the past to the terrors of the future. Soon,

Blacktalon would be coming for her – and when he did, she would do well to have her senses dulled as much as possible.

Father of Skies – would she ever feel clean again? Pouring more wine and taking the cup with her, Raven walked through the curtained archway into her bathing room, where a hollow with a drain-hole at the bottom had been carved out of the marble floor. A pull of a silken rope would send water cascading into the basin from the great peaktop cisterns that caught up rain and snow-melt from the mountain storms. Raven drained her wine and set the cup aside, then cast off her worn, much-mended leather tunic – the very one in which she had originally made her all too brief escape. She turned it in her hands, looking at Nereni's neat rows of tiny stitches with eyes that blurred with tears, then threw it away from her with a bitter curse.

For a time Raven splashed beneath the icy cascade. She had often heard Aurian speak wistfully of soaking in a hot tub, but such outlandish human customs were not the way of the Skyfolk. The snow-cold water helped to numb the ache of her bruises where Harihn's men had ambushed her, but did nothing to quell the pain within her heart. Inside, she was sick and shaking with fear at the thought of Blacktalon, and what he would do to her now that he had her in his power.

Once she had dried herself Raven returned to her chamber, and spent some time preening her disordered plumage, sorting the ruffled feathers with her clawlike fingernails, and pausing often to sip more wine. It was long since she had eaten, and the drink was making her head spin. The sensation alarmed her at first, but she soon became accustomed to it, and after a while began to welcome it. The glimmerings of a plan came into her head as she preened. Not much of a plan, to be sure, but it held out a slender hope that she might after all escape the attentions of Blacktalon. By custom, the Skyfolk mated for life, and not one of them would touch someone who had already bedded with another.

So deep in thought was she, that when Blacktalon entered Raven was slow to react. With hammering heart, she turned to face him. The High Priest said nothing. He simply stood in the doorway, running greedy eyes across her body, with a pair of goggling guards, warrior-priests in the livery of the temple, behind him. Witnesses, thought Raven. Perfect. Without the wine, she could never have done it. Though Raven's skin crawled to feel their eyes on her, and the blood rushed scalding to her face for shame, she did not trouble to hide her nakedness. She forced herself to lift her head and look the High Priest brazenly in the eye, though it was the hardest thing that she had ever done in her life.

'You come too late, Blacktalon,' the winged girl spat. 'That is, unless you care to soil yourself on one who is already defiled. Your fellow-conspirator beat you to the mark, High Priest. The human had me – not once, but many times.' Raven heard the gasp of horror from the temple guards, and forced herself to laugh in Blacktalon's face.

Then the High Priest joined in the laughter, and Raven knew she was undone. 'So Harihn told me,' Blacktalon chuckled, with a knowing leer. 'He said that you'd proved an apt pupil, my little princess, and he hoped he had taught you sufficient to keep me entertained during Aerillia's long cold nights.'

As though he had cut her throat, Raven's laughter came to a choking halt.

'You fool', Blacktalon sneered. 'Had you chosen one of the Winged Folk it might have been different, perhaps, though with the throne at stake I could still have forced myself to take you. But as it is, what difference does a human make? They are not our kind. You might just as well have been consorting with a mountain sheep – and to as much effect.'

He walked into the room, and poured himself a goblet of wine, glancing as he did so into the depleted flagon. 'For shame,' he mocked her, 'wantonness and drink. Is there no end to the vices you have learned among those groundling insects?' He shrugged. 'No matter. In the main, it is your hand I require – though your body I will take in due course. Joining with the heir to the throne will establish my claim on the kingship beyond all possible doubt – and by tradition, you must come to that joining a virgin – technically at least.' He snickered. 'Humans, as I said, can scarce be said to count. And since our joining may not take place until the moon has waxed and waned, because of the period of mourning for the late lamented queen, I must forbear until that time – though the anticipation may have pleasures of its own.'

While he spoke, Raven had been struck dumb by horror, but when she heard Blacktalon mock her mother's memory, her rage boiled up beyond controlling – and beyond all wisdom. 'You abomination!' She hurled her wine, cup and all, into the High Priest's face. 'You'll never lay a finger on me while I live, I swear it. And I'll see you rot in torment through all eternity before I'll join with you. Not all my folk are loyal to you, Blacktalon – you treacherous, murdering upstart – do you think you'll hold me with your bars and guards? I'll be avenged on you if – '

His blow sent the winged girl spinning across the room. 'Foolish, deluded child.' Blacktalon stood over her, shaking his head reprovingly. 'Did you think I would give you the chance to escape again, and lead an insurrection?' His eyes were pitiless and hard. Raven shrank away from him, and a shudder of dread went through her. The High Priest pressed her mercilessly, playing with his victim to prolong her torment. 'There are certain laws of the Winged Folk, my princess, that not even you can circumvent. Who, among your people, would follow a crippled queen?'

He beckoned to his warriors, and for the first time Raven saw that they were armed with heavy maces. Her heart turned to ice within her. 'No,' she whispered, as they advanced. 'No . . .'

Blacktalon stood watching, calmly sipping his wine and savouring the sound of her screams. The heavy iron maces lifted, over and over again, and came smashing down with all their weight upon the fragile bones of Raven's wings.

Afterwards, Anvar could remember little of his airborne journey to the citadel of the Skyfolk. All that remained in his mind were vague impressions; half-glimpsed shapes of four winged figures clasping the net above him, darker silhouettes against the dark night sky, and the ceaseless rhythmic drumming of their tireless wings; the discomfort of dizziness and nausea from the swinging net; the piercing cold searing into his face as Miathan's knife had done. The latticed pattern of the net's coarse rope digging into his skin. Fierce pain from the burn on his cheek and the dull throb of bruises where he had been struck and manhandled by his captors. But though the Mage was still half-stunned, fear and anger and desperation all combined to keep his consciousness struggling back to the surface, again and again.

Anvar's first clear memory was coming back to awareness as though waking from the clinging clutch of some dread nightmare, and seeing Aerillia in the dawn. For a little while, all thoughts of his plight vanished from his mind, for the first sight of the city was utterly breathtaking. Most of the sky was covered by a thick layer of ominous cloud, the purple-grey of slate; but the rising sun slipped through a narrow gap between the white-fanged backdrop of the mountain range and the darkly shrouded sky above. The delicate architecture of Aerillia threw back the level rays of sunrise into the Mage's eyes, gleaming like a filigreed coronet of pearls across the craggy brow of the mountain peak. Closer, and the towers and spires of the city took shape under Anvar's marvelling gaze – unbelievably delicate structures wrought in the palest of stone that looked, from this distance, as fragile as spun webs of milky glass. Now Anvar knew from whence had come the shimmering stone with which the ancient buildings of the Academy had been wrought. But the structure of Aerillia was so alien, yet so perfectly beautiful . . . Notwithstanding his own pain and peril, and his desperate fear for Aurian, the Mage was lost in wonder.

Carved from the living mountain, the pinnacle towers formed fantastic shapes and structures that no earthbound builder would ever have attempted. Clusters of dwellings seemed to grow out of the sheer rock faces like the delicate corals that Anvar had seen underwater in the warm southern bay where Aurian had taught him to swim. Others, of varying shapes, had been suspended like bubbles or drops of water or icicles; hanging from outthrust ledges over a terrifying drop. Yet others grew upwards in spirals or helices or fluted, tapering spires; their slender tips so high that they were veiled in tattered banners of low-hanging cloud. The stone of their construction glowed rose and cream and gold in the delicate light of dawn, against the grim and threatening background of

146

the slate-grey sky. Then the lowering cloud closed in like a lid, shutting off the sun; and the city became a wraith of its former self, sketched in brittle penstrokes of silver and grisaille.

The wind was blowing harder now. As the Mage, hanging in the net between his captors, neared the city, he became aware of a desolate, dissonant keening that ached in his teeth and ears, vibrating within the bones of his skull and chilling his soul with an overwhelming sense of oppression and terror. The sound grew louder and more shrill as they approached the city, until the clouds that veiled the top of Aerillia peak were swept away like a curtain drawn aside. Anvar looked up, and was transfixed in horrified disbelief.

There, on the utter pinnacle of the mountain, loomed a huge and ghastly structure of night-black stone. Every inch of the asymmetrical, buttressed monstrosity was carved with leering gargoyle images of demons, horned and beaked and breathing fire, and winged like great carrion birds with decaying corpses clutched between their claws. Anvar, fighting a desperate urge to vomit, found it impossible to look away. The hunched and twisted edifice was topped with five inward-curving spires that raked the sky like ebon claws – the source of the gut-wrenching plaint that throbbed with exquisite agony between Anvar's ears. Each of the spires was pierced with a multitude of holes, dark and round as the eye sockets in a skull, and through these the freely moving winds had been trapped and strained and twisted, then spewed forth in this distorted, tortured form to howl their agony at the unfeeling peaks.

The trembling Mage was relieved when his escort bore him lower, and the grotesque structure was lost to sight behind the towering walls of a precipice. The sound, unfortunately, still followed to torment him. Below the level of the city, the mountainside plummeted in a sheer, featureless cliff, curving round to the western face of the mountain, and after a time Anvar saw an opening in the rock ahead, a gaping black maw with bristling stalactite fangs. The meshes bit into his skin as his winged captors gathered up the net and flew directly at the aperture, moving at tremendous speed, and Anvar cringed, biting down on a scream as the jagged rocks around the mouth of the opening came hurtling towards him. *Too small! It's too bloody small! We're going to . . .*

The air was knocked from Anvar's lungs as his net brushed the lintel of the cave. As the Skyfolk let go, he went rolling over and over; carried forward by his own momentum; entwined in the meshes so tightly that he could hardly breathe. For an instant, the world turned dazzling black as he crashed into the wall at the rear of the cave.

The winded Mage heard a rustle of feathers as the Winged Folk stood over him, their half-spread pinions filling the space of the cavern and blocking the light from the entrance. 'Is he conscious?' one of them asked.

Wings folded. Anvar blinked in the light, and saw a sharp-boned face above him, upside down. It nodded once with a jerky motion. 'He wakes.'

'Then let us make haste.'

Anvar felt steel snick against his skin as they reached through the meshes of the net to cut the ropes that bound him. Then one by one they launched themselves quickly from the mouth of the cave – had the notion not been ridiculous, Anvar would have said they were afraid of him – leaving the Mage to struggle out of the net as best he could as the hissing thunder of their wings faded into the distance.

Stiff and numb as Anvar was with cold and fatigue and all his hurts, it took him a long, frantic age to free himself from the tightly wrapped meshes. So firmly was he entangled that more than once the Mage came close to throttling himself as he writhed and rolled on the cavern's uneven floor. Again and again he had to force himself, with a desperate effort of will, to cease the panic-striken thrashing that was only binding him tighter; to relax, and think it through, and try to twist himself another way until the ropes that cut into his body were slackened once more. Though the open cave was cold indeed, sweat was soon drenching his body and running down his face in rivulets, stinging the blistered skin of his burned cheek. And all the time, as he tired, his chances of freeing himself grew less and less.

When the Mage finally thought of the obvious solution, he was ashamed that it had not occurred to him sooner. What was

148

he doing, struggling like a mindless rabbit in a snare, or some common, helpless Mortal without magic? What would Aurian have said, if she could have seen him? Oh, gods, the thought of her in Miathan's power was an agony to him. Anvar swallowed hard. Not now, he told himself. You need all your concentration to get out of this accursed net.

But first he had to rest a little, to gather his strength. It was only then that Anvar became truly aware of the piercing cold within the cavern. He did his best to ignore it, and occupied his mind instead with how best to use his powers to achieve his escape. Reluctantly, he decided it would have to be Fire – not his preferred element, and decidedly risky, so close to his skin. After Miathan's torture, the thought of being burned again made his skin crawl with terror.

None the less, Fire it must be. Luckily, he would only need a tiny fireball. That was all he had the energy to produce, and, since his control was not too good, the smaller the blaze, the less fear there'd be of immolating himself. Craning his neck, the Mage looked down at his chest where the meshes were wrapped tightly, three or four times around. In order for him to get his arms free, that tangled mass of rope would have to go.

Biting his lip – how many times had he seen Aurian do that when constructing a spell? – Anvar reached deep within to find the wellsprings of his power. Ah. Compressing the magic that he found there with all the force of his will, he crushed it tighter and tighter until it formed a tiny spark of fiercely growing energy. In his mind's eye, the Mage placed it where he wanted it, where the meshes crossed each other on his chest – then he fed it with all the strength of his love of magic, nurturing it, encouraging it to grow and blossom – just a little at first – then a little more . . .

There was a sharp smell of singeing hemp, then a whiff of smoke. Before Anvar's eyes, strand after strand of the twisted rope began to blacken and glow red, breaking apart and unravelling thread by thread, with a little spark of fire gleaming like a dragon's eye at each fractured end.

Then the Mage became carried away with his success – or perhaps it was only that the rope was tinder dry. All at once, a section of the net the size of Anvar's hand burst into flames.

149

With a yell he rolled over, trying to douse the fire, and the net burst apart to free his arms. His rolling had almost quenched the flames, and he beat frantically at the smouldering remnant until he was certain that the fire was out. Half-cursing, half-laughing with relief, Anvar sat up and began to undo the tangle around his legs with shaky hands.

At last he was free, but he had been bound for so long that at first his legs would not support him. He crawled to the cave mouth, where a pile of windblown snow had collected at one side. His hands had not been badly burned by putting out his self-made fire, but he plunged them into the soothing snow until all the feeling of heat had been drawn away from his palms, and then plastered more of it on the tingling skin of his chest, where the flames had come too close for comfort.

That done, Anvar looked out from his prison, but the storms had closed in once more, and he could see nothing beyond the opening but dark grey cloud and thick, slanting curtains of snow. How far it was to the ground, he had no idea, but one thing was certain – if they had imprisoned him here, it must be too bloody far! At any rate, nothing could be done until he could see. Sighing bitterly, Anvar crept back into his prison, and found that it was better provisioned than he had expected.

Blacktalon, obviously, had sent messages on ahead. In one corner stood two great crocks of water, and a generous basket of food. Beyond them, stacked along the far wall of the cave, was a large pile of firewood and kindling. Very carefully, with the memory of his recent mishap all too clear in his mind, Anvar lost no time in lighting a fire. It took a little trial and error with a smoking brand to find the best spot for a blaze, where the swirling draught from the entrance would blow the smoke out of the cave without freezing the Mage to death in the process. After a time, he found the ideal place, where the left-hand wall of the cavern jutted out in a sloping spur, about half his height at its highest point. Behind this outcrop was a sheltered corner, where the smoke would blow over the top of the spur and out.

Anvar was cheered by his fire. The saffron flames brightened the gloom within the cavern, and the crackle and snap of the burning logs helped to cover the screeching, nerve-grating plaint of the hideous edifice on the peak. The

150

blaze danced and talked and needed to be fed – it seemed a living thing, and company. None the less, it was still bitterly cold within the cavern. Anvar wondered, for a time, why his enemies should go to all this trouble just to freeze him to death, until a more detailed exploration of his cavern provided the answer – an answer that froze his blood with horror.

Not far from the food, in a shadowy corner at the back of the cave, lay a thick pile of dark-furred animal skins; overlooked until the flames had thrown them into light. Anvar, much relieved, went quickly across to take one – and snatched his hand back with a vile and livid oath. How well he knew that fur – its depth and thickness and heavy, silky feel. Those bloodthirsty freaks expected him to wrap himself in the pelts of Shia's people!

'Murderers!' he howled. He struck his fist against the cavern wall. 'I'd rather freeze! I'd rather freeze to death a thousand times over, than wear the hides of these slaughtered folk!' Anvar thought of Shia; of her loyalty and courage; her understanding and her sharp, wry humour; the lithe and graceful beauty of her sleek, steel-muscled form; the glory of her glowing golden eyes. Shia with her fund of calm common sense, who would have been the first to tell him to be practical: to save his own life. He had no other choice.

Anvar steeled himself to place one of the furs around his shoulders, though his skin cringed away from its touch as though it were still steeped in blood, and its weight on his back was his burden of guilt for profiting from the poor creature's death. Had this been Shia's friend? Her mate – her *child*? With a shudder, he forced the thought away from him. The poor cat was dead, as were its companions. His sacrifice could do nothing to bring it back to life, and he had to survive. Somehow, he had to find a way to escape this prison and go back to help Aurian. And if in doing so he could strike a blow at the ones who had committed this atrocity, then by the gods, he would at least avenge these cats who, by their deaths, had saved his life.

Anvar hid his face in his hands, fighting back tears. He had been unable, until then, to think of Aurian – the agony of losing her had been so unbearable that his mind had shied away from

151

the pain. The memory of Shia, and the pitiful remnants of her poor murdered kin, had served to trigger all his grief at last – but survival was still the stronger imperative. His dying of cold and hunger in this accursed cave would not help Aurian. Anvar wiped his face on his sleeve, in an unconscious echo of his lost love, and got up to heap more wood on his guttering fire.

By now, the Mage felt dizzy and sick with hunger and thirst. He found a cup beside the water jugs and drank deeply, filling the cup again and again, before dragging his basket to the fire and rummaging through its contents. He found flat cakes of moist heavy bread, plainly not made from grain. But of course no grain would grow up here. Perhaps it was some kind of tuber, Anvar thought, as he wolfed it down. Nereni had experimented with similar foodstuffs in the forest. There were chunks of roast goat, and the meat of some enormous fowl that had been delicately spiced and smoked. No greens or fruit, but if Raven had spoken the truth Aerillia had been in winter's grip too long for such luxuries. At the bottom of the basket, Anvar found goat's cheese and, best of all, a flask of thin red wine.

When it came to it, the Mage could summon little appetite. His throat was dry and aching and his stomach churned, but he warmed the sharp wine with a little water on his fire, he made a nest of catskins in his sheltered corner, and curled up in them. Though he was hot and shivering with fever, Anvar fell asleep in a surprisingly short time, clutching the thought of Aurian to his heart like a talisman.

11
Words of the Goddess

After what seemed like hours spent in an agony of torment and despair, Aurian heard the dragging scrape of wood on stone as the door of her prison was thrust open on its solitary hinge. She ignored the sound. What more could they do to her? Anvar was lost to her, taken she knew not where, and Miathan had cursed her child. She shuddered, fighting nausea; wondering what manner of monster she carried beneath her heart. Trapped in wretchedness, her battered spirit shrank from facing her bitter defeat. Let them enter, whoever they were. Let Miathan do what he would with her – for he could do little worse than he had already done. How had she ever dared hope to defeat him?

Breaking into her misery, Aurian heard a horrified cry, and a stream of half-articulated curses aimed at the prince, his followers, his relations and ancestors. Nereni! It was Nereni, using profanities which normally would have made the little woman blanch and cover her ears. Aurian felt her lips twitch in a smile, and was suddenly ashamed. If timid Nereni could summon this much fire and fight, how dared she, Aurian, a Mage and a warrior, give way to despair?

Aurian felt cold steel against her wrists as Nereni cut the thongs that bound her, and stifled a curse as the blood returned to her hands in a scalding rush. With an effort, she opened swollen eyes. Nereni's face was ravaged with weeping, but her eyes burned with indignant rage as she gathered the Mage into her arms. 'Aurian! What have they done to you? And you with child?' Enraged beyond thought of her own plight, Nereni turned on the soldiers who had accompanied her. 'You – fetch some water! Bring wood for a fire. And get someone up here to mend that trapdoor. We may be prisoners, but we need not freeze to death – or starve, either. You, you son of a pig! Find some food for this poor lady.'

One of the soldiers laughed. 'We don't take orders from a fat old hag!' he jeered.

Nereni drew herself up to her full, insignificant height. To Aurian's utter astonishment, she advanced on the soldier, bristling. 'But you take orders from the prince, who told you that this lady was to be cared for. Now get your lazy backside through that door and fetch me what I need, before I inform his Highness of your disobedience!'

The soldier turned suddenly white, and scurried off to do her bidding. 'And while you're at it,' Nereni bawled after him, 'get someone up here to clean this pigsty!'

After that, things happened quickly. The corpses of the Winged Folk were dragged away, and soldiers came to wash the worn stone floor. Someone brought wood, and soon the air was filled with cheerful crackling as the growing blaze in the hearth began to take the chill from the room. One of the men brought a sack of provisions and utensils which was snatched from his hands by Nereni.

When their guards had gone, Aurian stripped off her torn robe with a shiver of revulsion, wrapping herself in blankets from the packs that had been returned to them. Nereni gave her a cloth soaked in cold water to hold against her battered face, then began to busy herself at the fire. Under the kindly fussing of her friend, Aurian felt the dreadful tension of her despair beginning to dissolve. As icy water numbed the ache of her bruises, she searched within for the shreds of courage; weaving them together into a cloak of adamantine will. Never again would she come so close to giving in. Had it not been for Nereni . . .

Aurian's chin came up in the old stubborn gesture. She would not give in to despair. She wanted her wits about her, ready to exploit any weakness in Miathan's plans. There must be a way to save herself and Anvar. Ah, gods, and her child! As if to remind her of its presence and its plight, Forral's son moved within her, and Aurian felt her heart go out to him in a flood of love and sorrow. After all he had gone through . . . 'Don't worry,' she whispered fiercely. 'No matter what form Miathan put upon you, you're mine and I love you. I won't let that bastard kill you.'

154

At the sound of her voice, Nereni turned from the fire and handed the Mage a steaming cup of liafa. 'You look better now,' she said softly. 'Aurian – did he . . . When I saw you lying there, I thought . . .' She bit her lip.

'No,' Aurian said wearily, 'I'm all right – so far. He won't risk bringing the babe early. But afterwards . . .' She sipped the stimulating drink, wincing as its heat stung her bruised mouth. Her hands trembled so that it took both of them to steady the cup. As a distraction from the memory of Miathan's unclean touch, she asked for news of the others.

Nereni scowled. 'Your so-called friend the cat fought her way out and ran, and that coward Yazour took the opportunity to follow her.' Her voice was edged with anger.

'Don't blame Shia – I told her to go,' Aurian replied firmly. 'The Staff of Earth is our one hope of defeating Miathan, and someone had to take it to safety. And don't blame Yazour for taking the chance to esape. Outnumbered as we were, it was the only thing to do. But are Eliizar and Bohan all right?' Aurian knew this was the real core of Nereni's anguish, and waited anxiously for her reply.

'They put Eliizar in the dungeon, with Bohan,' Nereni said shakily. 'He was wounded, by they would not let me go to him.' She shuddered. 'They threw me down, intending rape, but the prince stopped them. He knew I would kill myself, for shame, and he wants me alive, to take care of you. That is why his guards dare not harm me. Some winged Folk flew away with Anvar, and . . .'

'What did you say?' The cup shattered on the hearth, splashing liafa into the hissing flames. Aurian grasped Nereni's arms, until the older woman gasped with pain. 'Winged Folk took Anvar? Do you know where?'

'Aurian', Nereni cried out in protest, but the Mage did not loosen her grip.

'Where did they take him, Nereni?'

'I'm not sure,' Nereni whimpered. 'They spoke in the tongue of the Skyfolk but I heard them mention Aerillia. Then they put Anvar in a net and flew off with him. Aurian, you're hurting me.' She burst into tears.

'Nereni, I'm sorry!' Aurian gathered the weeping woman

into her arms. 'You've been so brave – I don't know what I would have done without you. But I'm so afraid for Anvar, and I didn't know where they had taken him.'

'I know,' Nereni sniffed. 'I feel the same about Eliizar, wounded and locked up in that terrible place. If only they would let me see him.'

'Don't worry – we'll work on it,' Aurian comforted her friend. 'If Miathan would leave Harihn alone sometimes . . .' She paused, wondering how to explain that the prince was not what he seemed. 'You see,' she began, 'Harihn is not . . .'

'Himself?' Nereni brightened a little at Aurian's look of surprise. 'I know,' she went on. 'Why do you think my folk have such a fear of sorcery? Tales of possession are common in our legends. When he saved me from his men, Harihn seemed normal, but then his face changed beyond recognition and another, evil soul looked out from his eyes.' The tremor of her voice betrayed her calm manner. 'Has the prince sold his soul to a demon?'

Aurian shook her head. 'I told you about the Archmage Miathan, who turned his power to evil. Well, he's in league with Blacktalon, but he is also using the prince's body. Miathan couldn't achieve such possession without Harihn's consent, so I suspect he offered the prince his father's throne. An ally in the south would benefit his own plans for conquest. But Harihn has no idea of the depth of Miathan's deceit. He is only a puppet now, dancing to the Archmage's every whim. I've no sympathy for Harihn, but your people will suffer, as we all will, if we can't find a way out of this.'

'But how can we?' Nereni cried. 'He holds Eliizar and Bohan captive, and he will kill them if we try to escape.'

'I don't know,' Aurian admitted. 'That is, I don't know yet. He's holding Anvar hostage too, but thanks to you I have an idea of his whereabouts now. Don't worry, Nereni. If we don't panic, we'll think of something.'

While she comforted her friend, Aurian was analysing the situation, as Forral had taught her. Her plight was desperate. She was helpless until her powers returned with the birth of her child – but would she have time to act before Miathan killed the babe? And if there was no way to free Anvar, so far away in

Aerillia, how could she move against the Archmage? Aurian's head began to ache. She was bruised, shocked, and utterly bereft; afraid to the core of her being – yet still she pushed herself to stay calm, to think. It was vital that she come up with a plan.

'Aurian!' The voice in the Mage's mind was tinged with desperation, as though its sender had been trying to gain her attention for some time. Joy shot through Aurian, so intense that it brought a lump to her throat. 'Shia! I'd forgottten about you.'

'So I noticed,' Shia said dryly. 'Idiot! I've been trying to penetrate that mess you call your thoughts for ages.'

'Idiot yourself,' Aurian retorted. 'I told you to get out of here.'

'I'm well hidden – and if anyone should find me, may their gods help them.' Her voice grew soft with worry. 'Aurian – how could I leave without knowing what had happened to you?'

Briefly, the Mage told Shia what had happened. Shia spat when she heard of Raven's treachery and subsequent betrayal. 'Little fool! I never trusted her. Not for nothing have the Winged Folk been our bitterest enemies for an age and an age. But Aurian, how can you ask me to leave you in such peril? Can't I do something to help?'

For a moment, Aurian dared to hope. Then she remembered Anvar, imprisoned in Aerillia, and all optimism perished. Even if Shia could free her and she could elude the Archmage, Miathan must somehow be in contact with Blacktalon. If she escaped, she knew that Anvar would die long before she could come to him.

Aurian sighed. Whatever move she made, Miathan had her cornered. 'No, Shia,' she told the cat. 'They have Anvar as a hostage, and if you free me, he'll die. All you can do is take the Staff and . . . By Ionor the Wise! Why didn't I think of it sooner?' Aurian laughed out loud, giddy with relief. Inspiration had come to her in a blinding flash.

'What?' Shia's tone was sharp with exasperation. Aurian made an effort to stifle her giggles, hushing Nereni's baffled protests.

'Shia, listen carefully. We believe that Anvar is being held in Aerillia. Find him as quickly as you can, and get the Staff to him. He can use it to escape!'

157

'Is that all?' Shia's voice was acid. 'I simply cross thirty leagues of mountains alone in winter, carrying this wretched magical thing that sets my teeth on edge. Then I penetrate the inaccessible citadel of the Winged Folk without losing the Staff, give it to Anvar – supposing he really is there and that I can find him – and trust you've taught him enough magic to somehow get us out. Have I forgotten anything?'

'I think you've covered it all,' Aurian replied with a smile. 'If anyone can do it, Shia, you can.'

Shia sighed. 'Very well, if this is what you want – but if I go to rescue Anvar, what will become of you?'

The hopelessness of Aurian's position returned to her like a black and choking cloud. 'Shia, I don't know. Things are bad, and likely to get much worse.'

'Then let me get you out. I know I can do it.'

Oh, it was tempting. Aurian though of Eliizar and Bohan, in the chill, damp dungeon. She thought of Miathan's threat to destroy her son, and the vile touch of his hands on her body. Then she thought of Anvar. If she gave in to her fears, she would have killed him. 'No!' she insisted. 'Get Anvar out, Shia, then Miathan will have no hold over me. He won't harm me until my child is born, and when that happens I'll get my powers back.' Her words sounded hollow to herself, but Aurian stiffened her spine. 'Come what may, I can bear it if only Anvar can be rescued.'

Shia sighed. 'Very well, we'll do it your way. But my heart quails for you, my friend. Be careful.'

'I will, I promise. And you be careful too. I know too well the difficulty of the task I've set you.'

'If I can get my teeth into some of those stinking Winged Folk, it will be worth it. Farewell, Aurian. I'll rescue Anvar, I swear, and we'll both come back for you.'

'Farewell, my friend,' Aurian whispered. But the cat was already gone.

In the ragged copse below the tower an ancient tree had fallen, its roots wrenched out of the ground by the weight of its snowy burden. Shia crept stealthily out of the little cave that had been formed between the roots and the rocky side of the knoll, every sense alert for signs of the enemy. She felt a surge of grim humour as she glided forth, a slip of darkness on the shadowed snow. How clever, to hide right under the noses of these stupid men. Aurian had insisted that Shia abandon her, and the cat's heart burned at the thought – but before she left, Shia had plans of her own. The enemy picket lines, for their horses and mules, were a short distance away through the tangle of trees. Shia crept close, her mouth watering at the luscious scent. Horsemeat was her favourite food, but while travelling with Aurian she'd been forced to restrain herself. Her tail lashed back and forth restlessly. That's not why you're here! Shia reminded herself. She laid the Staff down carefully under a bush, where she could easily find it again and tensed herself to spring – then dropped flat, muffling a snarl of frustration.

Two soldiers approached the horselines, the sound of their grumbling borne towards her on the wind, loud enough for Shia to hear every word. Communicating with Aurian had given her some understanding of man-speech, and while she lurked in the bushes, awaiting her chance to strike, she listened closely, hoping to pick up some useful information.

'By the Reaper, it's not fair!' one man whined. 'Why should we freeze out here, up to our balls in snow, while others toast their backsides in front of a roaring fire?'

'Someone must care for the beasts,' the second guard pointed out. 'Besides, I would rather be outside. That Priest of the Skymen made my skin creep.'

'All Skymen make my flesh creep,' his friend agreed. 'Why did the prince take up with them? And if he wanted to ambush the northern witch, why not just stick a sword in her and be done with it? Then we'd be in the Xandim lands by now, instead of freezing to death in this accursed wilderness. If you ask me, Harihn has lost his wits. He's never been the same since we left the desert.'

His friend hushed him hastily. 'Watch your tongue, Dalzor! If you're caught talking treason, they'll have your head. Anyway, we should be unloading these beasts and settling them. What if the captain comes and we've not yet started? It's too cursed cold to lose skin to a flogging.'

He began at the far end of the line, fumbling at buckles with frozen fingers and dumping the packs on the ground. Still grumbling, his friend began to work his way towards the other end of the line – and Shia. The animals were restless, their coats damp with fear-sweat as they scented the cat nearby. 'What's got into the beasts?' Dalzor muttered. As he approached the nearest horse, it swung around, snorting, and barged into him, knocking him flat in the trampled snow. Cursing, he struggled to regain his feet on the slushy surface, but it was too late.

Shia was on him in a flash, the hot ecstasy of enemy blood filling her mouth as her teeth sank into his throat. Then she was among the horses and mules; snarling and lashing out with her claws. The frantic creatures screamed and reared, panic lending them the strength to pull their tethers from the ground. They scattered, some heading back down the valley, but most of them, Shia noticed, fleeing straight through the pass. She'd feed on horseflesh yet!

The other guard was running, yelling for help. An uproar broke out within the tower, and the snow on the hill was washed with a gleam of dirty yellow light as the door swung open. Regretfully, Shia abandoned her plans for the second guard. Dashing back to seize the Staff, she sped down the pass like an arrow, congratulating herself as she went. She had let them unload most of the food, for she had no wish to starve her friends, but her attack had effectively trapped the enemy in the tower. Had Shia been human, she would have been grinning from ear to ear. The prince and his men were stuck in the bleak, hostile spot – and when Shia returned with Anvar, she would know exactly where to find them.

For all his determination to leave, Schiannath had stayed near the tower, unable to let go of this mystery. Why were the Khazalim fighting their own? And what, in the name of the goddess, had the misbegotten Winged Folk to do with it all? Since it was obvious by now that the fleeing man was not going to be pursued, the outlaw continued to lurk behind his boulders, his eyes fixed on the tower. The sounds of fighting ceased, and after a time he saw the Winged Folk leave, bearing between them a long bundle supported in nets. They headed north-west, towards Aerillia. So – they were taking a prisoner with them! The shape of the bundle was all too familiar. Schiannath shook his head. Fugitives from the Khazalim? Fugitives from the Skyfolk? Just what was going on here? 'Forget it, Schiannath,' he murmured to himself. 'You have more important things to think about. Like survival – and the provisions the Khazalim have left on those mules!'

The commotion in the horselines took Schiannath by surprise. He had been biding his time, waiting until the tower settled down to an uneasy peace. He suspected that the Khazalim – curse their name – would need some time to restore order within before someone remembered to unload the horses. He had been just about to make his move when the wretched guards appeared, jabbering in their uncouth tongue, and began to unload the horses. Schiannath swore bitterly. The chance of a lifetime, and he had lost it. What was wrong with him? All that food – and it had almost been his.

The outlaw's mouth watered. Damned if he would let it go so easily. The guards moved apart as they worked, the nearer coming closer to Schiannath's hiding place, and the scrubby thicket at the foot of the hill. If he could cross the intervening space and get under cover while the man was distracted by the horses, who seemed strangely uneasy . . . Schiannath awaited his moment. Leaving Iscalda, he darted forward, keeping low, and dived into the bushes.

The thicket exploded. Branches sprang back into his face as a huge black shape burst from beneath them. Roars and snarls mixed with the screams of horses assaulted his ears. The outlaw picked himself up, his heart hammering. Whatever it was, it had gone – out there. Schiannath groped feverishly for his bow, and discovered that he had lost it in the snow. Goddess! How could he survive without it in the wilderness? But his immediate survival was at stake now. Drawing his sword, he crept to the edge of the thicket – and stopped, transfixed in horror.

The guard lay dead in a spreading pool of blood, his throat and half his face torn away. Among the horses, wreaking havoc with teeth and claws, was the flame-eyed shape of a demon. Schiannath sucked breath through his teeth in a hoarse whistle. One of the fearsome Black Ghosts from the northern mountains. And he'd lost his bow!

161

Even as Schiannath watched, the cat leapt towards him. He flung himself backwards, knowing he was already dead; but the creature ignored him, pounced on something that lay nearby, and fled towards the pass. Schiannath's blood congealed. Iscalda! he scrambled to his feet, hardly daring to look; but the mare had gone. Unable to face the monster, she had fled down the pass – in the same direction as the cat was heading. Oh, goddess, save her.

Now that the dread beast had gone, men were venturing out of the tower – but would they dare the pass while the cat might still be there? Schiannath doubted it. He didn't relish the idea himself, but he had no choice. Some of the horses still milled in the lines, crazed with fear but unable to break free. The outlaw dashed to the nearest animals – a horse and a mule that still bore its pack. He leapt astride the horse, severing its tether and that of the mule with a sweep of his knife. The horse plunged wildly, but no ordinary horse could throw one of the Xandim. Clouting the maddened animal with the end of the rope, he sent it racing towards the mouth of the pass, praying that he would be in time to save Iscalda from the demon.

Schiannath bent low over the horse's neck, narrowing his eyes in an attempt to find tracks in the trampled snow. The sky was thick with curdled grey cloud, and though dawn was brightening the sky above, the cliffs on either side blocked out the early light. The floor of the pass was still in darkness, and shadows defeated his anxious sight. The outlaw strained his ears for any sounds of pursuit above the double set of hoofbeats and their bewildering echoes that reverberated from the surrounding stone. There was nothing. Fear of the cat had kept the Khazalim from following – for a time. With the frightened mule dragging behind him, Schainnath urged his mount to a faster pace, following the tortuous curves of the stony pass, until he heard a sound that turned him chill with dread. Somewhere ahead, a horse was screaming, raw and shrill, in an agony of terror.

Following the choked, despairing sounds, the outlaw found Iscalda in a narrow defile that branched off the pass. The shrieks of the mare echoed between the high walls; her flanks were streaked dark with the sweat of terror; her eyes rolled, white-rimmed, as she reared and backed away from the snarling shadow that stalked her.

Controlling his plunging mount with difficulty, Schiannath fumbled for his bow. Gone! Too late, he remembered losing it when the cat had scattered the horses. The feline's ears flinched back – it was aware of him. Schiannath lashed his mount, trying to force it onward against its will; steeling himself to take the terrible risk of riding this awesome creature down. The horse reared and wrenched itself away, afraid to approach the cat but goaded to a frenzy by Schiannath's blows. The mule went into hysterics, bucking and spinning on the end of its rope until the two creatures were tightly tangled. The outlaw barely had time to free his legs before the world flipped over as his horse went thudding down. He rolled clear, and landed on hands and knees, looking into the blazing eyes of the great cat.

'Festering ordure!' The curse was a whisper in his dry throat. The outlaw inched a shaking hand towards his sword, and the cat gave a low, warning growl. With a gasp, Schiannath froze. Then, suddenly, the awesome creature began to back away. Dear goddess – it couldn't be afraid of him?

The cat growled again, more softly this time, and began to paw at something – a limp, dark shape that had lain, unnoticed, in the shadow of the rock. So the beast had other prey. Remembering the warrior who had fled the tower, Schiannath felt a shameful surge of relief. If the cat had enough to eat, perhaps it would let him go. Was there a chance that he could sacrifice his fallen Khazalim mount and find a way to get Iscalda out of here?

The gigantic feline, still standing over the fallen warrior, gave a shrill yowl that sounded, to Schiannath's tight-strung senses, almost like impatience. Reaching down into the snow, it picked up something in its jaws. A stick, or some kind of twisted root, that glowed with a dazzling, pulsating emerald light. Once more, the flaming eyes seared into his own. Emerald and gold combined in a dizzying whirl, and Schiannath was falling, falling into the light . . .

The outlaw opened his eyes. One side of his face was a dull, numb ache where it had pressed into the snow, and his body was racked with shivers. His head throbbed as though it were

163

about to explode – but the cat, thank the goddess, was nowhere in sight. Loyal Iscalda stood over him, her nostrils flaring at the stench of blood. The other horse lay where it had fallen, its legs tangled in the pack-mule's tether, but the mule itself had vanished. All that remained was a trailing smear of blood; a rut in the snow where the body had been dragged away – and the animal's pack, left on the ground nearby.

'It's very stringy. I would have much preferred the horse.'

Schiannath leapt to his feet and drew his sword – but the voice had come from within his mind, not without!

'Even you would have tasted better than a skinny old mule – but I spared you for a reason. Take good care of the stranger, human, for your life depends on it.'

Shia spat out the Staff with a grimace, and tore off another mouthful of the mule's blood-warm flesh to take the taste away. The discovery that she could use the Artefact to communicate with this stupid human had been timely and fortunate – but oh, the magic in the wretched thing made her teeth ache. The thought of having to carry it for days on end made her shudder.

The cat peered out from her hiding-place – a narrow bay in the cliff where frost had cracked out a great chunk of rock. The stone had fallen outwards and shattered, the pile of fragments forming a lair tucked into the base of the escarpment. What was that human doing now? Oh, wonderful – talking to his horse! Shia flexed her claws and snarled with frustration. Stop wasting time on that brainless beast and help Yazour, she thought. She was bracing herself to pick up the Staff and tell him so, when he left the horse and knelt down beside the stricken warrior. Ah, good. Once she had seen him staunch Yazour's wounds and wrap him in a blanket, Shia turned her attention back to the mule, which was not nearly as stringy as she had claimed. She would need the sustenance. Now that Yazour would be cared for, she could concentrate on her own journey.

Wild with rage, Harihn dashed up the tower stairs. Ignoring the guards at the top, he flung the door open so hard that it

164

rattled and shook on its hinges. 'Accursed sorceress!' he shrieked. 'What have you done to my horses?'

Aurian's blanket-draped form rose from the hearth with surprising grace. Tall and regal, she faced the prince. 'Why, Harihn,' she said pleasantly. 'I see you're back in residence.'

He winced as her barb shot home, and she saw it and smiled. 'Can we offer you some liafa, perhaps?'

'Offer me some answers!' Harihn shouted, slamming the door on his smirking guards. 'Why did you bewitch my horses?' As he saw her struggle to suppress a smile, his rage and frustration overcame him. Forgetting Miathan's orders, he rushed at Aurian, intending to strike the smugness from her face. He discovered his mistake too late. At the last minute, her hand shot out, grabbed his wrist and twisted. There was a wrenching pain in his arm and Harihn went tumbling head over heels to hit the wall.

'You should be more careful, Prince. Miathan will be displeased if you damage his new body.' Aurian's cool voice was like a goad. The prince staggered to his feet, rubbing his wrist, his face contorted with rage.

'You'll suffer for this!' he shouted.

'Your new tenant would not permit it,' Aurian retorted. 'I know the Archmage, to my cost. Don't cross him, I warn you, or he'll make you sorry – as sorry as he has made me.' Her expression twisted with bitter pain, and something like pity. 'What did he offer you? Your father's throne? And you believed him. You invited him in, you poor fool, and now he controls you. Now he has a foothold, he can invade your body at will, forcing you to do his bidding. Whether you know it or not, you're as much a prisoner as I am.'

Harihn turned cold at her words. 'You're wrong!' he blustered. 'We have an agreement. You are *my* prisoner, and the days of your high-handed ways are done. By the Reaper, you will learn your place. You will obey me, or . . .'

'But of course, Harihn,' Aurian agreed sweetly.

The prince, staggered by her capitulation, stared at her through narrowed eyes. 'You lie,' he snapped. 'Do you expect me to believe this pitiful attempt to foil my suspicions, and let you go?'

Aurian laughed in his face. 'Harihn, you're a bigger idiot than I'd thought. The Archmage holds Anvar hostage, and you have Eliizar and Bohan. Do *you* think I'd let Anvar be killed? Would Nereni endanger Eliizar to help me? If I sacrifice my friends, how far would I get without a horse? You can't have it both ways. Had I planned to escape, would I have scattered your beasts?'

Harihn scowled. How this wretched woman twisted words! But, though it galled him, he had to admire her courage. Could he behave so calmly, in her position? Fleetingly, he regretted the ruin of their early friendship. If only he'd had the courage to seize the throne she had offered him. Why had he flinched from using her sorcery, only to accept it from another, grimmer source? At last, Harihn admitted the truth. It would have humiliated him to receive the crown from the hand of a woman. He looked up to see Aurian watching him, her expression grave and sad. 'Then what do you plan to do?' he asked in a gentler voice. She held out empty hands in a gesture more eloquent than words. 'For the moment, there's nothing I can do.'

Her words struck a chill through the prince's heart. 'What? You intend to let the Archmage slay your child?'

'Ah,' said Aurian sadly. 'I had wondered if you were still present, while Miathan possessed your body.' She shook her head. 'Oh, Harihn, this situation grieves me. We were friends once, and I haven't forgotten how much I owe you. Why has everything gone so badly wrong?'

To his astonishment, Harihn found himself moved by her sorrow. As his anger drained away, he was shamed by what he had done. He reached out to Aurian, his lips trying to form some kind of apology – and then he felt it. A slick, hideous probing within his skull, like icy claws sinking into his mind. With a wrench, his consciousness was shouldered aside to become an observer, detached and helpless; sunk without trace within the depths of his soul, as the Archmage returned to claim his body.

'How dare you subvert my puppet,' Miathan's voice came snarling from the prince's lips. Harihn, trapped within, saw Aurian's eyes stretch wide in dismay.

*

166

It wasn't much of a cave. With two horses inside, plus Schiannath and the man he had rescued, it was hopelessly overcrowded; but at least it boasted good venting for smoke in the crack-starred ceiling, and a large rock just inside the entrance that could be rolled, with a wrenching effort, to partially obscure the opening. Also, no one in their right mind would think of daring the narrow, crumbling ledge that led up here. The surefooted Iscalda could negotiate the perilous trail, but Schiannath had very nearly killed himself trying to get the wounded man and that bloody-minded bag of bones that the Khazalim called a horse up to the cave. After that, he'd had to go all the way down again, to wipe out their tracks.

The outlaw returned to the cavern, numb-witted with fatigue, and took one last look out from the entrance, set high in the cliff. To his left, the pass opened on to a ridge that dropped to a sweeping valley, with the crowded ranks of snow-clad mountains, awesome in their desolate grandeur, beyond. There, to the north, beyond that jagged barrier of stone, lay the Xandim lands. Schiannath spat into the snow and turned away. To his right lay the dark throat of the pass – and even as he looked, the harsh sound of Khazalim voices floated up to him, cutting across the snow-locked silence. He'd made it just in time. Gasping with the effort, the outlaw rolled the stone across the entrance, then sank to his knees, exhausted.

Schiannath was utterly spent, but there was no time to rest. In the dim light that slipped between the boulder and the top of the entrance, he groped his way to the back of the cave. It was well provisioned – all of his hideouts were. In the long months of his exile, Schiannath had been occupied with little else but survival. The mountains were honeycombed with caves, and the outlaw had a chain of several refuges reaching from the Wyndveil right across the range to the tower. Each was stocked with hay and wild grains for Iscalda, harvested from the valleys in a summer long gone; firewood brought up from those same vales; nuts and wrinkled berries, and smoke-dried flesh of wild mountain sheep. Their fleecy hides, together with shaggy wolfskins from his hunting, provided warmth.

Schiannath had toiled endlessly through summer and autumn to stock his havens. The labour had served to dull his

167

loneliness, and fatigue had taken the edge off his despair. Now, in this fell winter, the caves were his key to survival – but only today had he found the true reason behind his persistance in such seemingly pointless work. It had been the will of the goddess.

The outlaw could think of nothing else as he piled tinder in the ring of rocks that served as his fireplace, and lit a fire with the competence of long practice. He put hay down for the horses, then turned to the unconscious warrior. As he looked at that strong-boned Khazalim face, his wonder surged up anew.

The goddess spoke. She spoke to *me*! The words sang in his head as Schiannath tended the stranger's wounds. He stripped away the man's wet clothes and wrapped him in dry sheepskins; he snapped off the end of the crossbow bolt and drew it forth point-first. But when he seared the wound with the glowing tip of his knife, the man's eyes flew open and he began to scream. The outlaw clapped his hand over the other's mouth and got his fingers bitten for his pains, but still he held on until the screams subsided. He doubted that the noise would carry beyond the cave, but he was relieved when the man slipped back into unconsciousness. Making the most of the chance to work unhindered, Schiannath applied a wash of healing herbs to the wound, and did the same to the slice in the warrior's thigh. 'Any higher, my friend, and they'd have gelded you,' he muttered.

As Schiannath bound the wounds, he savoured the clean aroma of the herbs which dispelled the nauseating reek of scorched flesh. The scent brought back a memory of the day he had fled the lands of the Xandim with nought but his weapons and the clothes on his back, clinging dazed to Iscalda's neck and bruised and bleeding from the stones they had hurled to speed him on his way. As he passed the waystone on the Wyndveil ridge that marked the borders of his land, there had been a peculiar shimmer in the air, and Chiamh, the hated Windeye, had stepped forth.

Iscalda, her human memories still intact, had reared, screaming with fury. Schiannath had reached for his bow and fired, but his arrow went straight through Chiamh's body to embed itself in the snow beyond. 'I deeply regret my deeds this day,' the Windeye whispered, shamefaced. He sketched a blessing in the air, and vanished.

Apparition though Seer had been, there was nothing ethereal about the contents of the bundle that Schiannath had found beside the stone. Clothing, blankets, food; and best of all, the pouches of Chiamh's healing herbs, labelled with instructions in the blocky Xandim glyphs – some for fevers, others for infections or pain-ease. Though Schiannath had not been able to bring himself to forgive the Windeye, he had often had cause to be thankful for Chiamh's gift.

Coming back to the present with a jerk, Schiannath laid a cloth soaked in icy water across the livid bruise on the warrior's temple. That could be a hurt more dangerous than the other wounds, but he could only keep his patient quiet and hope for the best. For the first time in his life, Schiannath was confident that his prayers would be answered. Had the goddess not come to him, in the animal-guise of a Black Ghost of the mountains? Had she not tested him? And had she, herself, not spoken to him, telling him to save the life of this man, who should have been his enemy?

Schiannah was overcome by a thrill of religious awe. Perhaps there was a reason for his exile, and that of poor Iscalda! Oh, goddess, was there a reason after all?

Yazour opened crusted eyes, to see the face of an enemy. His stomach clenched in panic. I've been captured by the Xandim! Groping for his sword, he struggled to rise, and cried aloud in agony. It felt as though someone had thrust a flaming brand into his shoulder, and another into the muscle of his thigh. The Horselord pushed him gently down with an admonishing shake of his head. 'No. Do not.'

Yazour recognized the words – all Khazalim warriors who raided Xandim lands had learned the rudiments of their tongue. He squinted against the flicker of firelight that played across fanged stone – clearly, the roof of a cavern. A cavern that reeked of horses. Where am I? he thought. Who is this man? By his clothing and weapons he was plainly Xandim, yet the stranger seemed subtly different from those of his tribe that Yazour had seen before. His skin was fair beneath its weathering, and he had wary grey eyes, crinkled at the corners; a fine, high-cheekboned face with a curved and jutting nose; and a silver-threaded mane of black curls.

Yazour's rescuer smiled, and offered him a cup filled to the brim with water. Yazour had already discovered that if he moved his arm, it hurt like a perdition where the bolt had pierced his shoulder. He took the cup with his good hand and drank deeply, while the stranger supported his head with a gentle touch. The water was very welcome. When he had finished, the young warrior lay back in the nest of warm furs that had been wrapped around him, conscious of the terrible weakness that his wounds had caused. He wanted to ask the man a thousand questions, but before he could get the first one out, he had slipped back into oblivion.

When he awakened again, a savoury smell was tickling his nostrils. Yazour's mouth watered. The stranger must have been watching him. He was there at the warrior's side almost before he had time to open his eyes, offering a cup of broth. Once again he supported Yazour's head while he drank, with such solicitous care that the warrior was reminded of his mother, who had cradled him with similar tenderness when he'd been ill as a child. His mother, who had taken her own life when Yazour was fifteen, after his warrior father had been killed in Xiang's service, on a Xandim raid, by a Xandim lance.

With an oath, Yazour struggled away from the hated hand. Broth spilled down his chest as agony pierced his shoulder, and he muffled a whimper of pain with gritted teeth before falling back exhausted. He could feel a new flow of blood seeping stickily through the bandage on his shoulder. Bandage? Yazour had been too concerned with other matters to notice it before. His thigh was bound too, where a sword had caught him in his fight to escape from the tower. The warrior frowned. This enemy had rescued him, doctored his wounds, and was trying to feed him.

Yazour's enemy was shaking his head. 'No,' he said firmly. 'Do not . . .' he said an unfamiliar word, and imitated Yazour's struggle. 'Not prisoner . . .'

Ah, prisoner. That was a Xandim word the warrior understood, but he had never heard the word that followed it. The

170

Xandim frowned, thinking, then reached out a hand to clasp Yazour's own, smiling at him warmly.

Friend? Could he mean friend? Yazour was not prepared to befriend one of the murdering Xandim who had killed his father. He pulled back with an oath, then froze; wondering, too late, if he had made a fatal error. But his rescuer simply sighed, and offered him the broth again, and this time common sense prevailed. If Yazour wished to escape and help his companions, he must regain his strength. He snatched the cup, scowling at the stranger when he tried to offer assistance again.

This might be a foe, but by the Reaper, he could cook. Yazour was ravenous. He gulped the broth quickly, burning his tongue. Loath though he was to ask favours of a Xandim, he held the cup out for more, but the stranger shook his head. 'Bastard!' the young warrior muttered. Turning away, he pulled the furs across his face and pretended to sleep again. In reality, he wanted time to think.

Why? Why had this Xandim gone out of his way to help an enemy? Yazour hated the stranger's race with all his heart, yet the son of a pig had saved his life. The warrior turned restlessly, disturbed by the direction of his thoughts, and the wound in his thigh pulled painfully. The wound that had been dealt Yazour by his own people; his former companions and friends. Reaper's curse, what a tangle. The warrior wondered if that was why the man had rescued him. The Khazalim were enemies of the Xandim, so Yazour was a victim of the stranger's foes ... But no, he thought. Even had he not recognized me at first, he must have known me for a Khazalim when he brought me here – yet still he cared for me. In the name of the Reaper, why?

Yazour could stand it no longer. Rolling over, he pushed the furs aside to look his benefactor in the eye. 'Why?' he demanded in Xandim, wishing he knew more of the language. He gestured at the fire, the cave, the bandaged wounds. The man smiled, and held out his hand again.

'Friend,' he repeated.

Yazour was in the stranger's power, and besides, the man had saved his life. He forced a smile, and took the proffered

171

hand. 'Friend,' he agreed. For now, at any rate, you Xandim bastard, he thought.

Schiannath's patient was soon asleep again, but he seemed much improved, and the outlaw decided that it was safe to rest after his hours of watching. He stood up carefully – there was only one place in the cave where he could do it without knocking his head on the roof – and stretched the kinks from his limbs. Then he stirred the fire, prepared some tea from leaves and berries gathered in kinder months, and ate a scanty meal from his hoarded supplies.

Iscalda whickered from her place near the cave mouth, and Schiannath went to smooth her silken neck. 'Well?' he asked her. 'What think you of our new companion?'

The mare snorted in a manner so uncannily timely that the outlaw was forced to muffle his laughter so as not to waken his patient. 'I couldn't put it better myself,' he told her. 'A friend, indeed – that Khazalim scum!' But the goddess had commanded him to help this man, and so Schiannath would help him – for now, at any rate.

12
The Drunken Dog

The Drunken Dog, a typical dockside tavern if ever there was one, was the most squalid, insalubrious alehouse in Nexis. Its windows, broken time and again in countless brawls, had been nailed over with a clumsy patchwork of boards, and the taproom stank of smoke and grease and unwashed bodies. The floor was slick underfoot; a vile morass of sawdust, spilled drink and, more often than not, blood. When the river was low, the air was thick with the noxious stench of dead fish and sewage. The tavern's situation, down among the wharves and warehouses of the northern riverbank, would have been enough to make a strong man blanch, and a wise man turn hastily away; but even in this, the roughest of areas, the 'Dog' had a bad name – and was proud of it.

Only the desperate dared pass into the shadowy, reeking interior of the Drunken Dog, where the City Guard would rarely venture. Only the lowest of the low – the gangs whose haunt was the darkened alleyway, whose trade was the quick knife-thrust in the back and the chink of gold in a stolen purse. Only the homeless, stinking, red-eyed wrecks whose love of ale had become an addiction. Only the sorry, worn-out whores; pox-ridden, scarred and too long in the tooth to make an honest living from a better class of client. Only those who had already sunk so low that they had nothing left to lose – and Jarvas.

Jarvas sat in his corner near the ash-choked fireplace, his back to the wall and an unencumbered line between himself and the rear door. It was the best spot in the room; within easy sight of the serving-hatch to gesture for more of the raw, sour ale, and commanding a vantage over the entire taproom. It was his special place, and no one was prepared to dispute it.

Jarvas took a sip of the vile, cloudy brew from his grease-smeared tankard and grimaced at the taste. It was the sort of stuff, he mused, that was absolutely guaranteed to make a body ill – but that didn't stop him, or everyone else in the place, from drinking it. He was not usually the sort of man to waste his time wondering why he came here when he didn't have to – he knew his own mind, and was not much given to soul-searching. These days, though, with life in the city gone from bad to worse, and, more significantly, the recent loss of his brother, he was finding himself in an increasingly gloomy and pensive mood. He came here for several reasons; because it was safe – the mercenaries hired by the filthy Magefolk had only tried to come in once, and had regretted their rashness. He came because he could – he was a big man, and while he didn't go looking for trouble, anyone unwise enough to cross him paid for it sooner or later. People around here tended to respect him, and it was known that Jarvas made a good friend and a merciless enemy. Finally – and it said a lot for him that he would admit such a thing to himself – Jarvas came here because he was lonely.

It made life hard when you were ugly, and big besides. Jarvas avoided mirrors. It seemed that when the gods had made him, they had been in a hurry, and just picked up any features that lay to hand, with no thought for the result. His body was a gangling, uncoordinated, mismatched selection of parts. His hands and feet were too big for his frame, and that was saying a lot. His chest was too narrow for his broad shoulders and long legs, and as for his face . . . it was a nightmare. His nose was too long, and his ears stuck out. His pointed chin looked out of balance with his broad forehead and heavy brows. His eyes were a muddy grey-green and despite his best efforts his dark, stringy hair always looked unkempt. In short, he was a disaster. Men tended to look on him as a threat, and as for women – forget it. They wouldn't look at him twice. Given his appearance, it was difficult for Jarvas to make friends, yet friends he had, and it was all due to the greatness of his heart.

Jarvas had his own place, down near the wharves. It consisted of two decrepit warehouses and a disused fulling mill which adjoined one another on a piece of wasteground that had once held slums, burned down on the Archmage's order as a potential plague-spot in the Great Drought three years ago – just about the time that Jarvas had inherited the property, split between himself and his brother Harkas.

He been surprised by the bequest – his family had scraped a living as bargemen with an ancient, leaky craft; he had always discounted tales of a great-uncle, estranged by a family quarrel, who owned property on the riverside. Assuming that it was wishful thinking on the part of his parents, he had given the matter little thought. What sense did it make? No one wanted property along the north side of the river. In the past, perhaps, when the docks had been thriving and prosperous – before the weirs had been built and ships could come all the way upriver from Norberth – it might have been different, but now? Well, things had changed, that was all.

Jarvas was already in his late twenties when his uncle had died. He had given up the barge-trade by then, and had been earning his living in the city for the better part of a decade, turning his hand to any work that came along. While working as a warehouse foreman for the head of the Merchants' Guild, he had managed to scrape up a little education – Vannor believed in learning, and made sure it was available to those of his people who wanted it.

The merchant was a kindly man, despite his awesome reputation, and, having been poor himself, he was always keen to help his people get on in the world. He had gone with Jarvas and Harkas to inspect their bequest – and it was well that he had. When Jarvas looked at the abandoned buildings on the charred wasteground; saw the soot-stained walls, the patched, leaking roofs and the gaping windows like the empty eyes of a corpse, his heart had plummeted. His uncle had not been rich, that was for sure – these derelict shells were worthless. Harkas had cursed bitterly, but Vannor had said nothing – simply walked over to the fulling mill and looked inside, crunching through fallen rubble and moving aside bits of broken beam, his forehead furrowed in thought.

Jarvas smiled at the memory of the great merchant, as he spoke the words that changed the lives of two young men. 'Good solid stonework – this won't fall down in a hurry. Beams need replacing – you've woodworm there – but what a building!

175

See the thickness of these walls and the sturdy structure; and the warehouses are just the same, I'll be bound. Lads, it may not look like much now, but I would say you've struck it lucky.' He had grinned at Jarvas, whose eyes were round with astonishment.

Harkas, the elder of the brothers, was unimpressed. 'What do you mean, sir? How can these old heaps be of any possible use to anyone?'

The twinkle vanished from Vannor's eyes, and he gave Harkas a very straight look. 'Think it through, Harkas. I may be on the Council of Three, but I'm giving away no secrets if I say that this city is going from bad to worse. The drought, and the famine and riots that followed it, should be a lesson to us all. With this place –' he patted the soot-smeared stone – 'you'd be safe from anything. Lads, with a bit of hard work you could turn these buildings into a fortress. And burning was the best thing that could happen to this bit of ground. Look! Already it's starting to bear.' He pointed at the seedling grasses and patches of weed that had been quickened by the recent torrential rain.

'You could fence the land and build a stockade. The gods know, there's enough stone lying around from the hovels that were burned, and timber aplenty in the warehouses – those beams will need replacing anyway, so you might as well find a use for the wood. The fulling mill has a water supply piped straight from the river, and with a bit of work those old dye vats could be turned into pigsties. With the vegetables you can grow, and some chickens . . .'

'Just a minute, sir!' Harkas interrupted. 'You want us to become farmers? In the middle of the bloody city?'

'Why not?' Vannor's eyes were dancing. 'Do you know how I made my fortune? With vision. I dared to think differently from my fellows; to do things that got me accused of insanity by my family and friends – but, by all the gods, it worked. Vision, that's what you need, lads. Imagination.'

'And money!' Harkas snorted, before Jarvas could stop him.

Vannor had grinned, then. 'Don't worry about the money, Harkas – I'll see you have enough to get started.'

The merchant turned to Jarvas, and clouted him on the

176

shoulder. 'You impressed me, lad, while you were working for me, and though it pains me to lose a good foreman, you deserve to make something of your life. Besides, I'm intrigued by the possibilities of this place. Call it an indefinite loan . . .' His face grew thoughtful. 'With one condition. This place is too big for you, even with your families – don't look like that, Jarvas; you'll find someone someday – and putting it right is more than you can manage on your own.'

Vannor looked at the brothers. 'Have you seen how the poor suffer in this city? And their only recourse, if they sink too low, is bonding.' He scowled. 'It seems I can't put an end to it – but maybe there's a way around it. If the poor had somewhere to go, where they could be safe and supported, until they worked out some kind of future . . .'

Jarvas had leapt on the idea. 'Yes, by all the gods! They could help us grow things, and get the place straight – and do odd jobs in the city so we can buy what we can't grow. In those warehouses, there'd be space for dozens of families. Vannor, it's brilliant!'

The pragmatic Harkas had taken more persuading, but eventually Vannor's dream had taken shape. The brothers' seemingly useless bequest had been turned into a fortress; secure, inviolable – a self-contained smallholding within the city walls, with food and shelter, and the promise of a future. A place where there was a welcome for the lost, the homeless, the destitute and the desperate . . .

Jarvas felt his throat tighten with grief. Of three men who had set that dream in motion, he was the only one left. Vannor had vanished on the Night of the Wraiths – only to turn up, quite unexpectedly, leading the rebels who were sworn to end the rule of the evil Archmage. Jarvas and his brother had helped as they could with food and such, until the rebel base in the sewers had been attacked by Miathan's mercenaries, who had replaced the City Guard. Angos, their captain, claimed that the rebels had been wiped out to a man. Certainly their base was gutted and empty – Jarvas had checked.

Following the shock of Vannor's loss, Harkas had been taken – one of the mysterious 'disappearances' that were striking terror into the hearts of the citizens of Nexis. He had been on one of his usual nightly errands, collecting spoiled food, an increasingly scarce commodity in the city nowadays, for his beloved pigs. He had never returned. Those who had vanished were taken to the Academy – that much was known – but it was wise not to ask too many questions. Those who had tried had vanished in their turn.

Thanks to the Mageborn, two good men were lost for ever, and only the grieving Jarvas was left to carry on their work – and how long would it be before the hand of the Archmage stretched out to him? In the meantime, the Dog was one of his recruiting-places – as good a one as any. That was why he came here, night after night, to welcome the needy into his own special kingdom.

The Drunken Dog was not the sort of place that Hargorn would normally have chosen – to drink in a rat-hole like the Dog was simply asking for trouble – but the swordsman was past the point of caring. He'd been working his way down through the town, stopping at every tavern to pick up information for the rebels on what was happening in the city – and, more important, any word that might lead him to Vannor or his missing daughter. Now he was running short of options – not to mention silver with which to pay his way. Vannor's meagre supply of coin had not lasted long. At least this festering cesspit ought to be cheap, the veteran thought, as he stepped inside.

The fire and a scattering of feeble rushlights afforded the only illumination, but the fetid gloom of the taproom was a blessing in a way; for shadows hid the unwashed tankards, the cobwebs that festooned the low rafters, the splintered tables, the stained and knife-scarred walls. The smoky dimness also drew a merciful veil over the drinkers – for this was the roughest alehouse on the quayside, and its customers were rougher still.

In the absolute silence that followed his entrance, Hargorn glowered fiercely around the occupants of the crowded taproom, and fingered the hilt of his sword in what he hoped was a threatening manner. It usually was the best way to forestall any trouble, and, as he had expected, the talk started

178

up again very quickly as everyone suddenly rediscovered an interest in whatever they had been doing.

The soldier suppressed a smile. It never failed, he thought. Why buy trouble? He knew these folk – he'd met their like in every town he had ever seen in his wanderings. They were the scum of the city – dockhands, porters and scavengers; beggars, pilferers, and pickpockets; faded, ageing whores both male and female. Their squalid lives left them few expectations; the Dog was warmer than the quayside; it was marginally safer than the narrow, unlit alleys where a man's life was worth a copper or two, and a woman's virtue, nothing at all. The sour, watered ale was cheap, and the home-made grog – foul-tasting, but with a kick like liquid fire, as Hargorn soon discovered – was cheaper still. What more can they ask for? the warrior thought bitterly. What more could anyone want?

What more indeed? I know what I want, Hargorn thought ruefully. I want to find out what the blazes has happened to Vannor. It had been many days since they had entered the city, and then split up at the merchant's insistence. The veteran had told him over and over that it was a mistake, but Vannor, distraught over his wayward daughter's disappearance, had refused to listen to a single word of sense. 'We can find her far more quickly if we divide our efforts,' he had argued – and finally, when Hargorn had least been expecting it, had slipped away without trace into the labyrinths of the northern docks.

'The bloody fool,' Hargorn muttered to himself as he bought another flagon of cheap brown dishwater from the sour, pinch-faced little runt of a serving man. He would have preferred more of the grog, but ale would last him longer. Once this silver was gone, there would be no more – not in Nexis, at any rate. Word would be out on him now. Once Vannor's coin had been used up, he had taken service as a private guard for Guildsman Pendral – a fat, tight-fisted, money-grabbing little bastard with some very perverted habits, who had been one of the many merchants who had allied himself with Miathan's cause, in order to screw a quick profit out of the poor suffering folk of the city while there was still a profit to be had.

Hargorn sighed. I make a lousy spy, he thought. Vannor should have sent someone with less of a temper and better sense. Keeping his mouth shut in the face of Pendral's obscene greed had proved to be more than the warrior could stand, and he had taken to drowning his sorrows more than he ought, given his perilous situation. The last thing he needed was to draw attention to himself – but today Pendral had turned him off for being drunk while guarding a warehouse, and the insults of that arrogant lump of lard had been more than the veteran could take. Admittedly, it had probably been a mistake to dump the little turd headfirst into that midden, but . . . For a moment, Hargorn's black mood was lightened by a grin. By all the gods, it had been worth it!

To Tilda, on a raw black winter's night, the tavern seemed like a dream of comfort. Business, bad since the Archmage had taken control of the city, was slacker than usual tonight, for the filthy weather meant that few folk were out and about. The twisting, narrow streets of Nexis were shrouded in a thick, freezing fog that caught in her throat and set off the hacking cough that had dogged her all winter. Enough was enough, Tilda had decided – why freeze your backside off on a draughty corner for nothing?

On reaching the Drunken Dog the whore paused in the doorway to straighten the dripping hems of her petticoats and fluff out her damp, red-dyed curls. She'd be mad to ply for trade in the Dog. It was Dellie's patch, and Dellie was a mate – who wouldn't think twice about flattening her if business was involved. Still, in this trade, it always paid to be prepared. Sometimes, you just fell lucky . . . And as an ageing street-walker with a ten-year-old son to support, she needed all the luck she could get.

As soon as she entered, Tilda knew it wasn't going to be her lucky night after all. Evidently, she had not been the only streetwalker in Nexis to tire of the miserable weather – it looked as though the Dog was playing host to every drab and catamite in town. For a single evening, a truce had been declared, and many of the whores were chatting companionably around the tables, making the most of a rare hour's relaxation. If only it could always be like this, Tilda thought.

We're all in the same boat; we should be mates. But she knew better than to waste time on such daft ideas. They all had to live – and competition for customers, even in a city like Nexis, was fierce.

Tilda was forced to squeeze her way to the tables through the tight-packed crowd. In addition to the whores and regulars, a group of bargemen were playing dice near the fire, and she glimpsed a shadowy movement in the darkest corner, and heard the low hum of murmured talk. Tilda looked away quickly. After years on the streets, she could tell when something shady was afoot. If you wanted to survive, you had to know when to turn a blind eye.

The most interesting customer, as far as Tilda could see, was a weather-beaten, grey-haired man in a heavy soldier's cloak. He sat alone, blind to everything but his tankard. For a moment, Tilda had hopes – but as she drew near, she saw that his cloak was patched and threadbare, and he was scowling into his ale with an intensity that turned her cold all over. Forget it, she told herself. That kind of trouble, you can do without. Sometimes the soldiers got like that, she knew. All twisted up inside, poor bastards – but after a few drinks they would take it out on whoever was nearest, and once they started there was no stopping them. Gods, a friend of hers had been crippled for life by a drunken soldier. No thanks, mate, she thought, and was about to take her grog to a table near the dice-players, as far away from the glowering warrior as she could get, when suddenly she saw his face light up in the most mischievous of smiles.

How it changed him! Tilda, charmed by that quick, infectious grin, drew nearer to the stranger, her curiosity aroused. Well, it couldn't hurt just to speak to him, surely? 'Sir?' She laid a tentative hand on his arm.

He swung around, an oath on his lips, then turned away as though she had ceased to exist, and went back to glowering into his beer. He rubbed a hand across his eyes in a gesture so abjectly weary that Tilda's heart went out to him. Girl, what are you thinking of? she chided herself. You're as daft as he is. She'd seen grown men crying into their ale before now – it never meant anything. Still, it was worth a try. 'You look like you could use some company,' she said softly. 'Won't I do? Just for tonight?'

This time, the soldier's expression was wistful. 'Ah, lassie!' His voice was slightly slurred with drink. 'You'd do all right and more, but . . .' He shrugged, and, fishing in the pocket of his leather tunic, brought out a few scant coppers. 'Right now, I couldn't even stand you an ale.'

'Oh.' Tilda turned away, oddly disappointed and angry at herself for feeling so. Why, it had been years since she'd thought of a man as a *person*! A living, that was all they were to her, and no more. 'Tilda, you're a fool,' she told herself fiercely. 'Don't you dare go soft on me now!' She turned towards the dice-players instead, but they had pocketed their winnings and left while she'd been wasting her time on some penniless stranger. 'A pox on all bloody soldiers,' Tilda muttered. Well, she might as well go – she couldn't afford to buy herself another drink.

At that moment the tavern door banged open in a swirl of evil-smelling fog, and a dozen or so of the mercenaries who had replaced the original City Guard came hurtling into the room, followed by an obese, squint-eyed little man in the gold-stitched robes of a merchant. 'There he is!' he squeaked, pointing at Tilda's stranger. 'That's the man who tried to drown me. Arrest the blackguard at once!'

There was a thunderstruck silence in the taproom as Guildsman Pendral gave orders to his troops. At a curt nod from their captain, the guardsmen fanned out to approach the soldier. It reminded Tilda of a hideous scene she had once witnessed in the ramshackle slums, when a pack of street-curs had stalked and slain a helpless child. But this was no helpless child. With a steely rasp, the warrior drew his sword as he rose unsteadily to his feet.

Tilda noticed, out of the corner of her eye, a general movement towards the tavern's back door, as the skulkers in the corner sneaked away. The room emptied as if by magic – even the serving man had made himself scarce. The swords-man was plainly outnumbered. Not wanting to share his fate, Tilda thought it wise to make her own escape, while the guards were distracted. Quietly, she slipped out of her chair, and began to creep towards the door.

She had never intended to look back – but despite her instincts of self preservation, her eyes were drawn towards the unfolding scene. The guardsmen gathered themselves and rushed forward. Their swords crashed down – to embed themselves in the table in a deluge of ale as the stranger ducked and rolled, taking two of his assailants down in a tangle of arms and legs. Tilda gathered her skirts to run, but a shriek of agony stopped her in her tracks. One of the soldier's opponents rolled screaming on the floor, a knife in his belly. Tilda gasped. Who was this man? Even drunk, his movements had been almost too quick for her to follow.

He had obviously scared the others. No one wanted to be the first to approach him. The remaining guards merged in a loose semicircle around the stranger, who stood at bay with his back to the serving hatch. 'Well?' he taunted them. 'Which one of you bastards wants to be next?'

It was a standoff – the soldier seemed drunk, but after the speed of his reactions Tilda doubted it. Then she saw the serving man – a flicker of shadowy movement behind the hatch – holding a short sword in his hand. He lurked behind the stranger, prepared to do the guardmen's work for them; hoping, no doubt, for a reward. He raised his arm . . .

'Behind you!' Tilda yelled. The stranger dodged barely in time. The sword caught him a glancing blow on the side of the head, and crashed down to knock splinters out of the bar as its intended victim spun away, vanishing from sight as the guards closed in on him. By that time, Tilda had problems of her own. She had done the one thing she'd sworn not to do – attracted attention to herself. Hands grabbed her from behind, pulling her arms behind her back.

'Obstruct the City Guard, would you? You're under arrest, bitch!' The voice was harsh in her ear, followed by a glob of saliva that struck the side of her face and trickled, warm and slimy, down her cheek. Her arms were wrenched until she cried out with pain – then there was a sudden movement in the corner of her eye and the sound of a fist crunching into bone. The grip on her arms loosened, falling away so abruptly that

183

she staggered, and was caught by another pair of arms – gentle, this time, and supportive. Tilda looked up into the ugliest face she had ever seen.

'Jarvas!' she gasped thankfully. Her captor had staggered back, choking, with blood spurting between the fingers of the hands that were clasped across his face.

'That one won't be hurting any more women for a while.' As he spoke, Jarvas guided her to a stool in the safety of the corner. Tilda watched, open-mouthed, as he seized a heavy branch from the woodpile by the fire and waded into the fray.

The stranger was still holding his own, but barely. Blood poured from a headwound, where his left ear had almost been severed, and trickled down his ribs, staining his stout leather jacket. Though the fight had moved across the room, he was still at bay, with his back to a corner, but the guards – a dozen or so – were closing in on him, and Tilda could see that he was weakening. Already he was glassy-eyed and reeling, and at any moment . . .

Then Jarvas was among the guardsmen, wielding his sturdy bough in great, two-handed sweeps. The outermost guards, unaware that the flailing giant was descending on them, simply crumpled beneath the impact of his blows. The others turned, their swords upraised to make short work of this madman who dared accost them with only a branch against their long steel blades. It was a mistake. Seeing help at hand, the stranger seemed to find new strength. With a wild yell, he was on them, fighting like a dervish.

Jarvas was a man possessed, cracking his bough against arms and faces, dodging sword-thrusts, and wreaking havoc among the guards. It looked, against all the odds, as though the mismatched pair were going to pull off a victory between them, when Tilda saw the fat toad of a merchant who had started all this trouble creeping to the door, obviously going for help. The excitement of the fight had gone to Tilda's head. Without stopping to think, she picked up her stool and crept up behind Pendral to crack him hard across the back of the head. The flimsy wood splintered on impact, but the fat man went down like a felled tree. Tilda whooped with excitement. Thoroughly roused, she grabbed another stool and advanced on the

184

remaining guards, waiting until their backs were turned then clouting them.

It was easy – until the guards began to realize that their assailant was not a giant or a warrior, but a small and inexperienced woman. As one, they started to move in on her. Tilda backed away, cold inside with the knowledge that she had bitten off more than she could swallow.

'What in god's name do you think you're doing?' A strong arm wrenched her sideways as a blade came whistling down where she'd been standing. 'Get back, you idiot, and keep out of the bloody way!' Jarvas hurled her aside so hard that she fell, and brought his cracked and shortened cudgel crashing down on the wrist of the man who had attacked her. Tilda picked herself up with an oath, rubbing at bruises; grateful for her rescue, but absurdly annoyed that he had been so rough and slighting. *I was doing all right until then,* she thought angrily. *I'll show him!* She looked around for another stool, but the fight was already over. The stranger grinned at Jarvas over a pile of bodies. 'Good fight'!' he said, and crumpled.

'Oh, bollocks,' Jarvas said. 'Can you help me . . .' he frowned for a moment, then his face cleared. 'Tilda, isn't it? I'll have to take him home. It won't be safe for us on the streets tonight once word of this gets out.' He paused, looking down at her. 'I'm afraid that also means you, girl – you should have run when you had the chance. Now you're in this as deep as us.'

Tilda went cold all over. 'I can't go with you,' she protested, not wanting to accept the greater import of his words. 'What about my son? He needs me. Besides, I've got a living to make.'

Jarvas looked at her gravely and shook his head. 'Not in Nexis,' he told her. 'Not any more.'

13
Incondor's Lament

The great cat limped across the shattered rocks of the valley, her faltering feet trailing smears of blood across the cruel stones. Her massive form, dwarfed by the desolate immensity of the mountains, seemed pitifully frail to Anvar; her protruding ribs cast stripes of light and shade across the dull matted coat that hung on her sunken flanks. Her muzzle, where her teeth were clenched grimly around the Staff of Earth, was covered in blisters and scabs, and saliva hung from her jaw in thick slimy strands.

'Shia! Great gods, Shia!' Anvar cried aloud, unable to bear the sight of the great cat's suffering.

She glanced up at him, her yellow eyes dull and glazed. 'What do you want?' she said briefly, without a pause in her painful, monotonous plodding.

'Shia! Where are you? Are you all right? Dear gods, what happened to you?'

The great cat snarled around her mouthful of Staff. 'Do I *look* all right?' she snorted. 'To answer your other stupid question – what happened to me is that this thing I'm carrying is trying to kill me by slow degrees – but it won't succeed, whatever it thinks. And it does think – though not in the usual sense. The process is more like instinct – since I cannot wield it, it tries to destroy me. You Magefolk should know about that.' She staggered, grunting with pain, and began to speak again as she resumed her weary pacing. 'As to where I am – I'm on my way. Aurian asked me to bring this wretched object to you, so that you can escape Aerillia and go to her aid . . .'

The valley seemed to be filling with silvery mist that streamed along its floor like a relentless tide. Anvar was losing Shia . . . She was vanishing before his eyes . . .

'What are you doing here, anyway?' she snapped. 'Stop this

186

nonsense at once and get back into your body. A fine fool I'll look if I drag this horrendous thing all the way to Aerillia and you're dead. Don't you dare let Aurian down that way. She needs you . . .'

Shia and the valley were gone. All that remained was the clinging, silvery fog . . . which cleared to show him Aurian, huddled by the fire in the squalid little upper room in the Tower of Incondor, the weary droop of her shoulders betokening utter dejection. Anvar's heart went out to her. 'Aurian,' he called, longing to comfort her, but without her powers she could not hear him. After a time, she lifted her head, blinking, and he saw the yellowing bruises on her face, left by Miathan's hand. Rage boiled within him. It was vital that he escape and rescue her – but how? What had Shia said? *Get back into your body . . . If I drag this horrendous thing all the way to Aerillia and you're dead . . .*

Anvar gasped. 'Is that what's happening to me? But I can't die now!' Frantic, he blundered through the viscous fog, seeking a way back to his body; more panic-stricken with each moment that passed. *Help me, someone – oh, gods, I can't get out . . . Help me, please . . .*

'Come on, lad – brace up.' That gruff, gentle voice, with its memories of reassurance and long-ago kindnesses, cut through Anvar's fear; warming his heart and stiffening his resolve like a draught of strong spirits. Anvar's terror vanished as fierce joy exploded through him. 'Forral! But you're . . .'

'Yes, I am dead – and so are you, pretty nearly, which is why I can reach you.'

Anvar could almost see him now – the glimpse of a broad, shadowy figure through the swirling mists; the ghostly glimmer that could only be that quick, flashing smile.

'Come on, lad, we must get you back quick, before they find out what I'm up to. I'm not supposed to be doing this, you know!' There it was – that familiar wicked chuckle. Anvar did not have to see Forral to know that the old twinkle was back in his eyes – just as it used to be when he and Vannor had done something to outwit the Archmage. A calloused hand engulfed his own. How can I feel this, if we're supposed to be dead? the Mage thought wildly.

187

There was a whirling sensation, and Anvar found himself back in the cave, looking down at his own grey face, pinched and gleaming with fever. His body was twisting fretfully beneath the furs, and a white-winged figure knelt over him, frowning, one hand on his heart.

'Better get in there quick – you don't have long,' Forral's voice advised him. Though he could not see the swordsman, Anvar felt the pressure of arms around his shoulders, embracing him hard. Forral's voice was pleading: 'For the sake of all the gods, lad, take care of Aurian.'

Anvar's head throbbed, and his mouth was dry and foul. He felt queasy, and his body ached as though he had been brawling. It was only when he tried to struggle upright that he saw the low, fanged roof of the cavern, and the youthful, fine-boned face that frowned down at him beneath a mass of snowy, silken hair. The figure was cloaked in folded white wings, and beyond him, at the cavern's entrance, stood an armed guard clad in black.

'What . . .' Anvar's mouth was so dry that the word stuck in his throat. His chest was constricted, and he could only breathe in shallow gasps. He coughed, and pain knifed through his ribs. A cup pressed to his lips, and he felt his head supported by a bony arm. Anvar drank eagerly, choking, not thinking beyond the needs of the moment until his dreadful thirst had been eased. He opened his mouth to speak again, but was interrupted.

'Hush, now. Save your strength. You were fevered, from your journey here, and privations you had undergone before.' The winged man frowned, suddenly seeming older. 'The contagion settled in your lungs,' he went on. 'You were a feather's fall from walking the paths of the sky . . .'

Anvar shuddered. No matter how you put it, he thought, dead is still dead. Something was nagging at the back of his mind, but the Skyman was speaking again, driving all thought away. 'I must leave now,' he was saying, 'but I have built up the fire, and there is broth by the side of it, and wood to hand. At all costs, you must keep warm. There is medicine in this flask for your cough. I will return when I can,' he added, and with that he was gone, leaving Anvar gaping after him.

188

There was pain, and only pain. It encompassed her entire world. Raven lay crushed beneath the fearful weight and burden of the pain that rolled over her in pulsing waves. She opened her eyes to see the leg of her night table, a section of floor – and blood – so much blood – spattered over every surface that her tiny circle of vision could encompass. Clumps of mangled black feathers were embedded in the sticky mass, and tiny splinters of bone. Raven retched, and shrank from the sight, and the movement flayed her nerves with knives of fire as she tried to will herself back into unconsciousness, to escape the memory of blows pounding down on her; the agony of torn flesh and shattered bone. Oblivion had been welcome, then. Wishing for death, she had embraced the darkness as once she had embraced Harihn. A self-mocking laugh, as bitter as bile, bubbled in Raven's throat, and she flinched from the pain of it. Blacktalon had played her for a fool. He had duped her again. Given the refined cruelty of his nature, she should have known that death had been the last thing he had in mind for her. The last, no doubt, in a long line of torments.

But no torment could be worse than this fate, which had led Incondor to bitter ruin. She would never fly again. The free exhilaration of the skies was denied her for ever. Oh, but that blackguard of a priest was cunning! In wedding her, he might seize power as her consort, but she would still be queen, and always a threat to him. He could scarcely have kept her imprisoned – she and her mother must still have supporters within the Citadel. This way, however, he would have it all. She was the last of Flamewing's line, but crippled like this she would never be permitted to rule. It was against the law of her people. As long as Blacktalon could get a child on her, he could spend a lifetime as regent to a puppet heir. And to keep the royal line alive, her people would permit it. At that point, of course, she herself would become dispensable, unless he decided to keep her alive for his own amusement.

Raven shuddered. Live? As a cripple; an object of derision, or worse yet, of pity? And then it came to her, and her laugh – a real laugh of triumph this time – shrilled through the deserted room. Oh, but she could beat him yet – and how sweet it would be, to fulfill her only remaining desire while thwarting her enemy.

Even the smallest movement seemed to take for ever. *Oh mother, it hurts! Make it stop!* The room began to fade around her, and Raven bit her lip, blinking hard and breathing as deeply as she dared, until her vision came back into focus. In the background, she could hear the keening of the wind in the spires of the temple. Incondor's Lament, her folk called that sound. The nightmare edifice of the temple had been built to mark his fall – and his fate.

Incondor's Lament . . . Now Raven understood the anguish of a soul tormented that lay within that frightful sound. With dreamy detachment she watched her hand – a white spider streaked with rusty blood – as it crept, inch by painful inch, towards the spindly leg of the night table. At last the fingers touched, then circled, the smooth, cold metal. Good. The legs had always been unbalanced – she remembered nagging her mother to get it fixed. Raven braced herself and clenched her teeth. Don't pass out! she harangued herself. Princess of the Skyfolk, don't you dare pass out. Then, as sharply as she could, she pulled.

The shriek exploded against her clenched teeth; emerged as a whimper which was drowned by a crash of splintering crystal that receded as everything went black. *Blast you, Raven, don't pass out!* Somehow, the princess clawed herself back from the brink of the abyss by muttering every oath she had learned from Aurian, until the pain had reached the point of merely unbearable. She opened her eyes again. And there it was. The cup of her crystal goblet had splintered into shards, but the thicker stem had snapped off intact, as she had hoped, leaving a jagged, pointed edge.

She had wanted to drive it into her breast. But as she lay there, shaking, every muscle and bone unstrung, Raven knew she would not have the strength. Besides, the hearts of the Winged Folk were hard to find; protected as they were by the great, keeled breastbone that served to anchor the muscles of the mighty wings.

Oh, Father of Skies – why did they take my wings? At last, Raven permitted tears to escape her, for the glories she would never know again. The exhilaration of the hunt; soaring over endless changing cloudscapes; swooping through drifts of coldest grey to see the majestic mountains wheel below . . . And the light! The pure, lambent hues, that changed each hour of the day . . .

Drunk on the glory of a long-forgotten sunset, Raven groped for the broken stem of the goblet and gouged the jagged crystal across the veins of her outstretched arm . . .

Cygnus sat reading, perched on the solitary stool in his tiny cell in the vaults below the Temple of Yinze. At least, he was trying to read. The wind was still high, and the screeching wail from the spires above could easily penetrate the ells of solid rock that stood between the young physician-priest and the source of the appalling sound. Cygnus groaned, though the sound went unheard against the general background din. Incondor's accursed Lament! Not only was it interfering with his concentration, but the eerie howls had been setting his teeth on edge for some time. Much more of this, he thought, and I'll bid fair to lose my mind. Blackest heresy though it might seem, Cygnus wished that the creator of the temple might have considered the poor priests who had to live below.

Apart from the torture of the Lament, the young physician-priest had too much on his mind to concentrate. The chief physician Elster had also attended the queen in her last illness, and Cygnus knew that she must have recognized the effects of the poison he had given Flamewing on Blacktalon's orders. Only Elster's savage glare and her iron grip digging into the bones of his wrist had let slip the fact that she knew what he had done – yet the depth of his respect for his old teacher had prevented him from blurting out the truth and betraying her. It would have meant the death of his aged mentor – Blacktalon's spies were all over the Citadel, and he had ears in every room.

It was Elster who had been responsible for Cygnus eschewing his career as a temple guard for the path of light, as the Winged Folk called the pursuit of the healing arts. With a single act, the master physician had changed his life for ever. Cygnus, in those days, had been the carefree scion of a prominent family, blessed with a light-hearted spirit and quickness of both body and mind. As was to be expected in the caste-ridden society of the Skyfolk, he joined the Syntagma, the elite warrior guard of the priesthood, and had prospered – until the day he had almost caused the death of Sunfeather, his closest friend.

The accident took place during a training exercise, in a violent midair collision that was entirely the fault of his own inattention. Cygnus, with the airspace in which to correct his flailing spin, escaped the penalty of his carelessness. Sun feather, already unconscious from the collision, had plunged straight into the mountainside. Stricken beyond words, Cygnus had joined the sombre knot of his cohorts gathered round the victim, in time to see his friend stop breathing. It was then that Master Elster had appeared. Fragile, aged, and dishevelled from her hasty summoning, Elster had quickly cleared a path through the crowd with a few brisk words. Her frowning, fine-boned face was webbed with wrinkles beneath a mass of silken hair that was dramatically streaked in mingled black and white. Her bony, angular figure was cloaked in folded wings with pied and boldly patterned plumage. Cygnus, with an increasing sense of disbelief, watched awestruck as she smote Sunfeather's chest and breathed into his lungs her own breath of life, until his friend was breathing for himself once more.

Sunfeather survived that fall, and to Cygnus it seemed a miracle. Not only had Elster spared him much grief, but she had also freed him from the burden of a lifetime's guilt. His admiration for the elderly physician was little short of worship. How had she achieved the miracle of bringing the dead back to life? Suddenly, it seemed to Cygnus a far more worthy deed to save lives, rather than to take them, as he had been trained to do.

It had taken longer to convince Elster that he was serious in his newfound ambition. Only when he had resigned his post in the Syntagma, and had consequently been cast out by his family, did she finally and grudgingly agree to take him on as her apprentice. She was certain that he would never endure the long years of arduous and complex training. Cygnus had set out to prove her wrong, winning her admiration and affection in the process – until, with the coming of the fell winter, he had abandoned her for another, more sinister mentor.

When the White Death closed its jaws around their mountains, the Winged Folk began to perish. All around the beleaguered Cygnus, the population of Aerillia succumbed to slow lingering deaths from cold, disease and privation. The young physician could not defeat the monster – all the arts in which he had taken such pride were powerless against it. Cygnus began to doubt himself and his skills, and the futility of all his actions closed over him, leaving his spirit adrift in a sea of darkness.

Drowning in a morass of bitterness and despair, Cygnus clutched in desperation at the last, faint spark of hope. Blacktalon and his sacrifices. Because he had nothing left to believe in, Cygnus slowly came to accept the notion that if the High Priest could somehow restore the lost magical powers of the winged race, then at last it would be possible to perform the legendary feats of healing described in the ancient annals. Reluctantly at first, but with increasing willingness, he had come to accept Blacktalon's tenets – and methods of achieving his ends.

It had been some time now since Cygnus had thrown his energies behind Blacktalon's ruthless, ambitious schemes, but by Yinze, Flamewing's death had sickened him! She had fought for existence tooth and talon, incurring in her stubbornness much suffering that she might otherwise have been spared. Cygnus remembered her, black-faced and vomiting, choking for air; her limbs twisted and convulsed almost to breaking with her dreadful agony. And yet she had still found the strength from some inner depths of endurance to curse Blacktalon with her very last breath.

Later that night, in the confusion that attended the death of a queen, he had slipped away, flying in the snarling face of a newly returned storm, until he was safely far from Aerillia. There, shivering on a lonely pinnacle, he had finally begun to question his involvement with the High Priest – yet now, after the many days that had passed since that terrible night, he still had no answer to the promptings of his conscience.

Cygnus frowned. Despite Blacktalon's attempts to eradicate

it, rumour was always rife within the Citadel. The tale of the captive sorcerer – and of his mate who was imprisoned in the Tower of Incondor – must have first been spread by those who had assisted in their capture. None the less, Cygnus had been shocked beyond speech when Master Elster, in a tremendous hurry, had appeared in his chambers to tell him he was needed to attend the prisoner. 'I'd go myself,' the old physician added coldly, 'but the High Priest has forbidden it.' Her pied wings, with their intricate feathered fan-patterns of crisp white and shimmering blue-green-black, were half raised in anger as she darted the young man a significant glance beneath her shaggy white-streaked brows. 'In any case, do what you can.' Another pointed glare. The young man's breath had frozen in his throat. Elster's disapproval was tangible, and it still hurt him to think he had failed her.

Well, Cygnus had done his best for his old teacher. Squirming under his burden of guilt, he had reported back to Blacktalon that the prisoner's illness was beyond his own poor skills, and that Elster would be needed. It was the best he could do to ensure her safety, for since the death of the queen he had been concerned about her fate. Who knew what might happen to her if she started questioning Flamewing's demise?

Cygnus jumped as the door to his cell crashed open, and an ashen-faced temple guard appeared. 'Come quick,' he shouted, dragging the physician off his stool. 'The princess . . . Master Elster needs your urgent assistance!'

Cygnus could have wept when he saw Raven lying, tiny and frail and so alone somehow, in the gore-splattered chamber. Her skin had a ghastly pallor; her left forearm bore a ragged, gaping gash. And her wings – oh, Father of Skies – were a crumpled, mangled wreckage of bloody feather and bone. The murderous urge to take hold of the High Priest and twist his scrawny, wrinkled neck overwhelmed Cygnus.

'Pull yourself together! I can't keep this tourniquet on much longer.' Elster's terse words were like a drench of icy water in his face. 'Help me lift her. We must do our moving and manipulating while she's senseless.' The physician's voice was all brisk business, but one glance at her set, grey-tinged face

194

told Cygnus that Elster really needed to go straight to the window and vomit.

To the relief of the young physician, the girl made no sound as they moved her to her bed. 'Cover her as well as you can,' Elster muttered, frowning at the injured arm. 'Shock and blood-loss are our chief foes – she must be kept warm.' She gestured at the small brazier that she used to boil water for her needles and blades. 'Stoke that as best you can – it won't put out much heat, but . . .' She probed at Raven's ragged wound. 'Normally, I'd let you deal with this, but she made a dreadful mess of these veins, and time is of the essence.'

Cygnus straightened up from feeding wood into the tiny stove, his eyes wide with horror. 'The princess tried to take her own life?'

'What do you think?' Elster was flushing out the wound with a cleansing infusion. 'Look what those brutes have done to her wings.' Her hands had always been the steady hands of a master and a surgeon. Cygnus had never seen them shake before. Elster took a deep breath. 'Besides, she is not the princess, but the queen – and we'd do well to bear that in mind as we work,' she added waspishly. Like a true master, Elster had herself back under control. Cygnus wished he could have said the same for himself.

'Now . . .' Elster murmured, bending low over Raven's arm. 'Cygnus, will you be so good as to start cleaning up those wings before the poor girl wakes? Take the greatest care to piece together all that remains. The queen may never fly again, but cast me from the top of Yinze's temple if I'll amputate! The poor child has been mutilated enough.'

Cygnus could bear no more. The thought of one of the Skyfolk – the very queen – bearing two mangled stumps instead of her wings, was enough to finish him. At least he made it to the window before he started vomiting.

'Come on, boy! Are you a physician or not?' Elster barked. Cygnus made a superhuman effort to pull himself together. He took a long swig from the Master's waterskin, poured some of the cleansing infusion into a bowl to wash his hands, and bent grimly to the grisly, painstaking work of piecing together Raven's shattered wings.

*

'Well done, boy! I couldn't have done a neater job myself.'
Cygnus blinked, wiped sweat from his brow, and looked up – or
tried to. His neck and back seemed to have frozen in position.
Someone had filled his eyes with boiling sand, and his aching
fingers were rigid with cramp. A host of candles and small oil
lamps were burning around him, their twinkling flames
dancing in the gloom of a room gone dark; and outside the
window the sky was the rich and vivid blue of almost-night.
Then, with a jolt of shock, he realized that it was not dark, but
dawn!

The crack of his bones as he stretched was like the snapping
of kindling. Elster, red-eyed and haggard of face, was beaming
down at him, and gesturing at the wing that was stretched out
before him. Cygnus looked at it, shaking his head in disbelief,
and suddenly his weariness was forced aside by an expanding
glow of pride and satisfaction. Father of Skies, he marvelled.
Did I really do that? What had been a mangled mass of bloody
feathers and bone looked like a wing again; the major skeletal
framework firmly splinted; the fragile bones that supported the
structure of the pinions pierced together like a fledgeling's
puzzle and held in position by an intricate framework of
slender spills of wood – the lightest he could devise. Damaged
muscle and torn skin had been stretched back into place and
secured with hundreds of tiny stitches.

The wing looked like a wing again – almost. Cygnus,
thinking back over his handiwork, remembered bones chipped
and splintered beyond repair, and pieces never found. Slippery
curls of tendon that could not be reattached and muscles that
would be for ever weak, if they worked at all. Whether
circulation had been restored to the wings through the
damaged vessels, only time would tell. His painstaking work
might still have gone for nought. Cygnus felt his glow of
satisfaction wither to ash within him, and turned away with an
oath. 'What difference does it make in the end?' he said bitterly.
'She will never fly again.'

Elster, who had been completing a similar miracle of
restoration on the other wing, sighed. 'That's right,' she said
mildly. 'We might as well have saved our time and just hacked

196

the useless things off in the first place. The queen is crippled already – what difference will it make to her if she is deformed?'

Cygnus felt his face grew hot with shame. 'I never thought of that,' he confessed.

Elster raised an eyebrow. 'Ah, but that is why I am the Master and you are not. There are two things that the true physician must never be without. Skill, and compassion. Always compassion.'

Cygnus nodded, accepting the wisdom of Elster's words. 'But, Master,' he continued weakly, 'what will happen when she wakes and discovers the truth?'

Elster ran a distracted hand through her black-and-white streaked hair, and gestured bleakly at the bandage on Raven's arm. 'You think she does not know already?'

Cygnus nodded. 'I guessed as much. All the time I was working on that wing, I was thinking: What if it were me? And I knew then, that, in the queen's position, denied the skies for ever, I would have no desire to live. And it seemed to me that to save her life I *had* to fix that wing so that it could be used again, or it was all in vain.'

The master put an arm around his shoulders. 'I know,' she said gently. 'I watched you, as I worked – labouring on those tiny fragments with such determination on your face – and I bled inside for the grief that you must face. But all physicians, soon or late, come to this pass, where the best they can do will not suffice. My boy, only Yinze himself could make her fly again. It would have been kinder by far to have simply let her die where she lay, as she most surely wished. But she may not.' Her voice grew hard. 'Now that Flamewing is dead, that frail, crippled little girl is the queen – and she will be needed, if . . .' With a gasp, she caught herself up quickly. 'If our folk are to have a ruler. Unfortunately, someone must make her see that – and the task will fall to us.'

Cygnus opened his mouth, but after the murder of Flamewing and the mutilation of her daughter, he could find nothing to say. Though he had been acting under Blacktalon's orders, Flamewing's blood was on his hands. It was entirely due to his actions that Raven must live as she was: motherless, crippled – and queen.

197

Suddenly the sight of Raven's mutilated body vanished behind a blur of tears. Cygnus buried his face in shaking hands. 'I'm sorry,' he whispered. 'Oh, gods, I'm sorry!'

'So you should be sorry – but that isn't good enough.' Elster told him astringently. 'Yinze only knows what possessed you, Cygnus. You, a healer – my most talented pupil – to become involved in such evil. Why, with such skill at your disposal, did you turn to destroying, instead of healing?'

Like floodgates bursting, it all came pouring out of Cygnus – his doubts, his despair, his feelings of inadequacy when the evil winter struck down his people. 'You say I have skill,' he cried bitterly, 'but had I been any use at all, I could have saved them. I failed them, Elster – I failed my people when they needed me! And if my way – the way that you taught me – was no good, then what was left? I was so desperate to accomplish_ *something*, and Blacktalon seemed to hold out the only hope.'

Cygnus looked into Elster's eyes, and saw tears glinting faintly in the drear dawn light. 'Oh, you poor fool,' she whispered. 'Poor blind young fool. Why did you not talk to me, and share your doubts? My dear boy, there is not a healer in the whole of history that has not entertained such dark thoughts at one time or another.' She shook her head. 'There are ills and evils in this world that we cannot heal, for all our wishing – but that is no reason to adopt them.'

It was as though a void had opened beneath the young physician's feet – as though nothing in his world would be solid or secure again. 'I didn't know,' Cygnus whispered. 'Master, I didn't dare share my doubts with you. You were so reluctant to accept me at first. I didn't know you'd understand.'

Cygnus dropped to his knees at her feet, and held out his dagger in a shaking hand. 'Master, I've been an utter fool, and far worse than that.' His voice sounded cracked and distant to his ears. 'Take my life, I beg you, for nothing less will serve as restitution for the wrongs I have done, or wash the stain of evil from my spirit.' Closing his eyes and breathing deeply, he waited for his mentor to take the dagger and end his wretched existence.

'Oh no, my boy – that's very dramatic, but it isn't good enough!' At the sound of Elster's humourless chuckle, the young physician's eyes flew open in shock. Elster plucked the dagger from his limp hand, and with a flick of her wrist sent it flying out of the window. 'Death is too easy a way out – you can damn well live on and suffer, and take responsibility for your deeds like the rest of us.'

Shaking her head, Elster looked sternly down at her gaping pupil. 'A whole lifetime won't be long enough for you to make amends to this poor girl, so you had better start at once.' Pulling a resisting Cygnus to his feet, she looked deep into his eyes. 'That is, supposing you truly wish to make restitution for what you have done.' Her expression hardened. 'Cygnus, if you still feel any remaining shred of loyalty towards the High Priest after his deeds this day, then you should stay away from the queen in future – as far away as possible. I recognize poison when I see it, boy. I know you were responsible for Queen Flamewing's death, and I find intolerable the idea of that poor girl being attended by her mother's murderer. That aside, if you still support Blacktalon after what he has done, then you are unfit to associate with any decent being, let alone the Queen of the Winged Folk.' Elster's eyes burned fiercely.

The young physician, writhing with shame, found himself unable to meet his mentor's gaze. 'I'm done with Blacktalon,' he vowed. 'I'll do whatever you feel is necessary to convince you of that.'

Elster looked at him gravely. 'Brave words, boy, but can you put them into effect?' Her eyes glinted. 'I want you to take care of Queen Raven. Be her constant companion, her comfort, her support. She won't want to live, Cygnus – and so it will be up to you to convince her otherwise.'

Cygnus gasped. 'I cannot! Elster, please, ask something else of me. What can I say to her? I cannot face her, with her mother's blood on my hands.'

'Too bad.' Elster was inexorable. 'The more difficult you find it, the greater your chance of atonement. If you ever find the suffering too much for you, Cygnus, try putting yourself in her place.'

Her brutal words brought Cygnus up short. The chastened young physician bowed his head. 'I'll try, Elster,' he whispered.

'Don't try – do it!' Elster told him brutally. 'That girl's life is in your hands, Cygnus – don't make a mess of things. You've done enough damage already.' She tempered her harsh words with the ghost of a smile for him. 'If it's any consolation, boy, I have faith in you.'

'I can't think why.' Cygnus looked at Raven once more. He took a deep breath, and straightened his shoulders. 'But I promise, Master, that I'll do my best to be worthy of your confidence.'

'Thank Yinze – I have my pupil back.' Elster embraced the young physician. Though she grieved for his pain, she was somewhat reassured by his crisis of conscience. She had long been dismayed by his espousal of Blacktalon's bizarre ambitions, and had been appalled when she had realized his part in the murder of the queen. I ought to hate him, the master thought – but her understanding of Skyfolk nature and the frailty of Skyfolk spirit had persuaded her that matters were not so simple. She was convinced that Cygnus had not fallen irredeemably into evil – and that being the case, if she could save him and bring back his proper sense of values, it was her duty to do so. The thought of all the future good he could do with his skills was enough to make the effort worthwhile – and besides, though she would die rather than admit it, she was fond of him.

Breaking the embrace, Elster held her pupil away from her at arm's length. 'Now, go and eat,' she told him, 'and have something sent up here for me. And at all costs, stay away from Blacktalon until you can keep your feelings from your face. You've done good work tonight, but alas, there is no rest for the physician. Your other patient still awaits you, in the cave below.'

Cygnus gasped. 'I had forgotten the sorcerer!'

'Hush, boy,' Elster cautioned him hastily. 'Not so loud.'

'But, Master, I forgot to tell you.' Cautiously, he lowered his voice. 'I told Blacktalon his illness was beyond my skills, lest the High Priest should decide to kill you after you had seen what happened to Queen Flamewing.'

Elster gasped. 'You were thinking of me?' She was astonished that it should mean so much to her. Sentimental old fool! she scolded herself. Pulling herself together, she turned her attention back to her pupil. 'Is he, then?'

'Is he what?' Cygnus looked baffled.

'Beyond your not inconsiderable skills, of course.'

'No – though for a time I thought otherwise! It was a fever, brought on no doubt by cold and privation, and much mishandling by the temple guards. For a time I despaired of his life, but he is safe now.' For the first time in that long, weary night, Cygnus allowed himself to grin.

Elster returned his smile. 'Go and tend your patient, then. Afterwards, get some rest, then come back here to sit with the Queen, and I will visit our mysterious prisoner.' Her eyebrow lifted. 'Never having seen a human, let along a sorcerer, I must confess to some curiosity. A sorcerer, from distant lands, with powers such as we cannot fathom . . .' She shrugged. 'Oh, never mind. Just remember what he is, and take due care. And for Yinze's sake, boy,' she added in a whisper, 'get him on our side.'

Cygnus nodded. He hesitated, looking down at the Queen. Grief and rage twisted in his guts like a knife. 'Master, will she be all right?'

In that moment, Elster seemed to age so much that the young physician was sorry he had spoken. 'Her body? Yes, it will survive. Her mind? Yinze only knows what will become of that.'

14

Contest of Queens

As Shia picked her tortuous way from the Tower of Incondor, climbing up through the ever-rising chain of valleys that led into the heart of the mountains, the going became harder and harder as the snow grew deeper and the biting cold increased. It was a barren, menacing landscape, with its fanged and looming crags and bottomless, shadowed gorges through which the wind came shrieking like the death-wails of a thousand slaughtered cats.

At first, Shia sometimes found shelter in caves and crevices that afforded some protection from the merciless wind and its stinging burden of snow. She gladly stopped to rest in these havens, making the most of a welcome respite from her ceaseless battle with the mountains. Sometimes she found game – lean snow-hares or ptarmigan, or a cragfast sheep or goat – to ease her relentless hunger. But as the cat went on, shelter became more scarce and the snow piled ever higher on the stony trails and ledges, slowing her to a snail's pace, and making each step a greater torture.

Shia's neck and jaws ached from carrying the Staff of Earth. Its magic burned her, sending currents of prickling power swirling through her body to weaken her, and confuse her instinctive sense of direction. Her mouth, where her jaws clenched around the Staff, had become a mass of blisters and sores, making it harder to hunt and to eat on the rare occasions when prey could be found. Food was scarce and hard to come by on this freezing roof of the world. Day by day, the great cat grew more gaunt and hollow-eyed; a shaggy black scarecrow all skin and bone. Lacking the energy even to think, she hauled herself upward step by step, dragging the Staff in locked and frozen jaws. At night she made snow-nests to conserve her heat, but she never stopped shivering; wishing that Bohan and

202

Anvar were curled up beside her, and that Aurian could hold her close to warm her body with her own.

As time went on, Shia's suffering and wretchedness increased until she imagined she must be dying. Once, as she stumbled along in a kind of waking dream, she thought that Anvar walked by her side, and *he* was dying. None the less, he still found time to ask her a bunch of senseless human questions that irritated her beyond all bearing. She told him in no uncertain terms to cease his foolishness and get back into his body, and seemingly he had – or at least she hoped he had.

When Anvar vanished, Shia's boneless legs collapsed beneath her, and she lay for some time, quivering with shock and wondering if it could be true. Their powers were fey, the Magefolk, and there was no telling what they might do – but one thing was for sure. If Anvar had truly been on the brink of death, then she had only been able to see him because she was in a similar case!

Unclenching her jaws with an effort from around the Staff, Shia looked up at the leaden sky. Dying? But I cannot. I promised Aurian. Black specks were whirling in front of her eyes. Only when a harsh cry drifted down from above did her befuddled brain tell her they were real. Shia felt her heart kick into life within her. Eagles! And if the eagles were circling . . . The great cat picked up the Staff and tottered forward. Her mouth was watering.

Only the gigantic birds' fear of the weirdly glowing Staff permitted her to scatter them so easily. Otherwise, she might have joined the broken, frozen corpse of the sheep as their prey. Shia, wincing at the pain of her blistered jaws, spat out a wisp of oily, draggled wool and worried free a mouthful of icy meat, feeling it melt to a stringy succulence in her mouth. After the first few difficult bites, she felt new energy exploding within her like a fountain of fire, and bent to her meal in earnest, blessing her luck and the stupidity of herbivores who would wander along a narrow ledge in search of a mouthful of greenery and get themselves stuck, unable to either go forward or turn round. Going backwards was apparently beyond them, and they would either panic and fall, or starve in place until they toppled – for which Shia, at the moment, was profoundly thankful. When her shrunken belly had been filled, she found a niche in the broken rocks at the foot of the cliff and dragged the Staff and the remains of the sheep inside, then settled down, with enough food inside her to enable her to withstand the cold, for her first good sleep in days.

As she lost all sensation of where she was, her mind began to drift ... back to her kithood; to her first mating; to the monumental battle that had made her First Female of the Colony ... Back to the day the Khazalim had attacked with bows and spears, and she had sacrificed herself to save her kits and her people ... Back to her captivity, and the days of frustration, anger and hatred; the torment of the Arena ... Back to the fight with Aurian, and the utter relief of finding a mind that could communicate with her own, and the joys of friendship and freedom ...

It was only the thought of her beleaguered companions that kept Shia going in the days that followed. It was vital that she find a way to rescue Anvar, for otherwise Aurian would never escape. Her child would be slain by the Evil One, and she would remain in his power for ever – or be destroyed by him, when she refused to fall in with his plans, as the great cat knew she would.

Shia was torn. She neither knew nor trusted any direct route to the northwest – in that direction, the mountains became higher, steeper, and less and less passable. In truth, that land could only be colonized by Skyfolk, and that was where their population was thickest. For many a long age they had been the bitter enemies of Shia's people – she did not dare to risk going that way. That only left the route she knew, the western pass from the ravaged Steelclaw peak; a more roundabout way, and one that led directly through the central territory of the great cats.

In all her travels with Aurian, Shia had dreamed of going home. Much as she loved her friend and Anvar, she missed her own kind. It was lonely being the only cat. Yet here she was, returning from exile at last, and she could not stay. Oh, she could have forgotten her quest; just dropped the Staff down the nearest chasm – there were plenty of them – and gone on her way; but she could never have lived with herself afterwards.

The chief problem, the cat thought wryly, would lie with her own people. Though the route to Aerillia lay through their lands, they guarded their territory jealously even against the Chuevah – the solitary wanderers of their own species, who did not belong to the Colony.

These pitiful outcasts scraped a lone existence in the mountains, but usually not for long. They were the rejects of the Colony – the weak, the old and, in times of greatest hardship, even the very young. Those who had contested for leadership and been defeated were Chuevah; those who had transgressed against the law of the Colony; those of the lowest degree who had been expelled when times were hard, and food was in short supply. There would be many of those now, Shia thought. This dire, uncanny winter must have brought hardship on the Colony, even as it had crippled the society of the Skyfolk. The casting out of its burdensome members had originally been intended for the common good – a pruning of the weak and useless so that the Colony remained vigorous and strong to survive its harsh surroundings. But perhaps, Shia reflected, the custom had progressed too far. Why, she thought, with a twinge of unpleasant surprise – I am Chuevah now! I too am one of those poor solitary scavengers – I, who once was First.

The great cat knew that, according to the custom of her folk, she would be forced to fight the current First Female in order to win her way through to Anvar – and woe betide her if she failed, for even if she should survive the battle they would not permit her to pass through their lands. And look at me, Shia thought despairingly. Chuevah indeed! Exhausted, half-starved creature that I am – what chance will I have against such a strong opponent – the most powerful female in the Colony?

Shia had been travelling for more than half a moon, skirting carefully around the eastern boundaries of the Skyfolk territory, when she finally reached the highest passes that led over the crown of the northern range. The wind up here was so strong that she could barely keep her footing, and it was snowing so thickly that she could barely see to the ends of her whiskers. The great cat hesitated. Surely no one could come

205

through this and survive? Yet her instincts told her that the storm was steadily sweeping its way down the mountain. There would be no shelter back the way she had come – and she had passed broken ground laced with fissures and sudden drop-offs that would prove lethal to a cat who could not see her path.

'Get moving!' Shia startled herself with the words. 'If you stay here you'll freeze and die, and then what will become of your human friends? Everything depends on you.'

Snow-blind and snow-drunk, the great cat staggered forward, thinking of nothing beyond putting one weary foot before the other. If she could only keep moving, she might stand a chance.

Hours passed in an unchanging nightmare. Step by step, Shia staggered on into the teeth of the storm; not even sure, despite the uphill lie of the land, that she was heading in the right direction. Some buried instinct maintained her hold on the Staff; some lingering sense of self-preservation made her gauge each step carefully, lest she plunge blindly into a crevasse. Beyond that, Shia knew nothing. She was thinking, not of herself or her people, but of Aurian, of Anvar, and of her friend Bohan, who had always understood her without the need for words. For them, Shia kept going, walking a tightrope of life in the midst of conditions that would destroy her if she should falter.

The blizzard ended so abruptly that it took her unawares. Shia had no idea how long she had been ploughing grimly on, her eyes fixed blindly on her trudging feet, urging her weary, frozen body through breast-deep drifts. Suddenly she looked up, blinking rime-encrusted eyes, to discover that the snow had gone, and she could see at last. What was more, she had reached the end of the pass. The truncated, shattered face of the Steelclaw peak and the lands of her people lay before her. When she saw the familiar shape of Steelclaw, Shia's heart turned over in her breast. There were so many memories here. She was home at last, but she was still as much of an exile as ever.

'Hold, stranger!'

Shia froze, one paw uplifted in mid-stride. The sentinels

came bounding out; one from a ledge high on the cliff above the defile; the other from behind a broken, boulder-strewn ridge. She dropped the Staff and sniffed the air, her whiskers angling forward to pick up messages of temperature and the movement of the wind. It would help to know the identity of her opponents.

The two black females, sleek and well muscled, stalked her, bristling, the fur on their backs hackled up to a threatening ridge. One was a stranger to Shia; a youngster, lithe, delicate and wiry, who moved with the lightfooted grace of a dancer. The other, much older, was of stockier build, with powerful shoulders and a thick ruff of hair around her neck, almost like a male. Shia, hiding the surge of joyful recognition that flooded through her, looked the older cat in the eye – a deliberately challenging move. 'Do you not know me, Hreeza? You, my mother's den mate?'

The powerful old cat wrinkled her grey-flecked muzzle and bared her fangs in a snarl. 'My den mate bred well and often. Do you expect me to remember every last stray kit? You could be anyone, stranger.'

'What, you? Forget a kit that you helped to raise?' Shia's ears flattened. 'Don't lie to me, Hreeza – not even to save your own face.'

'Will you let her talk to you like that?' The youngster's eyes were blazing as she addressed Hreeza. 'And what manner of evil thing is that?' She sniffed carefully at the Staff of Earth, careful not to touch its glowing length.

Hreeza turned on her, one paw uplifted in threat. 'Stay out of this,' she hissed. Hesitantly, she advanced towards Shia, and ducked her head to rub faces. 'I never thought to see you again.' Her mental voice was gruff with emotion.

'Nor I you.' Shia was purring with delight, but the older cat was ill at ease, and Shia guessed that the chief cause of Hreeza's wariness was the Staff. Sure enough, her mother's former den mate raised worried eyes to Shia's face.

'What is that thing?' she asked.

Shia did her best to look unconcerned. 'A wretched piece of work, is it not?' she said brightly. 'Human nonsense, of course. Soon it will be gone, Hreeza, I promise you. It need not concern our people. Who is First Female now?' she added softly.

'Gristheena!' The word was a hiss. 'Shia, do you seek to contest the leadership? In your condition?'

Shia gave the mental equivalent of a shrug. 'Why else would I return?'

'Shia, you cannot!'

The great cat sighed – a bad habit she had picked up from her human friends. 'It may not be necessary. I hope it will not, for as you say, I am in no condition to fight. But I have a promise to keep – a debt of honour, to a friend who saved my life. All I need is safe passage through your lands, if Gristheena will consent.'

Hreeza snarled. 'You know she will not. You saved us all from the human hunters, Shia, with your courage and your sacrifice. To Gristheena, you will ever be a rival and a threat – and what better chance for her to finish you than now, while you are in this weak and weary state? Turn back, I beg you, before she finds out you are here.'

'Too late.' Shia's eyes glanced significantly over Hreeza's shoulder. The younger cat had vanished.

Though the vegetation on the lower slopes of Steelclaw had been burned away in the cataclysm that destroyed the peak, a new and vigorous growth had eventually come to take its place. Before this winter, the feet and knees of the mountain had been swathed in lush green skirts of aspen, pine and mountain ash. Dappled deer had sipped from limpid forest pools and salmon had flashed like slips of rainbow through the silver foam of the tumbling streams. The woods had been alive with birdsong, and squirrels had scampered with swift and fluid ease from branch to branch.

Now, Shia could barely recognize the place. Hreeza led her up the mountain between the shattered trunks of frost-cracked trees that leaned like dead black sticks, groaning beneath their burden of snow. The streams and pools were sealed and fettered in a prison of ice. No creatures moved within the stilted, brittle underbrush, or flickered through the straining boughs above. All was silent, still and dead; all colour, all life, all hope, had been throttled by winter's white-mailed fist.

208

There was no need for stealthiness on these lower reaches. No cats hunted here now – what was the point? Shia and Hreeza might have been the only living creatures in the world. Had the great cat ever wavered in her determination to help Aurian and Anvar, all such thoughts had vanished now. Gripping the Staff of Earth more tightly between her jaws, she snarled low in her throat, and vowed vengeance on those who had done this to her land.

The truncated peak of Steelclaw was shattered and pitted into a labyrinth of canyons and caverns. Crevices and channels honeycombed the rock where thick veins of ore had melted and run off in the intense heat of the mountain's destruction. Not that the cats were aware of Steelclaw's troubled history – they simply found the peak a safe and perfect place to rear their young.

Hreeza still dwelt in the same old den – a cavern that looked down into the rock-strewn shadows of a narrow draw – where Shia had been born and raised. As she tottered across the rocky threshold, the memories came flooding back of her mother, Zhera, long dead at the hands of the hunting Skyfolk, and her two siblings, brother and sister, who had both perished in the Khazalim raid that had made Shia a captive. Firmly, the great cat shrugged the memories away. She had no time, now, for such self-indulgence.

Hreeza was digging in a pile of dirt and stones at the back of the den, and emerged within moments, dragging the entire carcass of a mountain goat. 'Here,' she commanded. 'Eat! You have little time.'

Shia looked at the dead goat in startlement, then, at Hreeza's urging, fell upon it ravenously. 'You are well supplied,' she said. 'I feared that, during this winter, there would be hardship for the Colony.'

Hreeza licked at one of Shia's lacerated paws. 'There has been great hardship,' she said harshly. 'Gristheena has made many of our people Chuevah – mostly her own enemies.' She spat. 'In addition, the Winged Folk have attacked us many times, hunting for furs, until only a handful of our folk remain.'

'Then how comes this? A whole goat?' Shia indicated the

diminishing carcass. In her mind, she felt Hreeza's equivalent of a shrug.

'We were fortunate,' the older cat told her. 'Some days ago there was an avalanche down the side of the western ridge that brought down an entire herd of the stupid creatures – all we had to do was dig them out. For a brief time, there has been enough for all.'

For a time she was silent, grooming Shia while she ate, restoring warmth and circulation to the big cat's muscles with a brisk and rasping tongue. 'Shia, how did you come to return to us?' she asked at last. 'How did you escape?' She nodded at the Staff of Earth, which pulsed like a slender green serpent in the corner. 'And how did you come into possession of that dreadful thing?'

Shia, satiated now, was growing drowsy. 'It's a long and incredible tale,' she began dreamily, when . . .

'Come out, coward, and fight!' The cry of challenge – a long, blood-freezing yowl – echoed from outside the den.

Shia snarled; the hackles rose along her spine. 'I knew it would not take her long,' she said quietly. Stiffly, she got to her feet. 'Usurper, I come!' she roared.

When Steelclaw had been blasted, the force of the destruction had hollowed out the centre of the peak, leaving only the clawlike splinters of rock to snatch vainly at the sky. Beneath their shadow lay a bowl-shaped depression like the palm of that great grasping hand; its bottom humped and twisted in places by smooth runnels and strands of melted and recongealed black lava.

Unnoticed on his high perch, Khanu sat licking his wounds on a ledge above the canyon that for countless generations had served as the meeting place for the females of the Colony. He should not have been here, of course – this was no place for males, especially young, unimportant males – but Khanu's furiously wounded pride had been eased by his small act of defiance. Today, he had tried, ambitiously, to mate with Gristheena, First of the females, whose usual mate had been slaughtered in the last attack of the Skyfolk. To his utter dismay, he had battled his way through a mêlée of older, more

experienced suitors, only to be ignominiously, and painfully –
Khanu winced as he licked his paw to clean the smarting claw-
marks on his nose – rejected by the female herself.

Dusk was filling the snowy arena of the canyon with
shadows, but Khanu, cold as he was, made no attempt to move
away. He had something else to chew on besides his humiliation at the First Female's hands. With his rejection, and
Gristheena's open mockery, had come the crushing realization
that he was not as important to his Colony as he once had
thought himself.

'But I don't understand,' Khanu muttered sulkily to himself.
'Males are bigger – males are stronger. We take our pick from
the first fruits of the hunt, and the females stand aside until we
have eaten.' While the young bachelors lived in a loose-knit
group until they succeeded in winning mates of their own, each
of the older, stronger males selected and served his own cluster
of females – or so Khanu had thought until today. Now, it
seemed, his world had turned upside-down.

Males did not hunt, and provide for the Colony. Males did
not sit in the meeting place, and make the laws for the
wellbeing of all. Males took no useful part in the rearing and
nurturing of the kits. Males, it turned out – and Khanu flinched
from the memory – did not even select their mates. Oh, they
battled fiercely for the privilege; but the final choice, as
Gristheena had impressed upon him most forcefully, was
always the female's.

Following his rejection, Khanu had gone to talk with his sire,
Hzaral. A scarred, near-toothless oldster now, the veteran of
many mating fights, Hzaral had long ago decided to withdraw
from such fierce battles as attended the mating of a First
Female. He was happy with his own two ageing mates, one of
whom was Khanu's dam, and kept himself to himself.

'Is it true?' Khanu had demanded, bristling, and the whole
bitter tale had poured out. Hzaral had shaken his heavy, gold-
shot ruff, and turned his massive head away to groom the
dappled gold sunbursts on his flanks – the distinctive markings
that his son had inherited.

'What if it is?' he had said indolently, turning to pierce the
younger cat with his topaz gaze. 'Think. We are males. Why

211

trouble with hunting, when females do it for us? Why waste time fussing with their ridiculous laws, or wearing ourselves out minding unruly, squalling kits? If females believe such nonsense makes them more important, who are we to want to change things? We do very well as we are.'

'But we don't do anything!' Khanu had protested. 'Especially in these times of hardship, we should be . . . '

In a blur of speed, Hzaral's great paw lifted, and cuffed him, the force of the blow sending him rolling over and over. 'Learn wisdom, youngster!' Hzaral had snarled. 'The males are happy to have things as they are – and so, I suspect, are the females. Can you imagine Gristheena allowing you to meddle with her authority? Everyone has their place – how dare you try to alter that? Do you wish to end up Chuevah?'

Khanu was mulling unhappily over these matters on his ledge when he heard the harsh, discordant yowl of Gristheena's challenge. Within moments, the meeting place began to fill with females; emerging from the triangular tunnel-mouth in the southern wall of the bowl; leaping with dark, fluid grace down the rocky cliffs and pacing with dignified haste along the top of the spur that jutted out into the crater. Like a breaking wavefront, this gigantic ridge of black and glossy lava ran down from the northern rim of the natural arena, coming to an abrupt end almost in the very centre of the bowl. Here, perched in every niche and cornice in the rippled stone, the females congregated; brought together by Gristheena's strident call. Though he could make out few of their words, Khanu could hear the swelling background murmur of their excitement. One word, however, was repeated again and again. 'Shia!' they were saying. 'Shia has returned!'

Khanu had been about to creep quietly away; afraid of being discovered by the females in their own place. On hearing their talk, however, he abruptly changed his mind. 'They have no right to keep me out,' he muttered rebelliously to himself. 'This is as much my affair as it is theirs.' He shrunk down instead on his shadowy ledge, to make himself inconspicuous, and trembled with excitement. This was one contest that he meant to witness!

*

The meeting place was entered from below by means of a dark twisting tunnel that snaked through the cliffs at the southern end of the crater. Shia paced in stately fashion through the darkness, not hurrying, conserving her scant energy; tilting her head at an awkward angle to manoeuvre the Staff through the narrow space between the crowding walls. Hreeza followed, muttering imprecations under her breath.

The last of the grey twilight was glaring to Shia's eyes as she emerged into the meeting place. Though silence from the watchers was the rule on these occasions, she heard a murmur of amazement, and, if she was not mistaken, delight from the females on the spur; invisible in the shadows, except for a scattering of golden pinpoints where their eyes reflected the last light of day. Their joy changed swiftly to protest and consternation as they noticed the eldritch, pulsing glow of the Staff of Earth that she carried. I could have done without this – any of it, Shia thought wearily. Swiftly, she set her burden down at Hreeza's feet. 'Take care of this for me,' she said softly.

Hreeza gave the Staff an old-fashioned look. 'I'll guard it for you, Shia – as long as I don't have to touch the hideous thing.'

Then Gristheena was there. The First Female stalked into the centre of the crater: fit and muscular, and as heavy and big-boned as a male. Shia remembered that even as a kit, the younger cat had been a swaggering bully with scant concern for others and an even shorter temper. According to Hreeza, little had changed.

As contester and Chuevah, it should have been Shia's place to speak first. Instead she remained obstinately silent; never taking her eyes from the hulking figure of the First Female; holding Gristheena's glowering eyes with her own. Long minutes stretched by. The floor of the rocky bowl sank deeper into shadow. The two great females, hackles raised, stood eye to eye and glaring like raptors.

As Shia had expected, Gristheena was the first to weaken. 'Chuevah!' She spat the word in contempt. 'You do not belong here on Steelclaw, the territory and home of the Colony! Either fight or begone!'

Inwardly, Shia was laughing. By breaking the silence,

Gristheena had lost face – and everyone had witnessed it. Ignoring the swaggering cat as though the First Female was beneath her notice, Shia lifted her head and addressed her invisible watchers on the spur. 'I did not come here to fight,' she said, 'and I am not Chuevah, for I was never expelled from the Colony. All of you except the youngest know me. I am Shia, First Female, returned from the dead.'

'Save your breath, Chuevah, to fight.' Gristheena sprang. Shia tried to dodge, but her weakened body betrayed her. The other struck her heavily, and they rolled over and over, locked together, clawing, biting, snarling; one on top and then the other. Fur flew up, floating like clumps of black thistledown, but neither cat could gain a solid purchase. They broke apart and circled one another, sidling; eyes locked, fur erect and lashing tails abristle. Shia's flank was bleeding, scored and stinging, where the other cat had clawed her. Gristheena's nose had been laid open; she sneezed, spraying blood, and in the instant that her eyes were closed Shia cuffed her, left-right, across the head, ripping an ear. Snarling, her face contorted to a demon-mask, Gristheena lifted a threatening paw and yowled; a high-pitched, bubbling wail from deep within her throat.

Shia braced herself, expecting the heavier cat to rush her, but Gristheena was more wary now. Again they circled.

'Listen, fool,' Shia said. 'There is no need for this. Had you but listened . . . Gristheena, I do not seek to be First. My path lies elsewhere . . . '

'Elsewhere, in truth,' Gristheena spat. 'In oblivion, Chuevah, if I have my way!'

Again she sprang. There was no time to dodge; Shia met her headlong. Gristheena's greater weight crashed into her and bowled her over. Shia, pinned and struggling, felt hot, wet breath on her neck as the other's fangs sought her throat to crush and rend – but Gristheena had left an opening. Gasping, Shia embedded her hind claws in the soft flesh of the younger cat's belly and ripped down – but Gristheena was gone.

Shia rolled over and scrambled after her. Gristheena whipped round to face her – just too late. Shia's teeth met in her tail. Gristheena turned, hissing and screeching like a wounded eagle, but with her tail in Shia's jaws, she could not reach her opponent's body – nor Shia hers. Shia braced her legs and dug her claws into the crumbling stone of the crater's floor, but because of her opponent's greater weight and strength, she knew that she was likely to be overset at any minute. Regretfully, she chose her moment and let go of the tail.

Unbalanced, Gristheena went rolling over and over – right across the Staff of Earth as it lay on the ground. The great cat screamed as though she had been scalded and scrambled hastily backwards, her whiskers bristling, her eyes flashing fire. The western route out of the crater – up and over the spur, back and down the canyon rim – was suddenly unguarded, for until the contest was settled the other cats would not interfere. Shia seized the moment, snatched up the Staff, and ran.

Desperation gave such wings to her feet that she was on top of the spur in three great bounds, cats scattering from her flying paws. But Shia had been mistaken in thinking her opponent had been cowed by the Staff. The breath shot out of her body as Gristheena hit her from behind with all the force of a snow-slide. The impact knocked Shia from her feet, and the Staff fell from her jaws and went clattering across the stones.

Gristheena's claws scored her flanks like firebrands, opening bloody gashes, and one great paw raked across her face, missing her eyes by a hairsbreadth. Choking blood poured into Shia's nose and throat. She felt Gristheena's massive jaws, with their gleaming, ivory fangs, close around her windpipe . . .

Khanu had been watching the fight intently. He remembered little of the legendary Shia – he had only been a kit when she had been taken – but at the sight of her his golden eyes stretched wide in admiration. The cat was lean and scraggy, but hard-muscled still – and oh, she looked fierce! She was older than himself, but she was in her prime; at the height of both her fighting capacity and her sexual potential. Khanu, leaning out from his ledge at a perilous angle to get a better view of the struggle, and forgetting, in his anxiety, that he had no right to be there at all, willed her to win with all his heart.

Unfortunately, exhausted and half-starved as she was, Shia

215

could be no match for Gristheena. When the heavier cat brought her down on the spur, Khanu's heart plummeted. It was all over now. No one was more surprised than he when he found himself moving.

Aurian, I'm sorry. I failed you. Shia knew her death was very near now. Blue-steel claws pricked the tender skin of her belly, preparing to rip it open . . . And a massive shape, a blacker shadow in the gathering darkness, a whirlwind of teeth and claws, smashed into Gristheena from the side, sending her reeling, bleeding, toppling over the edge of the spur to the rocky floor of the crater below.

The furious protest of the watching females rose in a yowling crescendo.

'Run!' The voice came blasting into Shia's mind. 'They'll be on us in an instant!'

'The Staff!' Shia cried, groping with flailing paws among the flaking slabs of stone on the ridgetop.

'This?' said another voice. 'I have it safe. Now run!' It was Hreeza. Shia's heart leapt with joy.

Wasting no more time, the three cats fled; Hreeza, Shia, and the strange male who had saved her life. Leaping across chasms, streaking perilously between the boulders that littered the mountain's ravaged western face, they ran as they had never run before; the horde of females surging and raging at their heels.

Hreeza staggered the last few agonizing steps up to the top of the bluff, and swept keen eyes across the broken slopes that they had just climbed with such difficulty. 'I believe we've shaken them off at last,' she panted.

Khanu said nothing, but simply stopped amid the knot of wind-bent pines that crowned the bluff, and with a grateful sigh allowed his aching limbs to collapse beneath him as he flopped to the snow-flecked ground. He looked hopefully at Shia, whose jaws were clenched in a deathlock around the glowing object that she had taken from Hreeza on the first day, and had carried ever since. Khanu knew that only sheer willpower had carried her this far.

216

Shia heaved a heartfelt sigh of relief at Hreeza's words. 'I truly hope so,' she muttered. 'I can go no further.' She looked like death incarnate, and old Hreeza was little better. Khanu, a non-hunting male, who was unaccustomed to such exertions, admitted to himself that he, too, was in a woeful state.

For a day and a night, the furious cats from the Colony had clung to the trail of the fugitives, pursuing them relentlessly down the shattered flanks of Steelclaw, and on through the canyons and passes that threaded between the two peaks to the west, where the three had tried as best they could to keep below the snowline so as not to leave tracks for their hunters to follow. Since daylight, they had begun to climb again, and had penetrated into territories that were far beyond Khanu's ken. Above them loomed another mountain; a disquietingly different silhouette from the familiar shape that Khanu had been used to seeing all his life. Even as he watched, turgid snowclouds darkened the peak, rolling like massive grey boulders down the mountain towards him.

Khanu had interfered in the battle of the queens through bitterness towards Gristheena, who had humiliated him; through awe and respect for the legendary Shia, and her brave, hopeless challenge; and through a desperate desire to prove himself. He had never stopped to consider that his impulse would cost him his future within the Colony. Now he, too, had become Chuevah. The thought made him tremble.

'I won't think about it – not now,' Khanu muttered to himself. He shook his heavy bronze-black mane, as if to dispel such terrifying thoughts. 'Are you sure we've lost them?' he asked Hreeza, who dismissed him with a withering glance.

'Would I be stopping else!' she snapped. 'Keep your foolish kitten questions to yourself, youngster.' Her eyes flashed anger. 'Why did you follow us?'

Khanu had enough sense to realize that hunger and weariness were making Hreeza snappish, but he was weary too, and the old cat's dismissive attitude stung him. Lifting his head, he returned her stare. 'I *came with you* because that was my wish. I came because of Shia – because I want to help her.'

'You want to help her,' Hreeza sneered. 'You? A male? What possible use will you be? Shia has no wish to mate – she has

217

more important matters to attend to. Why should we burden ourselves with you? You cannot even hunt!'

Khanu's teeth clenched down on a snarl. 'I can learn,' he bristled.

'Pah!' Hreeza spat her contempt.

'Be silent, both of you!' With an effort, Shia unclenched her blistered jaws from the Staff. Laying the Artefact down, she looked from Khanu to Hreeza. 'It's no use you fighting,' she told them in the firmest of mental tones, 'because neither of you is coming with me.'

'What?' Hreeza looked thunderstruck.

'You heard me.'

For an instant, Khanu caught a glimpse of the stern and forceful will that had made Shia a leader and a legend among her people. Hreeza, however, was less easily overawed. 'Indeed?' The old cat's tail flicked scornfully. 'I say that I will come with you. If you would stop me, be prepared to fight!'

Shia's regal pose collapsed abruptly. To Khanu's astonishment, she sighed and laid her head on her paws. 'Hreeza, I couldn't fight a snow-hare at the moment, as well you know. But you should hear my plans before you decide.' She took a deep breath. 'I go to Aerillia, with the Staff of Earth, to save the life of a human – and to confront our ancient enemies, the Winged Folk.'

It was as if a thunderbolt had hammered into the earth between them. In the concussive silence that followed, Khanu, his mind almost paralysed by horror, could only think that Shia had gone mad during her long exile. To climb the unscalable Aerillia peak? To venture alone into the stronghold of their bitterest and most deadly foes? And all to aid a human?

He saw Hreeza rub a paw across her face as though Shia had struck her. For once the old cat was bereft of speech, and Khanu was shocked to see the shadow of doubt in her eyes; she who had always been Shia's most loyal supporter. Somehow, the old cat's reservations stiffened his resolve.

He sucked in the breath that he had forgotten to take. 'I will go with you, Shia. My siblings were killed by those wingborne monsters – I have some interest in this matter.' Khanu twitched his whiskers forward in a feline grin. 'I always wanted to taste Skyfolk meat.'

218

'You will not go, foolish cub! And neither will Shia.' The words exploded crimson in a blast of rage from Hreeza's mind. 'Aerillia! Humans! Never have I heard such moonstruck folly. You won't even get past the foothills of Aerillia peak. You will not go! I'll kill you first!'

Shia flicked her tail.

'Then you must kill me, Hreeza,' she said calmly, 'but why go to the trouble? As you said, the Winged Folk will likely perform that task – why have it on your conscience when you can let the Skyfolk bear the burden of my death?'

Hreeza recoiled, hurt and confounded. 'I just wish I understood,' she snapped. 'What is this Staff of Earth? Who is this human, that you should risk yourself for it? Your exile has changed you, Shia. What happened to you while you were so long away?'

'I will explain, old friend, while we rest and eat – for though we are weary, eat we must. So if you have sufficient energy to fight me, it would be better spent on finding us some food.' Her eyes twinkled wickedly. 'That is, if you're still up to it, old one!'

'Pah!' said Hreeza, unabashed. 'I'll find more food than you will – I who was foraging and hunting before you were born!' The old cat wrinkled her nose and curled back her lips, tasting the air. 'We must hasten. Snow is coming.' She turned to Khanu. 'Youngster, you had best come with us – if you truly wish to learn to hunt.'

As the cats crept through the stand of trees, Hreeza, still bristling, took the lead. Khanu, making the most of the opportunity, approached Shia. 'She will go with you, you know,' he told her softly. 'Hreeza will go, and so will I. Whatever you say won't make me change my mind.'

Shia looked at him. 'I know,' she said wearily. 'And fine fools you are, for not listening to me!' Then her harsh thoughts softened, and took on a warming glow. 'Shamefully selfish it may be – but in truth, I would be glad of your company. I have been far too long in exile, without the companionship of my own kind. But know this, Khanu – the matter is so urgent, that if I must sacrifice you both to the Winged Folk, I will do so without hesitation, should the need arise.'

The hair on Khanu's spine lifted as a shiver passed through

his frame. 'The Winged Folk will have to catch me first,' he said stubbornly.

15
The Refuge

'I know Remana is worried about the girl, Yanis, but I don't much like the notion of risking our ships so close to Nexis,' Idris grumbled.

Yanis looked across at Fional and grimaced. The young leader of the Nightrunners had never liked the pinch-faced, ill-tempered old captain, and he supposed it had been inevitable that it would be Idris who tried to spike his plans to return to Nexis in secret and look for Zanna and her father.

Yanis clenched his fists on the scrubbed, knife-scarred wood of the council table, which, being in the great kitchen cave of the Nightrunners' lair, was normally used for much less exalted purposes. The glowing cavern, with its row of great fires, was the warmest place in the smugglers' hideout; and the meeting was being held there for the benefit of Fional, who was still trying to thaw out. The archer had come staggering, half-frozen, out of a howling blizzard that morning, with the grim news that after all this time neither Vannor nor Hargorn had returned to the Valley.

Yanis glared at the bristling Idris. 'Our ships?' the leader of the Nightrunners demanded. 'Since when were they your ships, Idris?'

The wizened captain leapt to his feet and struck the table with his fist. 'Don't give me that, you young cur! I sailed with your father – aye, and your grandfather too. Fine men, both of them, and they knew this was a community. Just because you're your father's son, it don't mean you can't be replaced.'

'Oh, and can he, now?' Remana spoke softly, but there was poisoned steel beneath her tones. Idris caught her eye and shut his mouth abruptly, sinking back into his chair. No one among the Nightrunners would cross Remana, and the old captain knew it. To Yanis's surprise, his mother winked at him before

221

turning back to the bowman. 'Fional,' she asked, 'have you any idea what's happening in Nexis now?'

Fional shook his head, and poured more taillin from the pot on the table. He took an appreciative sip of the steaming beverage before continuing. 'Once I had returned Vannor's son to Dulsina, it took me ages to get back here from the Valley, what with all the snow – and we were isolated for some time before that. I thought that your information would be more recent than ours.'

'I don't think so,' Yanis demurred. 'After the Archmage took control, I pulled my agents out of there. It was just too dangerous to risk good men. Mark you,' he added, 'I've been having second thoughts lately. This winter-in-summer and the storms at sea have almost put an end to trade, and we're just about at the limit of our resources. We'll have to do something soon.'

'That bad, eh?' Fional said sympathetically. 'You know, if you run short, you could always send a messenger to Dulsina in the Valley. We've enough and to spare.'

Remana shook her head. 'I don't understand. You've told us that the winter seems not to extend to the Valley – but how can that be?'

'Dulsina thinks we're being protected somehow – by the Lady Eilin, presumably,' Fional replied with a shrug. 'But we can't work out why she won't show herself. According to Vannor, Aurian always said her mother was a very solitary sort, but all the same it seems strange to me.'

'Well, whatever the reason, I'm glad it's so,' Remana said, 'but this brings us no closer to helping Vannor and Zanna.' A frown crossed her broad-cheekboned face. 'I feel so responsible. If only I had kept a closer eye on the wretched girl . . . '

Yanis reached out to lay a comforting hand on her arm. 'Don't go blaming yourself, mam. It was my fault that Zanna left, and we all know it. If only I had agreed to her schemes for using our ships to help Vannor, instead of listening to Gevan, and Idris here . . . ' He scowled at the old captain. 'The least we can do now is help find her – and that is not a matter open to debate.' He paused, and looked round at the assembled faces. 'The question is: without our agents in Nexis, how do we go about it?'

Idris still looked unhappy. 'Very well. If we must, we must – if only so we don't lose the partnership with Vannor that has served us so well. But is there no way of managing it without putting our own folk in danger?'

Yanis shook his head. 'I don't see how . . . '

'I know!' Remana, who had been deep in thought, suddenly interrupted him. 'We need a contact who is already in Nexis, and I know the very man – your father's old friend Jarvas, who runs a refuge for the poor folk of the city.' She looked at all of them, her eyes sparkling with excitement. 'His place is right down by the river, so we can sneak in easily, after dark, and . . . '

'Now just hold on there!' Yanis shouted. 'What do you mean, we? If you think I'm taking you into the dangers of Nexis, you'd better think again.'

Remana smiled sweetly. 'But, Yanis – Jarvas doesn't know you. He would never trust a stranger, especially with things the way they are now.' Her eyes twinkled mischievously. 'He does, however, know me.'

Across the table, Fional was grinning. 'Did you know, Remana, you're just like your sister?'

Yanis put his face into his hands, and groaned.

The journey through the slushy alleys was swift and furtive. Even with Jarvas taking the stranger's weight – Tilda had done little more than carry his sword and bedroll, retrieved from the wrecked taproom, and keep his cloak from trailing in the muck – the whore had difficulty keeping up with the swift pace that the big man set. By the gods, she would be glad when they reached safe haven. The shock of her folly in the tavern was beginning to hit her. 'What have I done?' she moaned to herself. 'Why did I do it?' Some of the guards had only been wounded, but some were certainly dead – and once Pendral circulated her description, and that of Jarvas, they couldn't expect to elude arrest for long.

Tilda cursed under her breath. Being a streetwalker wasn't much of a life, but it was better than being a fugitive. In the last hour, her world had fallen apart. Her face set in grim and bitter lines, she trudged behind Jarvas through the labyrinth of alleys that led to his home.

The sturdy fence of the stockade towered above Tilda's head, and in spite of her growing dismay she was impressed. She had never been here before – she could look after herself, thank you, and took pride in doing so – but of course she had heard of the place. Jarvas and his good deeds! she thought. And where has it got him? When they reached the heavy gate, the big man whistled a complicated trill, and there was a hollow scraping sound as heavy wooden bars were lifted out of their sockets on the other side. The gate swung open to a blaze of haloed torchlight that made Tilda's eyes water, and a cloaked and hooded figure materialized out of the fog.

'You're back early.' Then the woman's voice faltered at the sight of the Jarvas's burden. 'Dear gods, what's happened?' Tilda saw her small, shrouded figure straighten as she collected herself. 'I'll fetch Benziorn at once,' she said briskly, and turned to go.

'Good lass,' Jarvas yelled after her. 'Tell him there's a wound needs stitching.'

'All right.' The woman vanished into the swirling mist.

Jarvas carried the wounded stranger into the nearer of the warehouses. Tilda, following, gasped as she slipped through the narrow gap in the massive door. The fog made it difficult to gauge the building's size from the outside, but inside the ground floor was an echoing vault, with shadows dancing on its walls from the torches attached to the eight supporting stone columns that marched, two by two, down the length of the hall. Tilda's first impression was one of warmth and light. Lamps and candles burned on ledges and niches in the rough walls of limewashed stone, and campfires burned at intervals down both sides of the spacious chamber. Woodsmoke rose in sluggish whirls, filling the room with a choking haze that stung Tilda's eyes and stabbed at her throat, setting off her cough again. She caught a brief impression of people crowding round and a buzz of questioning voices, but her eyes were watering so hard that it was impossible to see clearly through the smoky haze.

'Out of the way – I've an injured man here,' Jarvas roared.

'May the gods have mercy! Which lackwit closed the windows? Hey, you there!' He caught the eye of a skinny, smudge-faced urchin who came pelting through the haze of smoke. 'Lad, can you climb?'

''Course I can!' The scruffy brat nodded enthusiastically.

'Good. Over by the wall you'll find a ladder. Climb up to one of the high windows and open the shutters, and when you've done that, do the same with the window opposite. A good through-draught will clear this smoke in no time.'

'All right, Jarvas.' The child raced off, calling for his friends to help him.

'And don't go mucking about with that ladder!' Jarvas turned to the whore with a rueful grin. 'I'm wasting my breath, telling that to a lad his age. Are you all right?'

'Smoke!' Tilda managed to wheeze.

'Sorry about that – we'll soon get it cleared. Somebody boil some water – and scrounge up some clean rags from some-where,' he bellowed to the room at large.

Jarvas went to the far end of the room, with Tilda clutching blindly at his cloak-hem, and set the wounded man down on a pallet near one of the fires. 'Benziorn had better hurry,' he muttered, as Tilda covered the injured stranger with a blanket. 'He's losing a lot of blood.'

Tilda heard the squeak and thump of the ladder going up, and shrill squabbling in childish voices. Their cursing didn't bother her – she had grown up with such coarseness on the streets. After a few minutes her throat was soothed by welcome fresh air. The smoke was clearing, but the windows were so high – about the height of three tall men – that they kept the worst of the cold from getting into the room.

'All right – what have I got to patch up this time?' The voice was deep and smooth as velvet, but the tone was querulous, and ragged with fatigue. 'Some idiot victim of yet another drunken brawl?'

Tilda looked up to see a man of medium height and indeterminate years, his fair hair threaded with brighter strands of silver. His expressive face, though drawn and haggard with weariness, was pleasingly lean and well propor-tioned, but his light blue eyes were snapping with irritation.

225

Without waiting for an answer, he snatched aside the blanket that covered the stranger, and cursed. 'Melisanda have mercy – what a ghastly mess! Are you dimwits so impossibly dense that you can't contrive a simple bandage? You might as well have left the poor bastard to bleed to death, and allowed me a decent night's sleep for once. It would have come to the same thing in the end. At least he's unconscious, so I won't be plagued by the sound of his screams.'

All the while he had been talking, Benziorn was unpacking a bag he carried with him, and handing his instruments to the girl who had gone to fetch him. Emerging from her voluminous cloak as a delicate pale-haired waif with a ruthless streak of efficiency, she immersed the instruments and bandages in boiling water while the physician cleaned the stranger's wounds, all the while keeping up a continuous peevish grumble.

'His chest is no problem – the wound's a slice across his ribs, not a stab, and his jerkin protected him. He's in shock from blood-loss, though – couldn't you idiots have kept him warmer? Nasty head wound . . . If I move fast and we're lucky, we might be able to save the ear . . . What's keeping you, Emmie?' he demanded, but the blonde girl simply responded with a smile.

'Ready now, Benziorn.'

'You! Whoever you are,' the physician snapped. 'Fetch me more lights. Candles, lamps, whatever. Hurry!'

Tilda jerked upright as she realized that he was addressing her. Jolted into action by his peremptory tone, she scurried off to do his bidding. When she returned to place her handful of garnered candles, as instructed, around the head of the stranger, Benziorn was already stitching with deft, economical motions. As she came close to him, Tilda noticed a familiar smell on his breath, and realized, with a shock, that the physician had been drinking. Dear gods, she thought – what kind of place have I come to?

Jarvas surveyed his little kingdom, looking around at the scenes of squalor and poverty. Some three dozen families were camped within the hall, dividing the space with sagging

226

partitions of rugs, sacks, or whatever came to hand. Children slept together like puppies in tangled nests of blankets, while mothers tended stewpots and sewed hopelessly at clothing whose original fabric was indistinguishable beneath rainbow layers of patchwork. Old folk, wrapped in cloaks and shawls, snored in corners or competed with steaming laundry for space at the fires, while groups of men sat cross-legged in the lamplight, gambling for pebbles with knucklebones. The topaz eyes of several cats blinked and gleamed in the firelight. Somewhere in the shadows, a baby cried. Every face was scarred and haggard with hunger and hardship.

Jarvas felt a presence beside him. Tilda was looking at his people with horror and pity on her face.

'At least they aren't starving now.' There was a defensive edge to his voice. 'At least they aren't freezing in the streets tonight.'

'There are so many of them,' Tilda murmured. Compressing her lips, she looked away. 'Your precious physician is drunk!' she added.

Jarvas nodded. 'He usually is. Once, he was the best physician in Nexis. He made a comfortable living treating the merchants and such – until the night those hideous monsters struck.' He sighed. 'Benziorn was away from home, attending a sickbed, when one of the creatures got into his house and slaughtered his wife and children. Ever since then, he's been drinking – it cost him his house and his livelihood, and he was a stinking, starving wreck when I took him off the streets.' Jarvas shrugged. 'We're lucky to have him, though. Drunk or sober, he's still the best.'

'I'm glad to hear it.' There was a bitter edge to Tilda's voice. 'I'd hate to think we'd risked our necks for some stranger, only to have him finished off by a drunken physician. Why did we do it? We must have been mad!' There was a note of shrill desperation in her voice.

Jarvas shook his head. 'I'm blessed if I know.' At the time, it had seemed the only thing to do, but helping that one man had probably spelled the end of this refuge for all these others. 'It might take a day or two for Pendral to find out who I am,' he went on grimly, 'but after that, they'll be coming here, for sure.' He sighed. 'Get some rest now, Tilda. First thing tomorrow, I'll send Emmie to fetch your son – then we need to start thinking about getting out of here.'

Tilda's home was in a mare's-nest of squalid alleys, upcurrent from the great white bridge that leapt the river beside the Academy promontory. Having been sent by Jarvas to collect the streetwalker's son, Emmie walked quickly through the baffling maze, shivering in the chill of a damp grey dawn. Today, the stout stick that she always carried for protection was being put to the use for which it had been originally intended, for her sturdily shod feet kept slipping in the deep layer of freezing, slushy muck that slicked the cobbles. The alleyways stank of rot and mildew and decay; of human filth and human waste. Emmie knew it well – the stench of utter poverty.

The dark hulks of damp, half-derelict buildings with boarded windows towered over her on either side, cutting off most of the leaden morning light and turning the narrow ginnels into threatening tunnels of gloom. On each side of her were openings; some with cracked and rotting doors that hung drunkenly askew from a single rusting hinge; others merely dark and gaping holes that might have concealed any amount of dangers.

Emmie hurried past these, her nerves strung tight, cursing Jarvas under her breath for sending her on such an errand. This was the safest time to visit these poverty-stricken haunts, for most of the inhabitants would be sleeping after their desperate deeds of the previous night, but Emmie felt uneasy. Though the alleys were deserted, she imagined hostile eyes in every gaping doorway. Glancing around warily and checking the knife at her belt, she drew her concealing hood more snugly over her tangle of pale-gold curls and walked on, repeating Tilda's instructions to herself over and over again. Gods preserve us! she thought. What an appalling place to raise a child!

Suddenly, Emmie heard a bloodcurdling snarl. One of the tilting doors in front of her burst open to reveal a huge and shaggy white shape, its lips wrinkling back to reveal savage yellowed fangs and drooling jaws, its eyes kindling with a menacing fire. Never taking those glaring red eyes from her, the dog slunk out into the street, plainly nervous but determined. Blocking her way forward, it broke into a torrent of guttural barking.

Emmie froze in her tracks, her heart hammering wildly, and took a firmer grip on her stick. Time seemed to stretch as she noted the knobs and ridges of bone that stuck out through the creature's dirty, matted white fur, and the row of swollen dugs that hung from its hollow belly. Despite the danger, she felt her heart contract with pity for this poor starveling mother with a hungry litter to feed.

Emmie understood a mother's instinct. She'd had a little one of her own, and another on the way, when her husband Devral, a young storyteller, had been snatched by the Archmage's soldiers and vanished from her life. The shock and grief of his loss had made her lose the baby too, and in the hardship that followed, her little daughter had died of a fever. Suddenly she was swamped by a wave of fellow-feeling for the wretched creature before her.

For all its size, the dog was young – full young to be a mother, Emmie thought, noting its gawky appearance and the huge paws that seemed to promise further growth. This was probably its first litter. Despite its skeletal, filthy appearance, its eyes were clear and its matted coat thick. There was no sign of mange or madness. In the pouch at Emmie's belt was food – bread, cheese and meat – intended for Tilda's son. No doubt the animal had scented her provisions, and desperation had driven it to attack.

'You poor thing,' Emmie murmured. Well, she was sure that Tilda's brat could wait to eat until she got him back to the refuge. Stealthily, her free hand crept towards the pouch at her belt, but the movement was injudicious. A swelling snarl burst from the animal's throat as it leapt to the attack, followed by an agonized yelp as Emmie's stick whacked into its ribs with a hollow thud. Cowed and whining, the bitch slunk back towards her doorway, glancing frequently over her shoulder as if trying to pluck up the courage to attack again.

'Oh, turds!' Emmie muttered. She was shaking, and sick

with an irrational guilt. Swiftly, she fumbled in her pouch and drew out the package of food, ripping away the cloth that wrapped it. 'Here, girl,' she called, and tossed her provisions to the starving animal. The dog pounced on them, drooling, and suddenly looked up with bright eyes at her benefactor. The ragged, white-plumed tail wagged once, as if in thanks, and then the dog snatched up the food and was gone. From within the building came a shrill chorus of high-pitched whines as the mother returned to her litter.

Inwardly mocking her own soft-heartedness, Emmie went on her way, pausing to wipe her eyes, that had unaccountably filled with tears, on a fold of her cloak. 'You idiot,' she told herself. 'Haven't you seen enough human suffering, that you have to get in a stew about a starving animal?' She could imagine what Jarvas would say if he ever found out she'd given scarce and valuable supplies to a bloody dog. None the less, her heart had been warmed by the dog's seeming gratitude – and Emmie knew that if she had to live the encounter over again, she'd do exactly the same thing.

'Grince? Grince – are you in there? Your mother sent me to fetch you.' Emmie rapped hard on the flimsy door, wincing inwardly as she called the poor child's unfortunate name. ('I called him after his dad,' Tilda had said defensively. 'At least, I'm almost sure that was his dad.') Emmie shook her head resignedly, and knocked again.

She had been hammering for some minutes on the un-yielding wood when there was a grating noise, as if some heavy object was being dragged back from the other side. The door opened a crack and a dark, suspicious eye peeped out. 'My ma said don't open the bloody door for nobody!'

The young woman was just in time to get her stick into the gap before it slammed shut again. Such a string of curses came from the ten-year-old within that, even though she had thought herself inured to the language of the gutter, Emmie winced. For all his bravado, she could sense that the child was very much afraid – and not without reason, when his mother had failed to come home.

'Don't be daft,' she said crisply. 'Tilda ran into a bit of

trouble last night, and that's why she didn't come back. But don't worry; she's safe, among friends. My name is Emmie – she sent me to fetch you, so you could be safe, too.' With that, she forced the door open.

'Go away!' the child howled. 'I'm not going with you. I want my ma!' He was cowering in the furthest corner of the single room, in a nest of verminous rags that obviously passed for his bed; his dark eyes scowling up at her from behind a ragged fringe of black hair.

'Come on, Grince,' Emmie wheedled. 'Look, we don't have time to waste. Your mother is worried about you.' She looked down with pity at the small and skinny boy, and silently cursed Tilda. Why, the child looked as neglected, wild, and undernourished as that poor stray dog.

'Come on, now.' She approached his bedside and knelt down – and froze in horror as she saw the wicked glint of a knife in the small boy's hand.

'Bog off!' he shrilled. 'Don't come no closer, or I'll gut you!'

He meant it, that was certain. Emmie shuddered. What sort of life could do this to a child? Her mind was racing. If she could only get him to trust her. Fleetingly, she regretted giving her food to the starving dog. The dog! Emmie gave the boy her brightest of smiles. 'Oh, never mind old Tilda, then. She can wait. Would you like to see some puppies instead?' she asked disarmingly.

Grince's face lit up like a beacon. 'Puppies? Really? Are they yours? Can I have one?' Then the scowl returned. 'But my ma won't let me,' he added sullenly.

Emmie grinned, adopting the boy's own language. 'Stuff your ma,' she said briskly. 'If you'll put down that knife and come with me, you can have the whole bloody lot!'

At first, Emmie was afraid that the dog would be hostile. When she approached the building with the excited child in tow, she told Grince to wait outside, and crept into the hovel with great trepidation. She need not have worried. The white dog was delighted to see her – probably, Emmie thought, in the hopes that she might have more food.

'Good dog,' she said softly, and put out a hand to scratch

231

the soft white ears. She was rewarded by a whine, and much tail-wagging, as the dog pressed close to her and licked her hand. A good-natured creature at heart, the young woman thought, delighted that her assessment of the animal had been right. Once, this dog had had a kindly owner, but what had happened to him or her? A quick search of the room gave her the answer. The owner had died within the hovel – of age or sickness, most likely – and the dog had been living on the corpse ever since.

'Well?' Emmie asked herself. 'What was she supposed to do, with pups to feed?' None the less, she found it hard to suppress her retching as she took an old blanket and covered the well-gnawed heap of bones before calling the child into the room.

Grince went into raptures over the pups – a motley lot, one white beast like its mother, and the others splotched with black. When Emmie reached down to take the little creatures, the bitch, weak with hunger, reacted with a trust that touched her to the core. As they left the hovel, Grince danced around her, unable to contain his excitement. 'Are they mine?' he asked her, wide-eyed. 'Can I have them all?'

'Of course you can,' Emmie told him recklessly. She laid her free hand on the broad white head of the bitch who paced at her side, and smiled. 'But the dog is mine,' she added firmly. Suddenly, she felt lighter of heart and more at ease than she had done since Devral had died.

It was nearing noon when she trudged wearily back to the refuge, encumbered by her burden of five squirming pups, their eyes not yet open, tied up loosely in a rough bag that she'd made from her petticoat. Grince, who had been hugely impressed by her resourcefulness – and the fact that she had kept her promise – clung tightly to her free hand, and the big white dog followed trustingly at her heels. Dear gods, Emmie thought, imagining the whore's reaction on being presented with not one but five puppies – Tilda is in for a shock. And what on earth is Jarvas going to say when he sees this menagerie?

'What the blazes is that?' The horrified expression on Jarvas's face at the sight of the white dog was not encouraging.

Grince shrank nervously behind Emmie's skirts. She squeezed his hand and tilted her chin in defiance, but the boy could feel her trembling. 'It's only a dog, for goodness sake!' she protested.

'Dog? It's more like a bloody horse!' Jarvas snorted. 'Emmie, you should have more sense than to bring that creature here. Haven't we enough to worry about, after my idiocy last night? Aren't we in enough trouble? And how in the name of all the gods do you expect to feed the wretched beast? We've little enough to go round as it is.'

And my puppies! thought Grince. He swallowed against a tightness in his throat. Never in his short life had he possessed anything that really belonged to *him* – and never had he wanted anything more than those five tiny scraps of life. Above his head, the argument continued.

'I'll feed her from my rations,' Emmie said firmly.

'And that you bloody won't!' Jarvas spluttered. 'As it is, you don't eat near enough, without giving it away to some mangy dog. I'm telling you, Emmie – I won't have it.'

Grince saw his newfound friend look down into the trusting eyes of the dog. She took a shaky breath. 'Very well,' she said tightly. 'If we aren't welcome here, we'll go elsewhere.'

'No!' The howl of protest came from Grince. 'You can't go away. What about my puppies?' Before Emmie could react, he had dived out, kicked Jarvas hard in the shins, and dodged behind her again. 'Leave her alone, you rotten old pig!' he shrilled. 'It's her dog, and they're my puppies, and we're keeping them, so there!'

A long arm shot out, and the big man dragged Grince out from behind Emmie's skirts. Much as the boy wriggled and cursed, he could not escape from the bruising grip of those strong fingers. Jarvas's eyes were glinting with anger.

'It's all right, son.' The smooth, deep voice was firm and reassuring. 'Jarvas – is this really necessary?'

Jarvas let go of the boy and turned to confront the man with silver-gold hair who had walked up behind him, his booted feet silent on the snowy earth of the stockade.

'You have no right, Benziorn . . . ' the big man began angrily, but the other took him by the arm and dragged him

233

out of earshot. Grince looked up at Emmie. To his astonishment, her lips were crooked in a smile.

'Benziorn is a good physician,' she told the boy, 'and we need him here. If anyone can persuade Jarvas to change his mind, he can.'

Grince watched the two men talking, their heads close together, and bit his lip anxiously. Glad as he'd been of Benziorn's intervention, he only hoped the physician would be able to sway Jarvas in favour of his puppies. It looked as though Emmie was thinking the same. Kneeling, she put her arms around the thick-ruffed neck of the white dog. 'It's all right,' the boy heard her mutter to the animal. 'You'll have a home with me whatever Jarvas says.'

After what seemed an age to Grince, Jarvas stamped off across the stockade, grumbling, while Benziorn returned to the waiting pair with a wry shake of his head. 'At least I still retain some powers of persuasion. Really, if you weren't such a good assistant . . . ' the physician said to Emmie in mock-scolding tones.

'Benziorn, how can I thank you?' Emmie replied gratefully. 'I had expected Jarvas to be awkward, but . . . '

'Don't blame him too harshly, Emmie.' The physician sighed. 'Jarvas has too many other worries today to be concerned about one stray dog. He . . . '

'It's not just one stray dog,' Grince piped up indignantly. 'What about my bloody puppies?'

'Grince!' Emmie scolded. 'We're going to have to do something about your language!'

'What language?' the boy asked innocently.

Benziorn squatted beside him, frowning. 'I think you know what bloody language, you little wretch. Well, Jarvas doesn't allow swearing here – especially not in front of ladies like Emmie. So you'd better apologize to her, or she might just decide to take those puppies back.' He looked so ferocious that Grince gulped nervously.

'I – I'm sorry, Emmie,' he said in a small voice.

'That's better.' Benziorn smiled and ruffled his hair. 'Now, let's go and get those pups of yours settled. While we still have

234

time.' He said the last words in such a quiet, worried voice that the excited boy barely heard them.

Leaving Emmie – after all, it was her fault – to cope with Tilda's hysterics on being presented with five puppies, Jarvas crossed the echoing warehouse and looked broodingly down at the injured trooper who had caused so much trouble. He started as a voice behind him said, 'You know, our mysterious stranger's head-wound may be more serious than I thought. He should have regained consciousness by now.'

'Is this your day for sneaking up on me?' Jarvas snapped, but his irritation was dampened by the sight of the physician's haggard face and worried frown. For the first time since the big man had known him, Benziorn was sober. 'Is it really so serious?' Jarvas asked, feeling suddenly cold. 'By all the gods, if I've gone and put everyone in danger to save him, and then he dies on us . . .'

The physician knelt by his patient. 'His pulse seems a little stronger,' he said hopefully. 'Maybe it's just his age, and blood-loss – not to mention being hauled through the streets in that raw cold!' Scrambling to his feet, he put a hand on Jarvas's arm. 'Can I help?' he said quietly.

'Help? How?' The big man's voice was raw with bitterness. 'I've bollixed things up good and proper, Benziorn. Just look at this lot. What's going to happen to them when the soldiers come? So far, we've escaped much official attention – what do we have, that anyone should want to bother us? But now?' His arm swept out to encompass his ragged little band of destitute Nexians. 'It's only a matter of time before Pendral's troopers find out who I am. A face like mine is pretty recognizable.'

'And it's a short step from there for them to treat this place as a hive of dissension – and we know what that means.' Benziorn gave Jarvas a very straight look. 'My friend, I think we should prepare to evacuate.'

The big man flinched from Benziorn's words. 'But . . .' His protest subsided as the physician raised an eyebrow, and he sighed. 'You're right. I know we should. I'm not that daft. But to see the ruination of it all . . .' He looked again across the noisy, crowded, smoky hall – at the huddled old folk,

235

enjoying the first food and shelter and security that they had known in a long time; at the little ones who played between the fires, their present freedom from filth, starvation and disease giving them the energy to get under everyone's feet with their riotous games. Would this be the end of Vannor's dream, and his own? Not while Jarvas had a breath left in his body. Determined now, he turned back to Benziorn. 'There is,' he said quietly, 'another alternative. I could give myself up.'

'No, you fool! You can't do that.' Benziorn, his eyes wide with alarm, caught Jarvas's arm as though to detain him by main force. 'What about Tilda? What about the stranger you took such risks to save? Pendral must know you weren't alone in what you did.' His fingers pressed painfull into the big man's arm. 'Jarvas – they'll torture you to find out the whereabouts of the others – and in the end you'll have no choice but to betray them. Believe me, what you're suggesting solves nothing.'

'What can I do, then?' Jarvas shouted. 'Folk can't leave Nexis without permission these days – shall I just cast my people back out into the slums?'

'They may be safer there than here, for the time being,' Benziorn reminded him gently. 'Once this trouble has died down, it may be possible for them to return – but I think you must tell them to start packing up their belonging now. If the need should arise, they must be ready to leave. I would also look to the fortification of your stockade, and send the more sensible youngsters out into the streets, to give us early warnings of the approach of soldiers. Then, after dark tonight, it may be wise to start moving your people out of here.'

Jarvas knew the physician was right. But never, since his childhood, had he been so close to weeping. It was not long, however, before Benziorn's precautions turned out to be necessary. By nightfall, there were soldiers at the gate.

Guards, dressed in the achingly familiar livery of the garrison, dragged Vannor up the spiral tower staircase, their booted feet striking harsh echoes from the cold, hard marble. But even the stairwell was so much warmer than the chill outside . . . The merchant felt himself sinking into a drowsy oblivion, and fought to clear his mind, to stay alert, to struggle; but his limbs were bound, and too numb, in any case, to obey him. He was utterly helpless – and back in Miathan's power.

Vannor was taken to Miathan's chambers and forced down to his knees on the rich crimson carpeting. Waving the guards aside, the Archmage stood in silence, looking down at the captive with the glittering, expressionless gems that were his eyes. Vannor shuddered. Miathan's face had altered – the harsh hauteur of his former days had been recarved into deeper lines of bitterness and cruelty. The skin on his masklike face was waxen and unhealthy, and twisted into livid scars around his gutted eyes. Only his clawlike hands, rubbing and writhing against one another, betrayed his glee. The merchant knew fear, the like of which he had never before experienced. Not even the Wraith that had slain Forral had filled him with such terror, a terror which mocked at hope and drained his courage as though the lifeblood was being leached from his very veins.

'So,' Miathan whispered. 'I have you at last.'

'You won't have me long, you bastard!' Vannor spat at the Archmage's feet.

'Vannor, you would be amusing, were you not pitiful,' the Archmage mocked. 'You are correct, however: your presence will not plague me long. In your case, the end will come much sooner than you think – for who will help you now?' He smiled coldly. 'Here we are, back where we started – but there is no Forral to help you this time, and no Aurian to interfere. Your friends from the garrison are scattered or dead. You have no one, Vannor. No one but me. And before I am done, you will beg for death a thousand times. But first I shall require some answers – such as the names of your companions, and where they are hiding.'

The hissing voice, the malevolent face, struck chills through Vannor. The merchant gritted his teeth and closed his eyes, but he could not shut out Miathan's insidious, gloating voice, which turned him sick to his soul with loathing.

237

The worst of his horror was not for his own fate – that (he promised himself, and tried hard to believe it) he could stand. But he knew that, sooner or later, he would tell the Archmage everything he wanted to know.

Vannor shuddered. Blinded by his love for his daughter, he had betrayed his friends. Mortal men he could deal with, but this monster wielded powers that went far beyond Vannor's worst imaginings. A wave of nausea overwhelmed him as he remembered the hideous creature that had slain his old friend Forral, and only the stubborn core of courage that had supported him throughout a rough, hard life kept his limbs from trembling. Saving a miracle, his survival could be measured in days, at most. And Vannor knew that those days would be very bad indeed.

None the less, he intended to go down fighting. Scowling, he looked up into Miathan's expressionless eyes. 'Why?' he grated. 'You're the bloody Archmage. You know full well that you could pick whatever information you wanted out of my mind as easily as picking up a piece of fruit from that bowl over there. In fact . . . ' Another shudder convulsed him. 'In fact, you may have already done it.' *Was it true? Was it?* Taking a ragged breath, he tried to control his racing thoughts. 'So why are you threatening me with torture?'

'For revenge.' Miathan's smile reminded Vannor of the snarling wolf he had seen so long ago in the Valley. 'Revenge for all those years of being balked, hindered, and opposed on the council. And your suffering will be far greater when you hear the words that betray your companions coming from your own lips – and know that you have failed them.'

Again, the wolfish grin. 'But there is more to it than revenge, my dear Vannor. Consider the sources of magical power. Abandoning the Mages' Code has brought me certain – opportunities. Bear in mind, when you are dying in torment, that your terror, your agony and anguish, will all be serving to fuel my magic and increase my power.'

With that, he lifted his hand. Every nerve and muscle in Vannor's body went into spasm as a bolt of agony consumed the merchant's backbone like white fire. He toppled like a falling tree, writhing on the crimson carpet as his spine arced backward like a tensioned bow. Though he bit his tongue to keep from crying out, the last thing he heard as his senses left him was his own agonized cries.

16
A Shadow On The Roof

As Yazour slowly recovered from his wounds, his lessons in the speech of the Xandim continued. It was not so difficult as he had expected, for he already knew a little of the language – had been taught it, as all Xiang's officers had, to equip him for his scouting expeditions to raid the Xandim studs. There were certain similar roots shared by the two tongues, which made the learning easier. Besides that, the two men had only each other for company, they had nothing else to do but talk – and each of them was bursting with curiosity as to what the other was doing in this bleak and lonely place.

After several frustrating days, Yazour managed, in halting Xandim that relied heavily on both mime and pictures scratched with a charred stick from the fire on the smooth stone floor of the cavern, to explain that he and his companions were fugitives fleeing the wrath of the Khazalim king – and that their captor, who occupied the tower, was Xiang's son. On hearing this news, Schiannath broke into a torrential spate of Xandim that left Yazour completely at a loss. After a good deal of repetition, and many attempts to get his strange companion to slow down a little, the warrior finally understood that Schiannath too was an outlaw in exile from his people, though the nature of the Horselord's crime remained unclear.

Yazour suspected that Schiannath was being deliberately vague on this point, and it gave him some uneasy moments, until he remembered that this man had rescued him, fed him, and tended his wounds. After all, Yazour reflected, I never told him why we were forced to flee the Khisu. Schiannath may be thinking just as suspiciously of me – yet still he shows me unstinting care. It was a sobering thought.

Once the outlaw had discovered that Yazour was an exile like himself, Schiannath's manner towards him thawed a great deal,

240

and despite his own hostility the young warrior found himself responding in kind. Though the ghost of his slain father would occasionally rise in his mind to berate him for befriending an enemy, making him sullen and taciturn for a time, the level-headed Yazour could not help but realize that this former foe had proved a better friend than Harihn's soldiers, those ex-companions who had dealt the wounds that Schiannath was doing his best to heal. For Yazour's recovery was not straightforward. Sometimes, when his wounds flared into fever, Schiannath would mix soothing poultices and cool his burning face with icy water; when the bruise on his forehead throbbed, the Xandim would give him infusions of herbs to still the pain. And at these times, Yazour's confusion became so great that he felt as though his head – or maybe his heart – was threatening to break apart.

Yet the deepest part of Yazour's anguish was not for himself, but for the companions he had left behind in the tower when he fled. What had happened to Aurian and Anvar? What of Bohan, and Eliizar and Nereni? What had become of Shia, all alone in this wintry waste? And worst of all, why was he stranded here on his back, helpless as an upturned turtle, when he should be out there helping them?

As the days progressed, the warrior's frustration festered within him. His outer hurts were mending slowly, but the wounds to his spirit grew ever worse. Yazour grew terse and fractious, lacking the words and the inclination to explain to Schiannath that his anger was turned upon himself. The fragile bond of trust that had been growing between himself and the Xandim was strained to breaking point, and Yazour even resented Schiannath's hurt and bewildered expression as he tried to answer his companion's unspoken needs, and was rebuffed again and again.

Matters finally came to a head between the two men on a wild and bitter night, while the latest in a long succession of vicious blizzards was venting its spleen on the surrounding mountains. Schiannath lay sleeping near his beloved mare, but Yazour was tossing in the grip of a grim and stubborn wakefulness that refused to yield and let him rest. All his thoughts were on his lost companions; he was tormented by bloodcurdling visions of his friends being tortured and broken within the tower; of Aurian being used and manhandled by the prince.

All at once, it was too much for the warrior's guilty spirit to bear. 'Reaper take me – I can lie here no longer!' he muttered. 'I must overcome this weakness, and make myself strong enough to rise.' The timing was ideal. Schiannath was sleeping deeply – if Yazour was quiet, he could get himself up and moving before the Xandim became aware of what he was doing and tried to stop him.

Yazour sat up, catching his breath against the stab of pain from the arrow-wound in his shoulder. But it was better, he promised himself – a mere few days ago he would not have been able to move that arm at all. As he waited for the pain to subside to a background throbbing, Yazour looked around the cave, seeking something to support the weight of his injured leg. His sword had been his original thought, but Schiannath had prudently hidden all the weapons away beyond his reach. His plan seemed doomed to failure, but the young warrior had no intention of giving up so easily. The wall of the cave was sufficiently rough and broken to provide him with handholds. Yazour reached out with his unwounded arm, took a firm grip on a solid-looking projection, and began to pull himself slowly up.

Reaper's mercy! I had no idea it would hurt like this! Yazour clung to the stone as the cavern walls whirled dizzily around him. Sweat flooded his face and dripped stinging into his eyes. The weak muscles of his wounded thigh were a knot of screaming agony. 'Curse you for a whining weakling,' he goaded himself. 'Call yourself a warrior? You, the only hope of your poor friends.' Clenching his teeth, he let go his handhold, and tried to shuffle forward.

One step . . . two . . . The wounded leg gave way as though the bones had turned to water. The world tilted crazily – turned upside-down before Yazour could catch his balance. He was sprawling on the floor of the cave, one hand in the scattered embers of the fire. He snatched it back with a shriek of shock and pain, but his clothes were burning in a score of places. The horses screamed in panic, pulling at their tethers, then

Schiannath was there, wild-eyed and furious, shouting profanities in the Xandim tongue. He pulled the warrior out of danger, and flung the contents of his waterskin over both Yazour and his smouldering bedding. The fire went out in a choking cloud of smoke and ash, and the cave was plunged into darkness.

The warrior heard the click of flint on iron. A tiny flame bloomed like a flower on the end of a torch, and blossomed to illuminate the smudged and waxen face of Schiannath. The Xandim wedged the torch in a crack in the rock and scrambled over to Yazour, slipping a little on the slick and muddy floor.

'Fool! You were not ready.' Schiannath propped the trembling warrior in his arms. 'Are you much hurt?'

Yazour turned his head away from the Xandim, and sobbed as though his heart was breaking.

It took Schiannath a long time to restore order to the wreckage in the cavern. Yazour, wrapped in dry wolfskins, and sipping one of the Xandim's pain-ease infusions, could do nothing to help him. The young warrior, burning with humiliation, had reached the depths of wretchedness. What use was he, crippled like this? He had even become a plague and a burden to the man who'd saved his life. He avoided Schiannath's eyes, not knowing what to say.

Eventually, he felt a gentle touch on his shoulder. Looking around, Yazour saw that the floor had been mopped clean, and the mended fire burned brightly. A new bowl of snow was melting nearby, next to a bubbling pot of broth left over from their last meal. Schiannath, drawn and weary, was sitting beside him, holding out a cup of the savoury, steaming liquid. 'Come,' the Xandim said softly. 'Talk. What is this great need, that you must walk too soon?'

Yazour took a deep breath. 'My friends in the tower,' he said. 'They may be hurt, or even dead. I must know.'

Schiannath nodded gravely. 'I understand your torment. I should have thought of this sooner – but why did you not speak before? Set your mind at rest, Yazour. I will go myself, tomorrow night, and bring you news of your friends.'

'Here now – let me take that,' said Jharav. With relief, Nereni

243

surrendered the heavy basket, woven from withies that this same man, who was now captain of the troops in Yazour's place, had gathered for her from the outskirts of the coppice. Of all Harihn's guards, Jharav had been the most kind and helpful, keeping herself and Aurian well supplied with firewood and melting bowl after bowl of snow to let them bathe. Nereni felt sure, now, that his conscience must be troubling him. At first, she had despised Jharav as deeply as she did the rest of Harihn's men, but as the days of her imprisonment passed her resentment of the stocky, grizzled soldier had worn away until she no longer saw him in the same light as the rest of the prince's troop. Jharav was a decent man – and Nereni suspected that he had thrown his weight behind Aurian's persistent campaign to let her tend to Eliizar and Bohan. Some four days ago, Harihn had finally given in, and Nereni's heart had been eased, a little, by the daily contact with her husband. She felt that she owed Jharav a debt of thanks.

Jharav lifted the basket as though it was filled with feathers, and looked at her handiwork with an approving eye. 'This is a fine piece of work,' he told her. 'Your husband must be most appreciative of your skills.'

'My husband will be more appreciative of the stew if he gets the chance to eat it hot!' Nereni snapped. Kindness was one thing, but this amounted to flirtation. The little woman was breathless with indignation. Why, this man had a wife at home!

Jharav chuckled. 'Consider me chastened, Lady.' He sounded completely unrepentant. Taking her elbow, he helped her to descend the slick and narrow stairway that twisted down into the tower's roots.

The iron-bound door creaked slowly open, and a pale and ragged figure burrowed out of the pile of furs in the corner like a sand-rat emerging from its hole. 'Eliizar!' Nereni flew across the filthy floor to embrace her husband. Her heart seemed to catch in her throat as she felt the bony ridges of his ribs beneath his tattered shirt. 'But he's recovering now,' she told herself firmly. 'Each day, since they let me visit him, his wounds are getting better.'

'Nereni – are you well?' Eliizar held her out at arm's length, peering anxiously into her face. Though she really wanted to

244

bury her head in his shoulder and weep, Nereni forced herself to be brave for him.

'I am well, my dear.' From somewhere, she found a smile. 'And Aurian is also well, and growing bigger by the day!'

She knew what he would ask next, and dreaded the question. Why must he torture himself so? she wondered.

'Is there any news of Yazour?' the swordsman asked softly. Nereni shook her head, not trusting her voice at the sight of the hurt on his face. He had loved Yazour like a son. By the Reaper, it tore Nereni's heart to see him so unmanned by grief.

'Come,' she said firmly. She took his arm and led him back to his nest of furs. 'Come, Eliizar – eat some stew.'

As Nereni checked Eliizar's wound, a long shallow slice across the muscles of his belly, and applied salve and fresh bandages, she thanked the Reaper for the furs. She reflected, as she pulled bowls and spoons and the covered pot of stew from her basket, that undoubtedly these pelts had saved the lives of the two men in the damp and freezing dungeon. The Winged Folk had brought them two or three days after the companions had been captured, when she had complained to the prince that the tower room was too cold for Aurian. But when the dark, luxuriant furs had arrived, Nereni's blood had turned to ice, and she wished, on the Reaper's mercy, that she had never spoken. These were the pelts of great cats just like Shia! She tried to keep the Mage from seeing them, but she was too late.

Aurian had flown into a rage so terrible that Nereni had expected her to go into early labour on the spot. She had flown at Harihn with such violence that, though she had been armed with nothing but her bare hands, it had taken several of his guards to restrain her – and not before she had inflicted some telling injuries on them.

At the sight of those accursed pelts, something had broken within the Mage. Since that dreadful first night of their capture, she had remained as cool and firm as a bastion of stone, and Nereni had drawn inspiration from her courage. But after the furs had come, the little woman had been kept awake all night long by the storm of Aurian's bitter, heartbroken weeping.

245

Nereni blamed herself. She had gathered every single fur and brought them down here to Eliizar and Bohan, and the incident had never been referred to again. The following day, Aurian had been pale, but stern of face and calm as ever; but now, when Nereni looked at her, she saw an extra shadow of pain behind the Mage's eyes, and knew that she herself had put it there.

Once she was satisfied that Eliizar had mastered his emotions and was eating, she dished out another bowl of stew and took it over to where the eunuch huddled miserably beneath his own pile of furs. He had not been able to come to her – his captors, afraid of his tremendous strength, had fettered him to a ring in the wall with long but heavy chains. He had remained unscathed from the fighting, barring the many bruises where they had beaten him down at last, but his wrists, as thick as Nereni's arm above the elbow, had been chafed and scored by the heavy manacles where he had tried desperately to pull himself free. Due to the damp and dirty conditions in the dungeon, they were now a putrid mass of festering sores.

Bohan's plump face was grey now, and hollow-cheeked. Though he still had his enormous frame, he had lost so much weight that his wasted flesh seemed to hang from his bones like a beggar's suit of rags. Though the eunuch's hurts had been less serious than Eliizar's, he looked in a far worse state. Nereni knew why – she had seen the same thing happen to prisoners within the Arena. Chained and helpless, feeling that he had failed his beloved Aurian, Bohan had simply lost the will to live.

Thanking the Reaper that the Mage had been spared from seeing her friend in this appalling state, Nereni let him have his stew first – how could she refuse him, poor man? While he ate, she comforted him with news and messages from Aurian, which seemed to cheer him a little. Then, gritting her teeth, she bent herself to the nauseating task of cleaning his sores.

It hurt him dreadfully. Nereni saw the pain in the rigid set of the eunuch's face and the roll of his eyes; yet he sat there suffering patiently, and neither flinched nor moved until she had finished. What must it be like, Nereni wondered, to be in such pain and be denied the release of crying out? None the less, she forced herself to be thorough. By the time she had finished, and was bandaging the lacerated wrists as best she could beneath the manacles, both she and Bohan were shaking.

Nereni looked coldly at Jharav, who had been standing on guard by the door all this time, watching without saying a word. 'You are cruel to fetter him like this,' she snapped. 'How will he ever heal, with these iron bands that chafe and infect his hurts?'

Harihn's captain could not meet her eyes. 'Lady, take your anger to the prince, for this was not my doing,' he said abruptly. He bit his lip, and glanced uneasily at Eliizar. 'For my part, I agree with you,' he murmured. 'But if I value my life, there is nothing I can do, and you must not expect it of me.'

'Come, Nereni, he is right,' Eliizar put in harshly. 'You cannot blame the man for following orders – or if you do, you must also take the blame with me for all the atrocities that were committed in the Arena, to those poor wretches under our care.'

Nereni shuddered, and turned away.

While Nereni was visiting Eliizar and Bohan down in the cramped dungeon that was carved into the foundations of the tower, Aurian was making the most of her absence to take some welcome air on the roof. Usually, the little woman's protests about the state of the ladder were enough to deter the Mage from climbing up here, but she had reached the point, she felt, where one more day spent looking at the walls of that dingy, claustrophobic chamber would send her right over the edge into raving insanity.

Aurian sat, wrapped in cloak and blanket, beside the parapet of the tower, letting the crumbling wall shield her from the worst of the wind. Every once in a while, when she was tired of her thoughts, she would peer through a dip in the crenellations at the uninspiring vista below. Though no sunset had been visible through the heavy clouds, the light was fading rapidly, flattening the sweeping slopes and shadowed crags until it looked as though a gigantic sheet of dirty grey linen had been draped over the world.

It had been many days since the Mage's capture; fifteen, sixteen, more, she thought – she could no longer be sure. Aurian had never felt so desperate and helpless – not even when she was recovering from the wounds she had received in the Arena, and had been unable to go in search of Anvar. Even then, though she had been constrained by her wounds, she had known that Harihn was searching in her stead.

The thought of the prince fuelled Aurian's anger. That treacherous bastard, she thought. That monumental fool! I should have stuck a knife in him back then, when I had the opportunity, and taken my chances. The Mage fought against an overwhelming wave of despair. Why did he do it? she wondered. Why did he betray us? I saved his life when his father would have killed him. What did I do to make him turn against me like this?

Yet deep in Aurian's heart, buried amid her raging resentment, there lurked a shred of pity for Harihn. He had made his choice – had succumbed to Miathan's blandishments – and now, as she had told him, he was as much a prisoner as she. Had it not been for her own desperate situation, and that of Anvar and her child, Aurian might almost have forgiven him. As it was, however, she wanted to tear out his beating heart with her bare hands, and stuff it down his throat.

The Mage wished that she knew what had happened to those of her companions who were missing: to Shia on her long and lonely journey – oh, gods, how Aurian's heart had turned over when she had seen those accursed pelts! The thought that one of them might have belonged to her friend . . . But that was nonsense, she told herself firmly. If Shia had been slain, Harihn would never have been able to resist bragging about it. She thought of Yazour: was he even still alive? And Anvar, imprisoned in the Citadel of Aerillia . . . The Mage crammed her knuckles into her mouth, and bit hard to keep back tears. Oh, Anvar, she thought. How I miss you. And to make matters worse, though she had cudgelled her brains through every sleepless night since she'd been taken prisoner, she had been unable to come up with a single plan to save Anvar, her child, or herself.

The Mage froze, as the response of her child intruded into her mind. Even after all this time, it still startled her, and she was both alarmed and dismayed to find that her despair was causing him distress. Aurian sighed. 'Dearest, I'm all right . . . ' She sent out impulses of love and reassurance, but at the same time her mind was racing. As the time for his birth drew nearer, her son's thoughts were growing stronger and more articulate – and, unfortunately, more perceptive to the turmoil of her own emotions.

Aurian frowned. What could she say to him? How could she explain, in terms he could understand, why she communicated so much pain these days? Though she knew that he had access to her feelings, she had always tried to shield her most private thoughts from the child. Had the little wretch been eavesdropping? I'll have to be more careful in future, she decided.

Aurian wondered if this close mental link would continue to exist after her son was born. Less than a moon now, she thought, and I'll be able to hold him in my arms. Me, a mother! Dear gods, I don't think I'll ever get used to the idea. Less than a moon now, and you won't have the chance to hold him, she reminded herself, if you don't stop daydreaming and come up with a plan to save him.

What was that? Aurian tensed, hearing a new sound, from somewhere close at hand, above the wind's thin whine. A scratching and a scrabbling that could only be the scrape of leather boots against stone, followed by the spatter of falling pebbles and a muffled curse. The Mage drew in a sharp, hissing breath. Someone was climbing the outside of the tower.

Dusk was falling fast now. In the last remaining light, Aurian saw a huff of steaming breath rise above the parapet. Hastily, she rose to her feet and edged back towards the trapdoor – then cursed herself for a fool. Whoever was trying to sneak into the tower was hardly likely to be any friend of Harihn, or the Archmage. For an instant, Aurian's heart leapt in an absurd and desperate hope. Anvar! Could he have somehow escaped? 'Don't be ridiculous,' her common sense told her. 'Anvar is too valuable as a hostage to have escaped without aid – and it's too soon for Shia to have reached him.' Aurian frowned. Could it be Yazour? Her heart leapt at the thought, but none the less, the Mage had no weapon to hand, and because of the need to protect her child hand-to-hand fighting was out of the question. It would pay her to be circumspect. Silent as a ghost, Aurian slunk behind the tottering stack that housed the tower's

249

crumbling flues. Glad of the comforting warmth of the rough stones beneath her ice-cold hands, she peered out, round the corner, at the deserted stretch of parapet.

Aurian thanked all the gods that her night vision, along with her Mage's knowledge of tongues, were the only powers that had not deserted her in her pregnancy. The roof was shrouded in night's shadow – and then suddenly a darker shadow detatched itself from the gloom and dropped lightly down from the parapet. Aurian stiffened. A single glance at the man's stealthy, skulking movements told her that he was not one of Harihn's people. Tallish, though not as tall as herself, he had a lithe, wiry body and dark, silver-shot hair that fell in curls around his shoulders and glinted in the faint snow-glimmer; the white drifts that spread across the landscape for miles around the tower prevented the night from ever growing completely dark.

The Mage watched with increasing curiosity, barely daring to breathe, as he crept towards the trapdoor and knelt to peer down into the chamber that was her prison. He would find it dark and empty, Aurian knew, for she had forgotten to light a torch before coming up here, and Nereni was still below with Eliizar. The man paused, his head cocked, listening for the sound of voices below. 'Lady Aurian?' he called softly. 'Lady, are you there? Do not fear me – I come from your friend Yazour.'

Swift and silent, the Mage left her hiding-place and approached him from behind. 'I'm Aurian. Who are you?' she whispered.

The man leapt up with a startled oath, and Aurian hushed him hastily. Before he could grope for his sword, she had seized him by the elbow and dragged him into the shadowed lee of the chimney-stack. Still firmly holding his arm, she used her night vision to peer closely into his face. It was not a face to inspire trust in a stranger. It was angular, bony, and unshaven, with a jutting nose and crinkled crow's-feet at the corners of the hooded, light grey eyes, which were staring-wide with shock as he tried to see her in what to him was darkness.

Absurdly, Aurian found her mouth twitching in its first smile in many days. Dear gods, she thought – no wonder he looks as though he'd seen a ghost. If someone had crept up on me like that . . . 'I'm sorry,' she told him, surprised to hear the alien sound of yet another language coming out of her mouth. 'I didn't mean to startle you. I am Aurian.'

'Goddess be praised,' the man breathed. 'My name . . . ' for a moment he hesitated. 'My name is Schiannath. Yazour sent me to aid you, if I can.'

'Yazour is all right?' The weight of Aurian's worries suddenly grew lighter.

'Wounded, but recovering,' Schiannath told her gravely. 'The goddess herself told me to help him. I found him in the pass – he was being attacked by a great cat – and . . . '

Aurian was suddenly seized with a delightful notion. 'Did the goddess sound, well . . . more irascible than you had imagined she would?' she interrupted.

The man frowned. 'Why, indeed she did! But how did you know? Does she talk to you also, Lady?'

'You might say that,' Aurian said wryly. She swallowed a chuckle. I wonder how Shia managed that? she thought.

To the Mage's astonishment, Schiannath dropped to his knees. 'Lady, indeed you are blessed,' he said. 'In my land, we revere those who are with child as the special chosen of the goddess Iscalda. I swear myself to your protection, for this must truly be what the goddess intended for me, when she made me save Yazour.' He hesitated. 'But how may I aid you, Lady? I can scarcely fight a towerful of guards, but maybe if you were able to climb down . . . ' He looked doubtfully at Aurian's rounded shape.

'No, I can't,' the Mage said quickly. 'One of my companions is being held hostage elsewhere, and if I escape just now he will surely die. But there is one thing you can do, Schiannath, that would help me enormously. Do you have a weapon you could lend me? A knife, maybe? Something that could easily be hidden?'

'Of course.' Schiannath pulled a long, slender dagger from his belt. As she took it from him, a thrill of excitement passed through Aurian. At last, she was no longer unarmed and helpless! When her child was born, she could protect him.

'Schiannath,' she said gravely, 'I can't thank you enough for

251

this. But where is Yazour? Are his wounds too bad to let him climb? Can you give him a message from me?'

'That much I can do,' Schiannath said eagerly. 'He was desperate to come to you, to the point of endangering his healing – so I offered to come in his place, and take back news of you, if I could.'

Oh, gods! Aurian thought. I wonder how much of the language Yazour can speak? I'll wager this poor man hasn't the slightest idea what he's getting himself into.

The Xandim might have been reading her mind. 'It still seems a miracle,' he said. 'Yazour promised me that you could speak my tongue, but he lacked the words to explain, and I regret to say that I did not believe him. Lady, the likes of you has never been among the Xandim – that much I know. How came you to be fluent in our language?'

The Mage bit her lip, remembering the Khazalim distrust of sorcerers. Were the Xandim the same? If she told him the truth, would she alienate this unexpected benefactor? 'Tell the truth,' some inner instinct prompted her. 'If you lie, he's bound to know – and that will damage his trust in you just as much as the other.'

Aurian took a deep breath. 'Schiannath... Do you remember that you swore to protect me? Does that oath hold good, no matter what I am about to say to you?'

The dark-haired man was frowning. 'Lady, you ask a great deal. How can I answer you, on something I have not yet heard?' He hesitated. 'Yet I gave my oath – and I do have some shreds of honour left, no matter what some may say. Besides, the goddess spoke to me. I know she wanted me to help you, one of her chosen. Say on without fear. What dreadful secret can it be, that causes you such hesitation?'

Aurian looked him in the eye. 'I know your language because I am a sorcerer.' She stopped speaking abruptly, and frowned. The word that had left her mouth bore little similarity to the Khazalim word 'sorcerer', and had a slightly different meaning. It had come out as something that she could only translate as 'Windeye'. What the blazes did that mean?

Schiannath's face brightened with comprehension – he made a strangled sound deep in his throat, and Aurian, to her

252

dismay, saw his face light up with joy. 'A Windeye! Blessed goddess! Now I comprehend your plan. Oh, thank you. Thank you!'

To Aurian, his delight seemed out of all proportion, and the Mage's heart sank within her. Oh, no, she thought. Dear gods, please don't let him be another one like Raven, who needs my powers to help him. This is just too cruel.

'Wait,' she told him softly. 'How much of our story has Yazour told you?'

Schiannath shook his head. 'Little, in truth. He is learning my language, but as yet he lacks the words. I was hoping that you might make things clear for me, Lady.'

'Yes,' Aurian sighed, 'I think I should. You have a right to know what you're getting yourself into.' She sat down, her back propped against the warm stones of the chimney, and pulled her ragged blanket more closely around her shoulders. 'Well,' she said doggedly, 'this is how it goes . . . '

Though the hours that stretched by until Schiannath's return were the longest Yazour had ever spent, the Xandim's news, on his return, more than made up for the wait. Aurian was unharmed – for the present at least – and it was plain that Schiannath had fallen under the Mage's spell, Yazour thought wryly. The warrior had never seen his rescuer so excited. Glad as he was, however, to hear that Aurian was safe and well, the remainder of the Xandim's tale filled Yazour with alarm. Shia missing. Raven a traitor. Eliizar and Bohan hurt and imprisoned. Anvar a captive of the Winged Folk. Before Schiannath had finished speaking, Yazour was looking for a way to get to his feet, and demanding his sword.

'No.' Schiannath, shaking his head, was holding him down with gentle insistence. 'Aurian says we wait.'

'Wait?' Yazour was appalled. 'How can I wait, when my friends are suffering? They need help. Accursed fool, you misunderstood her!' Only when he saw the blank look on Schiannath's frowning face did the warrior realize that he had been shouting in his own language.

Schiannath's eyes glinted. 'She says we wait. When the child comes – then we fight!' His voice had taken on an edge of

253

stone, and his fingers dug into Yazour's shoulder with bruising force. 'Before you fight, you must heal,' he added pointedly.

Reluctantly, Yazour subsided. 'How will we know when the babe is born?' he asked sullenly.

'Each day I will watch. She will signal – a flame at the window. Then – we move!' His eyes were alight with excitement.

Yazour sighed. More waiting! But Aurian was right. They were badly outnumbered, but if she waited for her powers to return, she would be able to fight. In the meantime, it seemed, he must school himself to patience – and try to get back on his feet as quickly as he could.

17
The Challenge

Parric was drunk again. He had reached the point in his drinking where he knew he was drunk, but didn't care. It had been his only solace in the long, dull days that had been crawling by, since the Windeye had rescued him from the mountain. The cavalry master, sitting on a snowy log outside the great stone spire crowned by Chiamh's Chamber of Winds, looked over his shoulder at the looming Wyndveil and shuddered, remembering that nightmare descent. He had always thought himself tough enough to cope with any crisis, but he had never fought a mountain before. Oh, gods, that journey . . . Struggling through the endless snow, burdened by a dying old man, with the storm hunting at their heels, and his own constant fear that those monstrous cats might be tracking them . . . Fighting fatigue and frozen limbs, and the paralysing consciousness that one false step might mean a lethal plunge over the edge of a precipice . . . 'Dear gods,' Parric muttered thickly. 'Is it any wonder I'm drunk?'

For the first time in his life, the cavalry master had found himself unequal to his situation, and he was taking it badly. 'What am I doing here?' he muttered, for about the hundredth time. 'I'm a plain, honest fighting man, I am; give me a sword in my hand, and a good horse under me, and I can handle anything. But when it comes to mountains and giant cats and half-blind spooks who talk to the wind, and then turn into bloody horses in front of your eyes . . . ' He closed one eye and squinted carefully and critically at the leather flask he was holding. 'Not that he's a bad little chap, mind you – and he makes bloody good mead. A bit sweet for my taste, but it has a kick like a warhorse! Maya would have liked it.'

And there, of course, lay the true reason for his drinking. Parric was homesick for Nexis, as it once had been, and would

255

never be again. He missed the garrison, and his responsibilities as an officer. He missed using his skills, and teaching them to new recruits. Most of all, he missed the companionship; the rough-and-tumble of weapons practice, the comradeship of drills and patrols; the drunken nights spent in the Invisible Unicorn with Maya, Forral and Aurian. Parric was drunk because he was angry, frustrated and, at the moment, helpless. Though he was terrified for Aurian's safety, and desperate to reach her, the cavalry master was forced to bide his time until the dark of the moon, as the Windeye had so poetically phrased it.

'Wait,' Chiamh had counselled. 'You cannot go alone, across the mountains. Only wait until the time is right, and you can go to the aid of your friend with an army of Xandim at your back. I have a plan.'

There was nothing wrong with the plan, Parric conceded grudgingly. Well, he hoped not. The cavalry master knew nothing of Xandim customs, and had been forced to take Chiamh's words on trust – as he had been forced to believe the Windeye's assurance, gleaned from his vision on the winds, that Aurian would be found at the Tower of Incondor.

Despite his frustration, Parric found himself grinning as he thought of Chiamh's plan. By Chathak – the lad didn't lack for nerve. The cavalry master recalled the night when he and the young Windeye had sat discussing plans in Chiamh's cave at the foot of the spire. (If you could call it a cave. In Parric's experience, a cave was a hole in a cliff, or a sheltered hollow in the rocks, not a place where the furnishings – bed, benches, and table – had seemingly grown out of the living stone.) For sheer audacity, Chiamh's scheme had taken the cavalry master's breath away.

'You cannot count on aid from the Xandim,' the Windeye had said, waving the mead-flask vaguely in Parric's direction. His large, short-sighted eyes had been squinting slightly with drunkenness. 'While my folk are fierce and swift to defend themselves against the Khazalim marauders, aggression has never been part of our philosophy.' Parric fielded the flask with practised adroitness, and took a long swig as Chiamh continued: 'From my vision, of which I told you, I know that your

256

friends the Bright Ones must be helped. There is but one way to force the Xandim to fight for you – and that is to become their leader yourself.'

'What?' Parric choked on his drink, and spluttered. Blue flames shot high as a spray of mead hit the fire. Chiamh thumped him helpfully on the back.

'When the moon is dark, you must challenge the Herdlord for leadership, according to the way of our tribe,' he said. 'There may be difficulties, of course, for you are an outlander, and not as we are; but our law states that anyone may challenge, and the winner must be accepted as leader – until the next dark of the moon, at least, when he may be challenged again, by some other. Until that time, his word is law.'

'But, Chiamh,' Parric had protested, 'I dare say I can fight as well as the next man, but what if . . . '

'Yes, I know. Phalihas has the advantage of his ability to change into horse-form – but if you are a horseman, as you say – ' Chiamh shuddered at the word – 'then you will have an advantage over him. You see, our tradition is that the challenge must be carried out in equine shape, so if you can get on to the Herdlord's back and best him, the leadership will be yours.'

Parric frowned. 'It's not a fight to the death, then?'

The Windeye shook his head. 'Not necessarily – but in your case, it will be. As you are an outlander, the Herdlord will certainly try to kill you. Be warned. But to win the leadership, you need not slay Phalihas, only force him to concede defeat.'

'Oh, fine.' Parric sighed. This is the craziest thing I've ever heard, he was thinking to himself. Tomorrow morning, the young idiot will have sobered up and forgotten all about it . . .

Chiamh had done nothing of the kind.

The cavalry master was jolted out of his drunken memories by the sight of Chiamh and Sangra walking towards him through the snow. The Windeye looked cheerful as usual, but the warrior had a certain hard look in her eye that she had been reserving for Parric ever since he had taken up serious drinking. Didn't the woman understand that this endless waiting was enough to drive any man to the flask? Parric turned

257

to face her, determined to be friendly none the less. 'How's Elewin?' he asked.

Sangra's expression softened a little. 'Sitting up in bed, eating stew, and complaining bitterly about the accommodation,' she grinned. 'Gods save us, he's a tough old beggar! How Chiamh managed to pull him back from the brink of death like that I'll never know.'

She smiled fondly at the Windeye, and Chiamh grinned back at her through the flopping fringe of his hair, then turned his attention to Parric. 'Come.' With unexpected firmness, he prized the flask from the cavalry master's clutching fingers. 'It's time to sober up, my friend. The dark of the moon is only three days away.'

Meiriel, shivering in her hiding-place among the broken rocks at the head of the valley, was awakened from a doze by the cavalry master's whoop of joy. Snarling like a beast and muttering vile curses, she peered out to see what was afoot, and cursed again in disgust. Nothing. As usual. The three of them, Parric, the warrior-girl and the little Xandim man, were standing together in a group, waving their arms and talking excitedly. Talk, talk, talk – that was all they ever did. Imbeciles! Meiriel spat upon the freezing rocks. What was the point of following these useless Mortals all the way down the accursed mountain if they did nothing. She needed them to lead her to Aurian – and Miathan's blighted monster, which lurked in Aurian's womb . . .

The healer roused herself, and blinked. By all the gods, it was almost nightfall – what had happened? Her limbs had stiffened with cold and the expanse of trampled snow below her hiding-place was bare. A burst of panic forced the heat back into her veins. Had she lost them? Had they gone without her? But no. In the mouth of the Xandim's shelter in the base of the spire, she could see a slip of flickering gold where the firelight was reflected on the snow. Meiriel felt giddy with relief. As usual, they had done nothing. But this time it was just as well.

Crawling on her hands and knees until she was well out of sight, Meiriel slunk back to her own cheerless shelter among the broken rocks. Thanks to the Xandim's habit of burying his supplies in caches, so that the frozen earth could keep them fresh, she had found food and furs enough to ensure her survival. She could wait those wretched Mortals out, she told herself, if it took them for ever. Sooner or later they would set off again in search of Aurian – and when they did she would be close behind. Someone had to do what must be done. In the fetid darkness of her lair, Meiriel chewed on a sliver of raw meat and smiled to herself. Tomorrow would be soon enough to watch again.

'So what do we do now?' Parric knew he was chattering to keep his nervousness at bay, and despised himself, but he couldn't help it. The windsong keened across the shadowy vastness of the Wyndveil plateau like a soul in torment; the snapping tongues of the bonfires seemed to be reaching out for him; the hostility of the crowds of Xandim that surrounded him was a palpable wall of hatred and rage that combined with the dark and watchful presence of the standing stone that loomed above him. Parric was not an imaginative man, but this place made his flesh creep.

'We keep vigil,' Chiamh replied, to the question the cavalry master had forgotten he'd asked. 'Make good your questions now, Parric, for once the sun vanishes behind the shoulder of Wyndveil silence must be kept until dawn, or the challenge is forfeit. And when dawn comes, you fight!'

Parric shivered. 'How will you know when the sun sets?' he asked. 'You can't see it behind the cloud.'

The Windeye shrugged. 'We are the Xandim – we simply know,' he replied.

Parric snorted. 'Lot of nonsense, if you ask me,' he muttered under his breath. Elewin had heard him, though, and chuckled. The old steward, despite Sangra's protests, had insisted on coming, and was seated, a shapeless bundle wrapped in layers of furs, close to the fire. No doubt Elewin was feeling light-headed, Parric reflected, from the medicines with which Chiamh had dosed him to keep his cough from breaking the silence of the vigil. Stupid old coot, the cavalry master thought. I should never have let him come. If he messes everything up with his wheezing . . .

259

Instantly, he was ashamed of himself. Parric knew that his nerves were making him irritable, but he couldn't help it. This was not the way he would normally spend the night before a battle: no sleep, no food, no talk – and no drink. He thought back to the good old days, when he and Maya and Forral would find a tavern before a battle, or sit around a campfire just like this one with a shared wineskin – several skins, if they could get them. Parric sighed at the memory of his commander. *Oh, Forral,* he thought. *Wherever you are; wherever warriors go when they die, I hope you're watching tonight. Help me tomorrow if you can, because I'll need all the help I can get, and I'm doing this for Aurian . . .*

The shimmering sound of a horn rang out across the plateau. The Windeye, casting an eye towards the heavens, nudged Parric and laid a finger to his lips to signal that the silent vigil had begun. The cavalry master sighed, and tried to turn his thoughts to more positive subjects. So far, everything had gone as planned. Yesterday, the Windeye had come down here to deliver his challenge to the Herdlord, who had accepted, as by law he must.

'It was not a popular decision,' Chiamh had confided on his return. 'No outlander has ever challenged before, and the people were outraged. Had the Herdlord not encouraged his folk to mock, rather than protest, I would have been lucky to escape with my life. Folk are already calling me Chiamh the Traitor.' He had shaken his head sadly. Parric, looking at him, had thought that the Windeye had been lucky to escape in any case. He had come back covered in bruises and cuts from hurled stones, and caked from head to foot with pelted dung. Sangra, on seeing him, had almost wept with indignant rage – a rage that echoed Parric's own.

Chiamh had brought back a surprise from the fastness that had lightened Parric's heart a little. He'd come staggering back up the valley, long after nightfall, carrying a long, leather-wrapped bundle. Ignoring Sangra's protestations over his bruised and dung-spattered state, he had dumped his burden into Parric's arms.

'I wish I could have found your own weapons,' the Windeye apologized, 'but they were too well guarded. Still, at least you will not be forced to fight the Herdlord with your bare hands.'

When the cavalry master had unwrapped the bundle he had found two swords, one for Sangra and one for himself. They were nothing like the quality of his own lost blade, for the pastoral Xandim possessed little skill at forging. None the less, he was glad to have even this sharpened length of brittle, badly tempered iron between himself and the Herdlord's hooves and teeth. If only the Xandim hadn't found his hidden knives – but perhaps he could manage. Turning to the Windeye with a grin, Parric said: 'Do you by chance have a grindstone – and any blades I could turn into throwing knives?'

The cavalry master was brought back to the present by a crawling sensation between his shoulder-blades, as though he was the focus of unfriendly eyes. He looked across to the foot of the other stone, where Phalihas and his companions were keeping their vigil. In the firelight, he caught the Herdlord's eye, and scowled. Phalihas held the look, his own eyes glinting with anger – and already, it seemed, the battle had begun.

The brazen cry of a horn cut through the thick wall of mist like a shaft of sunlight, but it was the only indication that dawn had come. Parric stretched stiff limbs and rubbed his gritty eyes. By the balls of Chathak, he thought, that was the longest night of my life. Until this solid mist had hidden the camp of his opponent, the cavalry master had spent the night in staring contests with Phalihas, and so far the honours had come out about even. Chiamh handed him a waterskin and he took a sip – it was the only sustenance allowed him before the fight, though the Windeye had told him that a victory feast was in preparation down in the fastness. Well, Parric thought, I have every intention of enjoying that feast. Heartened by the thought, he tipped the remains of the waterskin over his balding head, in the hope that it might wake him a little, and wiped his face on his cloak. Chiamh nudged him. 'It is time to begin,' he whispered.

Parric was puzzled – he had expected speeches, or some kind of ritual. 'What do I do?' he asked.

'Walk out on to the plateau. When the horn sounds, combat will commence – so be ready.'

'What? The horn sounds and I fight him? Is that it? Shouldn't somebody say something, at least?'

261

Chiamh grinned. 'I did that for you yesterday. Today you fight. Now hurry – and may fortune go with you.'

Parric had barely walked a dozen paces, cursing the fog, when the harsh cry of the horn pierced the greyness once more. 'Damnation!' The cavalry master reached with frantic haste for his sword, but before the blast had time to die away there was a drumming of hooves on turf and a huge black shape came swerving out of the mist to his right.

It was on top of him before he could complete the draw. Parric glimpsed the flash of a white-rimmed eye as he dodged and rolled, expecting at any second to be smashed by the pounding hooves. He heard the harsh rasp of tearing cloth, and felt a hot and bruising agony in his shoulder where the great slablike teeth had torn out a mouthful of flesh. Something dug into his side – Great Chathak, he'd rolled on his sword – and where was that demon horse?

Parric completed the roll and sprang to his feet, tottering on knees gone strangely shaky. His foe had vanished into the mist again; playing cat and mouse, Parric thought bitterly – and it had the advantage. He couldn't see it, but with its sharper senses it could hear him – and smell the blood that streamed down his arm from his bitten shoulder. The cavalry master allowed himself a sour chuckle. His enemy had come at him from the right, to disable his sword arm – but the creature had not noticed that Parric was left-handed. Quickly, he reached to draw his sword, and his blood turned to ice. In rolling on it he had bent the ill-crafted blade – and the bloody thing was jammed in its scabbard!

There was no time to think as hoofbeats welled up through the fog. The sound was deceptive – he had no idea from which direction it was coming. Parric barely had time to dodge as the black stallion hurtled past, carving up clods of turf with its feet. A flying hoof smashed into his knee, wringing a curse from the cavalry master, but even as he swore Parric was groping in his sleeve for a knife, flicking it swiftly after the retreating figure in the fog. A scream told him it had hit its target, and a grin split Parric's face. The hours spent reshaping and balancing the blades with Chiamh's grindstone had been well spent. 'One for me!' he muttered gleefully.

Before the beast could come at him again, Parric reached down and slid another of the knives from his boot. The spilling of his enemy's blood had buoyed him; once again, as it had always done, the battle-urge overwhelmed him, singing in his veins, loosening his muscles and sharpening his senses. He no longer noticed his bruised and rapidly swelling knee, or the pain of his torn shoulder that dripped ribbons of blood on to the grass. Knife in hand, the cavalry master stood peering tensely into the blind, grey murk; awaiting the next onslaught of his enemy.

'Oh, gods, what's happening now?' Sangra pulled at Chiamh's sleeve. Absently, the Windeye plucked her hand away and held it in his own.

'I can see no more than you,' he told her, 'but I imagine the Herdlord is using the mist to screen his attacks. From that scream, I'd guess that Parric has wounded him, at least; but whether our friend has also been hurt . . . ' He shrugged. 'Who can say?'

Sangra growled a bloodcurdling oath, and fell to loosening her sword in its scabbard with her free hand. 'I hate this helpless feeling,' she muttered. 'If only we could see . . . '

'Even if we could, we could do nothing,' Chiamh reminded her, 'but I, too, would feel better if I knew what was happening. Besides, Phalihas is using this fog to his own advantage . . . ' His words were cut off by another rumble of hooves, and beside him Sangra tensed, her strong, calloused warrior's hand nearly breaking the bones of his own, so hard did she grip it. The hoofbeats faltered; the thud of an impact came clearly through the mist. A man's voice cried out in pain and on the heels of the cry came another enraged squeal of agony from the stallion. Sangra scrambled to her feet, taking Chiamh with her. From the Herdlord's camp by the other standing stone there came the slithering ring of drawn steel as the shadowy figures of his companions leapt up in answer to her sudden movement.

'Sit down!' Chiamh hissed, and pulled the frantic warrior back to the ground beside him.

'A pox on this festering mist,' Sangra muttered. She turned to the Windeye with wide-eyed appeal. 'Chiamh – you do some

263

kind of peculiar magic with the wind, don't you? Can't you get this wretched stuff to blow away?'

The Windeye was as shocked as if she had hit him with a stone. 'Me?' he gasped. 'Sangra, you don't understand. I can work with the wind, but I cannot make the wind work!'

'You're right, I don't understand.' Sangra glared at him. 'But by Chathak's britches, Chiamh, can't you even try?'

Once more, the Windeye heard the sound of hooves; stepping warily now, with a faltering rhythm. Through the mist came the sound of Parric's breathing; harsh, ragged gasps that caught in his throat, as though the warrior was in pain, and reaching the end of his endurance. The Herdlord was hurt, Chiamh thought, but so is Parric. Phalihas is circling; stalking; waiting his moment . . . Oh, blessed Iriana, help me . . . Help me bring a wind . . .

Without some kind of breeze to work with, even Chiamh's Othersight would not function. He closed his eyes, trying to reach out with his other senses. The moist, turgid air resisted him; thick and gelid, heavy and dead. Using his mind, the Windeye pushed at it with all his strength. It was like trying to push the Wyndveil mountain. Chiamh felt his heart beginning to labour; felt himself trembling with exhaustion. Sweat poured down his face and trickled, tickling, along his ribs. Oh, Iriana, he thought; goddess, help me. I need a miracle. And the goddess heard him.

There was the faintest of sighs, like a distant woman's voice that whispered his name. Chiamh felt the gentle touch of a breeze, like cool fingers laid against his cheek. His heart leapt within him like a river-salmon in the spring. More, it needed more . . . With all his strength, the Windeye pushed . . . and opened his eyes to see the mist dissolving, unravelling before his eyes in curling strands.

'Chiamh, you did it!' There was the sweet, firm pressure of a mouth on his own as Sangra kissed him, and for a moment Chiamh forgot all about the challenge.

Parric shook his head and blinked. Is it clearing? he thought. Surely . . . Yes, by all the gods – it is. The strengthening wind cooled the sweat on his hurt and weary body, and with the passing of the gloomy murk the cavalry master took new heart. His opponent must be tiring too – and on his last pass Parric had lamed him.

The stallion had come charging out of the fog, and Parric was under its feet before he had a chance to blink. The horse had reared above him, intending to crush his skull beneath those colossal hooves – and had met Parric's knife, instead, slicing down the inside of its foreleg and aimed at its unprotected belly. The horse had screamed and wrenched itself aside, landing a glancing kick in the cavalry master's ribs and spraying him with gore from the injured leg – not hamstrung, as Parric had hoped, for his stroke had somehow gone awry, but limping badly.

Since then, the Herdlord had treated him with greater respect. For a time they had been circling blindly in the mist, but now . . . There, close by, was the looming form of the black stallion; its head hanging, its sides heaving, as it blew puffs of steam from its snorting red nostrils and glared at him with furious white-rimmed eyes.

Parric gasped. For the first time, he had a clear sight of his enemy, and for a moment he forgot that this was not a true beast, but one who could take on human form. As a horse, it was the most magnificent creature he had ever seen. The cavalry master looked in awe at the clean, powerful limbs; the finely sculped head with its wild, dark, intelligent eyes; the tremendous curving sweep of the great arched neck; the liquid play of fine-etched muscles beneath the midnight coat that now was dull with sweat and blood, where Parric's first knife had lodged in the thick muscle of the haunches.

Thank the gods I didn't manage to hamstring him! To destroy such a creature . . . A horseman to the very depths of his being, Parric felt his heart melt within him in a surging wave of longing and joy – until this glorious creature gathered itself for one last desperate effort, bared its great white teeth, and charged.

Parric had been expecting something of the sort, and now instinct took over. As the horse came up to him, he sidestepped quickly, ignoring the grinding pain in his hurt knee; grabbed a handful of mane as the stallion hurtled by, and leapt. It was not a clean leap. The wrenched knee gave under him, and the cavalry master found himself hanging on by his tightly tangled fistful of mane, one leg half-across the horse's back, the other waving wildly as he strove frantically to pull himself up. Seconds stretched out into an eternity as Parric, tensing his arms until his muscles screamed in protest, clawed himself on to the surging back, pulling himself up inch by inch from his perilous position in midair. At last he made it; found his seat and his balance, as the horse went berserk beneath him.

The powerful body seemed to explode across the plateau in a series of jolting bucks that jarred every bone in Parric's spine and rattled the teeth in his head. Twining his hands deeply in the long, flowing mane, he wrapped his wiry legs around the horse's ribs and stuck to the stallion's plunging back like a burr to a dog.

The creature reared, shrilling its fury, but Parric clung tightly, refusing to be unseated. It tried to run, and made an incredible effort, despite its injuries. The cavalry master clenched his aching teeth and concentrated on staying on. From the tail of his eye, he caught blurred and dizzying glimpses of the plateau, the mountains – and the hundreds of Xandim, hidden by the fog until now, who had come to watch the challenge.

Dear gods, Parric thought incredulously; how fast would he be if he were sound? Never in his life had he ridden such a beast. Though the stallion's abrupt, arrhythmic paces were giving his own wounds a fearful jolting, the cavalry master was oblivious of the pain. He whooped aloud in his euphoria. 'Father of the gods! What a ride!'

But the stallion was tiring fast. His steps began to falter, and his sides were heaving as his breath wheezed in and out. Eventually, he came jerking to a halt in a series of stiff-legged bounces. With a sinking heart, Parric tensed as the horse dipped its head and rolled over, its long black legs flailing wildly. The cavalry master leapt awkwardly to the side, to avoid being trapped beneath. He landed clumsily, and felt his injured knee give under him with an agonizing crunch. Curse it! He rolled quickly aside, out of danger, but by the time he had climbed to his feet it was plain that his opponent was finally spent.

266

Parric felt his throat tighten as he watched the creature's pathetic efforts to rise. 'Perdition!' he muttered. 'I didn't want it to end like this!' But his attention was distracted from the struggling beast by an ugly murmur of rage from the watching crowd. The cavalry master swore, and attempted once again to free his sword, but it was no good. The wretched blade was . thoroughly jammed. Then a frantic figure burst through the milling ranks of the restive crowd, and came pelting across the grass towards him. Behind the Windeye, the crowd broke at last and came racing after him with weapons drawn.

Chiamh, to Parric's surprise, ignored him completely. Instead, the Windeye came to a panting halt before the stricken Herdlord and raised his hands in a series of intricate, flowing gestures as he began to intone some words in the rolling Xandim tongue. It was as though the pursuing crowd had run into some invisible barrier. To a man, they stopped dead, their faces blank with horrified disbelief.

Parric glanced back at the Windeye, and his stomach turned over. Chiamh's eyes had changed, horribly, from their usual soft brown to hard, bright, blank quicksilver; giving his normal, rather vacant expression a demonic, otherworldly cast. Parric shuddered. What the blazes was going on?

At last, the Windeye reached the end of his blood-chilling chant. Tears streaked his face, and he looked as though he had aged a hundred years. As he approached the cavalry master, sagging with weariness, Parric was relieved to see that the silver seemed to be draining away from his eyes, leaving them their usual, reassuring colour. With his bruised ribs knifing him as he breathed, and his injured knee stiffening now, and hurting like perdition, Parric could not have run away if he had wanted to – and he didn't want to, he told himself firmly. The Windeye took hold of his right hand – it was all that Parric could do not to flinch from his touch – and flourished it aloft.

'Hear me, my people,' the Windeye cried. 'This day a challenge has been given, and met, according to our ancient law. I give you, O Xandim, Parric – your new Herdlord!'

Jeers and curses came from the crowd, and Chiamh blinked anxiously. 'Quiet!' he yelled, abandoning his stately dignity of speech, and to Parric's amazement the roar of the crowd was

267

instantly hushed. 'You all saw what I did just now,' the Windeye continued. 'I spoke the words to trap Phalihas in his equine form, until the spell is removed again. I regret the deed, but it was the only way to ensure my own safety, and that of the new Herdlord and his companions. As yet, I have no heir to my powers . . . ' he blushed self-consciously, 'so I am the only one who can restore Phalihas to his human state – as I will, I promise . . . eventually. In the meantime, those who deny the new Herdlord will share the fate of the old one.'

Once again the crowd began to mutter restively, but he had them now. This time, Chiamh had only to hold up a hand for silence, and the Xandim obeyed. Parric, shaking with pain, and hunger and exhaustion, was wishing heartily that the wretched Windeye would just shut up, and let him go somewhere quiet where he could put his feet up and have a large and well-earned drink while his wounds were being tended, but even he was forced to listen closely, as though bespelled by the Windeye's words.

'My people,' Chiamh said sadly, 'you think me a traitor for siding with outlanders, yet I would not have done such a thing without a reason.' He straightened, eyes flashing, his long brown hair blowing back in the breeze. 'O Xandim – you must make ready for battle. The Khazalim have crossed the desert and formed an alliance with black sorcerers, and with our other foes, the warlike Winged Folk. I have seen this in a vision – and I swear it is true!'

Chiamh's next words were drowned in an angry roar of protest, and once again he was forced to bellow for silence. 'We are not a warlike folk,' he said into the hush that followed. 'Though we can defend ourselves fiercely at need, we lack the organization and battle skills that have permitted the Khazalim scum to raid us with impunity in the past. But this time it will be different!'

The Windeye turned to Parric, who was staring at him in amazement. 'This outlander can lead us; can teach us the skills we lack. He seeks companions who were captured by the Khazalim scum, and will offer us his aid until his friends can be released, and our lands swept clean again. At that time, he promises to relinquish the Herdlordship and leave us in our former seclusion, keeping the secrets of our folk for all time. O Xandim – for the sake of our lands and the future of our children – will you have him?'

This time, the roar of assent almost knocked Parric off his feet. 'Chiamh, you've a way with words,' he told the young man gratefully.

The Windeye shrugged modestly. 'Who would have thought it – least of all me.'

The crowd surrounded them, staring curiously at Parric. Some of the bolder ones reached out to touch his alien clothing. Sangra, who all this time had been standing at bay with her back to the standing stone, defending Elewin with drawn sword, came pushing with the steward through the throng, her face aglow with relief. 'Well done, Chiamh!' She pounded him on the shoulder.

Some of the Xandim had gathered in a knot around the former Herdlord. To Parric's relief, they were assisting the exhausted, injured beast to climb shakily to its feet. 'Now that the people seem to have accepted me, will you change Phalihas back?' he asked the Windeye.

Chiamh shook his head. 'Too dangerous,' he said flatly. 'Not everyone may be convinced – and in this state, Phalihas ensures our safety, for if he could speak, he would oppose you. Our former Herdlord is a proud and stiff-necked soul.' A grimace, like the memory of old pain, shadowed his face – then, with an effort, he brightened. 'It will be time enough to restore him when we have done what we set out to do – but now, O Herdlord, you have a feast to attend!'

'Thank the gods for that,' Parric said feelingly. Then his face fell. 'Chiamh – I won't have to make a speech or anything, will I?'

'Where's the problem?' Sangra teased him. 'After a couple of wineskins, we usually have trouble shutting you up!'

Chiamh, his lips twitching to hide a smile, hastened to comfort the dismayed cavalry master. 'Don't worry, Parric – I think I have said what needed to be said.' At last, his grin escaped him. 'What would you do without me?'

'What, indeed?' Parric agreed. 'And tomorrow, I'll need you again, my friend – when we prepare for battle!'

269

*

Meiriel watched from her hiding-place behind the standing stones as the last of the Xandim left the plateau to accompany the new Herdlord to his feast. 'Herdlord, indeed!' she snorted – but at least the wretched Mortal was finally doing something. The Mage smiled to herself. If Parric meant to use the Xandim to rescue Aurian, that meant he would be bringing her here – along with the monster she had spawned. 'Why, thank you, Parric,' she crooned, 'you've just saved me a long hard trip through the mountains. And when you return with Aurian – I will be waiting.'

18
Spirit Of The Peak

'And there you have it,' Anvar finished. 'That's the whole story – so far.' He took a sip of wine to moisten his throat.

Elster was looking at him, her head cocked slightly to one side, her dark, bright eyes fixed upon his face. She frowned. 'Now I see why it took you so long to trust me with this.'

Anvar nodded. 'I had to be convinced, in the first place, that I *could* trust you.'

'And you trust me now?' Elster's eyes narrowed.

'Gods, I've got to trust someone,' Anvar cried. 'Elster, I must get out of here!'

The physician sighed. Ever since she and Cygnus had begun to visit this fascinating alien prisoner, her sympathy towards him had grown at an alarming rate. But to her shame, she had simply lacked the courage to assist him in any of his increasingly bizarre plans to escape. 'Alas, Anvar, what can I do?' Her wings rustled as she shrugged. 'My own life hangs by a thread, and were it not for my skills, Blacktalon would have had me murdered long ago. As it is, he is depending on me to heal Queen Raven . . . '

'How is she?' Anvar interrupted.

Elster spread her wings helplessly. 'She lives – but she will not speak, and we must force sustenance down her throat. When we enter the room, she turns her face to the wall. I see your eyes harden when I speak of her, yet if you saw her I am certain you would pity her. Though it is difficult to tell, since she will not speak to us, I'm sure she is bitterly ashamed of what she has done.'

'As far as I'm concerned, she brought her suffering on herself.' Anvar's voice was hard. 'Don't ask me to pity her, Elster. Though even I was sickened by what was done to her, I can never forgive her for what she did.'

271

'Yet if you could only see the poor child, your heart might soften.' Elster shook her head sadly. 'I cannot imagine what effect your news would have on her. Perhaps it would do more harm than good for her to know that her lover's mind was in thrall to your ancient enemy.'

'Then you believe me?' Anvar relaxed a little. 'I wasn't sure that you would.'

Elster took the forgotten goblet from his hand, and drained the wine in a single swallow. 'Oh, I believe you, Anvar. Too much of your tale rings true.' Turning, she groped for the flask in a dark corner beyond the firelight, and refilled the goblet before handing it back to him. 'I can also believe that the High Priest has allied himself to an evil sorcerer,' she went on. 'He is desperate to restore the lost magic of the Skyfolk, which perhaps is understandable: but Blacktalon's mind has flown too high, and fallen into madness.' She grimaced. 'He is convinced now that he is a new incarnation of the doomed Incondor.'

'What?' Anvar's eyes opened wide in surprise. 'Aurian told me of Incondor, and how he brought about the Cataclysm.' He shook his head. 'No wonder Blacktalon and Miathan chose one another. Both have gone beyond the bounds of sanity in their pursuit of power.' Anvar leaned forward and grasped the physician's wrist. 'Elster, you've got to help me escape.'

'Anvar, I cannot,' Elster interrupted flatly. 'Not now. I would assist you, as would Cygnus, but Blacktalon keeps a constant watch on our movements. Besides, what could we do? The only way out of here is by flight, and Cygnus and I have not sufficient strength between us to bear you far enough to escape the warriors that the High Priest would send after us.'

'What about the other Winged Folk?' Anvar said. 'Surely there must be some who oppose the High Priest?'

'No one dares. The city is paralysed by fear and suspicion, Anvar. Blacktalon's spies are everywhere, and it is impossible to discern who they may be. You must understand that there are many among us who would wish to see the Skyfolk in the ascendant once more – at whatever cost.' Elster sighed. 'If there are those who would help us – and I'm sure there are – they dare not reveal themselves. Anvar, I truly wish to help you, but you must be patient. The time is not ripe to strike back at Blacktalon. If Cygnus and I were to contrive your release at this point, we would be unable to rally opposition against him. Not without the queen. And it would be clear to him who had done the deed. We would lose our lives for nought.'

'But you could come with me.' Anvar interrupted. 'The gods only know, we could use you.'

Elster's feathers quivered. 'What – and abandon our rightful queen? Without the skills of Cygnus and myself, Raven will die, for certain.' Seeing the flash of anger in Anvar's eyes, she rose to her feet. 'You may not care whether or not the queen survives, Anvar, but I do. I must.' Seeing him about to protest, she took her leave hastily. 'I will return when I can,' she promised, and launched herself, with unseemly haste for a master and a physician, out of the mouth of the cave.

It was still dark, though a faint glimmer of dawn was beginning to brighten the bleak sky beyond the mountains. Elster beat upwards, feeling the icy wind go whistling through her feathers, banking in a wide looping turn that took her well away from the cliff. To the physician's relief, a few scattered lights could still be seen among the towers of the city, allowing her to get her bearings and head for home. She hated flying by night – the dangers could not be overestimated – but if she wanted to visit Anvar undetected, it was the only time to do it; while the other Winged Folk were safely at rest.

Elster's home was located in a crumbling turret that clung to the side of an ancient building in the lower part of Aerillia. In Flamewing's day, the physician's quarters had been grander and close to the palace itself, but now she felt safer dwelling in obscurity and anonymity. A few leaks and draughts were well worth suffering, if it kept her out of the High Priest's way.

Landing with care on her snowy porch, Elster pushed open the door to her rooms – and hesitated, one hand on the latch, peering into the gloom within. Surely I left a lamp alight? she thought with a frown; and then shrugged. Perhaps it had gone out in her long absence, or been blown out by one of the whistling draughts. The physician had not gone three paces inside the room when she was seized.

*

'Why have I been arrested?' Bruised, bound and guarded as she was, and facing Blacktalon's hard, expressionless eyes, Elster had to fight to keep her voice steady. *He knows*, she thought despairingly. *Oh, gods – he must know!* The physician had never been inside the priest's high tower in the Temple of Yinze, and was unnerved by the tomblike blackness of the polished obsidian walls. Outside, the screeching plaint of Incondor's Lament swirled round the tower, sending shivers through the physician's body, and preventing her from concentrating her thoughts to form some kind of defence.

Blacktalon lifted a sardonic eyebrow. 'Did you really believe you were the only one prepared to fly in darkness?'

Elster stifled a gasp, and fought to keep her face expressionless. 'What do you mean, High Priest? A physician must often fly in darkness, if there is an emergency . . . '

Blacktalon burst into peals of mirthless laughter – the most chilling sound that Elster had ever heard. 'Elster, my spy was hiding just beyond the mouth of the cavern. He heard everything. Next time, if you insist on playing the innocent, I would suggest that you occasionally look outside whilst you are plotting with a prisoner.' His eyes glinted. 'Not, of course, that there will be a next time for you. I have Cygnus to keep Raven alive, though your unguarded words condemned him also.' He shrugged. 'For now, however, I will permit him to keep his life – for as long as he is needed.' Again, that mirthless smile.

The flash of rage as she realized that Blacktalon was savouring her fear was the only thing that kept Elster from collapse – until the High Priest's next words: 'It has come to my attention, Elster, that you are lax in your religious observances. I have never yet seen you attend a sacrifice within the temple.' His voice grew hard. 'Tonight, at sundown, we will rectify that omission. You shall experience the next ceremony – as the victim!'

Even by the standards of an Immortal, it had been a long time. Aeons had passed since the Moldan of Aerillia Peak had last been wakeful. She gauged the intervening centuries by the subtle differences in the society of the Winged Folk, who dwelt upon and within her body: the alterations in culture, in clothing, and above all in the language. The Moldan was accustomed to such shifts. For her, the passing centuries were an eye's blink apart. Nowadays, only events of great significance awakened her – momentous times; times of struggle and change.

What had wakened her this time? The Moldan cast her senses forth, surveying the domain that was her body, roaming the flanks of the mountain that was her flesh and bone, and outer skin.

Ah – significant. On the upper reaches of her pinnacle, the temple whose foundations were being laid when she had last lost herself in the mists of sleep had grown into a massive structure. The tortured rock, in the shape of a clawed and grasping hand, looked like melted, twisted bone, and the Moldan shuddered, reminded of the riven corpse of her brother, far to the east. What warped brain had designed such a hideous edifice?

Below the temple the city had prospered and grown. Here, the delicate beauty that she remembered as typical of Skyfolk architecture had blossomed into many new and incredible forms. In the past, the Moldan had been indifferent to the flitting Winged Ones who had colonized her after the departure of her own Dwelven population, looking upon them as trivial, ephemeral beings. Now, for the first time, she felt a smug sense of pride in their achievements. Apart from that hideous temple on her peak, their works had done much to adorn and accentuate her natural beauty.

With regret, the Moldan wrenched her attention away from her contemplation of the city of Aerillia. It was then that she felt it – the slow, erratic approach of a source of incredible power.

Dishes rattled in the upper city and possessions fell from shelves as a thrill of mingled terror and delight ran through the Moldan's massive form. In her lonely tower, the captive Queen Raven twisted in her sleep, and cried out in pain. In the Temple of Yinze, Blacktalon looked up frowning from the sacrifice he was about to despatch, as the menacing black edifice shuddered on its massive foundations. In the older quarter of the city, a crumbling parapet toppled, and went crashing down the mountain's face in a cloud of snow.

275

The Moldan paid no heed to the puny beings that infested her slopes. Her entire attention was fixed on the approaching Staff of Earth.

'Anvar? Anvar, can you hear me? For the last time, will you not answer?' Shia waited, her head cocked expectantly, for the space of many breaths, but no reply was forthcoming. Despondently, the cat turned back to her companions. 'The human must be asleep,' she sighed. 'I cannot wake him.'

Khanu shook his mane. 'So what do we do now?' he demanded. Hreeza lifted a heavy paw and cuffed him into silence. He whirled on her, eyes flashing balefully, but Shia stopped his retaliation with a sharp command. She knew that although the old cat was making a valiant effort to hold fast to her courage, Hreeza was dismayed, as were they all, by what they had found at the end of their journey.

Had Shia been human, she might have railed against the gods at the unfairness of it. The long struggle up the stony knees and snowy breast of Aerillia Peak had been difficult and toilsome, taking them several hard and hungry days of travelling under the cover of darkness to foil the farseeing vigilance of their skyborne foes. As the cats made their slow ascent, the cultivated terraces of the Winged Folk had given way to steep, sloping valleys clad in spruce and hemlock, which thinned at last to reveal a stark and lonely land of soaring crags and snow-scoured rock.

Shia and her companions had forced their way upwards, going ever more slowly as the snow grew deeper, and the whistling winds more chill. Despite their thick coats, the cats were pierced through and through by cold and hunger, for all animal life had long since fled from the inhospitable upper slopes of the peak. Grimly they had struggled on, Khanu and Hreeza driven forward by Shia's threat to leave them where they lay, should they founder.

This dawn had found the cats scrambling in single file between the jaws of a narrow, snow-choked gorge. As they reached the top, the fanged crags dropped away to their right, to reveal the lower mountains of the northern range spread out beneath them, their jagged, snow-capped peaks seeming to float like islands on a sea of blood-red cloud. The smouldering ball of the newly risen sun lurked beyond the hunched shoulders of the mountains, glowering beneath low brows of heavy cloud that capped the sky above.

The weather-wise Hreeza growled low in her throat. 'I don't like the look of that,' she muttered.

'If you don't like that, I suggest you take a look in the opposite direction.' Shia's mental voice was choked. The old cat turned away from the baleful sunrise, and her breath grew still in her throat. Up, she looked, and up, at soaring walls of stone . . .

'Well, what do we do now?' Khanu repeated, keeping a wary distance between himself and Hreeza. 'I can't see how we can possibly climb up there.'

'I don't know.' Shia glared at the Staff of Earth where it lay on the snowy ground, fighting the furious urge, born of pure frustration, to chew the wretched, troublesome thing into splinters. Her breath huffed out in a crystal cloud as she sighed. 'I suppose we must wait until Anvar awakes – perhaps he knows of some way up.'

Hreeza looked again at the smooth, sheer curtains of stone that soared straight upwards and disappeared into the clouds above. Shia could sense a strange reluctance in her old friend's mien, and wondered what was coming. 'Well?' she said at last. 'Are you going to chew on that thought like an old bone for the rest of the day, or will you spit it out and share it with us?'

The old cat refused to meet her gaze. 'Are you so certain,' she said slowly, 'that the human merely sleeps? What if he is dead?'

Flame kindled in the depths of Shia's eyes. 'I will not accept that.' Her voice was laden with quiet menace. 'Aurian's foes need Anvar as a hostage – why would they kill him?'

'Yet I sense your doubt,' Hreeza persisted. 'Anything may have happened. An accident – a change of plan . . . To stay up here, exposed to the weather and to our enemies, is folly.'

'Anvar is not dead!' Shia bared her teeth, advancing threateningly on the old cat.

'Why not wait a while and see?' Khanu broke the tension

277

between the bristling females. 'After all,' he added, 'we did not come all this way just to give up so soon. And while we wait for Shia's human to wake, we can always explore the foot of this cliff. Perhaps there may be an easier place to climb, further along.'

Shia looked at him gratefully. Khanu was beginning to develop both the sharper wits of a hunting female and the common sense of an older, more experienced beast. Right now, she appreciated his intervention. It was imperative that Anvar be released before the birth of Aurian's child, in order to give the Mage freedom to act to save the cub's life. The slow and difficult journey to this place had driven the great cat into a fever of anxious impatience, but that was no excuse for her unreasoning anger at Hreeza's intervention. With unswerving loyalty, the old cat had followed her all this way, only to be defeated, in the end, by this last unconquerable obstacle. Even if Khanu and I can find a way to climb that cliff, Shia thought, Hreeza cannot – and she knows it. That is the true reason behind her obstructive attitude – she can't bear the humiliation of being left behind.

'You think there might be an easier way up elsewhere?' Hreeza was demanding of Khanu. Bless him, Shia thought, for restoring my old friend's hope, if only for a time.

Khanu twitched his whiskers forward in the cat equivalent of a grin. 'Why not?' he said cheerfully. 'I certainly hope there is – for though you may be able to scramble up there, the climb is far beyond my skills.'

'Let us go, then, youngster, and try to find a place that won't overtax you!' Hreeza's eyes were bright again. Before Shia picked up her burden of the Staff once more, she briefly touched noses with the young male in a heartfelt gesture of thanks.

'Shia? Is it really you?' Anvar's mental tones were ringing with joy and relief, though the cat was certain that no one in the world could be more relieved than she at making contact with the Mage at last. It was worth this long and arduous journey to feel his hope blaze up, renewed, when she told him that Aurian had sent her with the Staff of Earth. 'Dear gods,' he cried. 'I

278

saw you, in a dream, as you were crossing the mountains – but I thought it was only the fever.' But Anvar was anxious for news of Aurian, and could listen to nothing else until Shia had told him what little she knew. Because of her stronger link with the Mage, she hoped to establish mental contact once Aurian's powers returned, as did Anvar himself. Whether this would prove possible over such a distance, only time would tell.

Unfortunately, Anvar could offer the cat no help with her present difficulty. 'The cliff is utterly sheer for as far as I can see,' he told her. 'To my left there's a waterfall, about the length of a bowshot away from the cave, but that won't be much use to you – the torrent is very swift, and it doesn't look as though you can get behind it.'

'At least it will tell us where to find the human,' Khanu pointed out to Shia. Although he could 'hear' Anvar, he had not yet found the confidence to address this alien creature directly.

'Your friend has a point,' said Anvar, when Shia passed on the young cat's contribution.

'He certainly does,' she agreed. 'We've been searching since sunup, and found no trace of any way to ascend. I was hoping for a tunnel, perhaps, but . . . '

'No, it won't be as easy as Dhiammara. I've explored this cave thoroughly, and there's no other exit. Gods, Shia,' Anvar's thoughts were tense with frustration, 'are you sure you can't scale the cliff?'

'Never fear, we'll keep looking,' Shia told the Mage. 'Those low clouds will shield us from any watchers above.'

'These low clouds are also ready to drop another lot of snow on our heads,' Hreeza pointed out, but no one was paying her any attention. Shaking her head in dismay, the old cat limped stiffly in the wake of the others as they set out to search once more.

An hour later, Shia was wishing she had listened to Hreeza's warnings. The cats had worked their way along the base of the cliffs until they found the massive waterfall, and it was then, as they explored the churning green pool at the foot of the cascade, that the snow began to fall.

Thick and fast came the whirling, heavy flakes. Whipped

into flurries by the rising wind, they drifted deeply in the angle at the foot of the cliffs, making it impossibly dangerous to seek refuge there. Indeed, the only shelter on this windswept plateau lay far behind them – the gorge where they had made their original ascent.

'Well, it's no use trying to get back there now,' Hreeza pointed out. 'We would perish long before we reached it.' Despite her thick, shaggy coat she was shivering violently, her black fur already plastered white with a clinging sheath of snow. 'We may as well keep going, and try to find a place to shelter somewhere along the foot of the cliff.'

Shia looked doubtfully at the growing drifts. 'Even supposing there is such a place, it will be buried out of our sight.' She took a tighter grip on the Staff of Earth. 'There's only one thing to be done. I must climb up the cliff to Anvar now, before this cold saps the last of my strength.'

'Shia, you cannot! No one could hope to climb that cliff.' Hreeza protested. 'Would you die for nought?'

'Far from it.' Shia held the old cat's eyes with an unwavering gaze. 'Hreeza, this matter is greater than all of us. Anvar must have the Staff, or not only the lives of my companions will be lost, but the entire world besides.'

Shia's quiet determination robbed Hreeza of words. She looked away. 'Very well,' she mumbled, her mental voice hushed with emotion. 'You must do as you must, my friend. But, Shia – be careful. If you lose your life in this climb, I must avenge you, and these new enemies of yours are too much for one old cat to handle.'

'Shia, I will come with you,' Khanu offered eagerly.

The great cat glared at the younger male. 'You will not!'

'Why not?' Khanu sulked. 'If you can do it, so can I – and you will need me when you reach the top. There are many foes upon that mountain, as well as Anvar.'

She sighed. 'You may be right. But hear me out. I have good reason for wanting you to stay behind, for if I should falter and fall, then you must take my place, and climb with the Staff in my stead.'

Khanu's eyes grew very wide, but he said nothing. Shia,

taking his silence for acquiescence, turned from her friends with soft words of farewell, and began to climb.

Anvar, safe from the blizzard in the cave above, was frantic. He cursed, and drew a weary hand across his eyes. During his illness, the Mage had lost track of how long he had spent in this accursed hole, but he was sure that the birth of Aurian's child must be imminent. Only sheer Magefolk stubbornness had prevented him from giving up hope over these last days, and Shia's sudden appearance with the Staff had seemed nothing less than a miracle. Now, however, it was as though the cup of hope had been offered to him by the capricious gods, only to be dashed from his lips once more.

Shia's sendings had become progressively weaker as the cats struggled on in the teeth of the storm, fighting their way forward against the bone-piercing blast of the wind that heaped the snow ever deeper in their path. Pacing back and forth across the stony floor of the cave, Anvar raged against his helplessness. Gods, if only I could help them, he thought. There must be something I can do. Then, as if to add to his torment, the rough old voice of a strange cat flashed into his mind with a message that turned him cold with dread.

'Human, we can find no other way up. Shia has decided to climb up to you, so it will be as well if you do not try to speak to her for a while. She will need all her concentration if she is to survive.'

'Stop her! She mustn't do it,' Anvar cried. 'It's not possible to climb this cliff!' In his mind, he heard the cat's dry, humourless chuckle.

'It's too late to stop her. Already she climbs. But bear in mind that what is impossible for a human may not be so for a cat. Her claws can find the tiniest crevices, and she can stretch her limbs beyond the distance that a mere human could reach.' Then Anvar heard a note of doubt creep into the old cat's voice. 'That is, if her strength holds out.' Hreeza's words faded into a sorrowful silence.

Anvar rushed to the cave mouth and hung perilously over the edge, trying to peer down through the layers of cloud and twisting veils of snow. It was hopeless. The storm obscured

281

everything. Realizing that it would take Shia some time to accomplish her climb, and that it would serve no purpose to stay out here and freeze, Anvar returned to his fire. Numb with horror, he sat down, staring sightlessly at the flickering, frost-blue flames, and began to pray.

At the foot of the cliff, the old cat turned from her conversation with the frantic human, and found herself alone. Above her head she caught a flicker of movement as Khanu's tail vanished into the blizzard. Hreeza's own tail lashed in anger. 'Come back, you young fool,' she roared. 'Shia ordered you to stay down here.'

From above her, Khanu's voice came strained and stilted as he struggled to maintain his hold on the sheer face of the mountain. 'Shia was wrong,' he said flatly. 'I have no doubt that she'll reach the cave – and when she does, she will need my help.' A note of cunning entered his voice. 'Of course, if you were to tell her what I'm up to, it might prove a fatal distraction, but that is between you and your conscience, old one. Now leave me alone – this climb is harder than it looks.'

Hreeza, snarling with frustration, turned away from the dreadful cliff. She had no gods to invoke, and lacked the human relief of cursing. Her companions, discounting her as too old, worn out and spent to attempt the climb, had not even thought of including her in their plans. Driven by the urgency of their quest, they had left her to survive the blizzard as best she might. Rage and resentment flashed through Hreeza, sending a surge of hot blood through limbs that were already growing stiff and numb. Leave her to perish in the snow, would they? Well, she'd see about that. There was life in the old cat yet – and she would sell that life dearly, and on her own terms.

How long had she been climbing? Shia had no recollection. Time had stretched so that eternity encompassed this icy stretch of cliff to which she clung with the strength of pure desperation; yet the boundaries of her world had narrowed and shrunk to a scant few feet of stone, and the next slight chip or chink in the rock which might provide a slender purchase for her blunted, shredded claws.

Shia's head was swimming with weariness, and the Staff, clenched in her aching jaws, interfered with her breathing and obstructed her vision. Her limbs, unnaturally splayed to hold her close to the cliff and locked for so long in that one position, felt as though they were strung together by strands of searing fire that ran into her body to bind her labouring lungs in a vicelike embrace. With her entire weight suspended from her claws, Shia dared not think of the endless plunge to oblivion that awaited her should she weaken even for an instant. She very carefully kept her thoughts away from the near-impossibility of the task that she had set herself. Instead, she simply kept on going, refusing to give in; fighting an endless series of small battles for each new burning breath, and moving laboriously, one paw at a time, inch by inch, like a small black fly up the face of that vast, unyielding wall of stone.

'Shia?' Anvar's tentative voice cut across her concentration like a whipcrack. Jerked abruptly from its trance of suffering, exertion, and endurance, the will of the great cat faltered. Shia's weight seemed suddenly to double, and her claws scrabbled frantically at the slick stone surface as she slid for several inches, almost dropping the Staff, her claws digging deep grooves in the crumbling rock, her heart leaping into her throat, until she reached a spot where the cliff leaned slightly inwards, and she could find her hold again.

Anvar's cry of horror still echoed around the rocks above her. When the pounding of blood in her ears had quieted, Shia heard him cursing himself in an uninterrupted stream of oaths, in a voice that shook more than a little. The great cat leaned her head wearily against the icy stone and waited for her breathing to steady and her limbs to stop trembling. In the meantime, she diverted her thoughts from her brush with death by telling Anvar exactly what she thought of him. It took quite a while, and by the time she had finished, Shia felt ready to go on.

Now that she was aware of her surroudings, the cat noticed that the blizzard was slackening – and she also saw why Anvar had been forced to risk distracting her.

'You need to move across to your left now, Shia,' he told her. 'You were going to miss the cave entirely.'

Shia forgave him at once. Above her, the cliff stretched on

and on beyond the dark blot that marked the cave mouth, and Shia shuddered at the thought of climbing endlessly, until her strength gave out and she fell . . .

'Stop that!' Anvar's voice cut firmly across her despairing thoughts. 'Come on, Shia,' he wheedled, 'you can do it now. Why, you're almost here.'

His words put new heart into the exhausted cat. Anvar was right, of course. Given the distance she had already come, this last little stretch would be nothing! 'At times like this, I can see why Aurian is so fond of you,' she told the Mage gratefully. Buoyed by the warmth of her friendship with this human, Shia gathered the last dregs of her faltering strength and began to climb again.

With one last weary heave, the great cat hauled herself over the lip of the cavern entrance, assisted by Anvar's strong grasp around her upper limbs. At long last she relinquished her precious burden, dropping the Staff of Earth at Anvar's feet with a soaring sense of triumph before collapsing bonelessly to the ground.

Shia lay, her chest heaving, her vision dim with exhaustion, as Anvar's hands gently smoothed the pain from her cramped and trembling limbs. His touch sent a tingling warmth through strained and weary muscles, and in its wake Shia felt a glow of wellbeing and energy renewed. As her vision began to clear, she saw the haze of shimmering blue round his hands, and realized that Anvar was using magic, as Aurian had done in the desert, to restore a measure of strength to her. After a few minutes, Shia stretched luxuriously and sat up, and Anvar ceased his ministrations to lay a gentle hand on her sleek, broad head. 'That was a mighty climb, my brave friend,' he told her softly, with a catch in his voice. 'Shia, I don't know how to thank you.'

'Well you'd better think of a way,' Shia retorted tartly, 'because I don't intend to do it again.'

Laughing with pure relief, Anvar threw his arms around the great cat, hugging her hard, and Shia rolled over on her back like a playful kitten, wrapping her great paws around him, and rubbing her head against his shoulder as the cavern reverberated with the booming rumble of her purr.

'Help me . . .' Had it not been for that anguished mental cry, Anvar would never have noticed the weak and pitiful whimper that accompanied it. The tiny sound would have passed unnoticed in the midst of his joyful and boisterous reunion with Shia.

'What the blazes was that?' the Mage demanded as he disentangled himself from the great cat's embrace.

'It had better not be who I think it is,' Shia muttered wrathfully as they rushed to the cave mouth to peer out.

'God save us,' Anvar cried. 'Another one!'

Shia peered past the Mage. 'It's Khanu,' she said. Anvar could see the young cat hanging by his forepaws just below the lip of the cavern – in trouble and plainly at the end of his strength. Already, his grip was beginning to loosen. 'Anvar, can you reach him?' Shia cried.

The Mage was already on his stomach, leaning out over the drop. 'Curse it, I can't – not quite . . . But wait. I know!' Scrambling up, he dashed back into the cave and returned with the Staff of Earth. Holding tightly to the head that bore the crystal, he lowered the other end down to the terrified young cat.

'Grab this, and hold on tight,' Anvar instructed. As Khanu grabbed the Staff in his jaws, the Mage linked his will with the mighty powers of the Staff and pulled, as though hooking a fish from a river. Khanu, the Staff held tight in his jaws, came flying up the last few feet of the cliff, impelled by Anvar's strength augmented out of all proportion by the power of the Artefact.

Unfortunately, the Mage had overestimated the amount of force he would need. Letting go of the Staff, the cat went hurtling into the cave past Anvar and Shia and rolled across the floor, narrowly missing the fire, to fetch up hard against the further wall, where he lay, stunned, bruised and breathless, as the others ran towards him.

'You wretch! You idiotic young fool!' Shia was already snarling. 'Did I not tell you to stay behind?'

Khanu, in no state, as yet, to defend himself, looked utterly wretched, but even as Anvar felt a twinge of sympathy for the young cat, the merest flicker of shadow across the bright cave mouth caught the corner of his eye. Damn! Skyfolk! Thinking quickly, Anvar picked up the pile of catskins that lay by his bed and flung them over Shia and Khanu in their shadowy corner. 'Don't move! Don't make a sound!' he warned the cats, as just in time he remembered to hide the Staff away out of sight.

The sound of Winged Folk entering stilled Shia's shocked and furious protests. Now that the blizzard had ceased, Anvar's guards were bringing his daily ration of food, and the Mage cursed himself for having forgotten. Thank the gods they didn't come any sooner, he thought.

As soon as Anvar's captors had left, Shia and Khanu emerged from beneath the pile of furs as though they had been scalded. Both were shaking with anger and revulsion, and Anvar didn't blame them. He knew how he would feel if he had been forced to conceal himself beneath a pile of human corpses. Dropping to his knees, he put an arm around each of the great cats. 'I'm sorry,' he told them softly, 'but it was the only way to hide you.'

Khanu slunk into a corner and began to retch, but Shia glared balefully at the pile of skins. 'How many would you say are there?' she asked Anvar. Her voice held the bite of ice and steel.

'Ten – a dozen, maybe,' Anvar told her. 'To be honest, I needed them in order to survive, but they filled me with such horror that I never wanted to examine them closely. I can't bear the sight of them.' He shuddered.

The great cat looked at him gravely. 'You are a friend of cats, Anvar. Those who once wore these pelts would not begrudge you their use now. But as for those murdering Skyfolk – ' Her gaze kindled like cold fire. 'You have the Staff now, Anvar – when do we start? I wish to kill today. The Skyfolk will pay for this atrocity in blood.'

Anvar had no quarrel with Shia's sentiments – he had wasted enough time kicking his heels in this accursed hole, and he too had debts to pay. 'First you and Khanu must eat, and rest a little more,' he told her. 'Once I start this, I want to be thorough.'

While Shia and her companion shared the meat brought by the Winged Folk, Anvar picked up the Staff of Earth and sat down beside the fire with the slender, serpent-carved Artefact in his hands. At the Mage's touch, the green crystal clasped in

286

the serpents' jaws began to bloom with a growing emerald radiance, and the magically charged wood vibrated and hummed with such power that Anvar had to exert every ounce of his will to keep the energy contained and dampened until it could be properly focused. The Staff was Aurian's gift, and the key to his freedom, brought to him beyond all hope by Shia's heroic journey. Buoyed by the thought of his love, Anvar began to formulate his plans of escape and vengeance.

Elster, though she dared not help him openly, had been lavish with her information. Anvar had only seen the edifice from a distance, but he knew that the menacing structure that crowned Aerillia Peak was the focus and seat of Blacktalon's power, and the place where he would most likely be found. With the awesome power of the Staff of Earth, Anvar would be able to strike directly at the temple – right through the heart of the mountain.

Briefly, the Mage's lips curled back in the grimmest of smiles. Too long had he and Aurian been helpless and imprisoned. Now it was time to turn the tables on their foes. By all the gods, he was looking forward to this.

19
Return to Nexis

Eliseth looked up from the scroll she was studying as the Archmage burst into her chambers without knocking. For an instant, Miathan saw the dark line of a frown between her brows, but she hid her irritation quickly beneath a mask of sociability. Pushing the scroll down the side of her chair, she stood to greet him, and gestured to her maid, who had been sewing in the corner, to pour wine.

'What has happened?' the Weather-Mage asked. 'I gather from your precipitate entrance that it must be something of importance.'

'Vannor has been captured.' Miathan swung around sharply at the brittle crash of splintering crystal. The little maidservant was standing by the cabinet, wide-eyed with horror, the knuckles of one clenched fist held to her mouth, looking down at the twinkling shards that strewed the floor. Crimson wine splashed her skirts and pooled like blood around her feet.

'You clumsy little wretch!' Eliseth grabbed the unfortunate girl by the shoulder and slapped her sharply, twice. 'That was one of a matched set! Hurry up and pour some more, and get this mess cleaned up. You'll be beaten for this.'

'And you'll enjoy it.' Miathan smiled cruelly as Eliseth returned to him. 'How very kind of her to give you an excuse.'

The Weather-Mage shrugged. 'Who needs an excuse? Which is just as well, for she doesn't provide me with many. To give the brat her due, she's the best maid I've ever had.'

'No matter.' Miathan shrugged aside such unimportant considerations. 'Eliseth, I have just made the most useful discovery.' He went on to tell her of his confrontation with the captured merchant, and his excitement when he found out the extent of the magical energy that could be transmuted from a Mortal's pain and fear.

288

Eliseth cursed disgustedly. 'What? So you mean that all those human sacrifices were unnecessary? We could have saved ourselves the trouble of procuring new victims by keeping a handful of prisoners alive and torturing them?'

'To a certain extent,' the Archmage replied judiciously. 'For magic requiring a massive boost of power, however, like possession from a distance, I should think that a sacrifice would still be required. None the less, this discovery presents some interesting possibilities. Some experiments will be in order, I believe – and what better subject than Vannor himself?' His voice sank to a purr. 'The man is tough-minded and physically strong. If we take care of him, I should think he'll last a good long time.'

The Weather-Mage nodded avidly. 'Where have you put him?'

'I had Aurian's old chambers cleaned up for him.' Miathan smiled at her astonished expression. 'We shall want him close to hand, and we must pamper him – for as long as he lasts. Besides, the only other place we could have put him is the archives beneath the library, and it would be easier for him to escape from there – or even be rescued. No, I have him this time – and he will not escape again!'

Vannor opened his eyes, and for an instant wondered where he was. Then his guts clenched with terror as he remembered his capture and subsequent confrontation with the Archmage. The aftermath of Miathan's assault was still with him: he felt weak as a newborn colt, and his body throbbed with an all-encompassing ache. But his discomforts were lost in surprise as he took note of his surroundings.

The merchant had been expecting a dungeon. Instead, he found himself in a soft bed that stood in a pleasant chamber with green and gold hangings on the walls, and a fire burning brightly in the grate. The furnishings were delicately wrought, their lines flowing and simple; all their richness in the deep glow of dark polished wood. Vannor shivered. What was the Archmage up to? Frankly, he would have preferred the dungeon. 'At least, that way, I'd know how things stood,' he muttered to himself.

A cup stood on the night table by his bed. An experimental sip proved that it contained taillin, still warm, and laced with spirits. Vannor could feel its heat all the way down to his stomach. His body craved the warm liquid. Before he had time to worry about whether the cup might contain anything worse, he had drained it to the dregs. The liquid seemed to put new life into him. Cursing, the merchant dragged his stiff, aching limbs, still marked in places from the ropes that had bound him, out of bed. Blessing the huge fire that blazed in the bedroom grate, he staggered across to the doorway that led into the next room.

A fire burned brightly in the living-chamber too. Everything was neat, clean and welcoming, just as he remembered it from long ago. The familiar surroundings brought back the past so sharply that Vannor lurched against the doorframe, undone. A groan wrenched its way from the very core of his being. He remembered dining with Aurian on several occasions, in this very chamber that had once been her own. Aurian – and Forral. And where was Aurian now? Vannor wondered. How was she faring? It must be about time for the poor lass to be bearing her child. And where was Zanna? Despite his best efforts, she was still wandering at large somewhere in the sink of vice and iniquity that the city had become. By the gods, if he ever got his hands on that wretched girl, he'd . . . His view of the room became suspiciously blurred. Vannor rubbed his eyes vigorously, and told himself he was suffering the after-effects of Miathan's attack.

Moving like a sleepwalker, the merchant checked the chambers thoroughly. The door was locked, of course, and he could get nowhere near the windows for Miathan's spells. When he tried to touch the crystal panes, there was a flash of light, and his hand was engulfed in burning pain that shot up his arm. It felt, for an instant, as though he had thrust his hand into a brazier. The fires in both rooms were guarded by a similar spell. Vannor found by painful experimentation that he could throw logs into the flames from a short distance away, but could approach no closer than the hearth itself. That ruled out using fire as a weapon, then – and there was nothing else in the chambers that could be used at all. Even the bedcovers, with which he'd thought to hang himself as a last desperate measure, simply slipped out of any knot he tried to make.

Swearing luridly and rubbing his stinging fingers, the merchant sank into a chair by the fire, buried his face in his hands, and cursed himself for a fool. Fear for Zanna must have blurred his thinking when he had set out to find her. His plan had seemed so simple at the outset. Return to Nexis, disguise himself, and make surreptitious contact with some of his old and trusted connections among the merchants. It should have been simple enough to trace one lost girl. What he had failed to take into account was that at least one of his old acquaintances was no longer to be trusted.

Vannor cursed. Which of those bastards had betrayed him? The city had changed so much in his absence – another thing he had not considered. New opportunities had arisen under Miathan's rule; new chances to prosper and make money, if you weren't too particular about the methods used. The rich and the poor were growing further and further apart in Nexis, and the merchant had been sickened to his very soul by the poverty, sickness and squalor he had witnessed. Others, it seemed, had less tender consciences. Miathan's immoral, self-serving ruthlessness was spreading like an evil canker through Vannor's city, and the merchant was helpless to stop it. Stop it? Why, he couldn't even save himself. Though he had never been a man to give up hope, Vannor could see no possible way out of this predicament.

All activity ceased as the Archmage strode into the kitchen. Janok, berating some hapless minion, broke off short in the midst of his tirade, his face betraying both astonishment and fear. What was Miathan doing here? He never lowered himself to enter the kitchen.

'Yes, sir? How can I help you?' Janok bowed low, almost grovelling. The head cook had never forgotten that dreadful day so long ago, when he had carelessly allowed the drudge Anvar to escape and fall into Aurian's hands – and how Miathan had punished him for his mistake.

'Janok,' the Archmage barked. 'I need a servant for a delicate and special task. Is there anyone among this disreputable crew of layabouts and slatterns who is reliable, trustworthy – and discreet?'

'I can do it, sir,' a small voice piped up from the shadows. Janok scowled. By all the gods, were it not for the fact that she had the Lady Eliseth's protection, he would teach that upstart little snippet a lesson she would never forget.

The Archmage was frowning down at the tangle-haired young girl. 'Are you not the Lady Eliseth's servant?'

'Yes, sir.' The maid bobbed another curtsey. 'But I can make up the extra time, and I'm ever so efficient, the Lady said.' Beneath her tangle of hair, she frowned. 'At least, I think that was the word she used.'

In spite of himself, Miathan found that he was smiling. What a droll little creature she was. 'Well,' he said, 'if you are sure you can do this without inconvenience to your mistress . . . '

'Oh, I can, sir, I promise you. I'll work ever so hard.'

Janok ground his teeth. Pushy little brat! Always toadying to the Magefolk and putting herself forward.

'Very well,' said Miathan. 'I must say, it makes a refreshing change to see such enthusiasm. Janok, prepare a tray with food and wine – the best you have. You, girl, will bring it upstairs to me as soon as possible.'

When the Archmage had gone, Janok turned on the maid. 'Why, you little . . . '

'You touch me, an' I'll tell the Lady Eliseth,' the girl shrilled, scrambling deftly out of his way. Janok cursed her, but he was defeated for the moment. He was terrified of the Lady Eliseth, as were all the servants. But one day this little bitch would slip up, and when she did . . . Thinking dark thoughts of revenge, Janok went to prepare the tray.

Vannor, exhausted, frustrated and in pain, had fallen asleep at last in his chair by the fire. But he had scarcely closed his eyes, it seemed, when he was awakened by the sound of the door being opened, and the rattle of crockery. Miathan entered, followed by a small, slight figure staggering beneath the weight of a laden tray. The merchant sprang to his feet, his first thought one of relief that the Archmage was unaccompanied by guards. Though where Miathan was concerned, that made very little difference. 'What do you want of me now?' he growled.

The Archmage shrugged. 'I merely came to bring you some food.' He smiled mirthlessly. 'We must take care of you, my dear Vannor. It would be tragic to lose you too soon.' Turning to the maidservant, he gestured to her to put the tray down on the table. She lurked behind Miathan, head down and face averted. Then Vannor caught a clearer glimpse of her. Though a ragged fringe of hair obscured most of the maid's face, there was something so familiar . . . The merchant gasped. Quickly, he swung away from the Archmage to hide his shock. The maid banged the tray down on to the table, almost spilling its contents, and with a scared glance at the Archmage darted from the room like a startled hare.

'If you've only come to threaten me, Miathan, I'm not interested,' Vannor snarled, to cover her retreat.

'Very well. The next time I come, you must be prepared for more than threats.' Stiffly, Miathan stalked from the chamber, locking the door behind him.

When he was gone, Vannor shot across the room to the tray, lifting the dishes with trembling fingers. Sure enough, under a plate he found a folded note, curling and damp from the heat of the food. Carefully, the merchant peeled it open, stifling his impatience. The ink was beginning to spread in fuzzy lines, but the hasty scrawl was still legible.

'Dad,' it said, 'don't worry. I'll get you out of here as soon as I can, but it may take a while before I think up some kind of plan. Be patient, I beg you. *Don't do anything to give me away*.
                                                          Zanna.'

Beneath the signature, blurred and dotted with tears, was a hastily added scrawl: 'I love you.'

A weight of worry lifted from Vannor's shoulders. Quickly, he read the note again, then threw it in the fire. 'Well, of all the sheer nerve! Of all the insane, ridiculous, dangerous notions . . . ' he muttered. Then his face broke into a grudging

293

smile. Zanna! The little minx was spying in the Academy, right under the very noses of the Magefolk.

Vannor shook his head, half aghast, half admiring. 'She's my daughter, all right,' he admitted to himself. 'Bless her and blast her for her courage!' With that, Vannor bent to his meal with a better heart than he would ever have thought possible.

The lean, fleet Nightrunner vessel, with its sails of shadowy grey, slipped into Norberth Port long after dusk and tied up to a derelict jetty on the south side of the harbour. This year's evil weather had all but put an end to trade, and the town seemed quiet and subdued, with few windows showing lights. There was no sign of activity on the handful of ships moored on the north side of the harbour, and the docks were silent and deserted. Remana, standing in the prow of the smuggler ship, snuggled more deeply into her heavy cloak, and shivered. Already it was getting on for autumn again, although this year they had never seen a summer.

Remana thought wistfully about Fional's description of the Valley, where this eldritch winter held no sway. From along the deck, she heard muffled rattles and scrapes, and the creaking of rope as the ship's boat was lowered in the darkness with a despatch that betokened long practice. A figure materialized at her side out of the gloom, and Remana, expecting Yanis, was surprised to hear the voice of Tarnal, the devoted young Nightrunner who had taught Zanna to ride. 'Are you ready to go, ma'am?' he whispered.

Remana nodded, feeling a twinge of excitement, then remembered that Tarnal could barely see her in the gloom. 'I'm ready,' she whispered. 'Where's Yanis?'

'Waiting in the boat – he's still not happy about you going,' Tarnal replied. 'Had it not been for Gevan whining about taking a woman to do a man's work, you'd have problems. But you know how Gevan gets under our leader's skin.' He chuckled. 'Yanis will take you now, just to spite him.'

'It's not up to Yanis – or that idiot Gevan!' Remana retorted in astringent tones. She scrambled down into the rowing-boat, profoundly grateful she'd thought of wearing britches instead of skirts, though her clothing had provided Gevan with another bone of contention. She sighed, annoyed because everyone thought that Yanis had included her just to irritate his irascible mate. Ever since her dearest Leynard had been drowned they had all wanted to wrap her in wool like a babe in arms.

'Come on, mam,' Yanis hissed. 'What kept you?' His words did nothing to improve Remana's mood, but she took a deep breath and bit back the acid comment that sprang to her lips. Only by her actions would she finally prove her worth to the men as a Nightrunner.

With Tarnal and Yanis at the oars and Remana, at her own insistence, steering, the ship's boat skirted the docks under cover of the shadowed wharves, heading towards the springing span of the great white bridge that marked the river's mouth.

Before long, the scattered lamps of Norberth had faded behind them. Curls of mist were rising from the dark water, shrouding the surface of the river with glimmering silk. Peering ahead into the gloom, Remana caught the tip of her tongue between her teeth and concentrated on her steering. If she ran aground or hit a rock, she would never hear the last of it from those wretched smugglers – especially Gevan.

Judging from the laboured breathing of the two men, it was hard work rowing upstream against the current. It also took longer than Remana had expected. When at last she heard the roar of water rushing over the weir, she was greatly relieved. Briefed by Yanis on what to expect, she steered the boat into a calm bankside pool beyond the swirl of the turbulent waters, and the two men scrambled to steady the craft while she disembarked. With muffled grunts and curses, they hauled it out and carried it up the sloping bank and around the weir, returning it to the water in a place beyond the pull of the ferocious current.

Remana lost all track of time as Yanis and Tarnal propelled the boat with rhythmic strokes along the river's upper reaches towards Nexis. Despite the warm gloves that one of the old Nightrunner grandmothers had knitted for her, the hand that grasped the tiller was freezing – almost as cold, in fact, as her feet and her face. She was very glad when the first straggling buildings of Nexis came looming through the mist. Suddenly Remana jerked bolt upright, peering at the torchlit scene that swung into view around a bend in the river. The boat gave a sudden yaw as her hand tightened unconsciously on the tiller. 'What in the name of the gods is that?' she yelped.

Yanis spat out an oath and grabbed for the oar that had been wrenched from his hand by the boat's abrupt jerk. From his scowl, Remana knew he had been about to deliver a blistering comment on her steering, but, luckily for him, had thought better of it. Tarnal, however, had looked over his shoulder, and his startled cry drew the Nightrunner leader's attention away from his mother.

'Yanis – look! They've rebuilt the old wall!'

In Remana's lifetime, the city of Nexis had long since burst the constraining bounds of its ancient walls. Their crumbling remains still existed to the north and east of the city, where the steep uneven landscape had discouraged further construction, but generations of merchants had taken to building their homes on the terraced slopes on the south side of the river, and the burgeoning city had also extended westwards, where the land sloped less steeply as the river widened and the valley opened out. But while Remana had been away, someone had been repairing and extending the original fortifications with massive blocks of rough-mortared stone, to about the height of three men.

A new bridge spanned the river; a continuation of the new wall which climbed the south side of the valley in a series of stepped lengths, to loop around the mansions of the merchants. Blocking the arch of the bridge was a huge barred gate that slid down into sockets on either side. Above it, on the bridge, was a sturdy building that presumably housed some lifting mechanism, to permit approved river-craft to pass.

'How could they have built it so fast?' Yanis gasped. Quickly, he paddled the little boat beneath the sheltering trees of the northern bank, out of sight of any guards who might be stationed on the bridge.

'The Magefolk have done this,' Tarnal asserted. 'It would take magic to get those blocks into place.' He frowned. 'But why did they do it? Surely, with the powers at Miathan's command, he can't be afraid of being attacked?'

Remana shook her head. 'Perhaps this wall was built, not to

296

keep people out of Nexis, but to keep them in.' Whatever the reason for its construction, the new wall presented them with a problem. Remana frowned, utterly at a loss. 'How can we get in to see Jarvas now?'

'Nightrunners can get in and out of Nexis unseen,' Yanis assured her with the wicked grin that reminded her so much of his father. He moored the boat in its hiding-place, and lifted something from a bundle of sacking in the bottom. To Remana's puzzlement, it was the shielded lantern that the smugglers used for signalling. Yanis led Remana and Tarnal along the bank towards the new bridge that formed a barrier across the river. Near the bridge, he scrambled down the steep bank, the others following with difficulty, clinging to tussocks of grass to keep their balance on the rough and muddy ground, and glad of the dappled tree-shadow that shielded them from view.

Though she had been hearing the sound of trickling water for some time, Remana only realized where Yanis was heading when an appalling stench almost sent her reeling. 'Oh, no!' She scrambled forward to grab her son's shoulder. 'Yanis, you can't be serious! You're taking us through the *sewers*?'

Yanis chuckled. 'Why not?' he said. 'Think of it as following in dad's footsteps.' Still chuckling, he led the way towards the dark, round hole in the bank that was the western sewer outfall for the city of Nexis.

'Pox rot it! Why didn't I listen to you, Benziorn?' Jarvas groaned. 'If I'd sent these folk away sooner, they would have been safe by now!' Peering through a chink in the stout wall of his stockade, he could see the glint of torchlight on swords and spears, where Pendral's troops had surrounded his refuge. Already, the captain had delivered his ultimatum. If Tilda, Jarvas, and the wounded stranger were not delivered into their hands before the torch in his hand burned down, his archers would set fire to the buildings within the stockade.

'You tried, remember?' Benziorn replied. 'Even knowing the risks, they wouldn't leave. They didn't believe anything could happen, they're so used to thinking of this stockade as a place of safety.' He shrugged. 'What more could you have done? It was their own choice to stay and take their chances.' The physician shook his head. 'Jarvas, you've fortified this place too well. Is there no other way out?'

'Only the bloody river!' Jarvas replied. 'And that's too deep and fast for most of this lot to manage.' Cursing bitterly, he slammed his fist into his palm. 'Benziorn, I'll have to give myself up. There's no other choice.'

'Wait.' The physician gripped his arm. 'Don't rush into this. Pendral is in the pay of the Magefolk, and we know the Archmage is behind these disappearances of people from all over the city. There's no guarantee that giving yourself up will save the rest of us. Besides, it's not just you they want – what about the others? By all the gods, there must be something we can do.'

Within the warehouse, folk were huddled together in terrified knots. Apart from the bawling of the youngest babes, who seemed preternaturally aware of the tension in the air, there was utter silence. When Jarvas entered the chamber, all eyes turned hopefully towards him, expecting answers. Expecting him to save them. Emmie came running up, the white dog a shadow at her heels. 'Jarvas,' she said urgently, 'you and Tilda and the stranger, and Benziorn, must get out of here. It's you they want. Maybe, with you gone, they'll leave us alone.'

The big man frowned. 'I don't like it . . . ' he began, but Benziorn interrupted him.

'Jarvas, she's right. It's the only way. The problem is . . . How do we go?'

'Through the sewers, of course.'

All three of them turned at the sound of the strange voice. Jarvas gasped. 'By all that's holy – it's Leynard's lass! Where the blazes did you spring from?'

The woman scraped a straggle of hair out of her face with a muddy hand and gestured towards her companion. 'This is my son Yanis, now the leader of the Nightrunners. I heard what you were saying. We'll get you out the same way we came in, and we've a ship moored at Norberth to take you to safety.' She spoke in a brisk, matter-of-fact way that reminded Jarvis of Emmie, and he respected her shrewd summing up of the situation.

298

'I'll find Tilda and the boy.' Emmie vanished into the depths of the warehouse, the white dog following.

'We've a wounded man to take,' Jarvas told Yanis. 'Can you help me with him?'

When she saw the face of the stranger, Remana went white. 'Hargorn! What happened to him? Will he be all right?'

At that moment, there came the thunder of heavy blows on the gate. Flaming arrows arched whistling overhead like a shower of shooting stars; some falling, still burning, to the ground within the stockade; some thudding into the wooden half-timbering of the buildings, or lodging between the rooftiles to set the beams smouldering beneath. The warehouse began to fill with smoke. A wooden feed-store in the stockade caught alight, and people were running, screaming. As the guards had planned, it was only a matter of time before someone panicked enough to open the gate.

Emmie blundered, choking, through thickening smoke, trusting the dog to guide her. With danger threatening, the animal would return to its litter – and where the pups were, Grince, and hopefully Tilda, would also be. It was her only chance of finding them now. Forcing her way forward blindly, eyes stinging and streaming, Emmie was buffeted and knocked by crowds of panic-stricken people struggling to reach the door. Without the white dog's large and steadying presence at her side, and the clutch of her hand on the thick ruff of its neck, she would have been knocked off her feet in no time. The panic was contagious. As she thrust her way to the rear of the warehouse, Emmie felt throttling tendrils of fear curling tight around her hammering heart, and constricting her throat.

'Emmie? Is that you?' Tilda seemed to erupt from the floor at Emmie's feet, her wild-eyed face distorted almost beyond recognition by fear. 'Is Grince with you?'

'I thought he was with you!' Emmie struggled to loosen the hysterical woman's grip on her arm.

'No – I sent him to find you. Then all the noise started, and the fires . . . '

Emmie swore with such crude savagery that Tilda gaped at her in shock. 'Which way did he go?'

'Don't know – I lost sight of him . . . ' Her words were cut short by a blood-freezing howl from the dog. Emmie's heart turned over. Near the scattered embers of the fire, the white dog stood, whining pitifully, over a mangled mass of blood and fur. The trampled remains of its puppies.

'I couldn't stop them.' Tilda gabbled. 'A whole crowd came running through here – there was nothing I could do.'

'You stupid bitch!' Emmie slapped her so hard that Tilda staggered. 'Can't you get anything right?'

Hating herself for taking her own anguish out on the streetwalker, Emmie stooped and put her arms around the neck of the whimpering dog, who was nosing in pathetic confusion at the limp little bodies. 'Come on,' she said softly. 'There's no point now.' The animal's distress tore at her. Dashing tears from her eyes, she pulled the dog away, and after a moment's hesitation it left its dead litter and followed her trustingly.

'Let's go.' Emmie grabbed Tilda's arm, pulling the woman along in her wake. 'We've got to find Grince.'

They found the boy with Jarvas, near the doors of the warehouse. 'Quick!' the big man said. 'The others have gone on ahead. Stay close to me.' Even as they followed him across the yard, the gates flew open, and the guards surged through in a swelling, relentless wave. Over the sound of screams, Emmie heard Jarvas cursing. He stopped, half-turned as if to go back.

Running forward, Emmie tugged at his arm. 'Jarvas, don't! There's nothing you can do for them now.'

Benziorn and Remana were waiting for them in the doorway of the cavernous building that had once been a fulling mill. 'Hurry,' Remana urged them. 'Yanis and Tarnal have taken Hargorn ahead.'

Then, to Emmie's dismay, Grince noticed that his beloved pets were missing. 'My puppies!' the boy howled. 'We can't leave them.' Tearing his hand from Tilda's grasp, he ran off across the yard and vanished into the crowd.

'Grince!' Tilda shrieked, and set off after him before anyone could stop her. She was recognized immediately. Emmie watched, transfixed with horror, as two soldiers pounced on her and hauled her, struggling and screaming, away. Tilda

300

managed to free one hand and gouged at the eyes of one of the guards, and the other plunged his sword into her belly. Emmie covered her eyes, and cried aloud in anguish. Remana's strong and comforting arm went round her shoulders. 'Grieve later,' the Nightrunner woman murmured. 'Right now, it could cost you your life.' She was right. Emmie nodded, and straightened her spine, though her throat ached with unshed tears.

Jarvas had started forward, his face a rigid mask of pain as the guards fanned out through the milling, terrified throng, laying about them with fist, boot and spear-butt; caring nothing for the pain they were inflicting on old and young, man and woman alike as they sought the fleeing fugitives. Emmie saw Benziorn's mouth tighten as he blocked the big man's path. 'Not you, Jarvas,' he cried. 'You're a marked man. I'll find the boy, and show others the way out.'

'Come back!' Remana yelled. She caught hold of Emmie as the woman was about to follow. 'No! Have you all gone crazy? You're his helper. Hargorn needs you.'

Somehow, Emmie and Remana hauled and cajoled the stunned Jarvas into the mill, and were almost knocked off their feet by the din from the fluttering chickens and terrified pigs and goats that were housed within. The light of the flames from the yard filled the dim building with a dancing, infernal light. In the lee of the great stone dye-vats, Remana stooped down to the floor. 'Here it is!' She tugged at Jarvas's arm. 'Feel for the ladder. Got it? Now get down there – quick.'

Looking over the older woman's shoulder, Emmie saw the square, dark opening of the floor-drain, an iron grating propped up beside it. At Remana's urging, Jarvas scrambled down, and Emmie, with a quick prayer that the drop was not too far, pushed the reluctant dog down after him before feeling for the crumbling, rusted rungs of the ladder herself. The descent was mercifully short, and as she reached the bottom, Emmie saw a glimmer of light.

Yanis stood with the blond young Nightrunner on the walkway at the side of the drain, carrying a shielded lantern that cast skull-like shadows on his pallid face. As Remana descended, he thrust the lamp into Emmie's hand and seized his mother by the shoulders.

'Where the blazes have you been?' he shouted hoarsely. 'Gods, I thought you'd been taken!'

'Don't be an idiot,' Remana retorted crisply, then hugged him hard. 'I'm sorry, Yanis. Really, I'm all right. Did Tarnal take Hargorn to the outlet?'

Yanis nodded. He looked hard at his mother, his jaw tightening. 'I'm counting on you to take care of them, mam. Once we get them to the river, Tarnal and I are coming back into the city through the sewers to look for Zanna and Vannor.'

Remana's reply shocked Emmie. Gods, this Nightrunner woman could swear just like a man! For an instant, she thought that Remana was about to argue, but instead the woman stopped short in mid-curse and nodded. 'I understand, Yanis. You lads take care of yourselves, and bring poor Zanna back safely.' Her mouth tightened ominously. 'I want words with that girl.'

Yanis grinned. 'If there's anything left when Vannor and I have finished with her.' He turned to Emmie with a quick flashing smile. 'Come on, lass, let's get out of here.'

Emmie was surprised at his smile, after all he had seen that night. For herself and Jarvas, there was no reason to smile – not now, nor for a long time to come. As she followed the others into the dark and reeking sewers, with her white dog close at her heels, Emmie wept for the ones she had left behind in Nexis.

Grince pelted back into the warehouse through the darkness and smoke, ducking and darting and worming his way through the mêlée of battling figures who took little heed of one stray child. Not for the first time in his young life, Grince thanked the gods that he was small and fast on his feet. Only his ability to slip between the larger adult bodies saved him from being trampled underfoot.

Inside the warehouse, flames were coming through the ceiling and clawing with greedy finger at the walls. The air was thick and stifling, and the heat was a solid, scorching wall. But at least the place was almost empty, now that folk had fled the fire. Choking, Grince groped his way to Emmie's little nest of blankets – and reeled back in horror from the carnage that met his eyes.

'No!' Sobbing, he beat the ground with his fists, and screamed out curses. His beloved puppies, all trampled to a mangled heap of fur! The heat was growing – it was becoming harder to breathe. An ominous roaring came from above. Grince glanced up through streaming eyes, and saw the flames beginning to consume the support beams of the roof. Panic seized him. He scrambled up and saw a corner of the blanket move.

Grince grabbed, and ran. Ran for his life, as the beams began to sag . . . ran gasping, breathless and blind, depending on pure instinct to guide him through the smoke to the door. Sparks and flaming bits of rubble landed in his hair and scorched his scalp, but he barely noticed.

With a triumphant roar of flame, the ceiling of the warehouse fell in upon itself. The boy erupted from the doorway not a second too soon, a cloud of smoke billowing out behind him and flames scorching his heels. He fell gasping to the ground, rolling instinctively to protect his precious furry burden, and with the last of his strength crawled away from the heat, one hand cradling the precious pup, alive or dead, to his breast.

Grince sat up, coughing convulsively, and wiped his streaming eyes. The warehouses were a blazing inferno; the courtyard was empty of people. Of the living, at any rate. Retching, the boy turned away from the dark and twisted lumps, most with their features still recognizable, that had been the folk who lived in Hargorn's sanctuary. Determinedly, he turned his attention to the scrap of fur that was still cradled in his arms. It was the white pup, his favourite. Grince's heart leapt, but he knew better than to rejoice too soon. The tiny creature huddled in his arms, shivering, weak, and wretched. It needed food, and warmth, and care. The boy looked wildly around him. Where was Emmie? She would know what to do. Where was everyone?

Grince put the puppy inside the scorched rags of his shirt, too concerned for the little creature to heed his own discomfort. Squaring his shoulders, he set off across the trampled, bloody courtyard to find Emmie. That she might well be one of the scattered corpses that littered the yard was a fact he was not prepared to accept. He did, however, find his mother.

Tilda lay in the mud, her guts split open like a butchered pig, her empty eyes staring in stark horror at the smoky sky. Grince stood there, reeling, too shocked yet for tears; unable to take his eyes from the ghastly sight. After a time, the puppy squirmed restlessly against his skin, its tiny scrabbling claws bringing his mind back to reality. This – this horror was not reality. This was not his mother. It couldn't be. She must be somewhere else, lost in the city . . . He would find her, he knew; and in the meantime, his puppy must be cared for.

Grince turned his back on the grim carnage of Hargorn's stockade, and moved slowly, like a sleepwalker, through the gates. Little more than a shadow himself, the young boy vanished without trace into the shadowy slums of Nexis.

20
The Sky-God's Temple

'Leave me alone!' They were the first words Raven had uttered since her wings had been destroyed. Cygnus sighed impatiently, and turned away from her. For days he had remained at her bedside, talking to her, coaxing her, comforting her; trying anything to pierce the shell of desolation with which the queen had surrounded herself. How typical that now, when he had troubles of his own, she should finally respond to his presence. A few moments ago, he had been visited by the High Priest, and was still reeling from the shock of Blacktalon's words. 'What fools we were,' he moaned to himself. Elster captured, and about to be executed; and himself a prisoner within Queen Raven's rooms, awaiting a similar fate when the priest was done with his services. Suddenly, Cygnus had stopped wishing for Raven's swift recovery. Once she no longer needed him, he could measure his life in minutes.

'Leave me alone, I said!' the sharpness of Raven's voice jerked Cygnus from his bleak thoughts, and he felt an irrational surge of anger.

'Willingly – if only I could!' he snapped at her. 'Don't tell me you didn't hear Blacktalon. I'm as much a prisoner here as you, so you might as well get used to it. I shouldn't worry, though,' he added. 'I doubt that I'll be around to trouble you for long. You have a longer life to look forward to than I.'

Stunned by the bitterness of his tone, Raven turned her head to look, for the first time, at the young physician who had tended her so patiently. 'I don't want life,' she said flatly. 'Would you want to live like this? Why did you not let me die, as I wished?' Her voice lifted in a childish whine, and tears of self-pity gathered in her eyes. The drops of moisture went flying as Cygnus slapped her hard across the face.

'You selfish little fool!' he yelled. 'Do you think you're the

305

only one suffering? What about your people? What about me? What about Elster, who saved your miserable life, and will die at sundown? You are the queen! Instead of lying there crying like a coward, why aren't you trying to revenge yourself against that black-winged monster?'

'Curse you! How dare you strike me? How dare you speak to me like that? Have you any idea what it's like to be crippled like this?' shrieked Raven. Incensed beyond all measure, she tried to raise herself to strike back at him, struggling against the heavy splinting that bound her wings.

Horror replaced the rage on the physician's face. 'Don't! For Yinze's sake, lie still.' Firmly he pushed her back to her pillows, avoiding the hands that clawed for his eyes. Raven struggled for a moment longer before hopelessness overwhelmed her, and she went limp. Cygnus let her go as though she burned him, and the two young Skyfolk glared at one another, breathing hard.

'Gods, I hate you!' Raven spat.

'I don't think much of you, either,' retorted Cygnus. 'But Elster and I put in a lot of hard work on those wings, and I won't have it undone by your hysterics. Try that again, and I'll strap you down.'

'You wouldn't! You . . . ' Raven was spluttering with rage.

'Would I not?' Cygnus spoke softly, but the winged girl saw the obdurate glint in his eye, and shut her mouth abruptly.

'At least you're fighting back at last,' the physician went on wryly. 'Had I known it would be so effective, I would have slapped you much sooner.'

'What's the point in fighting back?' Raven's despair returned to overwhelm her. Steeling herself, she looked Cygnus in the eye. 'I'll never fly again, will I?'

Cygnus shook his head, his eyes brimming with sympathy. 'Alas, Blacktalon was too thorough. We saved your wings, but . . . ' Eyes blazing, he grasped her hand tightly. 'Your Majesty – avenge yourself! Keep your hold on life until Blacktalon has paid for his misdeeds.'

'You don't know what you're asking,' Raven cried. 'What can I do, against the High Priest? I am crippled – helpless! I was betrayed . . . '

'The way I heard it from Anvar,' said Cygnus brutally, 'you got what you deserved.'

Beneath his accusing gaze, Raven writhed with shame. There was no escaping the fact that he was right. She had caused her own undoing, by betraying the Mages . . . Then the import of his words sunk in, and her eyes grew wide with horror. For a moment, time seemed to stop for her. 'What?' she gasped. 'Anvar is here?'

Cygnus nodded. 'Imprisoned below the city. Perhaps the gods have given you one last chance to redeem yourself,' he added softly.

Raven closed her eyes. How could she help Anvar? It was impossible. Yet for the first time since her capture, she felt a tiny seed of hope, buried deep within her, begin to grow. 'You're right,' she whispered. 'There may be no hope for me, but at least I can try to undo the damage I caused.' Opening her eyes, she looked at Cygnus, as though seeing him for the first time. 'Perhaps we can think of a way to save your life, too,' she added, with the faintest ghost of a smile.

Linnet crept around the edge of the parapet, her bare toes gripping the chill, crumbling stone; her brown wings fluttering to help her balance on the narrow ledge. Peeping around the corner of the old turret, she scanned the skies between her perch and the soaring, intricately structured towers of the royal palace beyond. Good. As she had suspected, there was nothing between here and the palace but empty air. She had chosen the perfect time for this forbidden adventure – while the grownups were all too busy preparing for the great ceremony that Blacktalon had ordered in the temple to notice what a stray child might be up to. Linnet grinned to herself, her face alight with mischief. The bizarre rococo forest of the palace's wildly elaborate architecture formed a mysterious and fascinating landscape – an irresistible temptation to an active, adventurous fledgeling. For as long as she could remember, Linnet had wanted to fly up there and explore this forbidden country, but normally the royal precincts were so well guarded that she couldn't get near the place. Today, however, her chance had come at last.

Ducking back round the corner, Linnet waved to her

companion, gesturing for him to come ahead. Lark hung back scowling, plainly uneasy about this expedition. Linnet bit her lip with vexation. She tried to make allowances for the fact that her brother was a whole year younger than herself, but honestly, he could be so dim at times. 'Come on,' she whispered. 'Hurry, while there's no one around!'

Lark came reluctantly, lower lip jutting unhappily as he dragged his feet along the ledge. 'We're going to get into trouble over this,' he warned her.

'Oh, stop whining,' Linnet snapped, 'or I won't play with you any more.' Without looking around to see the effect of her threat, she launched herself from the turret and swooped towards the tempting vista of rooftops beyond. He had better be following her, she thought; but was unconcerned. Sometimes it seemed that the brat had been following her around for the last six years – ever since his birth.

Ducking around the side of the first tower she came to, the winged child looked for a convenient niche to hide in. Finding an arched alcove within the shadow of a flying buttress, she slipped inside – and leapt back with a startled squawk as a hideous, contorted face leered at her out of the gloom. Flailing the air with frantic wings, Linnet caught herself from falling, and scowled at the horrid but harmless gargoyle that had startled her. 'Father of Skies!' she swore.

'I'll tell mother that you were swearing again.' Lark's voice was pert and taunting.

Linnet turned to glower at the little pest, who had followed her after all. 'And I'll tell her what you were doing when you heard me,' she retorted, grinning smugly as she saw his face crumple with incipient tears.

'I hate you,' Lark sniffled, 'and I'm going home. And I'm going to tell on you, see if I don't . . . ' His voice trailed away as he fluttered off.

'Cry-baby!' Linnet yelled after him. She was unimpressed with his threat – he knew she'd get him later if he snitched on her. In the meantime, she had some exploring to do. With a shrug, Linnet forgot her brother and plunged into the mysterious forest of towers.

Exploring, she admitted some time later, was not as much

fun without her little brother to show off to. Linnet was tired, dusty, and ravenously hungry; her nerves strained with looking over her shoulder for lurking guards. She found a ledge to perch on and took a last look around her, reluctant to admit the palace was not nearly so exciting as she had expected. 'It must be almost time for supper,' she consoled herself, 'and besides, I can always come back another day.' Linnet did not realize she had spoken aloud, until a voice came from the window above her head.

'Who's there? Yinze on a treetop – it's a child!' A long arm shot out between the bars on the window, and Linnet, poised to flee, found herself held fast by the back of her tunic.

'I'm sorry,' she wailed, her brain churning frantically in search of an excuse. 'I didn't mean to!'

'It's all right,' the voice said soothingly. 'Stop flapping, child – I won't hurt you. In fact, I'm very glad to see you.'

'You are?' Linnet craned her neck to look back over her shoulder at her captor. To her astonishment, he was smiling down at her. He had a kind face, she thought, and that shock of fine white hair that fell over his forehead was much prettier than her own brown curls.

'Listen,' he told her. 'I have some fruit here. If you'll do a small favour for me, you can have it all – and I won't tell anyone that you've been here.'

Linnet's mouth watered at the thought of fruit. She had not seen any since this horrible winter had begun. 'All right,' she told him quickly. 'What do I have to do?'

'Will you take a message from me to your father?'

'I can't.' The child's lip trembled. 'I don't have one any more. The High Priest sacrificed him.'

'I'm sorry,' the young man said hastily. 'Will you take word to your mother, then?'

Linnet's face fell. 'I'll get into awful trouble if she finds out where I've been.'

'No you won't – you'll be a hero instead. Listen, child – the queen is here with me, locked up in this room.'

'Don't be silly,' Linnet snorted. 'Queen Flamewing is dead.' She might only be a little girl, but even she knew that!

The man shook his head. 'Not Queen Flamewing – Queen

Raven, her daughter. The High Priest has captured her, and she's in dreadful danger, but if the people find out that she's here, someone might be able to help her.' He gave her a winning smile. 'And then you would be a hero, and the queen would give you a reward.'

'What sort of reward?' Linnet asked dubiously.

'Anything you want.'

'Anything?' She wasn't sure if she believed him, but he promised her so many times that finally Linnet allowed herself to be persuaded. The winged man handed the fruit to her through the window, wrapped up in a piece of cloth, together with a note for her mother, and, with his warnings to be careful and to hurry ringing in her ears, she set off for home once more, with deep misgivings. Maybe she should just eat the fruit, Linnet thought, and throw the note over the cliffs – for one thing was certain. Despite the man's assurances, her mother would punish her for sure, if she found out where her daughter had been.

Anvar stood at the rear of the cave, breathing deeply, willing his hands not to tremble. His hands grasped the Staff of Earth so tightly that his bones showed white through the flesh. 'Are you ready?' he asked Shia. Fleetingly, he was reminded of the last time he had said those words to her, when they had been stealing Harihn's horses in the forest.

'For goodness sake, get on with it!' The great cat's terse reply betrayed her nervousness. She was huddled with Khanu near the mouth of the cave, in the lee of the jutting spur of rock behind which the Mage had his fireplace.

'Brace yourself!' Anvar lifted the Staff. He felt its power pulse through him like the beating of another heart, as he prepared to blast his way through the core of the mountain. Excitement and exhilaration quickened his blood. At last! A chance to escape this place – if his plan worked. The Mage swallowed hard, and straightened his shoulders as he cast aside all thoughts of failure. What could stop him, when he held the Staff of Earth?

Anvar pulled back his arm and gathered his will to unleash the coiled forces of the Staff, but at the last moment something

310

made him hesitate. A shiver ran through him as he suddenly remembered the avalanche caused by his lack of understanding of the power at his disposal, and his close brush with death as he went hurtling to the bottom of the pass. If he tried to blast his way through to the temple with the Staff in the same unthinking way . . . The Mage shuddered. He could easily bring the mountain down on top of him. Yet what other option had he?

'Coward!' Anvar goaded himself, and raised his arm once more. His hand, holding the Staff, began to shake. Into his mind's eye came a vivid vision of Aurian, frowning and worried as she had been the day of the avalanche. She had begged him to be careful, then, but he had refused to heed her warnings. Slowly, Anvar lowered his arm. This time, he must do better. He would be no good to her dead. He frowned, thinking hard. How would Aurian proceed?

Well, first of all, she would find out more about the forces she was dealing with. Remembering the little that the Mage had taught him about healing, Anvar pushed his consciousness out a short distance beyond the confines of his body and probed into the rock with his healer's extra sense, much as Aurian had done with the crystal doorway that had blocked their path beneath the Dragon city of Dhiammara.

Like a probing tendril, his will slipped between the interlinking lattices of the stone's inner structure, as a serpent winds through the twining branches of a petrified forest. The stone was bonded in slanting layers which had cracked and slipped in places, leaving weaknesses in the structure. Anvar took note of them all, then, drawing back into his body, he summoned the powers of the Staff.

Shadows sprang up around the Mage as the cavern blazed with blinding green light. The measureless force of the High Magic swept through him like a great crashing wave, like the avalanche that had almost swept him to his death. Anvar gritted his teeth and strove to contain the power. A faint dew of sweat broke out on his brow. Releasing the Staff's energy a little at a time, he directed a narrow beam of emerald radiance at the weak place in the cave's rear wall where the layers of stone had slipped.

Smoke came curling up from the spot on the stone where the Staff's light blazed. The rock began to glow and sizzle, and flakes of glowing stone split away with loud cracking reports. Trembling with the tension of keeping so much magic contained and controlled, Anvar pushed with his will at the crumbling wall, trying to widen and extend the newly forming fissures. Piece by piece, the rock began to fracture and fall away, the aperture widening even as Anvar watched. The interior of the cave began to darken with the twilight outside, but Anvar, burrowing like a mole deep into the stony heart of the mountain, was oblivious to everything but the tunnel he created, and the vibrant, glowing light of the Staff of Earth.

In the secret heart of the mountain, the Moldan was awake; tracing the path of the Staff of Earth as it came closer and closer. She had felt it like the irritation of a crawling fly upon her outer skin as Shia had climbed the mountain. She had felt it enter her, when the cat had reached the cave. She had waited, with excitement and not a little fear, to see what would happen next. Only when Anvar took up the Staff did the Moldan become aware, for the first time, of the presence of a hated Wizard.

'No!' The mountain shook with the Moldan's rage. Anvar, preoccupied as he was with controlling and guiding the power of the Staff, paid no heed, except to believe that he was the cause of the disturbance, and to proceed with a little more care. Shia and Khanu, cowering beneath the backlash of the magic, had other troubles to concern them. High in the city of Aerillia, startled Skyfolk took wing like a flock of hunted birds as buildings cracked and shuddered, and boulders and snow were dislodged from the face of the peak. But earthquakes were not unusual in this range. The mountains had turned in their sleep before, and no doubt would again. Raven and Cygnus clung together in terror, briefly forgetting their animosity as they comforted each other. Elster, imprisoned in the cells below the temple, hoped that the walls would crack and free her, but to no avail. Even her prayer that death would cheat the High Priest of her sacrifice remained unanswered. Blacktalon, preparing for Elster's sacrifice in the sacred precincts, took the tremors as a sign of Yinze's favour.

312

The Moldan writhed in agony. The penetration of the Staff into her body was like a blade driven deep within her. Fighting for control, she at last took hold of herself, using her innate powers of the Old Magic to isolate and suppress the pain. Rage flashed through the ancient creature. What was that Wizard doing? How dared he? She traced the slanting path, marked by a sliver of residual pain, that reached far within her now. If he kept on in this line, the monster seemed bent on gnawing his way right to the top of her peak.

'We'll see about that!' The Moldan was unconcerned with the fate of the Skyfolk; uncaring about anything save this invasion by her ancient foe. And she wanted the Staff of Earth; had wanted it since the fall of Ghabal, but never had she dreamed that it would fall into her grasp.

The Moldan of Aerillia Peak tensed herself. After all these endless centuries, perhaps she would be the one to free the Dwelven, and release her people from the bondage of the Wizards. She only needed the Staff ... But she could not escape the fetters of her stony form without it – and in this shape, how could she accomplish her desires?

The powers of the Old Magic held the answer. The Wizard might, at present, be more than she could handle, but a lesser creature could be moulded and manipulated. Narrowing her vision down to the observation of the tiniest beings, the Moldan searched within herself for a creature that might suit her ends.

With growing confidence, Anvar clove his way into the heart of the mountain. Occasionally he would pause, and with an effort contain the power of the Staff while he stretched forth his will to probe ahead into the wall of rock, seeking the path that encompassed the natural weak spots, and would do the least damage to the structure of the peak. He conserved his energy; only making the tunnel tall enough for him to stand comfortably upright, though it tended to turn out wider because of the lateral bonding of the rock. Due to some trick of the Staff's power, he remained aware of his position as he went, and could feel himself climbing up and up; gradually homing in on the peaktop temple.

This cramped tunnel was a far cry both from the dark

313

labyrinthine catacombs that housed the Academy's archives, and the wide, well-lit spiralling tunnels beneath the Dragon city of Dhiammara. Both of those, at least, had been safe and well finished, their safety and solidity proved by the test of time. For the first time in a long while, Anvar thought of Finbarr. By the gods, he wished the archivist could be beside him now. Finbarr's delightful wit and boundless curiosity would have given him courage, and distracted him from the perils that pressed so close; for here the tortured stone creaked and complained around the Mage; the rough-hewn floor was uneven and the walls askew. Stones and dust continually spattered from the stressed and sagging ceiling. Water dripped down from pockets within the cliffs, and the air was dead and heavy with the dank scent of age and decay. The only illumination was the disconcerting and disorientating emerald light that emanated from the Staff of Earth; and thick, dark shadows thronged close in the gloom.

At first, Anvar heard nothing above the hum of the Staff's power, and the sizzle and crack of disintegrating rock. The rustling patter of a multitude of feet and the sibilant scrape of scales against raw stone escaped his notice. Only Shia and Khanu, following the Mage at a wary distance, saw the massive shadow that fell between themselves and the green light of the Staff of Earth.

Luckily for Anvar, the Moldan had never thought to take the cats into account – such creatures were beneath her notice. The Mage was unaware of any danger until Shia's warning cry ripped through his mind: 'Anvar! Behind you!'

Anvar whirled instinctively; his free hand groping for the sword that Elster, much against her better judgement, had smuggled down to him. As he saw the horror that confronted him, the Mage's mind went blank with shock, and the blade turned to ice in his lifeless hand.

A horror, an abomination, blocked the tunnel behind the Mage. All down the length of its black, segmented body ran a multitude of legs, each one ending in a barbed and deadly claw. Dark scales glistened slimily, picking up the emerald light of the Staff and throwing it back to Anvar distorted into flashes of the sickly luminescence of decay. Eyes glittered; pinpoints of

314

ichorous green, higher than the level of his head. Feathered antennae waved wildly; spiked compound mandibles clicked and clashed, cleaving the air as the creature reared up, hissing evilly and eyeing the Mage with malevolent intent. Anvar swallowed, his heart labouring with terror, his throat gone suddenly dry. Without volition, he began to back away, but it was too late. In a swift, scuttling dash, the monster was upon him.

Anvar hurled his body to one side, flattening himself against the tunnel wall. The saw-toothed maw snicked past him, carried inexorably down the tunnel by the momentum of the massive creature's charge. He struck out with his sword as it passed him, and a spray of green sparks were hurled into the darkness as the blade skidded off impervious black armour. As the backshock of the blow numbed Anvar's arm, he struck again, wildly, hewing this time at the multitude of scuttling limbs. It did him no good whatsoever. The creature was too tough to be killed by a blade – but it was also too clumsy to manoeuvre in the narrow tunnel, or so Anvar thought at first. Only as its sinister forked tail shot past him did he realize that the creature had vanished into the wall ahead, moving as easily through the rock as it had done in free air! Which meant that it was turning, even now. It could be coming at him from any direction . . .

Anvar waited, his damp skin prickling, attuned to the least cool whisper of air or the slightest sound that could betray the presence of the monster. Shia and Khanu joined him, moving soft and fleet on padded paws, and he welcomed their arrival, but found little reassurance. The young cat's thoughts were a churning maelstrom of terror, and for once even Shia was shaken and lost for words. 'Back to back,' Anvar told them, his thoughts, irrationally, a mental whisper. 'It could come from any . . . '

With a tearing crack of tortured rock, the monster erupted from the floor below his feet. Thrown aside by the buckling slabs of stone, Anvar and the cats evaded the deadly clutch of those clashing jaws. The Mage was caught up in a maze of writhing, chitinous coils as the creature tried to turn and get at him with its razored maw. Despairing, he struck out with the

315

Staff, but the magic was simply reflected from the slippery scales, dislodging a barrage of rocks from the walls and roof. Anvar, caught up in the creature's charge, was slammed against the tunnel wall as once again the monster overshot its mark and disappeared into solid rock.

'Khanu? Shia?' Dazed and disorientated, Anvar groped in the darkness. He felt the throb of incipient bruises, and registered the sting of many minor cuts and scrapes.

'I hear you, human.' The unfamiliar voice of the young cat echoed in the Mage's mind. 'Shia is here – just give her a moment to gather herself . . . '

It seemed as though Anvar had waited no time before Shia's voice rang crisply in his inner ear: 'Anvar, we must find a way to fight this thing.'

'I've already tried my sword and the Staff. I'm open to any suggestions – but you'd better hurry.'

For an instant there was nothing, then: 'If its scales are impervious, you must go for the eyes instead. They may be vulnerable – I hope.'

The Mage had no time to reply. The creature was on him again, roaring down at him; coming at him obliquely from above. 'Die, blast you!' Anvar had no idea he had screamed the words aloud. He had no conscious thought of directing the Staff. Yet in his hand the Artefact came to life, blazing into incandescent light. A high, thin scream tore through the tunnel. Steam began to erupt from the creature's compound eyes, which leaked tears of greenish ichor. The feathered antennae drooped, and legs scrabbled weakly on the stone. The hideous creature's momentum slowed, and finally stilled as its head came to rest against the far rock wall of the tunnel.

Yet Anvar knew he had only disabled the beast. Raising his sword, he dashed up close, and embedded the blade to the hilt in one darkly glittering eye.

The massive creature writhed, throwing the Mage to one side; but its death throes were short-lived. Soon it subsided, twisting within the confines of the tunnel; its ability to move through rock completely gone. In the dying light of the Staff, one massive compound eye glittered menacingly – then its light was doused for ever. The forked tail rasped once against the stone, and was still. As the last dregs of Anvar's energy ran out, the light of the Staff of Earth was quenched.

'Is it dead?' Khanu asked shakily.

'Gods, it had better be!' Anvar was breathing hard. 'I don't think I could go through another bout like that.' He pulled himself up into a sitting position, his back resting against the slimy wall of the tunnel. 'Shia – are you there? Are you all right?' He was shivering, both from physical cold, and from the chill of reaction.

'Both.' The great cat sounded subdued. After a time, Anvar regained enough energy to rekindle the Staff. Khanu was nearby, not far away by the opposite wall, but it took a few moments longer before Shia came into view, clambering over the dead monster's moribund coils. 'I sincerely hope,' she muttered, 'that there are no more of these creatures lurking within the mountain.'

Anvar shuddered at the thought – but he would not give up when he had come so far. Gathering the last shreds of his strength, he pushed himself to his feet and lifted the Staff once more.

The Moldan of Aerillia was both dismayed and incensed that her attack had failed so dismally. She had thrown all her power into the creation of her creature, and would lack the strength to enlarge another for some time to come.

Obviously, she had underestimated the power of this Wizard. She shuddered, as pain bit into her guts again. Did the wretch intend to hammer his way right through to the hideous edifice on her peak? For the first time, the Moldan began to wonder why. Over the ages, the battles and disputes of the puny Winged Folk had been beneath her notice: ever since the Cataclysm, when they had lost their powers of magic. Since then, they had been of little more account to her than fleas or lice. Now that a Wizard had become involved, however, not to mention the Staff of Earth . . .

What was this Wizard up to – and how could she turn it to the advantage of the Moldai? The Aerillian Moldan pondered; trying to ignore the painful pounding in her guts that kept threatening to scatter her train of thought. One thing was certain. Left at large, the Wizard would remain a threat to her for as long as he possessed the Staff of Earth. Her chief problem lay in the fact that the Artefact of the High Magic made him far more powerful than herself. Without the Staff, she was incapable of taking the Staff by force – a ridiculous and seemingly insoluble predicament.

The Moldan turned her attention back within her, to the puny creature that wielded such awesome power. Very well – so be it. For now she would watch and wait until she discovered the Wizard's plans. If force would not serve her, then she must take the Staff by guile.

The wailing of Incondor's Lament drowned the subdued and discontented muttering of the congregation in the temple. Blacktalon peered out from between the dark curtains behind the great altar, surprised and not a little gratified to find the massive chamber filling early, and fast. Skyfolk thronged the spacious nave, and were even filling the airy galleries above. At last! thought the priest. Finally, the Winged Folk must be accepting his rule. Flamewing's death had apparently tipped the balance, as he had hoped.

Blacktalon waited in the narrow antechamber behind the gold-stitched curtains, as his lesser priests carried out the service of worship for the Father of Skies. His heavily embroidered formal robes rustled stiffly, their weight dragging at his shoulders as he paced back and forth in the narrow space. The chanting and sung responses seemed to drag on endlessly, and the High Priest fought to stifle his impatience at such nonsense. Power was the only thing that mattered; however, if superstition kept the Skyfolk appeased, he supposed the end must justify the means.

At last the time arrived for Blacktalon's own part of the ceremony. Hearing his cue, he opened the wooden door at the rear of the chamber, and two temple guards came forth, supporting the physician between them. Elster's face was stark white, and her jaw was set. She remained limp in her captors' grasp; dragging her feet; refusing to assist them to take her on this final journey to the altar and the knife. As she passed Blacktalon, life returned briefly to Elster's stony face. 'May

318

Yinze blast you to oblivion!' she snarled. Eyes flashing, she spat into his face.

Elster had the satisfaction of seeing the High Priest recoil from her. He could not lose face by showing his disgust before the guards, and had to remain there, glaring fiercely as the slimy trail of spittle trickled down his chin, while she was dragged away. Elster smiled grimly. Considering the fate that awaited her, it seemed a puny victory – but it was satisfying, none the less.

As she was dragged beyond the curtains and out into the temple, she was further buoyed by the reaction of the congregation. As one, the crowd rose to its feet and hailed her. Elster blinked in confusion. Since Blacktalon had taken power, she had made a point of avoiding the temple, but from the tales she had heard, her reception was unprecedented. Even better was the crowd's reaction when Blacktalon appeared. The physician could not suppress a smile at the livid expression on Blacktalon's face as the Winged Folk hissed and jeered at him.

Without waiting for the High Priest's command, the temple guards fanned out through the congregation, seeking to identify and isolate the troublemakers. The restive crowd fell silent, but behind their stillness lay a palpable air of anger and resentment. Tension lay heavy on the temple like a brooding stormfront. Even as the guards fastened her down to the altar, the physician saw the look of baffled dismay on Blacktalon's face.

Dispensing with ceremony, the High Priest stood over her with lifted knife. For Elster, time slowed to a viscous crawl. The world sprung into vivid focus, her brain registering every detail. Each pore in Blacktalon's face; each line of ambition and discontent on his skin stood out like a scroll, unrolled for her to read. Elster felt the crowd's restiveness beating against her. The pulse of so many hearts beating together in a common cause thrummed through the temple like a vibrating harp-string. Then the world narrowed and dimmed, as the physician's attention focused with hypnotic intensity on the glistening blade that hovered above her, ready to strike. The knife arced down . . .

'Coward!'

319

'Traitor!'

'Where is Queen Raven?'

'We want the queen!'

Elster was amazed to find that she was still alive, and further astounded to find that the Skyfolk had discovered Raven's presence in Aerillia. How had Cygnus managed that? She opened her eyes to see the knife poised and trembling, a scant inch above her heart. Blacktalon's eyes flashed ire. 'Curse you!' he gasped. '*How did they know?*' He lifted the knife once more. 'This time, there will be no reprieve for you,' he hissed. Elster saw his upraised arm begin to move, and shut her eyes . . .

'We're close,' Anvar turned to the cats, who waited at his heels, at a respectful distance from the Staff of Earth.

'Then finish it!' Shia's voice was thin with tension. The Mage nodded agreement, knowing that the Artefact was causing her distress. At least she was better off than Khanu, who had remained strained and silent for some time, suffering the unfamiliar discomfort of the Staff's magic.

At last, however, they had reached their goal. Only a thin skin of rock remained to bar Anvar's access to the Skyfolk temple. And the priest was there – he knew it! Somehow, the Staff had made him sensitive to evil. The Mage could feel it, like a stream of fetid waste, seeping through the rock above, and was seized with an unconquerable urge to blast through the intervening stone. He raised the Staff, and . . .

Lethal fragments hurtled through the constrained space in the tunnel as the rock blew apart above him. Shia and Khanu cowered, snarling. Seeing the lip of stone and open space above him, Anvar leapt, his fingers finding purchase. Hauling himself upward, he found himself hanging on to a rim of rock, peering up into a vast chamber.

Panicked Skyfolk were screaming, running, taking to the air; their wings colliding in the constricted space. The High Priest stood over a bound victim on the altar. Anvar saw the blade flash down . . . Vaulting from the hole, he launched a bolt of emerald fire at the roof of the temple. Flaring, the bolt impacted. Rocks rained down as the ceiling cracked and crazed. Blacktalon cursed, glanced up . . . In that instant's

320

distraction, his blow was deflected, and flew wide to slice the victim's shoulder.

Two winged guards swooped down on Anvar from above. Shia gathered herself and sprung aloft in a mighty leap, taking one foe neatly from the air, ripping at him with her claws as he hit the ground. Flashing into Anvar's mind came a vivid picture of the pathetic heap of skins within the cave. Khanu caught the other guard as he landed, his jaws closing around the Skyman's throat. The air was full of blood and feathers. As Shia whirled, seeking another victim, the remaining guards drew back hastily, and fled – only to come face to face with another flame-eyed shadow that stood snarling in the open doorway. Hreeza. As he closed the distance between himself and the shocked High Priest, Anvar caught the old cat's triumphant thought: 'Ha! There *was* an easier way up after all!'

Blacktalon shot one terrified look at Anvar, ablaze with the power of the Staff of Earth, and whirled and fled behind the curtain. Anvar followed, reaching the anteroom in time to see the door slam as his foe escaped. Wild with wrath, he pursued the High Priest, almost wrenching the door from its hinges in his haste. With the Staff of Earth to light his way, he hurtled down a narrow stairway and raced through the maze of catacombs beneath the temple, following the sound of running footsteps.

Coming to a place where the passage forked, the Mage hesitated. Which way had Blacktalon gone? He thought he heard the faintest echo of footsteps coming from his right, and went that way. At once, the passage began to climb again, and soon Anvar found himself winding his way up an endless spiral of narrow steps. Up and up he climbed, until his legs were aching and he was gasping for breath. There had been no sight or sound of Blacktalon for several minutes, and Anvar began to wonder whether he had taken the right path after all. The sharp bang of a door slamming far above him erased his doubts.

A single window in the final landing showed Anvar that he had climbed to the top of a lofty tower. As the Mage had expected, the door at the top of the stairway was firmly locked. Cursing with impatience, he unloosed a bolt of energy from the Staff and blew it into splinters, charging into the chamber beyond before the fragments had time to settle, realizing his mistake too late as a knife came flashing at him through the air. As cold shock drenched him, time seemed to slow for Anvar. The blade floated towards him, turning slowly end over end . . . And went clattering to the floor as he activated his shield just in time. Gasping, Anvar looked up to see the High Priest, hunched over a carved pedestal, screaming into a glittering crystal. 'Archmage, Archmage – the prisoner has escaped . . . Curse you, answer me!'

Somehow it seemed cowardly and wrong to use the Staff to slay this evil creature. With a ring of steel, the Mage drew his sword. As Anvar stalked him, Blacktalon backed away from the unresponsive crystal and, whirling, raced towards the window, his wings already half-extended. Even as his hands stretched towards the ledge, Anvar's blade came arcing down to bite into his neck. Blacktalon's body crumpled at the Mage's feet. His head rolled a little way further, the eyes staring wide and aghast, marking that last frozen moment of horror when he met his end.

Anvar wiped his bloodstreaked blade on a corner of the High Priest's robe, and turned away with a shrug. So much for Blacktalon – now for Miathan. Rash as it might seem, he wanted his enemy to know of his escape, because Miathan would tell Aurian. Sheathing his sword, he picked up the High Priest's crystal, and summoned the Archmage.

The gem flared into dazzling radiance which suddenly cleared to show Miathan's face. His astonishment turned to horrified rage as he caught sight of the summoner. 'Anvar! How . . . '

'Blacktalon is dead, Archmage.' Anvar's mental tone was hard as ice. 'Now I'm coming after you.' Before Miathan had a chance to reply, he threw the crystal out of the window, and turned to leave the chamber.

All this time, the Moldan had been watching. Now, with the Wizard isolated in the pinnacle tower, she could seize her chance at last! Sharply, the giant elemental twitched her outer skin, concentrating on the rocks beneath that slender spire of stone. The entire mountain shuddered as Blacktalon's tower rocked, and cracked, and toppled with a thunderous roar to smash upon the rocks below.

21
Night Of The Wolf

As the moon waxed and waned again, Schiannath found it impossible to stay away from Aurian, much to Yazour's dismay. Although the outlaw should have been watching the tower from a safe distance, he would often creep closer in the dead of night and scale the crumbling walls to talk with the Mage again. Though Schiannath denied the visits, Yazour always knew when one had taken place. The outlaw would return to the cave bright-eyed and excited, and lie wakeful in his blankets when he should have been resting before resuming his watch.

Folly! Yazour found such rash behaviour difficult to countenance. Schiannath was placing himself, the Mage, and their entire plan in jeopardy. Yet, until he was back on his feet again, the warrior could do nothing to intervene. What concerned him most was the fact that Schiannath was lying about his actions. As far as Yazour was concerned, such secrecy boded ill. All he could do in return was to indulge in a secret of his own. Whenever the outlaw was absent, he would exercise and work the muscles of his injured leg; always testing, always pushing himself to the limits of pain. He had carved a forked and sturdy bough from the firewood pile into a makeshift crutch, and already he could manage to shuffle slowly around the cave. But to his increasing frustration, the long road through the pass to the tower remained beyond him – until he finally found the answer on a rare, still, moonlit night, when the snow was all diamond dazzle, and the lonely cries of hunting wolves swooped between the glimmering peaks.

Schiannath was going to the tower again. Though he had denied it as always, his face a picture of innocence, Yazour had sensed his concealed excitement as he hurried away, and the warrior had been hard-pressed to keep himself from violence. Oh, the fool. The utter fool! Climbing the tower was one thing beneath the black shroud of a clouded sky – but tonight! Everything that moved against this bright backdrop would be visible for miles around.

Just what was Schiannath's fascination with Aurian? The outlaw refused to say – but Yazour could not believe that the Mage would be encouraging such arrant folly. Unfortunately, without giving Schiannath away, she would be unable to prevent his coming. Yazour cursed the outlaw roundly. Somehow, Schiannath had to be stopped. Turning, he groped beneath his blankets for his crutch.

Tonight, Iscalda was both irritable and worried. Schiannath had been leaving her behind when he went to watch the tower, taking the spare mount instead, and – oh, humiliation! – tethering her within the cave lest she try to follow him. He was afraid of risking her, she knew. An increasing number of wolves were now hunting in the vicinity; drawn, in these desperately hungry times, by the scent of the tower garrison's food. Schiannath was also afraid that the Black Ghost was still somewhere in the area, though Iscalda, had she been able to speak, could have told him the great cat was long gone.

Men and their folly. The white mare snorted. And what was he up to with this woman in the tower, the one who claimed to be some sort of Windeye? Iscalda had her doubts about that. It seemed too good to be true. She did not dare let herself hope that one day she might be returned to her human shape, yet Schiannath plainly believed it – and as his excitement had increased with the passing days, so had Iscalda's disquiet. Was he truly so fascinated with this Windeye because of her powers? Or had it something to do with the woman herself? Was she truly a Windeye? Had she bespelled him? Why else would the idiot have risked going to her tonight, when there was no darkness to hide him?

To distract herself, Iscalda turned her attention to Yazour. The Xandim were mistaken in their belief that when members of their race were trapped in their equine form, they became mindless beasts – she knew that now. True, the animal instincts took over when danger threatened, such as the attack of the great cat. The only thing in her mind then had been

325

flight. But by and large, Iscalda's thoughts remained her own. It was simply that, in this form, she had no way of communicating; and besides, it was easier on poor Schiannath to think of her as a beast. At least he only had himself to worry about, without tearing himself apart over her anguish.

Iscalda wished she could communicate to Schiannath her trust in this young Khazalim warrior he had rescued. This was one occasion when her animal instincts had proved a blessing. Horses knew a good man from a bad; a friend from a foe; and this one, she knew beyond all doubt, possessed great goodness of heart, despite the fact that he had been born a foe of the Xandim. Iscalda had been observing him closely. He interested her more and more. She had kept an approving eye on his progress as he willed himself back to mobility, for she knew that he, too, was worried by Schiannath's behaviour – and that he had been horrified by the outlaw's plan to scale the tower on this moonlit night.

The white mare watched intently as the young warrior came staggering across the cave, still propped by his crutch. The leg was beginning to bear him now, but from the twisted expression on his face, and the sweat that sheened his pallid skin, she could see that the pain was still intense. If he wanted to follow Schiannath, he would have little chance of even getting down from the cave, let alone travelling through the pass.

It was then that Iscalda had her idea. Why not? She also wanted to follow Schiannath – and Yazour could untie her halter. They could help one another. Yet the white mare shuddered at the sudden realization of what she was proposing to do. It was a rare thing for a Xandim, in human shape, to ride another in horse form. It was a matter of the greatest intimacy, and only ever done in times of need, such as when one of the parties had been injured – or when the two concerned shared the closest of relationships. To let a stranger – a human – mount her! It was unthinkable.

Yet was Yazour truly a stranger, after all this time they had spent together, mewed up within the cavern? Did she not find herself liking the young warrior? And was this not a time of direst need? Iscalda braced herself. I can do this, she thought. I

326

can do it for Schiannath. Yazour was tottering towards her, plainly heading for the cave mouth. Iscalda whinnied to catch the young warrior's attention, and dipped her knees, so that he might mount.

She heard Yazour's surprised exclamation and wondered what he had said, for he had spoken in his own language. At a guess, he might be cursing Schiannath for a liar – for the Xandim had told him she was a one-man horse, and warned him, at his peril, not to approach her. Then she felt his touch on her neck, and shivered; struggling with the overwhelming instinct to fight or flee. Yazour spoke to her softly, urgently; and though she could not understand him, Iscalda concentrated with all her might on his soothing voice.

Yet when she felt the warrior's weight on her back, only the halter restrained her. Iscalda shied violently, to be brought up sharply by the painful tug of the rope. The crutch that Yazour carried with him banged against her flanks, and she felt his weight lurch forward as he ducked to avoid the low roof of the cave. She heard him curse sharply. Then he spoke again; low and gently. His hand smoothed the damp arch of her muscled neck. Trembling, the white mare submitted.

After a time, she felt Yazour relaxing, and at last he trusted her enough to untie her halter. Anger flashed through Iscalda as he looped the length of rope around and fastened it to the noseband at the other side, to form a crude rein. Did he not trust her? Yet she had seen the horses of the Khazalim at the tower, and remembered that these humans draped all kinds of pads and straps and buckles over their poor mounts. Very well, Yazour, Iscalda thought. Keep the wretched rope if it makes you feel better – but if you start pulling at my head, I'll pitch you off on to yours. With that, she took a tentative step; adjusting to the unfamiliar presence on her back. Yazour seemed as nervous as herself – and she would need to be careful, she knew, because he could not grip with his injured leg. Blinking, the white mare emerged into the dazzling moonlight with her new rider, and began to make her way towards the tower.

Aurian had finally fallen into an uneasy doze. Sleep was hard to come by, these days – her child, nearing the time of his birth, had been growing ever more restless. The babe had turned now, and Aurian had been bothered, this last day or two, by a nagging backache and twinges of cramp. Did this mean that the infant was due at last? With no experience of childbirth, Aurian had no idea. Stubbornly, she had refused to confide in Nereni, for she was out of patience with the little woman's ceaseless fussing. The Mage knew that this was mainly due to concern for Eliizar and Bohan, but it didn't help. Aurian had worries enough of her own to cope with, for she knew that, as the birth approached, the margin of safety for herself and Anvar, not to mention her son, was severely limited.

These days, the Mage was increasingly out of patience: with her pregnancy, her inability to come up with a useful plan, with Nereni – and with that idiot Schiannath, who would insist on visiting her, breaking her necessary rest to talk through the night, though she had stressed the danger time after time, and forbidden him to no avail.

Tonight, though, when she had looked out at the glimmering moonscape from the parapet on the tower roof, Aurian had been certain that he would not come. Perhaps because for once she feared no disturbance, she had fallen asleep at last. And simply could not believe it when she was awakened by a familiar scratching on the trapdoor. With a curse, the Mage turned over awkwardly in her blankets, and struggled to her feet. 'Has he lost his mind?' she demanded.

'Don't open it!' Nereni hissed from her corner. 'Let him take his chances, if they discover him!' She neither liked nor trusted Schiannath – a Xandim; an enemy. The Mage knew she feared reprisals if Aurian was caught with him, and was concerned lest Eliizar suffer.

'Oh, don't be daft,' Aurian said wearily. 'Schiannath is our contact with Yazour, and our only chance of outside help. It won't do us any good if he's captured. I just wish I could knock some sense into his head. Do me a favour, Nereni, and listen at the door for me while I get rid of him.' With a struggle, she hauled herself awkwardly up the creaking ladder, fumbled with the latch of the trapdoor, and felt Schiannath's firm, strong grasp around her wrist as he helped her on to the roof.

With the skies so clear, it was bitingly cold outside, and the grey stones of the tower glistened with a network of rime. The Mage could hear the eerie cries of the wolfpack, coming closer and closer.

'What the blazes do you think you're doing?' Aurian snapped in a furious whisper, pulling Schiannath into the shadow of the chimney-stack. 'Tonight, of all nights. If the Winged Folk come, you'll be visible for miles.'

'But, Lady, the Skyfolk only fly during the day – you told me so yourself.' His disarming smile flashed white in the moonlight.

'I said they don't fly in the *dark*, you jackass! It's as light as day tonight – and I know that Harihn is short of supplies. What in the name of the gods possessed you, Schiannath?' Aurian could cheerfully have strangled him. Already she knew what his reply would be, and she was right.

'Lady, you are my only hope of restoring my sister Iscalda!' His fingers bit tightly into her wrist. 'Your time is so near now. You will not let me rescue you, yet how can I stay away, never knowing if you are safe . . . '

'I'd be a bloody sight safer if you would stop pestering me, and watch for my signal from a distance,' the Mage replied through gritted teeth. 'Schiannath, get out of here, and don't come back until it's . . . '

'Aurian – someone comes!' Nereni's voice was an urgent whisper. Aurian cursed, and tore her hand free from the Xandim's grasp.

'Stay quiet until they've gone,' she hissed at Schiannath, and scrambled towards the ladder. Clumsy with haste, she felt her foot slip on a worn rung, and landed with a jarring stumble, barely catching herself upright with a hand on the splintery wood of the ladder. Somewhere within, she felt a catch of pain – but its import was lost in the wave of horror that overwhelmed her as she turned towards the door.

Miathan was coming! She knew the sound of those ominous footfalls on the stairs; and though her powers were gone, she could feel, even through the closed door, the pulse of his mind, ablaze with a deadly wrath. Outside, the wolves were gathering; their shrill, lonely plaints sounding all around the tower while the footsteps came closer.

The door flew open. On the threshold, wearing Harihn's body like an ill-fitting cloak, stood the Archmage.

Harihn's handsome features were pulled down into harsh, grim planes and hollows. His dark eyes were overlaid with a furious, fervid glitter. 'Out!' He snapped the word at Nereni. White-faced, and with a terrified glance at Aurian, the little woman scurried to obey. Kicking the door shut behind him, Miathan turned slowly to face the Mage.

'How did Anvar escape?' His voice contained such a depth of deadly fury that Aurian trembled, even as her heart leapt for joy. Anvar was free! Her plan must have worked. Breathing deeply, she tried to calm and marshal her roiling thoughts, but she could not, could not, keep the joy from showing on her face.

Red fire kindled behind Miathan's eyes. 'Curse you! You knew of this.' His headlong rush carried her with him across the room. Careless of her condition in his rage, he slammed her against the wall and held her there; his fingers, tensed like claws, biting like iron into her shoulders. Once again, Aurian felt that stabbing clutch of pain within her, and gasped.

'How did Anvar escape?' Miathan's hand lashed out, knocking her head to one side. 'Tell me! How did he throw down the Temple of Incondor? *What did you find on your travels that could so increase his power?*'

His eyes blazed into her own, and buried within their scalding depths Aurian saw a flicker of doubt – a shadow of fear. Miathan struck her again, and seized a handful of her hair at the nape of her neck, twisting cruelly. Aurian clenched her teeth. Though her eyes were blurred with tears of pain, she would not cry out. She laughed instead, harsh and shrill, for the tension of the moment demanded some release; and drawing back her head, she spat into his face.

'Can this be fear I see?' she taunted. 'The great Archmage Miathan – afraid of a lowly half-breed servant? Your one mistake lay in underestimating Anvar – which surprises me, since you fathered him yourself.' She flung her knowledge in Miathan's face, and watched him turn white.

'Liar!' he howled. 'I know the extent of Anvar's powers! I possessed them myself long enough. What did you find on your travels, to match the power of the Cauldron?'

Aurian was cornered; driven to desperation by her need to protect the secret of the Staff of Earth. 'Nothing!' she shrieked. 'Anvar needed nothing, save his hatred of you. And that's all you'll ever get from me, Archmage. Nought save hatred, and undying contempt!'

Miathan seemed to shrink before her. Since he had lost his eyes, the subtleties of his expression had become difficult to read, but the Mage was astonished to see his features drawn down in lines of anguish. 'It hurts, you know,' he said softly. 'You have no idea how much it hurts when you turn away from me and shudder at my touch.'

The Mage was staggered by his admission. 'Good,' she snapped. 'Now you know how it feels. You never cared how much you hurt me when you murdered Forral – you don't care that you're hurting me now, with what you've done to my friends and Anvar, and what you're threatening to do to my child. Did it never occur to you that I would despise you for your foul deeds? Are you really so lost to all sanity?'

Aurian steeled herself, waiting for the storm of his wrath to break over her. It did not happen. Sadly, Miathan shook his head. 'You loved me once, when you were younger – remember that. And notwithstanding all that I have done, Aurian, I have never stopped loving you.'

Aurian's mind was reeling, refusing to accept that in his own sick, twisted way, Miathan still cared for her. Images flashed through her mind of her youth, when the Archmage had been a father, her beloved mentor. Before Forral had returned, and come between them. Was that when the good in Miathan had begun to wither? Or had the sickness started long before? The Mage ached inside for those first, good years – but that did not change her feelings now. The thought of her child and the memory of Forral's dead face strangled any pity for Miathan. 'And I have never stopped hating you,' she hissed. 'Not since the day you murdered Forral. I'll loathe you until I die.'

Miathan's expression hardened once more. 'We'll see about that!' His hand came up to clench around her throat. 'Move a muscle, and I'll choke the lying breath from you,' he hissed. With a chilling certainty that lodged like a stone within her breast, Aurian knew she had pushed him too far.

With his free hand, Miathan grasped her loose robe at the neck and jerked it until it ripped apart. Twisting her arm in a cruel grip, he yanked her away from the wall and flung her down on the thin pallet that served as her bed. Again, the pain shot through her, worse this time; making her cry out. In that helpless moment, Miathan was upon her, kneeling over her, one hand around her throat again, pinning her with all the strength of Harihn's fit and youthful body.

Aurian, choking, her heart hammering wildly, scrabbled frantically among the tangle of blankets beneath her. Her hand closed around the long, cold shape of Schiannath's dagger and she struck at Miathan's throat – but in that instant another spasm of pain disabled her, sending her arching and writhing beneath his hands.

The blow went wide – the dagger grated on Miathan's collarbone, and drove into his shoulder. The Archmage shrieked in agony, and his hand around her throat went limp, but Aurian was in no state to take advantage of his disablement. Doubled and gasping, she felt warm wetness flood the blankets beneath her.

Miathan sprang to his feet with a vile curse, wrenching the knife from his shoulder, and looked down on her with hard and merciless eyes. 'Now comes the moment at last,' he grated. 'Believe me, Aurian, payment is only put off – and not for long!' He rushed to the door, and flung it open to bellow down the stairs. 'Woman – get up here! The child is coming!'

Yazour had never guessed that it would take so long to traverse the twisting mountain pass. Seething with impatience, he tried to urge the white mare to a faster pace, but Iscalda would have none of it. Had the idea not been so absurd, it seemed as though she was being careful of his injuries as she picked her way along the snowy defile. Yazour, shivering in the unaccustomed cold away from the cave's warm fire, tucked his hands into the tatters of his travelworn cloak, and wondered what to do when he reached the tower. Desperate as he was to see Aurian, there was no way he could climb the crumbling outer walls with his wounded leg. And supposing Schiannath was still up there – how could he persuade the outlaw down

from the roof? 'I'm a fool to come at all,' the young Khazalim
admitted to himself. None the less, he made no attempt to turn
back to the cave. Yazour had a feeling, unplaceable but strong,
that he'd be needed at the tower that night.

As the warrior's eyes made out the streak of moonbright
hillside beyond the dark walls of the pass, Iscalda's pace began
to quicken. Soon Yazour could make out the tree-clad mound,
so familiar yet so strange after his long absence. He could see
the blunt top of the tower thrusting itself above the scrubby
woodland, but could make out no details at this distance. Then
with a jolt that almost dislodged him from her back, Iscalda
pricked up her ears and leapt into motion. Fleet and silent as a
shadow on the snow, the mare burst out from the concealing
cliffs and raced across the intervening stretch of valley floor
towards the shelter of the copse that cloaked the tower's hill.

Oh, the thrill of that wild ride beneath the dazzling moon!
When it was over, Yazour came back slowly from the
exhilaration of Iscalda's speed. Branch-whipped scratches
stinging on his face, his trembling fingers still locked in a swirl
of the white mare's mane, he peered out from the hoary thicket
at the top of the hill and looked across the trampled clearing
towards the tower door, shut tight against the cold. Aurian was
in there – and Eliizar, Bohan and Nereni. Yazour twined his
fingers more tightly in Iscalda's mane. It was all he could do to
control himself like a seasoned warrior, and not draw his sword
there and then to storm that guarded tower like a fool who
knew no better.

But the tower guards were not Yazour's only problem.
Cutting sharply across the moonlit silence, the grim howling of
the wolfpack broke out once more, making Iscalda stamp
restlessly, and shudder. Yazour bit down on a curse. The
wolves were far too close for comfort – and where in the
Reaper's name was Schiannath?

The wolfsong must have drowned the whir of wings. Before
Yazour knew what was happening, he was plunged into
darkness as great winged shapes came between himself and the
moon. 'Reaper save us!' The words were whipped from his lips
in a gust of frigid air, and Iscalda reared and backed into the
shelter of the thicket as the Skyfolk banked down towards the

clearing. Struggling to keep his seat on the mare's plunging back, Yazour glanced up in time to see one of the two Winged Folk cry out sharply, and point towards the tower roof. He must have seen Schiannath! The warrior cursed again. That idiot of an outlaw must be up there, plain in the moonlight for the enemy to see.

One of the Skyfolk let go of the bundle that they bore between them and angled towards the top of the tower. His companion struggled on alone for a moment, dipping sharply, then, with an uneasy glance at the rooftop, dropped his burden, which hurtled down into the clearing's hard-packed snow and burst open, scattering hunks of venison and other forest foodstuffs in all directions. As the winged warrior went soaring to the aid of his compatriot on the roof, Yazour could only look on helplessly, ice-cold with dismay. How could he help Schiannath now?

Schiannath, once Aurian had left him, crouched tensely by the trapdoor, listening intently, lest the moment should come when he must go to Aurian's aid. Frozen in horror, he heard voices in an unknown language, and the sounds of a violent struggle. With all of his attention on the room below, he never heard the sound of approaching wings. The outlaw was just reaching out to the trapdoor when there was a blast of cold air and something hard and heavy hit him from behind, hurling him to the ground. Wiry arms clutched at him, and from the corner of his eye he caught the cold glitter of a blade.

Gasping as a taloned hand tightened around his throat, Schiannath rolled, trying to dislodge his foe. Throwing wide one arm, he knocked away the assailant's other hand, which was driving the dagger towards his breast. Though instinctively he wanted to claw at the Skyman's throttling hold, he reached back instead, over his shoulder, and drove his fingers into the enemy's eyes. With a shriek the winged warrior loosed his grip, and Schiannath scrambled round to lash out at him, but as he spun his feet slipped on the frost-slick rooftop and his blow went awry. The Skyman, however, was reeling, his hands clasped over his eyes, his fallen dagger spitting sparks of moonlight. Schiannath recovered his balance, snatched up the knife and lunged. With another tearing shriek, the winged man

334

tottered backwards and vanished over the low parapet, leaving a black smear of blood behind to mar the icy stones. Schiannath rushed to look down over the edge – and realized his mistake too late as a dark shadow fell across him, blotting out the moon's pristine rays. The Skyman had not been alone!

Aurian knew only pain, a crimson sea in which she twisted and struggled, striving desperately not to drown. A wave of agony would take her, lift her screaming, and finally cast her gasping on the shore – only to be picked up and snatched back by another wave of pain, and lifted into torment once more. Her only link to reality, it seemed, was the slender thread of Nereni's calm voice, soothing her and chanting advice – and the burning gaze of the Archmage, whose presence loomed over her like a black and ominous thundercloud over the crimson sea. Once, during a brief interlude from pain, Aurian's misted vision caught the chilling gleam of a dagger, ready in his hand for when her child should come.

But birthing, for Magefolk, was never easy – and this babe did not want to come. The child's mind had caught Aurian's terror, and with all the stubbornness of his Mageborn heritage, he struggled against his fate.

'Aurian, for the Reaper's sake, push!' Nereni's voice was lost in the tide as the Mage was swept up by another great wave of pain. She was snatched back by slaps that stung her face, and caught a bleared glimpse of Nereni, tousle-haired, white-faced and frantic. 'Aurian, you must help him. Help him to be born, or you both will die!'

'No.' Aurian turned her face away from Nereni. 'Not for this. Not for Miathan. I won't.' The Mage's mind fled her body; fled the sea of pain; fled through an endless grey waste seeking Forral. Always, he had helped and comforted her. 'Forral,' she shouted desperately. 'Forral . . . '

From somewhere ahead, she seemed to hear the echo of a reply. Aurian strained towards the distant sound – but suddenly her way was blocked by a vast black shadow.

'You may not seek him here. It is forbidden.' With a chill, she recognized the bleak and dusty voice of Death.

'Let me come to him,' Aurian cried, struggling vainly against the cloud of icy blackness that constrained her.

'Aurian, go back.' Death's voice was inexorable, but not unkind. 'Now is not your time, nor that of the babe you carry. Go back, brave one – return and bear your child.' With that, he cast her effortlessly forth, and Aurian went spinning down into blackness.

Biting his lip, Yazour cast desperately around in his mind for a way to save Schiannath from the attacking Winged Folk. Wounded as he was, how could he reach the top of the tower? Then the night was split by a shrill, wailing cry from the rooftop, and a dark, crumpled shape came twisting down through the air to smash into the snow. The young warrior, his heart in his mouth, collapsed over Iscalda's neck, limp with relief to see an explosion of dark feathers as the body hit the ground – and then Yazour stiffened, as the howl went on and on. Looping up through the woodland around the side of the spur, the wolf pack burst into the clearing, drawn and maddened by the scent of blood.

The warrior's first panicked thought was for the mare, but the starving wolves had sufficient to occupy them. The stream of shaggy bodies divided, some pausing to tear at the Skyman's bloody corpse, while others went for the contents of the Winged Folk's bundle – the chunks of venison that lay strewn across the snow. Yazour saw a thread of light as the tower door opened a crack, then shut hastily once more. The warrior grinned to himself. So, the guards had no taste for fighting the wolfpack? Now that gave him an . . .

Yazour's grin vanished abruptly as a scream ripped out from the tower above. Aurian! Forgetting Schiannath, Yazour drove his heels into the white mare's sides and forced her out of the spiny undergrowth and across the clearing at full gallop, riding down any of the wolves who stood in his path. With the maddened pack snapping at his heels, Yazour rode the mare at full speed into the tower door. The brittle old timbers splintered beneath Iscalda's weight and she leapt inside, springing lightly over the shattered planks, Yazour lying low along her neck to avoid the lintel. Behind her, the wolves came pouring into the tower, attacking any human in sight. Drawing his sword, the warrior dropped from Iscalda's back and waded, limping, into the startled guards, cleaving a path towards the staircase. The wolves, however, were more mobile. Yazour, fighting for his life, caught a glimpse of great grey shapes leaping up the stairs and bit down on a curse. The wolves could reach Aurian before him!

Down, down Aurian plummeted, screaming, to fall back into the sea of pain. She was brought back to herself by loud and terrified cries from below, which were drowned by the snarls and howls of wolves. At that moment, her agony peaked – she was drowning at the crest of the crimson wave – then abruptly the great sea drained away, leaving her spent and gasping; the only crimson now the blood that pulsed behind her closed eyelids. Distantly, Nereni's voice cried: 'A boy!' – and then Aurian heard the woman's terrified scream, and Miathan cursing.

The Mage wrenched her eyes open to see a stream of lean grey shapes come hurtling through the door. Then, for an instant, the world wrenched itself apart in a blinding flash of dark-bright power, as though reality itself had been hurled upward like a child's handful of jackstraws, to come down again and settle in a brand new pattern.

The terrified wolves hesitated in the doorway. Nereni screamed again, and dropped the child into the furs as though it had burned her. Miathan, distracted for an instant by the animals, turned back to the hapless babe, unseen among the bedding, and as he lifted his dagger . . .

Aurian realized that she was free at last. Reacting quickly, she reached for her powers, lost for so long, and summoned the wolfpack. Newly freed from its fetters, her magic blazed up within her like a fount of glorious fire. At her bidding, the great grey shape of the foremost wolf leapt forth, striking Harihn's possessed body and hurling him to the floor. The dagger went flying in a glittering arc as the wolves closed in. Aurian had time for one last glimpse of Harihn's face; stark terror in his eyes; his soul his own once more. With a snarl of rage, Miathan's bodiless form fled the chamber, as the wolf ripped out Harihn's throat in a fountain of blood. Downstairs, Aurian could hear the dwindling screams as the remainder of the wolfpack finished her guards. Nereni was cowering in a corner, sobbing and hiding her face.

Aurian, trembling with reaction and sickened to her soul by the carnage, hauled herself upright, driven by one last desperate imperative – to see whether Forral's child had survived its horrific birth. Hardly daring to breathe, she turned the furs gently aside – and what she saw there tore a scream of agonized despair from her very soul.

Aurian's mind refused to accept the reality of what lay before her. Her sight blurred and darkened as she crumpled, and her spirit fled wailing into the blackness.

22

The Darkest Road

He had been dreaming that the mountains had come alive. Anvar groaned, and opened his eyes to utter blackness that even his Mage's vision could not pierce. What the blazes happened? he thought hazily. One minute he had been heading towards the door of the tower: the next, everything was disintegrating around him . . . Memory flooded back, and with a gasp the Mage sat bolt upright – or tried to. He couldn't move. He was sprawled, face-down, on a rough, uneven surface that sloped away beneath him so that his head was lower than his heels. His left arm, trapped under his body, was completely numb. Anvar hoped that the lack of feeling was only due to constricted circulation. His right arm was outstretched in front of him; his hand still with its stranglehold around the Staff of Earth.

The Mage took reassurance from the fact that he had not lost the precious Artefact. Extending his will, he summoned the Staff's power until a faint green glimmer lit his surroundings. Anvar's breath caught in his throat. For an instant, his mind went blank with shock. All around him was a mass of broken rock that was trapping him with its weight.

Eventually common sense penetrated Anvar's panic, and it occurred to him that, far from being crushed, he could feel no pressure at all. Then he remembered. The tower room. The High Priest's knife hurtling towards him . . . And his shield. In his haste to destroy his enemy, he had forgotten to lower it again. A wave of giddy relief surged through the Mage. Close to hysteria, he laughed aloud, then shuddered at the narrowness of his escape. If Blacktalon hadn't thrown that knife . . . Then it occurred to Anvar that his relief was premature. The shield had saved him from being crushed, but he was still trapped beneath the ruined tower; pinned down by solid rock. And his air supply must be running out . . .

With an effort, Anvar forced himself to stay calm. It was ridiculous to panic. With the Staff of Earth, he could easily blast his way out of this predicament. Well, the sooner the better. Taking a deep breath of the stale, stagnant air, he concentrated his will . . .

'*Wizard – wait!*'

Anvar blinked, and shook his head. Hearing things? Maybe the air was running out faster than he'd realized. I'd better hurry, he thought. Gathering his scattered wits, he tried again, and the green radiance brightened as power thrummed through the Staff.

'*Wait! There is a better way.*'

The Mage started violently. Mind-speech was the last thing he had been expecting, but there could be no mistake. The pitch of the voice, though definitely not human, had been distinctly feminine. 'Who's there?' he asked sharply.

'*It was no dream, Wizard. See – the mountains do awaken!*'

The voice, though it was only in his head, seemed somehow to resonate through the rocks all around him. Anvar felt his heart begin to race. 'Who are you?' he demanded. 'What are you?'

'*I am the elemental spirit of this peak.*' As the Moldan explained her nature to the Wizard, she felt his growing astonishment, and found it hard to suppress her anger that his people had so quickly forgotten the once proud and mighty race that they had subjugated. Her determination to wrest the Staff away from him hardened.

'Forgive me,' Anvar interrupted her. 'I would like to hear the rest of your tale, but first I must get out of this place. Humans need air . . . '

'*Of course.*' The Moldan gloated. The fool was playing right into her hands. '*Perhaps I can assist you.*' Using the Old Magic, she could lure him out of the mundane world, in which she had no physical form save slow, constricting stone, and into another dimension; the Elsewhere of such elemental beings as the Moldan and the Phaerie. Her form was mobile, there, and her powers would be unconstrained.

Anvar's eyes widened with astonishment as a bleak and pallid light began to delineate the narrow space that held his

340

body. The rocks around him were fading; slowly retreating into the cold grey glimmer until they vanished entirely, and the Mage could see nothing around him but a featureless silvery haze.

'*You may stand, now.*'

Stand on what? Anvar thought, looking down with a shudder. There was nothing beneath him but that grey nothingness. With an effort, he pulled himself together. He was obviously lying on something . . .

'*Yes, it will support you.*' The Moldan sounded dryly amused. Incredulous, Anvar scrambled to his feet, badly unnerved by the fact that, despite his shield, she had been able to pick his private thoughts out of his head so easily. For an agonizing moment, he was preoccupied with rubbing the blood back into his stiff and tingling limbs. Then:

'Where are we?' he demanded. 'What is this place?'

'*Elsewhere,*' the Moldan answered softly, in a cold tight voice that sent prickles sheeting over Anvar's skin. '*No longer in the world you know.*'

Anvar tensed, suddenly aware of the threat that lay behind the elemental's tone. 'Why did you bring me here?' He struggled to keep his mental voice level. It would be a grave mistake to let this creature become aware of his fear.

'*Can you not guess?*' The icy tone took on the sneering sibilance of menace. '*In this world, I possess another form, unfettered by the bonds of stone. Here I can move, and kill, and take the Staff of Earth from you!*'

The grey blankness vanished. Anvar found himself standing on a slope of long, tawny grass, that seemed to shimmer in a rippling pattern, like windblown corn – except that no wind cooled the air against his face. Silence, a thin oppressive absence of sound, hung over the landscape like a pall. There was no sign of the Moldan. The Mage was completely alone. Anvar, braced for a fight that had not materialized, found himself at a loss. Where was the Moldan? What form would it take? From which direction would it come? With an oath, he looked wildly around him.

He was on the high, sloping side of a mountain meadow, gazing down to where a river, its water gleaming with an odd,

341

greenish, milky hue, rushed swiftly along the bottom of the vale to vanish over a precipice at the valley mouth to his left. To his right, the meadow ended at the feet of a tall, dark pinewood; above the trees was a broken mass of jumbled rocks and crags. Before the Mage, on the opposite side of the vale, was a rough, heather-covered hillside that swept upwards to a towering ridge. Behind him towered soaring cliffs with the mountain's peak looming dizzily above.

There was something unsettlingly odd about the light. Anvar blinked, peering up at the sky and down at the valley again. The cloudless sky was a peculiar shade of gold, flooding the landscape with amber light, as though the Mage was looking through smoked glass. There was no sun – there were no shadows to lend depth. Instead, the earth itself was suffused with a faint but burnished glow; each stone, each blade of grass standing out clear and shimmering with its own inner light. All except the pinewood. The huddled trees were a pulsing knot of smoky darkness. Anvar shuddered – yet of all the parts of this weird landscape, the forest, with its broken crags above, was the one place where he could hope to find some cover when the Moldan decided to stop playing with him, and attack.

The thought shattered the dreamlike spell of this eerie land, and galvanized the Mage to action. He had better come up with some kind of plan – and fast! Grasping the Staff firmly, Anvar straightened his shoulders, and set off up the valley towards the wood. He had not taken half a dozen strides when –

THUMP! The sound boomed across the valley, smashing through the silence like a battering ram. The earth shuddered under Anvar's feet, and an avalanche of small stones came rattling down from the crags above.

THUMP! Anvar's heart leapt into his throat and stuck there. He whirled wildly, trying to place the location of the terrifying sound.

THUMP! From the pinewood came the crack of splintering branches. Treetops waved wildly, as though tossed by a violent gale.

THUMP! Something was emerging from the forest, hurling broken pines aside like kindling . . . The Mage looked up and up, a scream of terror frozen in his throat.

Standing upright on two heavy, muscled legs, the creature was immense. Clad in tough grey-green hide, it was taller than the Mages' Tower in Nexis. Two great paws, unnervingly like human hands, were held close to the monster's chest on stumpy forelegs. Balanced by a long, thick tail that was held above the ground, the blunt and massive head, larger than Anvar's body, held great jaws lined with the sharp white spikes of fangs. Two wicked, glittering eyes, brimming with arcane intelligence, scanned the valley and came to rest on the Mage.

'*I see you, little Wizard!*' The familiar, gloating voice came, not from those horrific jaws, but from within the confines of Anvar's own mind. It was the voice of the Moldan.

There was no point in running – there was nowhere to run to. For one indecisive second Anvar stood rooted to the spot – and then he remembered the Staff of Earth. Gathering his will more swiftly than he had ever done before, he called up the Staff's powers, and hurled a bolt of energy at the monster . . .

And nothing happened. His will was unresponsive, and the Staff was dark and dead within his grasp. Stunned and unbelieving, the Mage tried again. Still nothing. He might as well have been holding a plain stick of wood – and what had happened to his own powers?

The vast jaws of the monster yawned wide in a grinning void. In his mind, Anvar heard the hideous, mocking laughter of the Moldan. '*Would you like to try again!*' the elemental sneered. '*The Staff of Earth is of your world, Wizard. Like your own magic, it has no power here, where the forces of the Old Magic hold sway.*'

THUMP! One great leg swung forward, the massive clawed foot sinking deep into the earth beneath the creature's weight. Anvar turned, and fled. With deadly speed, the monster was after him. Anvar could feel the jarring thunder of its footsteps shake the ground beneath him as it ran; its great legs devouring huge gulps of ground as it rapidly closed the distance between them.

Terror lending speed to his flailing limbs, Anvar hurtled downhill towards the river; knowing, even as he fled, that he was doomed. There was no cover that would hide him; there would be no outrunning the Moldan in its monstrous shape. Before him there was only that strange, green river – and a

343

plunge to oblivion at the end of the valley where the churning green waters vanished from sight in a cloud of spume. Well, so be it. Rather a quick death, pounded on the rocks at the bottom of the fall, than the slow agony of the monster's jaws. And at least the Moldan would be cheated of the Staff of Earth . . .

As Anvar neared the river bank, he could hear the monster pounding closer and closer. Its hot breath surrounded him in a noisome cloud . . . With one last, desperate spurt of speed, Anvar gained the bank and leapt. The moiling green flood took him, snatching him right out of the creature's snapping jaws. A bellow of rage receded down the valley as the Mage was spun away.

Gods – how could this water be so cold, and not be ice? Even if Anvar had been a swimmer, he would have stood no chance in that swift, icy current. Gasping, choking, he was whirled and buffeted in the flood, snatching a breath when his head broke surface, trying desperately to hold that breath when he was tugged beneath. Luckily the water was deep, and there were few rocks in this stretch. Already, Anvar's limbs were achingly numb. For a moment his head cleared the water, and to his utter horror he glimpsed the massive shape of the Moldan, running fast along the bank, keeping pace with him; its glittering eyes two burning pinpoints of rage in that expressionless, armoured face. But that was the least of Anvar's worries. He was losing his battle for breath in the chill water . . .

Aurian! He thought of her yearningly as the icy water seared into his lungs. There was a moment's dark confusion, then . . . Anvar found himself, not drowned, but breathing! Belatedly, he remembered Aurian telling him of her escape from the shipwreck, when her lungs had adapted to the water. Lacking his own powers at that time, he had been unable to make the change, but this time, mercifully, it had happened.

And happened too late. The current became swifter as the river narrowed between strait banks of stone. Ahead, he heard a thundering, booming roar. The falls! As he reached the lip, the Mage had time for one swift glimpse of the endless drop below, and at the bottom a lake that looked, from this height, like a small green eye. Then he was going over . . .

A paw like a great scaled hand caught him, squeezing the water from his lungs as it snatched him from the very brink of the precipice. Again, there was that moment's pain and darkness – then Anvar, breathing air once more, found himself being lifted, up and up, until he was on a level with the great toothed cavern of the monster's jaws. The eyes glittered down at him, inhuman and pitiless; and once again, Anvar heard the Moldan's voice:

'*So, little Wizard – I have you at last!*'

In the unearthly realm of the Phaerie, the Earth-Mage Eilin sat in the Forest Lord's castle, gazing through the window that showed what was passing in the human world. The deep, dark forest she saw: the wildwood that had replaced her own well-tended Valley. Her gaze fell on the bridge that crossed her lake, and followed the slender wooden span across the shimmering water to her own, dear island. But it was desolate and deserted now; her tower gone; replaced by the massive crystal, disguised by magic as an ordinary rock, that held the Sword of Flame.

Sadly, Eilin turned her gaze back across the lake, and saw, through the window's magic, the beautiful unicorn, all formed of light, that was invisible to other eyes. Sighing, she thought of the brave warrior Maya, who had dwelt with her for a brief, happy time, before being turned into this dazzling creature whose purpose was to guard the Sword.

Eilin's gaze sped onwards, through the forest, to where the young Mage D'arvan, Maya's lover and the Forest Lord's son, watched unseen over the little camp of rebels that had sought sanctuary in the wildwood. Onward went her seeking gaze again, to the city of Nexis, home of the Magefolk, where Aurian had once dwelt.

Suddenly Eilin started, gasped, and peered into the window more intently. What was the Archmage doing to the city? All around the ancient walls, the townsfolk were labouring; urged on by gruel guards with swords and whips. Great arches, equipped with barred water-gates that could be raised or lowered, had been constructed across the river on either side of Nexis.

The Earth-Mage growled a curse that would have

astounded her daughter, had Aurian been there to hear it. Miathan was rebuilding the city walls! What was that evil creature up to now? Quickly, she turned her attention towards the Academy . . .

'Eilin! Lady, come quick!' With a sound like a thunderclap, Hellorin, Lord of the Phaerie, materialized right inside the chamber. Eilin spun; startled by his unprecedented breach of Phaerie manners, and even more amazed to see the Forest Lord so agitated.

'Quickly!' he repeated, reaching for her hand. 'You must come with me. Something untoward has happened.'

'What!' Frowning, Eilin pulled back from him, but was no match for his strength. He pulled her from the window embrasure, and into the centre of the room.

'I feel the presence of High Magic.' His voice was tense with excitement. 'A Mage has somehow found a way into this world!'

'Aurian?' Eilin cried. Hope leapt like a flame within her. Hellorin squeezed her hand.

'We will go at once, and see,' he told her.

In a blinding flash, the Great Hall of the Phaerie vanished around the Earth-Mage. She and Hellorin seemed to be flying through the featureless amber heavens, the landscape nought but a dizzying blur, far below her. Eilin's heart heat faster. Her grip on the Forest Lord's hand tightened convulsively, and she swallowed hard and closed her eyes tightly. It helped. 'Is – is it far?' she faltered. Their speed snatched spoken words away as soon as they were uttered, so she switched to mental speech, and repeated her question.

'Far, near . . . ' she felt his shrug. 'Lady, in this world, the rules of human distance do not apply. I am searching for traces of the alien magic, and as soon as I find it, we will be there.'

It seemed an age to Eilin before she felt herself being set down on the blessed ground, as gently as a falling leaf. As soon as her feet touched the earth, sound returned – the thunder of massive feet, followed by a hideous cacophony of blood-chilling snarls. With a startled cry, the Earth-Mage opened her eyes – and saw a monster. A huge, terrifying, fanged abomination that stood on its hind legs, towering up and up . . . And held in its great forepaw was a tiny human figure, its identity unguessable from this distance. Eilin's mouth went dry. Was it Aurian? 'No!' she cried, and leapt towards the monster, not knowing what she would do when she reached it, but knowing she must do something.

A hand caught her, and hauled her roughly back. 'Stay here, Lady. I will deal with this!' Hellorin's eyes flashed dangerously. Then he vanished, to reappear on the river bank, confronting the monster – but now he had cast off his puny human form. Tall he towered, far higher than the creature; cloaked in cloud and shadow with stars glinting like jewels in the branches of his great stag's crown. Eilin gasped in awe. This was the first time she had seen the Forest Lord revealed in all his might and majesty. Lightning flashed from his angry eyes, and his great voice thundered across the valley. 'Moldan – do you dare?'

The monster recoiled. Great fangs flashed white as it bellowed its defiance. Though it was using mental tones, its thoughts were so powerful that Eilin could hear them clearly. *'Stay out of my business, Forest Lord. Let the Phaerie seek their prey elsewhere! This Wizard is mine!'*

'I think not,' Hellorin said quietly. Eilin took an involuntary step backwards; her heart chilled by the depth of menace in those few soft words. 'Would you pit your power against the might of the Phaerie?' the Forest Lord went on. 'Give me the Wizard, Moldan, and slink back into your mountain – ere I blast you beyond the bounds of oblivion!'

'This prey is mine!' Eilin heard a sudden note of doubt in the creature's voice.

Hellorin smiled. 'Put it down, then, Moldan, and fight me for it.'

'Never!' The word ended in a snarl. The monster snatched the tiny figure towards its mouth, opening those dreadful jaws . . . And from Hellorin's hand sprang a great bolt of blue-white fire that struck the Moldan, sizzling, right between the eyes. With a shriek, the monster dropped its prey. Eilin cried out in horror, but the Forest Lord's great hand reached out and caught the falling figure, laying it gently aside on the grass, out of harm's way.

The monster, meanwhile, seemed to be shrinking in on

347

itself. Smoke and bluish flame leaked from its eyes and the jaws that stretched wide in an endless scream as its great tail thrashed in agony. Vivid lightning crawled, a lethal network, across its body, searing where it touched. With one last shriek, the Moldan toppled, falling into the swiftly racing river. The chill green waters snatched it greedily, and hurled it over the edge of the falls.

As if released from a spell, Eilin dashed forward and flung herself down on her knees beside the prone form of the Mage. For a moment, hope burned bright within her . . . But the figure was not Aurian. The Earth-Mage frowned in puzzlement, taking in the dark-blond hair; the blue eyes that flew open in that moment, their gaze wide and stark with terror. 'I don't know you,' she accused.

Anvar was aching, bruised, and chilled to the bone from his immersion in the river. His battered body would not stop shaking, and his thoughts were awhirl with shock. His mind simply refused to encompass the reality of what had happened. That vast shadowy figure; the giant hand that had caught him and borne him to safety . . . Surely it had been a dream – some kind of hallucination brought on by an extremity of terror. The words of this strange woman seemed so incongruous, so – so *ordinary* after his last bizarre and terrifying ordeal, that Anvar burst into hysterical laughter. Her angry scowl and her exclamation of impatience only served to make him worse. Hugging the Staff, which he had clung to desperately even in the monster's grasp, Anvar laughed until the tears ran down his face; until his ribs ached; until he ran out of breath and began to wheeze.

A shadow fell across his tear-blurred vision; another figure had joined the woman. Wiping a sleeve across his eyes, Anvar looked up, and recognized the gigantic figure, diminished now to almost human proportions, that had defeated the Moldan. The Mage's laughter cut off abruptly. 'It was real . . . ' he gasped. Above the stranger's head, like an illusory shadow, hovered the image of a branching antlered crown. Then the Mage's eyes fastened on that hand, the same size as his own now. The hand that had been vast enough to encompass his body . . . Slowly, he looked up from the hand to those fathomless, inhuman eyes. 'Who are you?' he whispered.

The man did not answer him, but looked across at the woman instead. 'My sorrow, Lady,' he said. 'I had so hoped for you . . . But as this is not Aurian, then who . . . '

'Aurian?' Anvar's fear was forgotten. 'What do you know of Aurian?'

The woman's hand shot out to grasp his arm, her fingers digging like claws into his skin. 'What do *you* know of her?' she rasped. Her eyes were blazing with a savage intensity. 'Hellorin said you were a Mage, but I know all the Magefolk. You aren't one of them. What do you have to do with my daughter?'

'You're Eilin?' Anvar gasped. 'Aurian's mother? Then where the blazes am I?'

'In my realm,' the deep voice of the man announced. He looked across at Eilin. 'I think we'd better take him home.' With that, he laid a hand on Anvar's forehead, and the Mage knew no more.

When Anvar awakened, he was curled in a deep, soft chair before a blazing fire. A blanket of some peculiar fabric, light but warm, was draped around him, and he was dressed in a shirt and britches made from similar stuff, their hue a shimmering, changeful greyish green, with a leather jerkin on top. For a panic-stricken instant, he looked wildly for the Staff of Earth, but to his relief it was propped against the chair beside him. Only then did he notice the low table of food and drink set before the fire, and the figures of his two rescuers seated opposite. Looking beyond them Anvar's eyes widened in amazement. 'Why, it's like the Great Hall at the Academy,' he gasped.

The man chuckled from his seat across the hearth. 'D'Arvan's words exactly! Do you still doubt, Lady, that he is a Mage?'

'D'Arvan?' Anvar interrupted in perplexity. 'D'Arvan is here?' It was becoming more obvious by the minute that this must be a dream.

'You know my son?'

'What about Aurian?'

The two strangers spoke together. Anvar looked from face to eager face. 'I don't think I know anything any more,' he sighed.

An expression akin to pity softened the stern, sculpted face of Anvar's rescuer. 'Here.' He handed the Mage a brimming crystal goblet of wine. 'Drink, eat, refresh yourself. You are still not quite recovered from the shock of the Moldan's attack. I will tell you what you want to know, and then ... ' his expression grew hard again, 'you will answer our questions, Mage. I am especially anxious to learn how you came by one of the Artefacts of Power.'

'And where my daughter is,' Eilin added urgently.

The explanations took some time. Anvar, desperately anxious now to return to Aurian, was forced to take comfort from the Forest Lord's assurance that time held no sway here in this Elsewhere that was the Phaerie realm – and in truth, he wanted to learn what the Archmage had been up to in Nexis, in the absence of himself and Aurian.

If the Mage was staggered by the tale of Davorshan's death, and what had happened subsequently to D'Arvan and Maya, he was more shocked by Eilin's news that Eliseth was still alive. 'Are you certain?' he asked. 'Aurian and I were positive that we'd killed her.'

Eilin nodded. 'I have seen her, in Hellorin's window which looks out upon the world. I imagine that you must have felt the death of Bragar – I saw the Archmage conduct his burning.' She leaned forward anxiously. 'But how did you come to believe you had slain Eliseth? Tell me of yourself now – and of Aurian.'

The Earth-Mage cried out softly in astonishment as Anvar told her that he was Miathan's son, a half-blood Mage, who had started off as Aurian's servant, until he recovered his powers after he and his Lady had fled to the Southern Lands. Anvar wished, however, he had remembered that Eilin would not know about Aurian's pregnancy, and Miathan's curse on the child. He never thought to prepare her, but simply blurted out the news. Witnessing the shock and distress that he had caused, he curse himself for a clumsy fool.

The Forest Lord gave her wine, and comforted her, and when Eilin had recovered sufficiently for him to continue,

350

Anvar brought his tale up to the present – his defeat of Blacktalon in Aerillia, and the trap that the Moldan had set for him. 'And now,' he finished, looking pleadingly at the Lord of the Phaerie, 'if you could only return me to my own world, I must get back to Aurian. Surely the child must have come by now, and she . . . ' The look on Hellorin's face stopped him in mid-sentence. To Anvar, the room suddenly seemed very cold. 'You can get me back, can't you?'

Hellorin sighed. 'Alas, I cannot send you back to your own world. It is beyond my power. But . . . ' A gleam brightened his fathomless dark eyes. 'I can send you beyond. Along the darkest road, Between the Worlds, to the Lady of the Mists. I warn you, the way is fraught with peril; but she has the power to return you, if she will – and she also holds the Harp of Winds: one of the lost Artefacts that you seek.'

Excitement quickened Anvar's blood. The Harp! Another Artefact. Already he knew that he would dare the danger and take that darkest road – but as he nodded his assent to Hellorin's questioning gaze, it was not the Harp that occupied his thoughts. It was the thought of returning, as quickly as possible, to Aurian.

Would that I could weep. But when Aurian blasted my eyes, she destroyed all hope of healing tears. Miathan sat before his fire, weary, stooped, and suddenly feeling every year of the two centuries he had lived. Until their last confrontation, the Archmage had been able to delude himself concerning the magnitude of Aurian's hatred. But no longer – the look in her eyes had pierced him like a spear through the heart. How could he win her back in the face of such deep and deadly loathing?

Now that he had been forced to face the truth, the magnitude of Miathan's errors appalled him. I should never have killed Forral, he thought. That was my first and greatest mistake – and my first step on the path that led us to this wretched day. The commander was a Mortal – much though it galled me, I need only have waited . . . Had he not fled with Aurian, Anvar would never have regained his powers. He would have remained here, a lowly servant, and under my control. And the child – had it been born with Aurian's powers,

351

it might have become a great Mage, an asset to our depleted ranks . . . But here Miathan's spirits revolted within him. He simply could not countenance Aurian's half-blood Mortal mongrel joining the exalted Magefolk ranks; no more than he had been able to bear the notion of Anvar . . .

Yet – and Miathan gritted his teeth, forcing himself to face the truth – Aurian and Anvar were practically the only Magefolk he had left. Thanks to his blunders on the night of the Wraiths, Finbarr and Meiriel were gone, and D'Arvan – well, he had been little use in the first place, but he was lost now for certain. Davorshan was dead, and Eilin had vanished from all knowledge. The only Mage left to Miathan was Eliseth, and the Weather-Mage was not to be trusted.

Aurian was now his only hope – the only full-blooded Mage that he still might influence – and besides, she was Aurian, and he had desired her from the first. I must win her back, Miathan thought desperately. I must – but how? Not by killing Anvar, that was certain, even if the Mage could be found. That would finish his chances completely. No, repugnant as the notion might be, Anvar must be spared for the time being, at least. That should earn him Aurian's gratitude, and later, he could think of a way to come between them. And the child? Miathan shuddered, but pulled himself together. He glanced across at the secret hiding-place behind the wall, where the tarnished, corrupted remains of the Cauldron lay concealed. Was there a way to reverse the curse? Could he find it in time?

'Damn you a thousand times over! How could you let her escape you!' The door slammed hard against the wall, shuddering and rebounding on its hinges. Eliseth stood there, white with anger. 'Curse you!' she spat. 'I should have known all along that you intended to betray and supplant me!'

The years fell from Miathan's shoulders like a cloak. Springing up straight and tall, he flung a bolt of power at her that cracked across her face like a whiplash, leaving an ugly, livid mark. 'Be silent! For all your machinations, I am still Archmage here!'

Eliseth staggered, half-turning, flinging her arms across her face. When she lowered them, tears of pain were in her eyes, but she gathered herself to face him squarely, her lovely features contorted with rage. 'Archmage of what?' she sneered. 'Have you looked out of your windows lately, Miathan? Have you ever thought, in all your endless travels of the spirit, to look down and see what is happening in your city? In the lands you now rule? You are Archmage over a handful of ignorant, grubbing Mortals – starving, sullen and bitter with resentment. Is this the power you sought so avidly and at such cost?' She laughed shrilly. 'While you waste your time mooning over that bitch like some drooling, foul-minded dotard, your new-won empire is falling apart around you!'

Inwardly, Miathan recoiled from the venom in her voice. He was careful, however, to let no trace of his dismay extend to his countenance. Rage, normally a flashfire explosion of wrath, was building within him like a slow red tide, steeling his will and swelling his powers. For a moment he lingered, savouring the sensation.

The Weather-Mage, clearly expecting his usual swift response to such baiting, seemed taken aback. Her instant of doubt and hesitation was her undoing. Miathan snared her eyes with his glittering, serpent's gaze, holding her motionless and aghast as he began to intone the words of a spell in a whispering, singsong voice.

'No!' Despite his control of her will, the word, no more than a whimper, forced itself from Eliseth's throat. Her eyes were wild and wide with terror, her slim white fingers clenching and unclenching at her sides. As Miathan looked on, smiling coldly, her face began to change; its clear and perfect outlines starting to crumple, blur and sag – until, abruptly, Miathan cut the spell off short.

Eliseth, freed from the fetters of his will, sagged and stumbled, catching at the side of the door to keep herself upright. As she regained her balance, her hands flew instantly to her face, and her expression altered. Gasping, she flew across the room to the nearest mirror and stared at what she saw.

Miathan chuckled. 'Ten years, Eliseth – ten small years. A droplet in the endless ocean of Magefolk immortality. But what a difference ten years make to that flawless face. Is your body a little less firm, perhaps? A little less straight and slender?' He smirked. 'It's almost worse than being a crone, is it not, to see those relentless signs of disintegration and the marks of time.'

Eliseth faced him, speechless and trembling, and Miathan knew that he had cowed her. 'The last time, when I aged you and you outfaced me, you could do so because you had nothing to lose. But I have learned from that mistake, my dear. This time it will be different.' His voice grew hard as stone. 'Each time you transgress against my will, ten more years will be added to your age. I suggest you think about the repercussions very carefully before you dare to cross me again. And Eliseth – leave Aurian alone. If you so much as raise a finger against her, I will not let you die – but you will wish a thousand and a thousand times again that I had.'

As Eliseth, beaten, turned to slink away, he threw a sop to her with deliberate and malicious cunning. 'Incidentally, I have not discarded you in favour of Aurian, whatever you think. For all those ten additional years, you are beautiful still.' Crossing the room, he cupped her face in his hands. Eliseth glared back at him, but he saw the steely wall of hatred behind her eyes suddenly pierced by a sliver of doubt.

The Archmage smiled inwardly. 'Yes,' he murmured, 'you are beautiful indeed. I may want Aurian to increase our dwindling race, and I may need her powers to further my plans, but she will always remain wayward and wilful. I could never trust her, Eliseth, and so she must remain a prisoner – while you are free, to come and go and work at my side.' Deliberately, he let his smile reach his face. 'You would make a fitting consort for an Archmage – if you prove that I can trust you.' With that he released her.

'Liar,' Eliseth breathed, but there was a new light behind her eyes.

The Archmage shrugged. 'Time will tell,' he said. 'For both of us.'

As he heard the door close softly behind her, Miathan chuckled. Had she taken the bait? Time would tell, indeed.

Hearing the Weather-Mage come storming down the stairs, the little maid fled on silent feet, back round the curve of the staircase. Flinging herself through Eliseth's open door, she grabbed her rag and began to polish the table industriously, breathing deeply and schooling her features into their usual expressionless mask, while elation bubbled over within her heart. She had come up to clean Eliseth's chambers as usual, but hearing voices from the floor above she had crept as close as she dared, to listen. And by the gods, the risk had proved worthwhile!

Eliseth came stamping into the room, holding a hand to her face. 'Inella!' She recoiled at the sight of the forgotten maid, and then collected herself. 'Is this all you've done, you idle slattern?' She aimed a blow at the maid, who ducked adroitly. Eliseth scowled, but seemed disinclined to pursue the matter further. 'Fetch me some wine,' she snapped, and vanished into her bedchamber.

'Yes, Lady.' The girl bobbed a curtsey at her vanishing back, and ran to do her bidding. Though her face remained expressionless, her heart was singing. The Lady Aurian had escaped. By the gods, such news was worth the risk of being here!

23

The Bridge of Stars

Iscalda, terrified by the ravening wolves, had fled the tower. Not even her love for Schiannath could override her animal instinct to escape so many foes. Down the hill she raced, flattening her ears at the cries of the startled guards who were battling with the wolves. Hands reached out to grab her as she thundered past the beleaguered men, but she was moving too fast to be caught. Across the flat ground towards the cliffs, then through the narrow stony gates of the pass, Iscalda sped across the snow as though her feet were winged. The white mare had no idea where she was going. She simply knew she must flee, as fast as possible; far from the howling pack and the scent of blood. Her hoofbeats echoing hollowly in the narrow slot between the cliffs, Iscalda hurtled through the pass, up and along the ridge beyond, and down into the valley on the further side.

Concerned only with her fear, she was not looking out for danger. No sounds reached her ears above the drumming of her hooves. So it was that Iscalda rounded a rocky outcrop that thrust far into the valley floor, and ran headlong into the troop of riders.

Xandim! These were her people! Even as she reared and tried to plunge aside from the leading horses, Iscalda recognized old friends and companions. Shamed by her exile, ashamed to be seen in such a state of unreasoning fear, she whirled on her hind legs and tried to race back the way she had come. But a horse, black as midnight's shadows, leapt out from the knot of riders and raced after her. One terrified glance over her shoulder told Iscalda the worst. Phalihas was after her! In her consternation at seeing her former betrothed once more, she gave no thought to the strange figure perched astride his back.

The mare was trembling with weariness now. As the white-heat of panic cooled from her blood, her sweating limbs began to stiffen in the chill of the mountain night. The black horse was gaining; she could hear his hoofbeats coming closer and closer, and from the corner of her eye she saw his great dark shape move up beside her shoulder.

Suddenly a hand reached out, and caught the rope that the wretched Khazalim had fastened around her head. Her neck wrenched cruelly, Iscalda came bucking and skidding to a halt in a spray of snow.

'Whoa, whoa now. Easy, lovey – there's a girl.' The rider, still clinging tightly to the rope, jumped down from the Herdlord's back and came round to her head. Iscalda leapt back with a snort of surprise. This wiry little man was no Xandim! Why had Phalihas consented to carry such a creature? The stranger continued to stroke her gently, and the mare stood trembling, her ears twitching at the sound of that rough voice that crooned soothingly in some foreign tongue. She rolled one white-rimmed eye to look at the Herdlord, and wondered, with a flash of anger, why Phalihas had not reverted to human form.

'He cannot. He is bound with the same spell as you.'

Iscalda let out a squeal of rage as the Windeye came into view. The outlander who had been riding Phalihas dodged to one side as her forefeet flailed around his ears. Iscalda jerked the rope from his hands and charged at Chiamh; teeth bared, eyes flaming. The Windeye did not flinch. Instead, he held up his hand, and began to speak the words of a spell . . .

And Iscalda was sprawling, face-down in the snow, as her four legs suddenly changed to two. Stunned, she struggled up on her elbows, looked down at her hands – two human hands – and burst into tears of joy. When she lifted her head again, she saw a hand extended to help her up. Chiamh was looking down at her, his expression both apologetic and compassionate. 'Phalihas is no longer Herdlord,' he said softly. 'I have waited so long for this day. You've been on my conscience ever since you were exiled. Welcome back to the Xandim, Iscalda.'

Iscalda ignored the outstretched hand, and looked at him coldly. 'And Schiannath?' she demanded.

357

The Windeye nodded. 'Schiannath's exile is also revoked.' Narrowing his nearsighted eyes, he peered around him. 'Where is he?'

'Light of the goddess!' Iscalda scrambled to her feet. 'I left him in the tower, with that woman.'

'Woman?' Chiamh's gaze suddenly became intense. 'A captive?'

Iscalda nodded. 'How did you know?'

But the Windeye was no longer looking at her. 'Parric!' he yelled. 'I think we've found her.'

Schiannath, in his equine shape, met the Xandim army on the ridge. He had finally bested his second winged opponent on top of the tower, only to look down, alerted by the commotion below, to see the wolves wreaking carnage among Harihn's struggling guards – and the white shape of Iscalda, streaking away into the woods. With an oath, he had scrambled back down the side of the tower, forgetting Aurian and Yazour – forgetting everything in his anxiety for his beloved sister. Once away from the guards and wolves, he had changed into his equine form and galloped after her, following the line of tracks that stitched the long, clear sweep of snow between the bottom of the hill and the pass.

As he breasted the top of the ridge Schiannath stopped and stared, amazed at the array of horses and riders picking their way up from the floor of the valley. While he was still hesitating, unsure whether to stay or to run, he heard a clear voice calling his name. A beloved voice that he had never thought to hear again. 'Iscalda!' he cried, forgetting, in his joy, that he still wore his equine shape. The word came out as a long, high-pitched whinny, and Schiannath changed hurriedly back to his human form as his sister came running up the hill towards him.

It was too much to take in all at once. Schiannath, an outlaw no longer, looked incredulously from face to face as the Windeye began to explain the changes that had been taking place among the Xandim since his exile. Iscalda, nestled into the curve of his arm, was grinning more and more broadly at her brother's bemused expression.

Suddenly a balding, bandy-legged little man thrust his way to the front of the crowd. 'Where's Aurian?' he demanded sharply. His words, despite clearly being in a strange tongue, were somehow understandable, and Schiannath realized that the Windeye must be using some form of spell to translate the foreign speech.

'Aurian?' Schiannath gasped. 'But how . . . '

The stranger was scowling. 'Who else?' he barked. 'We can waste time with pleasantries later. Show us the way to the tower that your sister mentioned.' Turning on his heel, he sprang in one fluid motion to the back of the great black stallion that was Phalihas in equine form.

'What do you think of the new Herdlord, then?' Chiamh chuckled softly in Schiannath's ear.

He turned to gape at the Windeye. 'That is the new Herdlord? He defeated Phalihas? Light of the goddess – how did it happen?'

Chiamh shrugged. 'We live in strange and momentous times, my friend – and as well for you that we do. At least, by the grace of Parric, you and Iscalda are no longer exiled.'

'Are you two going to stand there talking all bloody year?' roared the new Herdlord. With a guilty start, Schiannath remembered Aurian, at the mercy of the wolves. Wasting no more time, he changed back into the shape of a great, dark grey horse. Waiting only for Iscalda to leap on to his back, he set off at a gallop, back towards the pass.

Aurian awoke. An obscure, bitter darkness clouded the edges of her mind like the dregs of a nightmare beyond recollection. She had no wish to remember. Her mind was numb, registering only the simple, immediate messages of her senses: the dank, mildewy smell of the tower room; the rough walls of grey stone stained black with soot above the bracket where a torch burned with a fitful, smoky flame. The dying embers in the hearth, like a scattering of rubies. Pain, discomfort, and an urgent need to relieve herself.

The Mage struggled across the chamber to the draughty drain in the corner, still carefully guarding the numbness in her mind. She mustn't think – not yet. To think would send her over the precipice of madness . . .

Using the wall as a support, Aurian made her way to the hearth, where a bowl of water was keeping warm in the ashes, and cloths to cleanse herself lay nearby. Methodically, Aurian healed the damage to her body; concentrating hard upon the task. It was difficult. She was still very weak, and the effort left her drained and shaking.

Only then did it suddenly come home to the Mage that her powers had returned. With a cry of triumph, she leapt up, ignoring her staggering feet, and launched a bolt of fire at the ceiling to explode in a vivid shower of sparks. Oh, the sheer, breathless, glorious relief! Laughing and crying for joy, she followed her starburst with a blue fireball, another in red, then a green; juggling the spheres of incandescent light as she had done when she was a child.

Only exhaustion limited her exuberant display. Aurian sank to her knees on the cooling hearth, belatedly wondering where everyone was. Concern overshadowed her triumph. Whether the battle with the guards had been won or lost, surely Nereni should have been here? And who had removed the prince's body, and washed her chamber clean of blood? As soon as she caught her breath, she would investigate . . .

From the nest of cloaks where she had been sleeping came a muted whine. Aurian froze, appalled; the hand that had so joyously loosed her magic clenched in a white-boned knot. Oh gods! It had been no nightmare: she had known that from the start. But to face it now, so soon . . .

It came again – the fretful whimper of an animal in distress. The sound, too urgent to be ignored, stabbed like a knife into her heart. The Mage braced herself, walked slowly across to the makeshift bed, and looked down at her son. Her breath congealed in her throat.

He was tiny. Small, pathetic and bedraggled; his eyes sealed shut like all newborn wolf cubs, his body covered in dark grey fuzz. He crawled weakly in a blind circle, whimpering, seeking the lost warmth of Aurian's body. The Mage, responding automatically to his helplessness, reached out a hand towards the cub . . . It hovered, trembling, just above his body. She couldn't touch him. She couldn't. Anger scourged through her: rage and grief and grey despair. Was this what she had carried beneath her heart through long months of struggle and anguish? Was it for this that she had lost her powers, when she needed them? Was this blind, mewling scrap of fur the sole legacy of the love that she and Forral had shared? It was all too much for her. Retching, shaking, sick to her very soul, Aurian turned away . . .

And, for the first time since he had left the haven of her body, she felt the bright, tentative touch of the child-mind on her own. He was cold. Cold and lost and blind and hungry – and human. *Human!* Aurian had known wolves from her childhood, and these were not wolf-thoughts. Not animal thoughts at all. His body might be that of a wolf cub, but his mind was the mind of her son. Her son.

'My baby!' Aurian's voice broke on the words as she lifted the wolfling, cradling him to the warmth of her body. Warm tears of relief flooded her face. His joy, the joy of her child, flooded her mind as at last he found his mother.

Gods, but he was cold! And no wonder. Aurian, appalled by her neglect and suddenly fiercely protective, was galvanized into action. Cradling her son close, she crossed to the dying fire. Feverishly she hurled logs into the fireplace with her free hand and ignited them with a quick-hurled fireball; feeling again the incandescent blaze of joy as her newly recovered power surged through her. Then she returned to her bed and sat down, awkwardly pulling one of the cloaks around her shoulders. How could she not have noticed before how cold the room had become?

Hunger. Ravenous hunger pulsed from the thoughts of her child, and for a moment Aurian hesitated, at a loss. This business of motherhood was all new to her. But the cub was hungry . . . Aurian shrugged, and put her son to her breast. Well, she thought, I expect we'll learn together . . .

It was a struggle, but the instinct to feed was strong in the wolfling, and Aurian, with her healing magic, could adapt herself a little. They managed eventually, helped by their unique mind-bond, and the deeper bond of love that lay between them. Aurian looked down at her son as he fed.

Little wolf, she thought, remembering an old childhood tale that Forral had told her, about a Magechild who had lost his parents in the wildwood, and had been reared by wolves. He had gone on to become a mighty hero, and his name, in the Old Speech, had been Irachann – the wolf. Aurian smiled wryly to herself at the way the tale had been reversed. Irachann, she decided. I'll call him Wolf.

The cub had fallen asleep in her arms. As the Mage sat, looking down at him, she cast her mind back over the confusing welter of events that had attended his birth. The wolf, she thought, remembering the great grey shape that had leapt, snarling, across her chamber. It was the wolf that saved me from Miathan, when it tore out Harihn's throat. But surely, before the wolf had come to her aid, she had heard her child's first cry – *the thin, unmistakable wail of a human infant!* And she remembered – oh, now she remembered – Nereni's voice crying: 'A boy!'

The Mage recalled the day of her capture, when Miathan, in Harihn's body, had revealed that her child was cursed. 'When you see it,' he had said, 'you will beg me to put it out of its misery.'

Aurian swore viciously as the meaning of those words became all too clear. Her child had been born human – *before she'd seen the wolf!* Forral's son had taken the shape of the beast. So that was the nature of Miathan's curse!

There must be a way to change him back. But though Aurian tried and tried, probing the tiny cub with her healer's sense, the child remained in the form of a wolf. I *will* change him back, though, Aurian thought. When Miathan cursed Wolf, he had the power of the Cauldron to draw on. Once I regain the Staff of Earth . . . Her thoughts flew to Anvar and Shia. How could she have forgotten them? Aurian tried to reach out with her mind to her missing friends, but to her dismay she could not find an echo of response, no matter how hard she tried.

She was interrupted in her attempts at communication by the sound of a sudden commotion in the room downstairs. Not more fighting, surely? Carefully placing the cub back in its nest of blankets, Aurian ran to the door – and as she opened it, it suddenly struck her that she was free. Miraculously, unbelievably free! At last she could leave this hated chamber, and never have to look on it again!

Aurian ran to the top of the stairs and looked down into the lower room of the tower. She saw Schiannath in the doorway, arguing with Yazour. And behind the Xandim, sword drawn and cursing impatiently . . . 'Parric!' Aurian shrieked. 'Yazour, let him in!'

For a moment, Parric simply stood there gaping, taken aback by the subtle changes in the Mage. What a fool he had been! All the time he had been searching, he had entertained a romantic picture of himself as the dauntless hero coming to rescue a lost and frightened young girl. He was completely unprepared for the new maturity in her haggard face: the firm, wry set of her mouth and the grim and steely glint in her eyes.

Suddenly, the years rolled back and the cavalry master remembered returning from his very first campaign. The face that had looked back at him from the mirror then had reflected these same changes. So she had been tested by pain and adversity – and by the looks of her expression, had given back as good as she'd got. Flinging wide his arms, Parric gave a whoop of joy, then he was running upstairs and she was running down. They met in the middle with an impact that threatened to send both of them crashing to the bottom, and stood there, hugging the breath from one another.

'Parric! Oh gods – I must be dreaming!'

The cavalry master felt Aurian's tears soaking his shoulder, and that made him feel better about his own streaming eyes. Before she and Forral had come into his life, he had spurned tears as a sign of weakness, but now he knew much more about love – and loss. It was not the only way in which he had grown, he reflected. He had commanded an army, however unwilling, of his own, and had brought them safely through the perilous mountains to . . . What?

Aurian was trying to tell him so much, all at once, that Parric couldn't comprehend it all. The most startling piece of news was that Anvar also seemed to be one of the Magefolk. Despite the fact that Meiriel had told him about Miathan's

363

curse on the Mage's child, he was alarmed at first, thinking she had lost her mind, when she dragged him upstairs and showed him the wolf cub. Dismayed, he was trying to take her arm, to steer her out, when he felt a gentle hand on his shoulder.

'The child is there. It is human.' It was the voice of the Windeye. Parric turned to see Chiamh standing behind them, his eyes once more that alarming, reflective silver, as he gazed at the cub with his Othersight.

Aurian's eyes widened. 'Who's this?' she asked Parric.

'A very good friend,' the cavalry master told her. 'He saved our lives when we were captured by the Xandim.' With that, he introduced Chiamh, whose eyes, by now, had cleared to their normal shade. To Parric's amusement, the Windeye looked awestruck.

'Lady.' Chiamh bowed deeply. 'I am greatly honoured to meet, at last, one of the Bright Powers that I saw so long ago.'

'You saw me?' The Mage's brows creased in a puzzled frown. 'Where? When?'

Chiamh told her of his Othersight, and the vision he had beheld that stormy night so long ago. Parric could see that Aurian was fascinated by the Windeye's brief account of his powers. 'I must hear more about this,' she said. 'In fact, we all have so much catching up to do . . . But first, I want to try again to contact Anvar.' She bit her lip. 'I'm worried, Parric. I thought I'd be able to reach him once my powers returned, but so far I can't. If you want to wait downstairs, I'll join you in a little while.'

'Lady?' Chiamh caught hold of the Mage's arm. 'May I assist you? My Othersight can reach across many miles.'

Aurian smiled at him gratefully. 'Why, thank you, Chiamh. Right now, I'm so anxious to find Anvar that I'll take all the help I can get.'

The wind was gusting fitfully as Aurian and Chiamh climbed up through the trapdoor to the tower roof. The brooding sky in the east was beginning to show the pale glimmer of dawn, and the Mage could feel the hint of moisture in the air that presaged another fall of snow. As she rounded the corner of the chimney-stack, Aurian was startled to hear a faint moan, and see the figure of a winged man, rolling and writhing in a glistening, dark patch of what looked to be his own blood.

'Skyfolk!' Chiamh hissed. Aurian heard the scrape of steel as the Xandim drew his knife.

'No, wait!' She stayed the Windeye's hand. 'We may need him to take a message to Aerillia.' Squatting down beside the Skyman, she reached out with her healer's sense to determine the extent of his injuries. He was not hurt as badly as she had feared. The sword cuts from which he had lost the blood were not life-threatening, though he had taken a very hard knock on the back of his head which had left him struggling for consciousness. Quickly, Aurian tore strips from the hem of the blanket that she was using as a cloak to bind him, hand, foot and wing, before she bent to her work of healing.

Once she had attended to the winged man's wounds, the Mage crossed to the parapet with Chiamh, and stood looking out across the mountains, facing northwest where the sky was darkest. For a time, she tried with all her strength to stretch her will out across the miles to Aerillia, calling and calling for Anvar and Shia, then straining with all her might to hear an answer. But there was nothing. Dismayed, she turned back to the Windeye, who had been waiting patiently beside her all this time. 'I can't hear a thing,' she whispered. 'Maybe the distance is just too great for mental communication, but – Chiamh, I think that something has gone terribly wrong.'

The void was grey and featureless; sheathed in ghostly, clinging mist. Anvar hesitated, momentarily at a loss as to which way to proceed. Behind him, he heard the comforting tones of Hellorin's voice. 'Take three steps forward, Anvar, and do not look back. You'll find that the way will become clear to you.'

Anvar shuddered at the thought of stepping out into that formless nothingness, yet ... The Forest Lord must know what he was doing. He had opened the way into this Place Between the Worlds, cleaving the fabric of reality with an outstretched hand to produce this eerie doorway.

'Take courage, young Mage; this is a safer road than the

one you travelled with the Moldan – which admittedly is saying very little.' The rueful humour that lurked behind the Forest Lord's words heartened Anvar. Besides, the Mage reminded himself, this was the only way back to his own world – and Aurian. He had already said his farewells to Eilin and Hellorin, so there was no reason to linger. Anvar swallowed hard, and stepped forward into the grey mists. The glimmer of warm light from the Forest Lord's chamber was cut off abruptly as the Door Between the Worlds closed behind him, destroying all hope of return or retreat.

From somewhere, Anvar found his courage and marshalled his racing thoughts. Three steps, had the Forest Lord said? Well, so be it. The ground, if ground it could be called – certainly it was not earth – had a soft, clinging resilience beneath his feet. Counting, Anvar began to pace . . .

At the third step, the grey mist vanished. The uncertain surface beneath his feet took on the reassuring solidity of stone. Anvar, startled, raised a hand to his face, and saw his fingers, as he had seen them once before, wreathed in a ghostly glimmer of blue Magelight, as though his magic had taken on a physical form of its own, to cover his earthly flesh. He experienced a fleeting flash of memory – a vision of a carven grey door – and then the thought was gone. Grimly practical once more, Anvar lifted the glimmering hand to illuminate his surroundings.

He was in a tunnel: a narrow corridor roughly hacked from some gleaming, faceted black rock. To his astonishment, it was scored along its length, at roughly eye level, with strange, indecipherable runes and angular pictures. Anvar, moving slowly along the length of the tunnel, gasped. There, outlined in the gleam of his Magelight, was the entire history of the Cataclysm!

Marvelling, the Mage followed the tale to its end, where Avithan, once the son of the Chief Wizard but now called Father of the Gods, had led his followers, the six surviving Wizards, to seek sanctuary Between the Worlds, by the Timeless Lake. And in the final picture . . .

The depiction was in a different style from all the rest. It showed a face – female – surrounded by a swirling mane of hair, cunningly carved so that it caught up Anvar's Magelight and glowed back at him with a frosty gleam. The face, hawkish and high-cheekboned, reminded the Mage of Aurian, but it was older, somehow, and different, in a way he could not place. The great, fierce round eyes were not the eyes of a human, but an eagle. They seemed to hold Anvar's gaze, piercing deep into his mind, uncovering his innermost thoughts . . .

The Mage had no idea how long he stood there, spell-bound and entranced. He looked up at last to see a different light before him, framed in a yawning maw of blackest stone. A sky of deepest indigo, sprinkled with bright stars. With a gasp of relief, Anvar left the unnerving carving and hastened forward.

Another shred of memory, vivid and brief, flicked through Anvar's mind. The black, curving backs of hills, shouldering one another, outlined against a starry sky . . . But this time, it was mountains. A peaceful valley, its swelling flanks clothed in a fragrant patchwork of bracken and pine; and, cupped like a jewel, a calm and starlit lake.

As he reached the tunnel mouth, some sense of circum-spection returned to Anvar. He crept cautiously out, looking about him and listening hard, to emerge upon a narrow beach, all covered with smoothly rounded stones about the size of his clenched fist, sloping down to a strip of shingle that fringed a deep-cut bay at the head of the lake. There was not a sound, except the murmurous lapping of wavelets and the rhythmic rasp of rolling pebbles at the water's edge.

At first, the Mage felt horribly exposed upon the open beach, yet as the peaceful stillness of this place seeped gradually into his soul he felt his spirits lighten, filling him with a calm confidence and sense of certainty. The dark lake seemed to draw him; washing away all the pain and anxiety that had been his constant companions over these last months, and replacing them with a lulling sense of warmth and welcome.

Anvar walked down to the edge of the mere and looked into the still, dark waters. For a moment he experienced a giddy sense of disorientation. Stars, he saw – depth upon depth

367

filled with endless stars, as though, instead of looking down, he looked up and up into the infinite night sky. Just stars, reflected in a lake – and yet . . .

It took a moment for Anvar to identify that nagging sense of *wrongness*. With a gasp, he looked wildly up at the sky, then down into the lake again. Then, cursing, he scrambled back, away from those waters as though they had been deadly poison. The stars. The stars were wrong. The sky that was reflected in those obsidian depths was not the clear night sky above!

The wind was rising. A clump of reeds at the water's edge began to rattle and whisper, hissing with wild laughter. The lake's reflected stars were lost as the surface grew choppy. Small waves, growing larger, charged the strip of beach like cavalry; white tossing manes at their crests. Anvar, still backing, turned and ran for the secure shelter of the tunnel – only to fetch up against a blank, black wall of stone.

A grating rumble, growing to a thundrous roar, made the Mage turn back again, towards the lake. In the centre, the waters were boiling, bubbling, rising up in a sleek and twisting hump. A great black fang broke through the tortured surface, flinging the waves aside in a vast white blossom of foam. Huge arcs of spray glittered skywards, clawing at the stars with silver fingers before crashing back, spent, into the lake.

Up from the wind-tossed waters of the mere, an island rose. A towering black crag like a decayed and jagged tooth. Lake waters, churned from black to vibrant white, cascaded from its rising flanks.

Anvar, flattened against the sheer cliff at his back, shrank away as great waves thundered up the beach towards him. His old fear of water, of drowning, almost swamped his senses – until, after a moment's choking terror, he realized that, though the waves were crashing at his very feet and spray and spume leapt up around his head, his skin and clothes were still dry, as though protected by some invisible barrier beyond which the waters dared not go. The breakers stopped just short of him, like ill-used curs that darted in to snap at his boots, but were afraid to come any closer. Was he being warned? Gritting his teeth, the Mage reminded himself why he had come here. Only the Cailleach, the Lady of the Mists, could send him back to his own world. Only through her grace could he win the Harp of Winds. He could only accomplish these things by meeting with her – and now, it seemed, he had attracted her attention.

Well and good . . . or so Anvar tried to convince himself. But the Lady of the Mists was one of the Guardians: far above those that Magefolk legend had named as gods. Her powers transcended even those of Hellorin, for the Phaerie merely wielded the powers of the Old Magic. The Cailleach was one of those powers incarnate – and she had the Wild Magic, most dangerous of all, at her call besides.

By this time the island had emerged completely, and the waters were beginning to settle. Anvar's strip of shingle was slowly appearing, oddly reconfigured, as the lake grew calm. The valley became still once more, but without its former sense of peace. Now the atmosphere was tense with brooding anticipation.

Anvar waited . . . and waited, until he could bear the suspense no longer. It seemed as though time, and reality itself, must snap, twanging like a frayed and taut-stretched bight of rope. Then the Mage remembered how Aurian had won the Staff of Earth, and what she had told him of her encounter with the dragon. Nothing had happened until she had taken action, and broken the spell that took the golden Fire-Mage out of time . . .

Anvar braced himself. It was obvious that the Cailleach was aware of his presence. The next move, then, must be up to him. 'Lady, I am here,' he called. 'In the name of the ancient Magefolk, the Wizards that once you sheltered, I greet you.'

There was no reply – not in human tongue, at any rate. Instead, just as Anvar was beginning to wonder what to do next, a skein of fragile music crept out across the lake. An alien music so wild, so ethereal, so heartbreakingly beautiful that the Mage found his throat growing thick and tight. Tears streamed down his face, and, all unknowing, he wiped them away with his sleeve in an unconscious echo of Aurian's childlike gesture.

It was the music of a harp. As each note drifted, clear and

perfect, across the darkling waters, it became visible to Anvar's sight; a cascade of music like a starfall with each crystal note a clear and perfect point of light. The Mage watched, lost in wonder, as a bridge of song arced forth across the stillness of the mere.

As the last, entrancing phrase chimed to a close, a final cluster of stars fell to the stony beach; grounded, and took hold. The Mage took a deep breath, closed his fingers tightly around the Staff of Earth, and stepped on to the bridge of stars.

24
Lady of the Mists

The Windeye patted Aurian clumsily on the shoulder, and she welcomed his gesture of sympathy. 'You say your companion, the other Bright Power, is in Aerillia?' he asked her. The Mage nodded, unable, despite her worry, to keep from smiling wryly at his description of Anvar. She'd taken an instant liking to this round-faced, shy young seer with the delightful smile.

'You said earlier that you might be able to help me. How?' she asked.

'I will use my Othersight to ride the winds to Aerillia,' the Windeye told her. 'There, with luck, I should be able to locate your companion.'

Aurian watched, amazed, as silver flooded Chiamh's eyes. Leaning on the parapet, he relaxed, all expression leaving his face, and the Mage realized that his consciousness had left his body. Suddenly, she was seized by an idea. Breathing deeply, she relaxed her own body and slipped easily out of her mundane form.

Chiamh was still hovering above the tower: a golden swirl of incandescent light. She saw his astonished flicker as he noted her presence. 'Can you hear me?' Aurian asked him. In their physical form, she had not thought to try mental communication with the Windeye, and, for a moment, entertained some doubt about the extent of his powers.

'Lady, yes!' His mental voice rang out, clear and joyous. 'How beautiful you look: a being of light, just as I first saw you in my vision.'

In her anxiety, the Mage had little time for compliments, however pleasant, but she could not bring herself to be angry with the seer. 'I wondered, Chiamh – could you take me with you when you ride the winds to Aerillia?' she asked him.

'Let us try.' As if he were extending his hand, the Windeye

371

held out a glimmering, luminescent tentacle, and Aurian stretched out a similar strand of her own being to touch it. The two lights met in a flash of warm brilliance, and suddenly the Mage perceived the world as Chiamh saw it with his Othersight. She gasped with amazement to see the mountains, like translucent, glittering prisms, and the winds as turbulent rivers of glowing silver.

'Are you ready?' Chiamh's voice rang proudly in her mind, and Aurian knew that he had sensed and appreciated her delight.

'I'm ready,' she replied.

'Then hold on tight!' The Windeye stretched out another glowing limb and snatched at a strand of silvery wind. The next minute, they were being borne aloft over the mountains at an incredible pace, riding on a stream of light.

'This is wonderful,' Aurian cried exultantly. Attuned to Chiamh's thoughts while they touched, she could also feel his joy in the wild and exhilarating ride.

'I never knew it could be like this,' he replied. 'Always, before, I have voyaged alone, and it was lonely and not a little alarming. But this . . . Lady, what a gift you have given me. I will never fear my powers again!'

Aurian was glad that she had helped him, for he, too, had enlarged her experience by taking her on this journey. It was one of the most incredible sensations of her life, only marred by the shadow of concern, always at the back of her mind, for the fate of Anvar and Shia.

'Here is Aerillia,' the Windeye said at last. To her astonishment, Aurian saw what seemed to be a cluster of brilliant sparks far below her, and recognized them, with a start, as the myriad life energies of the Winged Folk who dwelt atop the soaring peak.

As the Windeye swooped down closer, Aurian strained to make out details of the peaktop city. Now, the weird, prismatic effect of Chiamh's augmented vision was a decided disadvantage. 'Is there any way I can get my normal sight back?' she asked him.

'Surely.' Chiamh's mental tone was tinged with regret for the end of their journey. 'You are here now – at least, your inner self is here. Simply let go, and you will see normally. I will stay close at hand, to take you back when you wish to go.'

Thanking the Windeye, Aurian withdrew the attenuated tentacle of light, severing her connection with Chiamh's inner form. Looking down, she gasped. On the highest pinnacle of the mountain was the shattered shell of a great black building, with Winged Folk wheeling all around it in panic. It certainly looked as though Anvar had regained the Staff. But why in the world would he not answer her?

Lowering her inner form towards the ground, Aurian tried calling for Shia instead, and at last she got an answer. 'Where the blazes are you?' the Mage demanded, brusque in her anxiety. 'What happened? Where is Anvar?'

'I'm hiding,' Shia replied grimly, 'with Khanu, another of my people who came to help me. We are in the passages below the temple. There is no one to explain to these winged monsters that we came to free them . . . '

Cold dread swept through Aurian as she heard the hesitation in the great cat's voice. 'Why can Anvar not explain to them? Where is he?' Her mental tones began as little more than a whisper, rising to an anguished cry. 'Where is Anvar? He can't be dead. I would have felt it!'

'You are right.' Shia's matter-of-fact voice helped to calm the distraught Mage. 'I kept in contact with him while he pursued Blacktalon from the temple. The priest fled to a tower, where Anvar slew him. Then there was an earthquake – not a natural phenomenon, I'm sure . . . ' Shia's voice betrayed her puzzlement. 'When the tower collapsed, I lost contact with Anvar's mind, but it did not feel like death. It was similar to that time in Dhiammara, when you were caught in that magical trap and swept away into the mountain. It was as though he simply vanished.'

'Dear gods!' Aurian was stunned. What could have become of Anvar? Was it some trap set by Miathan, to steal the Staff? But surely the Archmage was currently out of the reckoning, having been hurled so abruptly from Harihn's body when the prince was slain. 'Listen, Shia,' she said abruptly. 'I must find a way to get to Aerillia. I'm not in my body right now, but . . . '

'Then the child has been born?' Shia asked anxiously.

'Yes, and we're all free now. Harihn is dead – but I'll tell you later. I'll find a way to reach you as quickly as I can.'

'I hope so. We are trapped down here, and soon must be discovered. Aurian, before you leave . . . ' Quickly, Shia told the Mage what had happened to Raven. It made grim hearing, but the Mage had too many other anxieties to waste pity on the girl who had betrayed her. Still, the information could come in very useful. The seed of an idea began to form in Aurian's mind.

'I must go now,' she told Shia hastily. 'Take care, my friend, until I return.' With that, the Mage sought Chiamh once more, to return her to her body as quickly as possible.

The reunion that took place within the tower was boisterous. Bohan rushed to embrace Aurian, tears streaming down his face, while the Mage tried to conceal her dismay at his wasted appearance, and the sores that disfigured his enormous limbs. Her heart hardened against Harihn all over again, and in that mood she found it quite easy to think ruthlessly of Raven.

She had Parric and Schiannath bring the winged prisoner down from the roof, and while a reluctant Nereni served hot soup and liafa to revive him, the Mage told him, without preamble, of Blacktalon's death. Though he turned white at the news, Aurian thought she detected a glimmer of relief in his eyes, and hoped it would make it easier to gain his cooperation. In fact, she had already won his gratitude for healing the wounds that Schiannath had inflicted, and when she offered to set him free to return to Aerillia, if he would deliver a message to Raven, he gave his promise readily.

As she stood in the doorway watching the Skyman take off into the snowladen clouds, the Mage felt a presence behind her. Yazour was at her shoulder, plainly troubled. 'Aurian, is it wise to put your trust in Raven once more?' he asked her.

Aurian shrugged. 'I have no choice,' she replied. 'I must get to Aerillia in person if I want to find out what happened to Anvar. Besides, what choice has she? From what Anvar told Shia about the damage that had been done to Raven's wings, my healing powers are the only hope she has of ever flying again. And if she wants my help, she'll bloody well have to cooperate and send her winged warriors to bring us to Aerillia.'

'And who will you take with you?'

Aurian smiled at the warrior. 'That sounds like one of Anvar's questions – not really a question at all.'

Yazour nodded. 'I will go – unless you do something drastic to stop me.'

'Yazour, I don't have to do anything drastic. Your wounds would be enough.' Seeing the grave expression on his face, Aurian stopped teasing him. 'Now that I have my powers back, however, I can heal those for you in no time.' She laid a hand on his arm. 'I want you to come with me, Yazour. Apart from Anvar, there's no one else I'd rather have at my side. As for the others – ' She sighed. 'Well, I'll certainly take Chiamh, but I don't know about anyone else. Not Eliizar and Nereni, for certain. After what they've been through I can't part them, and I need Nereni to stay here and take care of Wolf . . . '

The Mage heard Yazour's sharply indrawn breath. 'Lady, you may have trouble there,' he said.

'Tell me.' Aurian appreciated the warning. Since her return, she had been puzzled, and not a little hurt, by the reticence of Eliizar and his wife. Though he had clearly been genuinely pleased to see her, the former swordsmaster said little, and seemed to shrink away from her touch, while Nereni had managed to avoid the Mage by pretending to busy herself with the supplies that their guards had left behind.

With a light pressure on her arm, Yazour drew Aurian to one side to look back through the doorway into the firelit tower room. 'Have patience with them, Lady. They are troubled by the wolfling.' He indicated the sleeping cub, now snuggled in a blanket and cradled in the arms of the beaming eunuch, who was delighted with the tiny creature. A slight frown creased the young warrior's forehead. 'I must admit, Aurian, when you told me . . . ' He broke off his words and the Mage felt a shiver pass through his lithe frame.

'It'll be all right, Yazour,' Aurian reassured him. 'Once I get the Staff back from Anvar, it should be possible to revoke Miathan's curse.'

'I hope so.' Yazour looked sadly at the wolf cub, and put an arm around the Mage's shoulders. 'Poor Aurian! After all your long waiting, and losing your powers, to be faced with this, instead of the child you longed for . . . '

In the face of his sympathy, Aurian felt a tightness in her throat. 'There's nothing wrong with Wolf!' she said fiercely. Yazour recoiled in surprise at her vehemence, and she shot him an apologetic look. 'I'm sorry,' she sighed. 'How could I expect you to understand? And worse still, how can I reassure Eliizar and Nereni, with their fear of magic?'

That was only one of Aurian's problems. Before the Skyfolk returned, as she prayed they would, to bear her to Aerillia, she had somehow to reassure the swordmaster and his wife, find some form of sustenance for her child in her absence, and make some provision for Harihn's surviving guards, who, thanks to the cavalry master and his peculiar army, were now locked safely away in the dungeon below. And where would Parric and the Xandim fit into her plans? With a wry smile, Aurian remembered Forral's advice from long ago: *'Take things one step at a time, and deal with the first thing first. Then you'll find, more often than not, that the rest will fall into place.'*

Unconsciously, the Mage resumed the burden of command that had slipped from her while she was without her powers. 'Right!' she said decisively. 'Yazour, I want you to go now, and talk to Harihn's troops. You commanded them once – they should still trust you. According to Parric, it's more than even he can do, as Herdlord, to persuade the Xandim to give sanctuary to their foes, but all is not lost. Many of them left loved ones behind in the forest, and it's a rich and sheltered land between the desert and the mountains. Say that we'll set them free when we depart, and tell them to return to the forest and settle there.' For an instant, her face lit up in a mischievous grin. 'Who knows – we may eventually be responsible for founding a whole new kingdom!'

'Lady, thank you!' Relief was plain in Yazour's face. Aurian knew he had been worrying about those of his people who had remained in Harihn's service. With alacrity, he left her, heading for the dungeons.

As for her son . . . Aurian walked out alone into the thicket that surrounded the tower, and sent forth her will to summon the wolves once more.

The pack had not strayed far from the tower, and were back with the Mage in a very short time. After a brief conference with the dominant pair, Aurian found another couple (for wolves, like hawks, had a life-bond and stayed together) who would be willing to leave their brethren and tolerate humans, in order to help her rear her son. Though the wolves were between litters, Aurian's healing powers soon made it possible for the female to produce the milk that the tiny cub needed. Leaving the pack leaders with her heartfelt thanks, Aurian returned to the tower, Wolf's new foster-parents gliding like silent shadows at her heels.

Unfortunately, persuading Eliizar and Nereni proved to be more difficult. Only by threatening to leave the little one here in the wilds with the wolf pack did Aurian finally succeed. Nereni's doubts helped solve the problem of Bohan, however. Aurian did not want to take him to Aerillia with her, yet she had envisioned having difficulty in persuading him to leave her side again, and was reluctant to hurt his feelings. As it was, the eunuch had already become fiercely protective of the wolfling, and readily agreed to stay as bodyguard to the cub.

By the time she had also dealt with Parric, who was fuming because, as Herdlord, he was forced to remain with the Xandim and could not come to Aerillia with her, Aurian was heartily sick of all the wrangling, and in a fever of anxiety over the fate of Anvar. To distract herself, she healed Yazour, and did the same for Eliizar (despite his obvious reluctance), Bohan, and Elewin, who was suffering from the effects of long, swift journey through the mountains with the Xandim. Parric had wanted to leave the old steward behind at the fastness, but Chiamh and Sangra had persuaded him otherwise. Not all of the Xandim had come with Parric's force, and not all were convinced of his right to the Herdlord's title. Had Elewin been left at the fastness, he would probably not have survived to see his friends return. As it was, he insisted, just seeing Aurian again had rejuvenated him beyond belief. Aurian knew, however, that he was deeply disappointed at not seeing Anvar, and shared her concern over the fate of the missing Mage.

Nereni had prepared a meal, and while they all ate, crowded into the tower room and halfway up the stairs, the companions

377

had a chance to catch up on what had happened to one another during their long separation. But while Aurian rejoiced in her reunion with her long-lost friends, her relief, when she heard the thunder of wings that presaged the returning Skyfolk, knew no bounds.

The bridge of singing stars was a scintillating lacework rainbow that leapt the dark waters of the Timeless Lake from shore to island. As Anvar had expected, the stars were as solid as stone beneath him. What he had not expected was their response to the touch of his feet. With each step that Anvar took across the bridge, the starstones rang with their unearthly music. Each footfall struck a different chord, until he found himself stepping deliberately, here and there, with varying rhythm; creating from this magic bridge his own song: his soul-signature.

The nearer Anvar drew to the island, the more he felt a presence, great and powerful, brooding on the other side. The closer he came, the more his self-song developed, and the more the presence seemed to awaken, hear and approve of the music he created.

The bridge grounded on the island, on a ledge of obsidian stone. With a wrenching pang as profound as grief, the Mage stepped off the arch of song. At once, the music was cut off. Silence fell like a hammer blow. Before Anvar's horrified eyes, the bridge shimmered, shivered, and disintegrated with a gentle sigh. A shower of stars spattered hissing down into the mere, filming its surface with coils of misty steam, and leaving nothing behind but an aching absence in the depths of Anvar's soul. Turning sadly away from the destruction, he saw a curving path that sloped up from the ledge and vanished from view around the flank of the island. The Mage sighed and, leaning heavily upon the Staff of Earth, he began to climb.

Round and round the pathway twisted; cut smooth into the craggy cliffs as though the basalt had been soft as butter. The way seemed endless. The Mage was giddy and gasping for breath by the time he reached the summit, where the path ended abruptly at the face of one last, sheer pinnacle – and the black mouth of a cave. Anvar felt the tingle of magic in his fingers, and lifted a hand that was limned, once more, in flickering blue Magelight, to illuminate his way into the cavern.

It was as well that he had the light. A few short paces within, the cave ended abruptly in a solid wall – and a gaping pit that plunged down into darkness at his feet. His heart hammering wildly, Anvar knelt gingerly at the brink. The glowing blue light reflected off the edges of a spiral of steps, cut into the rock and leading down and down into the core of the isle.

'I don't bloody believe it!' Anvar exploded in a flash of temper to rival the worst of Aurian's rages. Cursing viciously, he set off down the stairway, dwelling with dark and baleful thoughts on the benighted idiot who couldn't just make a tunnel straight through the rock at the base of the island.

Anvar's grousing was cut short as he realized that he was no longer within the isle at all. At the bottom of the steps, he found himself in the midst of a forest. A perfect forest – carved in stone. The Mage stopped dead, gaping. The illusion was flawless. Each bough, each twig, each delicate jade leaf was perfectly and intricately carved, right down to the tiniest detail. Stone birds perched here and there, caught with throats swollen in mid-song; their wings half-opened as though poised to take flight. Minute granite caterpillars looped along the slender twigs. Blossoms of translucent quartz opened in shining clusters along the boughs and a cool, silvery light filtered down between the trees, its source obscured by the lacework of leaves above.

The voice, when it came, was feminine, and most unusual: not old, not young, it managed to sound lilting and melodic, yet deep, harsh and rasping, all at the same time.

'Welcome to the wood in the heart of the stone – or the stone in the heart of the wood. Which is it?' the weird voice chuckled. 'Come, young Wizard. Follow your nose, for in this place, all paths lead to me.'

The sense of power in that voice was overwhelming. Though all of Anvar's instincts were screaming at him to turn and flee, as far and as fast as possible, he knew there could be no going back. With a little shrug, he began to walk, on and on, between the endless ranks of trees.

Stone trunks, stone branches, birds and insects – all were

379

clearly and eerily outlined in that deceptive dappled light that came from somewhere beyond the wood. The Mage felt overawed by the vastness of this place; as though he were a little child strayed into some great ruler's pillared hall. Though the magic of this timeless spot kept him from being troubled by hunger and thirst, his legs were growing weary and his feet throbbed in his boots. Anvar strove to ignore the discomfort. He must keep his mind alert and ready for the coming confrontation.

The trees came suddenly to an end. Anvar stumbled out into a vast open space – a gigantic cavern, perhaps, though it was difficult to tell, for the place was so huge that its boundaries –if boundaries there were – were lost in the farthest shadows. The ground, furred to resemble moss by tiny, prickling spikes of crystallized minerals, swelled upwards in a gently curving slope from where he stood. At the summit was the most gigantic tree that Anvar had ever seen; its girth greater than the massive weather-dome at the Academy; its trunk far taller than the Mages' Tower, soaring up and up to be lost in the shadows far above. And Anvar had found, at last, the source of the diffuse silver light that illuminated the forest. Though all the space around was enfolded in the wings of shadow, the tree itself glowed richly from within, as though filled with captured moonlight.

The immensity of this ancient titan outraged Anvar's senses. In order to maintain his reeling wits, he looked only at the lower part of the tree, concentrating on details. Stone or wood? Even as the Mage drew closer, it was impossible to tell. The fabric of the tree had that same dense grey graininess of the carven Door Between the Worlds, that had led him to the Well of Souls.

'Well perceived, O Wizard! The Portal of the Well of Souls was indeed made from a bough of this tree. But how came you to tread that perilous road? And why are you still here to remember it?'

Anvar, startled by the voice, looked up into the tree. And there, at about the height of three men from the ground, where nothing had existed save the plain and featureless trunk, was a door – a circular door that resembled a knothole in the wood. A rough stairway, seemingly a natural part of the tree, rather than

380

steps that had been cut there, slanted in a curve up to the entrance from one of the immense roots. The stairway curved out and widened at the top, to form a ledge or platform at the threshold.

The door swung slowly open. There, framed in the shimmering golden light that shone from the tree's interior, was a . . . Anvar blinked, and rubbed his eyes. The figure was an eagle – no, an ancient crone . . . No. It was the most beautiful woman he had ever seen.

The deceptive figure was clad from head to foot in a cloak of black feathers, cowled and fringed with white. For an instant, Anvar's vision blurred and he perceived an eagle once more, then his attention shifted and he saw a woman, with the face of the carving he had seen in the tunnel that led to the Timeless Lake. What he had mistaken for a cowl of white feathers was her swirling mane of snowy hair. Her eyes . . . Anvar had expected them to be hawk-dark, or eagle-gold, but instead they were pale, almost colourless, matching and blending into her white face and wintry hair. They fixed upon the Mage with unnerving regard.

'Well? I asked you a question. How came you to pass Death's portal, and survive?'

In the face of the Cailleach's impatience, Anvar scrambled together his scattered wits. He bowed low before he answered. 'Madam, the answer to your question I think you know already. Did you not search through all the contents of my mind while I was captivated by your image in the tunnel?'

'Captivated, eh?' The moonstone eyes held a gleam of approval – and something more. 'As well as being perceptive, you have a clever way with words, young Wizard. And you are right, of course. Otherwise, I might have thought you had come to relieve my lonely exile.' Her brief smile was cut off before it could reach her eyes, and her expression grew cold. 'As it is, I am well aware that you have come to steal the Harp from me.'

'Steal, madam?' Anvar strove to keep his fear from showing on his face. 'That is harsh. I had hoped, yes, to persuade you to give it to me. It was made by Magefolk in the mundane world, and there it truly belongs. I desperately need to take it back with me, to save my world from evil.'

'What, all by yourself? Are you some mighty hero, then, all set to save your world?' There was no disguising the mockery in her tone. Anvar, almost stung to making some rash retort, controlled himself just in time. It would not do to forget how powerful, how dangerous, this creature truly was.

'Not a hero,' he told the Cailleach. 'I never wanted this –any of it – except my powers, and Aurian. Especially Aurian. But it's better than using the Harp for destruction, is it not? It's better than letting such a thing of wonder moulder here, unloved and unused, far from the world of its creation. Even now, I hear it, calling out to me like a lost child, begging me to take it home.' As he uttered those last words, he realized that they were the truth. The thrilling starsong had not died with the bridge, but still murmured softly, somewhere in the back of his mind. But now the music carried words: half-comprehended yet but coming clearer all the time.

The Cailleach raised an eyebrow. 'The Harp sings to *you*?'

But Anvar heard the tremor of doubt behind her mocking tones; saw her eyes flick away, infinitesimally, before coming back to pierce him. And yes, the Harp was singing to him, with the crystal starry music of the bridge, from the hinterland beyond his consciousness. And it told him how to answer her. 'Of course it sings to me. You know it does. Who kept the waves of the lake from harming me? Who built the bridge of stars to bring me here? At first I thought that was your doing, but now I know better.' Anvar lifted his head, and looked her in the eye. His glance flicked across the Cailleach's pitiless raptor's gaze, and they clashed like two slender blades of steel. The Lady was the first to look away. When she looked back, she was smiling.

No trace of the crone, now. No trace of the eagle. Her face was flawless, youthful, and alluring. Beautiful. Irresistible. Anvar's heart beat faster. '*Fool,*' sang the Harp in the back of his mind. '*Dupe. Beware deception . . .* ' Just as the power of the Staff of Earth had a distinctly masculine aspect, the tone of the Harp felt indisputably feminine.

'Where are you?' the Mage called back to it, using mind-speech. 'How can I find you?'

'*Within. Within . . .* '

Anvar grinned up at the Cailleach. 'Why don't you invite me

inside?' In her eyes, he surprised a flash of victory. She beckoned him up the curving staircase, and as he entered the numinous golden glow beyond the portal, he heard the door spring shut behind him like the steel jaws of a trap.

The golden light was much brighter inside. It dazzled his eyes, burned into his brain. It was like falling into the heart of the sun. Anvar staggered forward; blind, dazed, disorientated. He heard the triumphant cackle of an old hag's laughter – or was it the harsh cry of a brid of prey? Arms twined around his neck, pulling him down; clawed nails like talons impaled his skin. An undulating body clung to him, pressing against his flesh. Moist lips fastened on his mouth, sucking at his breath, drawing the life-force from his body. Anvar struggled, fighting for control, drowning in the tidal wave of the creature's lust . . .

'The Staff, fool! Use the Staff, before she takes it from you!' The song of the Harp cut shrill across his reeling consciousness. Such was its power that Anvar obeyed instinctively. He lifted his right hand, and brought the Staff of Earth crashing down upon the head of the clinging succubus.

The vampire lover vanished. The air was split asunder by a hideous shriek, and the world plunged into blackness.

25

Healing

It was full night by the time Aurian and her winged escort reached Aerillia. The Skyfolk who were bearing her were plainly unhappy about the risk of flying in darkness, and to compound the problem, the peaks were smothered in low-lying banks of cloud, reducing visibility to nothing.

The Mage could hear the muttered complaints of her bearers as she dangled perilously below them in the swinging net. And they thought *they* had problems. She snorted in disgust. Of all the insane, ridiculous ways to get from one place to another . . . The rough rope meshes dug into her body and the raw damp chill had pierced her to the very bone, despite the blankets in which she had wrapped herself. And for someone afraid of heights, this was definitely not the way to travel. Aurian was wholeheartedly glad of the darkness and obscuring cloud, so that she could not see how far she would have to fall, if these idiots should accidentally drop her.

'Aurian? My friend, is that you?' They must be nearing Aerillia at last. Hearing Shia's mental call, the Mage forgot her fear in her concern for her companion. Shia sounded unhappy, and unusually subdued. 'Are you all right?' she asked the cat.

'Khanu and I are cold and cramped and hungry. We daren't even try to dig our way out, for fear of attracting attention. There are Skyfolk down here searching . . . for Anvar as well as ourselves.' Shia's despairing tone told the Mage that Anvar had not yet been found. Shuddering, she tried to banish the cold hand of fear that clamped around her heart. I'll find him, Aurian told herself stubbornly. I know he isn't dead – I would have felt it. Firmly, she put that worry out of her mind for the present and turned her attention back to Shia. 'But in the message I sent, I told Raven to tell the Winged Folk you weren't to be harmed.'

'Pah!' spat Shia. 'She already betrayed us once. I'd put as much trust in Raven as I would put in the rest of these murdering skyborne fiends!' There was a long pause, so long that the Mage began to worry; then an unknown voice – another cat, for sure, but definitely male – broke in: 'They killed Hreeza.'

'We failed her,' Shia added bitterly. 'We could not come to her in time.' Into Aurian's mind came a vision of a great cat standing at bay in a ruined building. Her black muzzle was frosted with grey and her movements were stiff with age, but her eyes were still ablaze with courage and defiance. A crowd of Winged Folk were closing around her, armed with stones and knives. 'It took her a long time to die.' Shia's mental tones were almost inaudible. The picture broke up and vanished as Shia lost control of the vision, and Aurian's heart was overwhelmed by the great cat's grief. A wave of anger rose up in her against the ones who had done this dreadful deed.

'Can't you fly any faster?' the Mage shouted at her winged bearers. She was desperate to reach Aerillia now, to comfort her friend. 'I'm coming,' she told Shia. 'We're almost there. Just hold on a little longer.'

Eventually, Aurian saw the haloed gleams of many lights shining dimly through the pervasive murk. Aerillia at last! Relief washed over her, but it was shortlived. A great dark shape came hurtling at her through the fog. A leering gargoyle face loomed close, and hard stone struck her hip as the net crashed into the edge of a buttress. Aurian heard her bearers curse as they skimmed the top of the tower with which she'd collided. Her heart leapt into her throat as the sound of wingbeats faltered above her and the net gave a downward lurch. Then the Skyfolk steadied themselves, though the net, with its horrified passenger, was spinning beneath them from the force of the impact, while the Mage indulged in some inventive cursing of her own.

Aurian's invective was cut short as she was dumped, none too gently, on a pile of excruciatingly sharp-edged rocks. Blast these bloody Winged Folk! she thought sourly, trying to scramble her way out of the tangled meshes. They're supposed to be expecting us. Why didn't they bring out some lights? Her

385

escort seemed to be thinking along the same lines, judging by the choice, unflattering phrases that were being called out in the Skyfolk tongue. By the time that Aurian had managed to disentangle herself from the net, she saw some half a dozen lanterns, faint glimmers in the swirling fog, bobbing towards her at ground level.

In the growing light, the Mage saw Chiamh and Yazour struggling out of their own nets, and breathed a sigh of relief. Then she turned her attention to her surroundings. There was little to be seen through the mist, but Aurian could make out the looming shapes of broken pillars above piles of shattered stone. She recognized the ruined temple that she had seen when her spirit had ridden the winds to Aerillia with Chiamh.

There was no time for further thought. The Skyfolk delegation was approaching. Walking between four armed guards were two figures of a different stamp – an ageing woman with a strong-boned face and a determined expression, her wings and hair pied in dramatic patterns of black and white; and a pale-skinned, white-winged man with dark hollows of sleeplessness beneath his eyes, and a shock of snowy hair that was belied by the youthfulness of his face.

The guards drew back as the two approached the Mage, inclining their heads and extending their wings in the Skyfolk equivalent of a bow. 'Lady Aurian,' the woman said. 'I am Master Physician Elster. Queen Raven sent us to greet you. She cannot move from her bed – not with her wings so badly injured.' She glanced behind, to make sure that the guards were out of earshot. 'Nor would it be wise,' she added softly, 'for her to appear in public in her current condition. Thanks to the unlikely assistance of a straying child, who took a message out for Cygnus – ' she indicated her white-haired companion – 'the people of Aerillia know that the queen was held prisoner by Blacktalon. They do not know, however, that she is incapable of flight, and therefore of ruling. Should this be discovered, trouble would ensue, for this fell winter is still upon us, and not all our folk were opposed to the High Priest. Some saw him as the harbinger of a golden age, when the Skyfolk would regain their old supremacy.' She threw up her hands in a gesture of despair. 'Lady, we stand on the brink of civil war, and only you can save us.'

386

Aurian thought of the death of gallant Hreeza, and Shia's grief. She remembered the pile of catskins brought by the Winged Folk to the Tower of Incondor, where she had been imprisoned through Raven's treachery. In that moment, she cared little whether or not the Skyfolk civilization collapsed . . . Except that, against Miathan, she needed all the help she could get. And, as a price for helping Raven, she could put an end to the slaughter of the cats once and for all, and perhaps make peace between the two warring peoples.

Aurian brightened. At least Shia's poor friend need not have died in vain. Feeling much better about the whole business, the Mage turned back to Elster. 'Of course I'll help you,' she promised, 'but before I see Queen Raven, I must locate some friends of mine.' The white-haired Cygnus moved as if to protest, but Aurian quelled him with a steely glare. 'As soon as I've found my friends – and not a minute before,' she said firmly. 'Now, show me the way to the passages beneath the temple.' She beckoned to her companions. 'Chiamh, Yazour – come with me, please.' The words had scarcely left Aurian's lips, when:

'I come!' Suddenly the Mage was bowled off her feet by a massive flame-eyed shape that was blacker than the darkness. As she went down, Aurian glimpsed, from the corner of her eye, another cat that pulled up just short of Shia's joyful leap – then Shia was on top of her, purring like approaching thunder, her dark muzzle rubbing Aurian's face as the two embraced.

'No!' The voice belonged to Chiamh. It was followed by a tearing, high-pitched scream. As the Mage and Shia leapt apart, Aurian saw the winged guards cowering, arrows dropping from their crossbows and clattering to the ground. The Windeye was standing at bay between the cats and the terrified Skyfolk, his eyes flaring bright silver and reflecting the flickering torchlight, his hands twisting skeins of the mist-heavy air. Looming over the Winged Folk was a hideous shape of a demon.

'Drop your weapons,' Chiamh shouted, 'or my creature will attack!' As swords and crossbows clattered to the ground, the Windeye glanced back towards Aurian. 'Lady, they were about to kill your friends,' he grated. Red rage coursed through the

387

Mage, but she had no time to indulge it. She could see the strain on Chiamh's face as he strove to maintain his dread apparition in the sluggish air. Aurian looked at the demon with a shudder. It was far too reminiscent of the Death-Wraiths for her liking, but she had to admit that it was incredibly realistic.

She turned to the cowering Skyfolk. 'If anyone so much as threatens the lives of these cats, we will turn this abomination loose on the city of Aerillia. Have I made myself clear?'

'As you wish, Lady. I give my word that the beasts will not be harmed.' Elster was ashen, her face taut with anger, but Aurian suspected that the physician's wrath was aimed at the guards with the crossbows, rather than at herself. Sure enough, she turned at once and began to berate the bowmen, and Aurian smiled. She knew that the woman was masking her fear with anger.

With a sigh of relief, Chiamh dispersed with airs that had formed his monster, and the silver drained from his eyes. Aurian put a steadying arm around him as he sagged with exhaustion. 'Thank you, my friend,' she said softly.

The Windeye looked at Shia, his brown eyes wide with wonder. 'When you told me of the cat that was your friend, I had no idea you meant the savage Black Ghosts of our mountains!'

'Savage, my eye!' snapped Shia. 'All we ever had from your kind was arrows and spears – ever since the day you first invaded our mountains and took our lands! True enough, most of your folk have neither the wit nor the wherewithal to communicate with us, but you and your predecessors could have done so!'

'Mother of the beasts!' Chiamh cried, putting a hand to his head. 'She *did* speak! When she leapt on you, Aurian, I was sure I heard her cry out to you in friendship. That was why I helped – else I might have thought she was attacking you, as well.'

Aurian smiled. 'You two can talk later, and work out peace between your peoples, I hope. Right now, though, our hosts look impatient. I think we had better see Queen Raven.' A hard edge crept into her voice, and, at her side, Shia snarled. The Mage laid a comforting hand on the great cat's head. 'I know, my dearest,' she sighed. 'But if we're to find Anvar, we need her support, and that means helping the wretched girl.'

'Aurian?' Chiamh tugged at her arm. 'I think I may be able to assist you in your search. May I stay here and make some investigations while you are with the queen?'

The Mage glanced questioningly at Elster, who nodded. Aurian thanked the physician, and turned back to Chiamh. 'What do you mean, investigations?'

He shook his head. 'I would rather not say at this point, and there is no time for long explanations. I will return to you as soon as I can – certainly before the dawn.' With that, Aurian had to be content. She knew the young Windeye could be trusted. She looked back at the sturdy winged bearers, who were readying nets to take her with the rest of her companions across the gulfs of air to the royal apartments, and sighed.

Raven had been dreading Aurian's arrival. She had always been considerably in awe of the tall, flame-haired Mage, and now that she had given Aurian cause to hate her . . . Raven shuddered, and gasped with pain. Even that small movement sent agony lancing through her ravaged, splinted pinions. If only she can help me, the winged girl thought desperately. Unfortunately, despite Aurian's promise, she had no confidence that the Mage would do anything of the kind. Were our situatins reversed, Raven mused, I would not help her . . . Then the door of her chamber opened, and the subject of her thoughts walked in.

For a moment, their eyes locked, then: 'Don't pity me!' Raven snapped, before the Mage could turn away, as others had, with *that* expression in her eyes.

Aurian merely shrugged. 'You brought it on yourself,' she said coolly, and the winged girl clenched her teeth with anger. It was even more galling that the Mage had noticed. Aurian raised an eyebrow. 'Make your mind up,' she said brutally. 'I didn't come to waste sympathy on you, Raven. I came to heal you, as I promised – and then we'll see what you can do to make amends for betraying us all.' The stern words were echoed by a low and menacing growl, and Raven's heart sank to see that Shia, together with another strange cat, had accompanied the

389

Mage into the chamber. She was further dismayed to see Yazour behind them, his eyes like a naked blade. The winged girl flushed beneath his withering glare. As far back as the forest, the young captain had made it clear that he was attracted to her. When she had repeatedly spurned his tentative advances, his feelings for her had soured. She was astonished, therefore, to see his face turn pale with shock as he took in the extent of her dreadful injuries. He shook his head, dismayed, and tightened his lips as though he did not trust himself to speak.

'Lady, must these animals be in here?' Cygnus, entering with Elster, was frowning. He sidled across the chamber, putting the widest possible space between himself and the intimidating cats, to hover protectively by Raven.

'Yes, they must,' Aurian replied shortly. 'Now get out of the way, and let me get on with this.'

'What?' Elster looked startled. 'You intend to heal her now? Just like that – with no preparation or anything?'

'Well, I must admit, a hot drink would have been welcome on this freezing night, but since no one has offered . . . ' the Mage shrugged. 'Yes, I'm going to do it now, and I want you two out of here.' She looked hard at the remains of Raven's wings. 'This will be tricky, and if I'm interrupted or distracted she could end up in a worse state than before I started.'

Raven saw the bitter disappointment on Elster's face, and a flash of angry denial in the eyes of Cygnus. For a moment she was tempted to insist that they stay. Alone, she would be utterly at the mercy of Aurian and the cats.

The Mage was looking at her with one eyebrow raised and a challenging tilt to her chin. 'Well, Raven?' she asked softly. 'Will you trust me to keep my word, or not?'

'Do not permit this, your Majesty,' Cygnus urged. Elster said nothing, but she also looked unhappy. The winged girl hesitated, but only for a moment.

'I owe you my trust,' she answered softly, 'and much more than that.'

The Mage nodded briefly, accepting the sentiment behind the words. Raven turned to the protesting physicians. 'Out,' she said in imperious tones that she had learned from her mother. 'Do not return until you are summoned.'

'Actually . . . ' Aurian was frowning thoughtfully, 'one of you must stay. In order to repair that wing, I'll need a perfect example to work from.' She gestured to Elster. 'It had better be you – you're less excitable than your friend.'

'Lady – no!' Cygnus protested. 'I too am a physician. Would you force me to miss such a miracle? It isn't fair to exclude only me, out of everyone in this chamber.'

Aurian sighed. 'Oh, very well.' She looked at Yazour. 'If our physician here utters a single sound, I want you to cut his throat.'

Yazour, grinning evilly as he slipped a long keen dagger from his belt, looked as though he would be only too happy to oblige, and the protest that Raven had been about to make died abruptly on her lips.

As the Mage began to work, there was complete silence in the chamber. Afterwards, Raven had few clear recollections of the healing, but what stood out ever afterwards in her memory was the sudden, shocking cessation of pain as Aurian laid a gentle touch upon her wings. In the absence of the agony that had been her constant torment, Raven was bathed in a warm, floating wave of euphoria, her body gloriously relaxed as though it suddenly had become weightless. Nothing in her life had ever felt so wonderful. Drowsily, she let her mind float free, barely feeling the lingering tingling glow as the Mage's hands passed over the shattered pinions, and the force of Aurian's magic sank into mangled tissue and splintered bone; straightening and mending the damage Blacktalon had wrought.

If only she could also heal my mind, Raven thought, of the grief I feel for my mother – and for Harihn, despite the fact that he betrayed me. If only she could heal me of the guilt I feel at betraying her, and poor Nereni . . . Yet under the benison of Aurian's healing touch, even such bitter thoughts had little power to hurt the winged girl. Perhaps, if she could find a way to make amends, she might be truly forgiven . . . On such a note of hope, Raven's mind drifted away into dreams.

'That's it – finished.' Aurian straightened her aching back, and rubbed the last traces of blue Magelight from hands that had

391

begun to shake with tiredness and tension. The repair of Raven's intricate wings had been by far the most difficult healing she had ever attempted. The gods only knew how long it had taken. Rubbing her stinging eyes, the Mage glanced out of the window. Although it was still dark outside, she could sense that peculiar lightening of the air and the spirit that comes when the night has turned towards the dawn.

Aurian turned away from the window, belatedly aware that no one had replied to her comment. Raven was asleep already. Shia and Khanu were also asleep, curled tightly together in a corner, black on dappled black-and-gold. Yazour was rummaging behind embroidered curtains, peering into the alcoves they concealed. 'They must keep some wine somewhere in this room,' he muttered. Cygnus and Elster were staring, mouths agape, at Raven's wings. 'Impossible!' whispered the young physician.

Elster shook her head. 'No,' she contradicted. 'It was truly a miracle.' For the first time, she smiled at Aurian with genuine warmth. 'My Lady, how can we ever recompense you for saving our queen?'

The Mage grinned back at her. 'Well, to begin with some food and wine and a warm place to rest would help.' Having expended so much energy in healing Raven, she was sagging with exhaustion. 'Tomorrow,' she added wryly, 'I'll talk to Raven, and let you know what else.'

'What now, Aurian?' Yazour, about to fling himself on the spindly couch, took a second look at its delicate construction and lowered himself more circumspectly. The Mage eased her worn boots off and lay back in the central hollow of the peculiar, circular bed. 'Let me eat and rest for a little while, and as soon as we have some daylight, we'll try to find out what happened to Anvar.'

She reached out to the low table that stood by the bed, and took another piece of the heavy, soggy bread that seemed to have been made from ground-up tubers. She grimaced as she swallowed. 'Gods, they *are* short of food,' she commented. 'If the Winged Folk are so desperate, no wonder Blacktalon managed to gain such a hold over the city.'

Yazour grunted a sleepy response. His eyes were already closing, and briefly, Aurian envied him. Forral had taught her, long ago, the warrior's trick of snatching brief moments of sleep wherever possible, but though the circular tower chamber, with its thick, draughtproof hangings, woven matting and smouldering iron brazier in the corner, was the warmest place she had encountered since leaving the desert, and she was finding it increasingly difficult to stave off the urge to sleep, she knew there would be no real rest for her until she had found her fellow-Mage. Aurian took a sip of the thin, sour wine that was all that was left in Aerillia, and wished in vain for liafa. When a disturbance on the landing platform outside heralded the arrival of Chiamh, she welcomed him with undisguised relief.

Shia opened a sleepy eye as the Windeye entered, and came sharply to attention. The cat was as anxious as Aurian to find some trace of Anvar. Chiamh dusted flecks of snow from his cloak and stood shivering by the brazier, warming his hands. The Mage passed a cup of wine to him. 'Did you find anything?' she asked urgently.

The Windeye shrugged. 'I have news indeed – but good or bad? I cannot say. Have you heard of the Moldai, Lady?'

'The giant earth-elementals?' Aurian frowned. 'Only in the ancient legends of the Cataclysm. I thought the ancient Magefolk had sent them out of the world, along with the Phaerie. What have they to do with anything?'

'More than you think,' Chiamh answered. 'The Moldai were not sent out of the world, but merely imprisoned, sleeping, in the mountains that are their mundane flesh and bone.' He laid an urgent hand on her arm, his nearsighted brown eyes blinking up at her earnestly. 'Aurian, the Moldai are awake once more. In my own lands, I have spoken several times with the Moldan of the Wyndveil Peak. And do you know what has awakened them? The finding of the Staff of Earth.'

Aurian stared at him, aghast. 'What? You mean these things are on the loose again? And it's all my fault?'

'Not on the loose, exactly – not in this level of existence, at any rate,' Chiamh told her. 'But they are awake now, and powerful – and not all have the good intentions of my friend Basileus, the Wyndveil Moldan.'

Aurian saw his hesitation, and shuddered. Aready, she had a sinking feeling that she knew what his next words would be. 'Are you trying to tell me,' she said softly, 'that there's one of these elementals here in Aerillia?'

'There is,' the Windeye answered grimly. He could barely meet her gaze. 'The Staff of Earth would prove an irresistible temptation to such a creature. Though this peak is unmistakably a Moldan, its consciousness is absent from this world. I fear it wanders other realms, far beyond this mundane plane – and if you say your friend is not dead, I am afraid that it has taken Anvar with it, to wrest away the Staff. If it succeeds . . .' The Windeye shuddered. 'Who can say what will become of our poor world.'

26
A New Day Dawning

Aurian leaned against the icy stone balustrade of the landing porch, watching the sky grow pale in the east. In the bleak dawn twilight, the city of Aerillia looked alien and mysterious, with its buttresses, and carvings both grotesque and beautiful; its lacework arches that pierced the stone at random; its spires and hanging turrets, and its utter lack of streets or any structure that was regular or level, and would give a sense of order to the human eye.

The Mage pushed back the hood of her cloak and shivered, letting the icy dawn wind cut through the cobwebs of fatigue in her mind. She was trying desperately to think of some way of reaching Anvar in time to help him – if it wasn't already too late. If her fellow-Mage was already beyond the confines of the mundane world, she would not know if he died there. Wretchedly, Aurian dropped her head on to her outstretched arms. 'Damn you, Anvar,' she sighed. 'Why did you have to go and do this, just when I had finally admitted to myself that I loved you?'

Aurian felt helpless and frustrated. Chiamh's words had filled her with dismay and dread, for without the Staff of Earth, she could not pass into the realms of High Magic, to go to Anvar's aid. And mixed with the dreadful, clutching fear she felt for the Mage's safety, there was an even deeper terror. If the Staff of Earth should be lost, she had nothing left to fight with. No matter what she did, Miathan would have won already.

The Mage blinked in the brightening light, and tried to tell herself that the blurring of her vision was just tiredness, and not tears. Suddenly, Aurian froze, narrowing her eyes against the dazzling dawnlight. That was not the light of the sun. It was brighter; more colourful. Great spars of jewelled light leapt skywards like an aurora. It was coming from the wrong direction: not east, but northeast – from the ruins of the temple!

With a stifled curse, Aurian whirled, shouting for the Skyfolk that Elster had provided to be bearers and messengers for the unwinged visitors in their lofty, inaccessible tower. 'Hurry,' she cried, as they emerged from their chamber rubbing sleepy eyes. 'Bring your nets. I must get to the temple at once!'

The interior of the Cailleach's massive tree was dark even beyond the compass of a Mage's night vision. Anvar groped in panic for the door, to let some light into the chamber, but flail though he might through the cloying blackness, his seeking hands met only empty air. With a muttered curse, the Mage poured his powers into the Staff of Earth. The gem between the serpents' jaws flared into life, sending shadows fleeing from its emerald blaze. But its magic did not belong within this timeless world. Some other will opposed it: a power much older than the Staff, and far, far stronger. The great gem flickered, its radiance sinking to a wan, sickly, firefly spark. Before Anvar had even had time to take note of his surroundings, the darkness crowded round him once again – except for one pale slip of light at the edge of his vision.

The Mage turned, frowning. What was that? As his eyes fell on it, the phantom glimmer brightened and expanded, the slender bar of light widening like a casement being slowly opened from another world. Anvar stiffened. Was this another of the Lady's tricks? The line of light writhed, becoming curved and fluid, transforming into a succession of familiar shapes: a swan; a crown; a rose; a leaping salmon. And finally, a harp.

The light flared to incandescent brilliance, leaping out in a thick, dazzling, opalescent beam that fixed upon the Mage like a pointing forefinger. Anvar gave a wordless cry of rapture. The unearthly song of the star-music flooded his mind as the power of Gramarye coursed through his body, consuming him, turning his racing blood to molten fire. Not even when he'd wielded the Staff had he known such glory! A sense of rightness, of belonging, washed over him from some external source, and was echoed in his heart as he accepted the power of the Harp, and the Artefact claimed him for its own.

With a wrenching snap like a whiplash across his soul, the light shut off abruptly. It was as though his heart had been torn out of his breast. Anvar, dazed and bereft and tingling from the aftershock of so much power, came back to his senses with a jolt. He still did not possess the actual Harp. Even though it had claimed him, it was not yet his to wield. And where, in all this time, was his enemy? Had he destroyed her with the Staff? Anvar doubted it. No doubt she was somewhere nearby, recouping her powers – and when she returned, he had better be ready.

'I will unseal your eyes,' whispered the starry voice of the Harp. The dazzling afterimages of the beam cleared from the Mage's sight. Anvar, blinking, saw a vast, circular chamber that encompassed the interior of the treetrunk. He perceived the walls with a different vision now. No longer that silvery amalgam of wood and stone, they were translucent, like sunlight shining through a shell. Within, he saw the pulse of the tree's life moving up, in slender, nacreous streams, through channels in the trunk. And there, on the opposite wall from where he stood, he saw the silver outline of a harp. It glittered dimly, as though submerged within the wood like a salmon beneath the surface of a river. Anvar's heart leapt. Running across the chamber, he thrust the Staff into his belt and pressed his hands against the wall, feeling for the outline of the Harp. To his utter astonishment, his fingers sank into the wood, as easily as slipping into water. The song of the Harp swelled to a climax in Anvar's mind. 'Free me,' it sang. 'You must free me . . . '

The Mage took a steadying breath, and plunged his fingers deep into the tree. His hands closed on an irregular shape, and his fingers felt the smooth swirling outlines of carvings. A paean of joyful starsong flooded Anvar's mind as he lifted the Harp free from its prison and held it aloft in triumph.

The Mage could not take his eyes from the Artefact. He was spellbound and awestruck by such beauty. The Harp was formed, not from wood, but from some strange, translucent

397

crystalline substance that glittered like diamond in the fire of its own internal light. Carved around the frame was an endless, ever-changing series of winged shapes: birds of many different species from lowly wrens and sparrows to great, majestic eagles and swans. Turning the frame in his hands, Anvar saw owls, bats, glittering moths and iridescent dragonflies. His fingers passed, not without a shudder, across the tiny shape of a winged woman. All creatures of the air graced the Harp of Winds, framed in fluid swirls of silver that seemed to be the very wind incarnate. In all his life, Anvar had never seen anything so perfect. Except for one thing. The glittering frame bounded nought but empty space.

'Oh gods – where are the strings?' In his dismay, Anvar did not realize that he had uttered the words aloud. A cackling laugh came from behind him, and the Mage whirled in alarm. The Lady of the Mists stood there, her face young and flawless, her hair frost-white against the blackness of her feathered cloak.

'Did you really think it would be so easy, Wizard?' she mocked him. 'Just reach into the tree and take it? Why, any idiot might have done the same!'

'I think not,' Anvar retorted coldly. 'Not without the Harp's consent.' He detected a gleam of approval in the Cailleach's eyes.

'As I remarked earlier, you are a most perceptive Wizard,' the Lady answered, 'and an honourable opponent. I would have you know I do not fight you willingly – but I am charged to protect the Harp, and that I must do. Only one who is truly worthy may win it, for it is a perilous thing indeed to be returned to the mundane world.'

'And?' Anvar's reply was a challenge.

The Lady smiled. 'So far, you have succeeded in your first two tests. You overcame the succubus, and then won the Harp's acceptance so that you could free it. Believe me, Anvar, had the Harp not willed it otherwise, you would have died in agony the instant you put your hand into the tree. Now, like the Staff of Earth, the Harp of Winds must be recreated. You hold the frame, Wizard – with what would you string this Artefact of the High Magic?'

The Harp was no help. In the back of his mind, it sang: 'You must complete me – make me whole once more.'

'How?' asked Anvar.

A shimmering sigh came from the Harp. 'I may not tell.'

Anvar looked at the Cailleach, aghast. He knew in his heart that she spoke the truth. He had known it all along. But how to accomplish his task, and win the Harp? Remembering Aurian's tale of her encounter with the dragon, he asked: 'May I ask questions?'

'No,' the Lady said. 'You may not.'

'Then give me time to think.' But for all the churning of Anvar's restless mind, he could come up with nothing. This was ridiculous, he thought. When Aurian had described her ordeal, it had sounded so much easier than his own.

'Why not give it up?' the Cailleach interrupted his train of thought. 'Stay here, instead, and be my love. I can be any woman – all women . . . '

Before Anvar's eyes, she began to change, her flawless features altering, her hair changing colour, time after time . . . With a pang like the twinge of an old wound, Anvar saw Sara. He saw Eliseth's cold and perfect beauty, and saw his mother as Ria must have been in her youth . . . The succession of women went on and on, each more beautiful than the last. Angrily, Anvar turned away. 'Stop doing that!' he snapped. 'Fair you might be, Lady, but I have no interest in remaining here with you. My heart is already given – elsewhere.'

'Indeed?' the Lady said silkily. 'From what I gleaned of your thoughts as you approached the Timeless Lake, your loved one's heart is also given – and not to you.'

'That's a lie!' Anvar cried. 'She needs time, that's all!'

'How much time? A month? A year? For ever? Your Lady is intractable, Anvar, and grief has turned her fey. Can you be certain she will ever betray the memory of her dead lover? And with the one who, indirectly, caused his death?' The power of the Cailleach's voice was insidious. Her moonstone eyes held the Mage's gaze; hypnotic and glittering as a serpent's stare. He wanted to protest – to deny what she was saying, but he could frame no words, for she had touched with cruel precision on the dark core of doubt in the depths of Anvar's soul.

399

'Why risk it, Anvar? Why take such a chance, when I can be everything that Aurian is – and more!' As the Cailleach spoke, she was changing form again – and the Mage found his beloved standing before him. Aurian, as she had been long ago in Nexis, before hardship had made her haggard, and grief and her desire for vengeance had put that steeliness into her gaze. Instead, Anvar found her looking at him – *him* – with an expression in her eyes that had always been reserved for Forral. Anvar tightened his fingers around the frame of the Harp, to stop his hands from shaking. Aurian took a step forward, her arms outstretched to embrace him. 'My dearest love . . . ' she breathed.

' . . . *As long as I have you, I have hope.*' As Aurian's last true words to him echoed in Anvar's mind, the Cailleach's spell was abruptly broken.

'Get away from me,' snarled the Mage. 'What need have I for a shallow substitute, when I have my Lady's love in reality?'

In a blinding flash, the vision of Aurian vanished. The Cailleach stood before him in the form of an old woman – and to Anvar's amazement, she was smiling. No longer the seductress, no longer a mighty figure of awe and majesty, she looked like a wise and kindly grandmother. 'Wizard, you have passed the test,' she said softly. 'Indeed you are worthy of the Harp – for only someone with a loving, faithful heart could be trusted to take such power out into the world once more.'

Taking a silver knife from her belt, the Lady of the Mists cut off a lock of her long hair. Reaching out to the Harp, still locked in the startled Mage's grasp, she passed her hand across the glittering Artefact. The snowy lock vanished, transformed into a waterfall of silver strings that bridged the crystal frame. Power blazed up within Anvar as his mind was flooded with joyful starsong. Green light blazed up from the Staff of Earth in his belt, to join the silver incandescence of the Harp. The Lady raised her hand in farewell . . .

And Anvar found himself standing on a snowy mountaintop, looking at the sun rising over the city of Aerillia. One last message from the Cailleach echoed in his mind – and in his hands was the Harp of Winds.

The Skyfolk bearers were terrified of the growing blaze of incandescence within the shell of the temple. Only the fact that they were even more afraid of Aurian made them take her there at all. They dropped her, net and all, into the midst of the ruined building, and fled as if for their very lives.

The Mage released herself from the meshes of the net, and began to pick her way across the stretch of rubble and shattered stone towards the source of the unearthly light. Her sword – her dear, familiar Coronach that she had recovered safely from the Tower of Incondor – was in her hand, but she found herself desperately missing the reassuring power of the Staff of Earth. She had no idea what lay behind the flaring knot of rainbow brilliance – but for certain, it would be beyond the scope of any human weapon. But despite the fear that set her heart racing, Aurian went on into the heart of the blaze, irresistibly drawn, like a moth to a candle.

As the Mage walked forward, the scintillating radiance began to shrink and coalesce to form a human shape, clad all in blinding light. A long-limbed, rangy, heartbreakingly familiar figure . . .

'Anvar!' Aurian cried. Then she was running forward, ignoring the stones that tilted perilously beneath her feet, her heart flying ahead of her across the intervening space. Then they were embracing, both of them laughing and crying and trying to talk all at once.

'I thought I'd never see you again!'

'Thank the gods you're safe!'

'Is the child all right?'

'Where have you *been*?'

As their words tripped over one another, both of them started laughing again, clinging to one another as they rocked with the slightly hysterical mirth that stemmed from pure relief. Aurian dashed away happy tears, and looked into Anvar's face. His blue eyes connected with her own like a flare of lightning, and Aurian trembled, half-amazed by her own longing. 'My dearest love . . . ' she breathed.

Anvar pulled her towards him, and as his lips touched her own she felt the sudden flashfire of desire spark between them – that same explosive, powerful surge of love and longing that she had used unknowing, so long ago, to release Anvar from the clutches of Death in the slave-pens of the Khazalim. And, just as it had happened then, their very souls seemed to touch – to meet and meld, as Aurian felt Anvar's joy, and her own, commingling to lift them both on the brightest of wings . . .

Aurian gasped. No one had ever told her it would be like this between Magefolk! Having formerly had a Mortal lover, she had never known that this deep, intense linkage of hearts and minds and emotions existed. The Mage felt Anvar's amazed delight in her mind, matching and augmenting her own dizzy joy. His mouth fastened on hers with a greed that matched her own as his hand explored her face and body, kindling the desire she had missed for so long. They never noticed the sharpness of the stones as they sank to the ground, their cloaks their only shelter. And there, in the remains of the temple of Yinze, in the ruins of an evil priest's dream, Anvar and Aurian fulfilled at last a love that had started with the seeds of need and mutual dependence, and taken them halfway across the world, through friendship, into passion.

By the time they were ready to notice anything beyond each other, the sun was already high enough to peep over the shattered walls and into the ruined temple. Anvar sighed contentedly and reached over to brush a wayward curl from Aurian's glowing cheek. 'You were well worth waiting for,' he murmured softly into her ear.

Aurian grinned wickedly. 'Suddenly, I can't imagine why I made you wait so long!'

'You weren't ready, my love,' Anvar said seriously – then he grinned back at her. 'Apart, of course, from being the most irritating, stubborn, contrary wretch . . . '

'Well of all the nerve!' Aurian spluttered, but he stilled her protest with a kiss.

'What happened to the child?' he asked her, when they could breathe again. For an instant, Aurian's expression clouded – then she lifted her chin determinedly.

'He's beautiful,' she said firmly. 'And he'll be all right, I know he will, just as soon as we work out a way to lift Miathan's curse.'

Anvar listened, with increasing sadness and concern, as Aurian told him about Wolf. He was about to reply, when:

'Welcome back, Anvar!' The voice in his mind came from Shia, of course, and Aurian's wry smile told him that she was listening too. 'Aurian – I should warn you that they have started to look for you,' the great cat went on, and then her voice grew smug. 'Otherwise, of course, I should never have dreamed of interrupting you . . . '

'You were listening?' Anvar felt his face growing warm and, looking across at Aurian, he saw her blushing too.

'One could hardly help but hear you,' Shia snorted. 'I would say that your emotions were broadcasting clear to the lands of the Xandim!' Her mental voice grew softer as she stopped teasing them. 'I am so very happy for you both. Unfortunately, the world will not wait for you. Raven wants to talk . . . '

'All right, we're coming,' Aurian sighed resignedly. 'That is, as soon as we can flag down some Winged Folk to bring us across.' She rolled over, and swore. 'Ouch! What on earth am I lying on?'

'Oh gods,' yelped Anvar in dismay. 'It went right out of my mind. The Harp, Aurian! I have the Harp of Winds!'

'What?' Aurian yelled. 'Why the bloody blazes didn't you tell me before?'

Anvar grinned. 'Well, I was somewhat distracted before . . . Here, let's get some clothes on before we freeze, and I'll show it to you. But first things first.' Anvar returned the Staff of Earth to Aurian with a flourish. 'I believe this belongs to you, Lady.'

Aurian's expression of joy and relief as she took the Staff made Anvar smile. Then he held out the Harp to her, and her eyes went wide with wonder as she beheld its shimmering beauty.

'Oh, Anvar . . . ' Aurian reached out to take the Harp of Winds – and as she did so, Anvar was seized with a strange and powerful reluctance to let the Artefact out of his hands. The Harp too seemed to object to a change of guardianship. Jangling vibrations ran through Anvar's body as it thrummed discordantly. 'No . . . ' it sang to him. 'No!' Almost of its own volition, it seemed to jerk away from Aurian's outstretched hands, and Anvar went rigid with alarm as he saw her frown. A shadow seemed to fall between them. Then Aurian relaxed, and shook her head with a wry grimace. Once more they stood in sunlight, and Anvar breathed again.

'Well, it certainly knows what it wants – and that doesn't seem to be me,' said Aurian ruefully. 'How daft of me – I should have known. Everything fits, Anvar. You won the Harp, just as I won the Staff – and frankly, of the two of us, you're the musician.' She took a deep breath. 'It couldn't have worked out more perfectly.'

Anvar was amazed and humbled by such generosity of spirit. 'But you were supposed to find the Artefacts,' he protested.

Aurian shook her head. 'No one ever said that, neither the Dragon nor the Leviathan. They just said that all three were needed. The Dragon did say that the Sword would be mine, but as for the others . . . Anvar, I'm truly glad you have the Harp. After what we've just shared, I couldn't bear to think of the Artefacts coming between us.'

Anvar hugged her – gods, it seemed that he couldn't get enough of touching her. 'You'll be able to use the Harp, if need be,' he promised. 'I'll make it behave – it's just that it's new to me yet.'

Aurian nodded gravely. 'I know just what you mean. When I think of the struggle I had to master the Staff at first . . . ' She sighed. 'And speaking of struggles, it's time we were moving. We need to have matters out with Raven, then I must get back to Wolf. And if we can enlist the help of the Xandim . . . ' she hesitated, her green eyes seeming to look far off into the distance.

'Then what?' Anvar prompted gently.

Aurian's expression grew hard. 'Then we go back north, to Nexis, and deal with Miathan once and for all – and Eliseth.' She shivered. 'Gods, I'm so sick and tired of this endless winter of hers.'

Suddenly, Anvar knew what he must do. He was so brimful of wonder, and joy that Aurian had accepted their love at last, that he wanted to give her something – some great, and wonderful, and special gift . . . He turned to the Mage and grinned. 'Your wish,' he said cheerfully, 'is my command.' And, lifting the Harp of Winds, he began to play.

The wild, unearthly starsong of the Harp swirled forth, as the power of the High Magic pulsed through Anvar and went spiralling out into the world. High on the roof of the world, the snow of Eliseth's winter began to melt, and the thaw spread out and out, across the territory of the cats and the lands of the Xandim. In the Jewelled Desert, the lethal, raging sandstorms faltered, and gem-dust fell to earth like pattering rain. Warm winds alive with shimmering music spread across the ocean, as spring, at Anvar's behest, came to the northlands at last.

As Aurian realized what Anvar was doing, a slow smile spread across her face. For an instant, she remembered the filthy, beaten, cowering servant she had rescued so long ago, and she thought her heart would burst with love and pride. And she, too, wanted to give him a token of her love.

Putting a hand on Anvar's shoulder as he played, Aurian summoned the powers of the Staff of Earth, and placed its heel upon the ground. And as its emerald radiance blazed forth, the mountains and the lands beyond grew green. Trees burst into leaf and blossom, and flowers sprang up beneath them, cloaking the earth in vibrant hues as the chains of sorrowing winter fell away, and the land, like her heart, was reborn.

Aurian's mind was awhirl with exultation. She grinned, imagining the wrath of the Archmage. Though much remained to be done, at last, at long last, she and Anvar had struck the real first blow against Miathan.

And far away to the north, in a high tower in the city of Nexis, Eliseth trembled.